Martina Reilly is the author of eight successful novels: *Flipside, The Onion Girl* and *Is This Love?* published by Poolbeg in Ireland and *Something Borrowed, Wedded Blitz, Wish Upon a Star, All I Want is You* and *The Summer of Secrets* published by Sphere. She has also worked as a columnist for the *Irish Evening Herald*. At the moment she writes a column for the *Irish Independent* while concentrating on her novels. She is a mother of two and in her 'spare' time she teaches drama at the Maynooth School of Drama, writes plays and helps out with her son's under-11 soccer team! Look out for Martina's new novel, *Second Chances*, coming from Sphere in autumn 2008.

For more information on Martina and her books, please visit www.martinareilly.info.

Praise for Martina Reilly

'Has all the elements of an excellent read: mystery, drama and romance' *Woman*

'Like Marian Keyes, Reilly takes a cracking story and adds sharp dialogue and buckets of originality' *Scottish Daily Record*

'Clever, frank and funny' *Bella*

'Martina Reilly's characters are so well observe a substantial read' *She*

'Hard to put down, laugh-out-loud funny . perfect holiday reading' *Woman's Way*

'Reilly is a star of the future' *Belfast Telegra*

'A rollicking good yarn' *Irish Evening Hera*

'Reilly has a wonderful comic touch, both in the way she draws her characters and in her dialogue . . . A brilliant read' *U Magazine*

Wish Upon A Star

MARTINA REILLY

SPHERE

First published in Great Britain as a paperback original
in January 2006 by Time Warner Books
Reprinted by Sphere in 2007
Reissued by Sphere in 2008

A CIP catalogue record for this book is available from the British Library.

ISBN 978-0-7515-4104-5

Typeset in Baskerville MT by
Palimpsest Book Production Limited, Polmont, Stirlingshire
Printed and bound in Great Britain by Clays Ltd, St Ives plc

Papers used by Sphere are natural, renewable and recyclable
products made from wood grown in sustainable forests and certified
in accordance with the rules of the Forest Stewardship Council.

Mixed Sources
Product group from well-managed
forests and other controlled sources
www.fsc.org Cert no. SGS-COC-004081
© 1996 Forest Stewardship Council
FSC

Sphere
An imprint of
Little, Brown Book Group
100 Victoria Embankment
London EC4Y 0DY

An Hachette Livre UK Company
www.hachettelivre.co.uk

www.littlebrown.co.uk

For all the McCann family

Acknowledgements

Thanks to everyone thanked before, with the addition of Aideen Sutton (the *Liffey Champion*) and Henry Bauress (the *Leinster Leader*) who have been there from the start – loadsa thanks!

Thanks also to Maynooth Veterinary Clinic for their invaluable input into the various dog diseases! Read on and see what I mean . . .

Prologue

'*Well,*' Mam asked once she'd sat herself down on the hospital chair, '*any names?*'

'*Fáinne,*' I said without hesitation.

'*What?*' Mam's jaw dropped. '*What sort of a name is that – a makey-up one, is it?*'

'*It means "ring" in Irish,*' I explained. I looked down at my new sleeping daughter and a rush of emotion went right up through me. For the first time in a long time, I didn't care what my mam thought. '*I think she looks like a Fáinne.*'

'*I think she looks like she doesn't want to be saddled with a makey-up name,*' Mam pronounced. '*And what's the point in calling a child "ring"? D'you think you're like a pop star or something that you can go about inventing silly names—*'

'*Now, Dora.*' Dad, who'd spent his time gazing at his new grand-daughter and trying to ignore the building tension between me and my mother, patted her on the back. '*It's Lucy's baby, she can call her what she wants.*'

'*Thank you, Dad,*' I said back.

He coughed and turned away again.

Mam shot him an annoyed look, which was nothing new. Though, surprisingly, she didn't attack him. '*I'll never get my tongue around it.*' She puffed herself up. '*Huh, I'll probably end up calling her Phone-ya or something because that's what it sounds like.*'

'*It sounds like Fawn-ya,*' I said back. *Jesus*, I thought, *why couldn't*

1

she give it a rest? There she went spoiling my lovely baby's name. 'Fawn-ya,' I said again. Fáinne cried a little then, a short sort of a moan, but the three of us turned to look at her and for an instant I saw my mother's face soften. It was as if all the hard lines disappeared, just for one tiny instant. She reached out and rubbed my baby's face and then spoilt it all by saying, 'God love you, child, being saddled with a name like that.'

1

Seven years later

I'M TORN BETWEEN the Bratz Supervan and the Bratz castle. The Supervan is cheaper – if I buy the van, I can perhaps get Fáinne another little present for Christmas. If I get the castle, that's all I'll be able to afford.

But she wants the castle *more* than the van.

No, I tell myself, she *thinks* she wants the castle more than the van.

'Can I put a deposit on the Bratz Supervan?'

The old woman behind the counter flicks me a disdainful look and then, turning back to her magazine, she snaps out, 'You can – you'll have to make the final payment the week before Christmas though.'

'OK.'

I gaze again at the Supervan. It's enormous. It comes in a big cream box, with a picture of the cool, ultra-trendy dolls on the outside. It has lights THAT REALLY WORK, a radio THAT REALLY WORKS and engine sounds. It is every little girl's dream and every single mother's nightmare. It costs well over a hundred euro.

But it's cheaper than the castle.

'What's your name?' the woman barks as she flips some pages.

'Lucy Gleeson.'

'Address?'

I give her my address and she scribbles it down before holding out her hand for my twenty-euro deposit.

'I'll put one by for you,' she says. 'You can collect it once you make the final payment. If it's not made by the week before Christmas we'll sell it off.'

'OK.' This woman intimidates me. She reminds me of my mother. 'Kids don't know how lucky they are,' she continues as she picks up one of the boxes and affixes a tag to it. 'Honestly, in my day we were lucky to get a doll – now it's these enormous toys.'

In my mind's eye, I can see Fáinne on Christmas morning going into our little front room and gasping, thrilled that Santa hasn't let her down. I hope she feels lucky – I've done my damnedest to make her feel lucky ever since I had her. Maybe I've spoilt her a bit in the process but so would you if you met her. She's so exactly right for her sweet-sounding name: all petite and fawn-like, with the big eyes inherited from her dad and the dark hair of my side. She is truly gorgeous though I suppose all mothers think the same of their children.

Now that I've actually made a payment on the Bratz van, I feel a little flutter of excitement. I ask the woman to put aside a Barbie make-up set for me too. She shakes her head and mutters something else. I watch as she tapes the make-up set to the box. I'm tempted to tell her to forget it, that I can buy the toy in another shop, but I don't. I'm no good at confrontation and, besides, the Bratz van is cheaper here than anywhere else.

Instead, I mutter a 'thanks' and make a face once I'm in the street. I wonder why she was so snappy – probably because she's a businessperson. In general, business people

– I mean *real* business people – are a bit hard. They make money and don't tend to be all soft and warm and personal. Mind you, Doug, the vet I work for, is nice. He doesn't charge some of his customers – though that's confidential. In fact, he barely makes the rent payments on our premises each month and you'd think vets would be loaded, wouldn't you? And the old woman who runs the sweetshop up the road from my house is nice, she always gives Fáinne freebies. And when I studied drama, I had a lovely teacher who was a businesswoman. And later, when I studied Drama in college, I'd got on with my tutors, who were business people. I'd even graduated with honours.

Though it hadn't done me much good – as my mother likes to remind me.

It's hard to break into acting. I do have an agent and he gets me the occasional casting – I've done a Lotto ad, a detergent ad and sometimes I've been an extra on *Fair City*. But my main job, the one I had to look for after Fáinne was born, is as a receptionist in a vet's surgery. Of course, when I landed it, my mother predicted that I'd catch all sorts of germs working with sick animals. Or I'd get bitten and catch rabies. It wasn't a responsible job for a single mother, she kept saying. What would happen if I got sick, she said. Who'd mind Fáinne then?

'Maddie,' I'd retorted, knowing she'd go ballistic. Maddie was my best friend, had been for years, but she wasn't exactly conventional – well, not back then.

'Maddie can't mind herself, never mind a baby,' Mam had snorted. 'It'd be left to me and your father to mind her, wouldn't it?'

'No.' I shook my head. 'She could go to an orphanage.'

Mam gave me a sneery look. She knew I didn't mean that. To be honest, I'd hate her to bring up Fáinne. I'd hate my child to end up like me and that's what would happen if my mother had a hand in her upbringing. Anyway, seven years on, I still haven't caught a fatal dose of anything. I'm still working away, still hoping to be spotted by some film producer, still single and, thankfully, still not living at home. My parents gave me a deposit for a small house near the surgery where I work. It has two small bedrooms, a living room, a tiny kitchen and a teeny garden: all in all about seven hundred square feet, but we love it, Fáinne and me. It's home.

2

I'M A GREAT believer in fate. I guess I'm a great believer in anything really. Well, if I'm honest, I believe in everything except people, which makes me sound cynical, though I wouldn't consider myself a cynic. For one thing, I cry loads. I cry at soppy films and at really good ads. I cry when I'm happy and when I'm angry and especially when I'm sad.

But I do believe in *things*. Like fate and fortune-tellers and psychics. Gullible is what my mother calls it and maybe she's right. I especially believe in destiny. At first, I didn't think much of finding the diary. Yeah, I was a great believer in keeping a diary for every day of my life too until one day my sister found an old one, one from my Leaving Cert, and read it out loud at the tea table. Of course she deliberately chose a piece where I was describing how some lad had walked me home from a night out and how he'd ended up thinking he was on to a good thing when I'd told him that I saw nothing wrong with sex before marriage. Two seconds later I was pinned up against a wall being shown just exactly what *was* wrong with sex before marriage. Not that the poor bugger had a chance to get that far. I'd walloped him across the face, hitting him in the eye, and made a run for it. Tracy, that's my sister, had read this whole story out to Mam and Dad in her perfectly clipped voice, her eyes laughing across the table at me. I'd cringed. Mam had launched into a marathon lecture on decency and morals (forgetting of course that her darling Tracy aka Mona Lisa had stolen my diary to begin with) with Dad nodding and shrugging every so often in a feeble attempt to back her up. I pretended to listen to her but was really waiting for my chance. When Tracy cockily handed me back my diary, I hit her hard on the head with it.

She'd screamed that I'd scraped her face, that her looks were ruined.

If only.

I'd been ordered up to bed and from then on, keeping a diary was a sketchy business. The diary I'd found is one from my second year in college. A *very* sketchy one. I'd written in it about twice a month and pictures and letters and notes fall out of it, even as I pick it up. Just inside the cover is a photo: me with scraped-up hair, wearing a pair of jeans and a tie-dyed pink sweatshirt. I'm standing beside a tall guy in navy football shorts and a white jersey. His head is turned so that his face is in shadow. I'm staring up at him with such a look of love on my face that even to gaze on the photo now, eight years later, makes my heart twist something rotten. Just to the side of the photo is Maddie. She's in her usual hippie garb. She looks so young. We both do.

I touch the guy's face gently with my index finger. I begin to trace the line of his body. Forgotten feelings spread out from somewhere in my chest. Sad, gentle, tender. Jesus, it hurts all over again.

I don't even hear the front door opening downstairs.

The next thing I'm aware of is that Fáinne is crying and my mother is doing her best to calm her down. Of course, if Fáinne cries, I start getting all worried. I jump to my feet, the diary landing back among the debris of my room. 'What's wrong?'

8

'Mammy!' Fáinne hurtles up the stairs and into the room. 'You're home.' Big fat tears are eking from her eyes.

'Hey, what's the matter?'

She throws herself at me and wraps her skinny arms around my legs. I can't make out what she's saying. 'Come on,' I say jokingly, 'what happened?'

'A right mess sending her to that drama class,' my mother calls up.

Please don't let her come up, I pray. Please don't let her come up.

Up she comes. She stands just inside my bedroom door and glances about. Her face puckers at the war zone that meets her eyes. There are clothes and books and bits of broken toys and teddies all strewn about the room: I'd decided to clean out the wardrobes. 'A right mess,' Mam says again, though I don't know if she means Fáinne's drama class or my bedroom.

'What's wrong?' I ask Fáinne again. There is no way I'm going to give Mam the satisfaction of listening to her disapproving sniffs.

'The girls at – at – at—' Fáinne heaves. 'At – at – at—'

'The girls at her drama class were teasing her,' Mam finishes, striding further into the room. 'Oh, a right bunch of stuck-up little madams, they are. I don't know why you insist on sending her to drama, it didn't do you much good.'

I ignore her and look at Fáinne. 'What were they teasing you about?'

'About her having no daddy,' my mother answers with what I think is a note of triumph in her voice.

'But I do have a daddy, don't I, Mammy?' Fáinne asks. 'Doesn't everyone have a daddy?'

I'd dreaded this day.

'I'll leave you to it,' Mam says.

I don't acknowledge her. She comes towards Fáinne and tousles her hair. 'Don't you worry, pet. Don't you worry.'

Not for the first time I think how nice my mother could be. Fáinne brings out the best in her.

Fáinne buries her head into my shoulder and I hug her harder. I'm trying to hug it all away but I know it won't work. Mam stands for a second or two, studying us. I think she's half afraid to leave. I don't think she trusts me with my own child. Anyway, neither Fáinne nor I say anything and eventually she turns around and goes. Even after the front door closes neither of us talks. I'm frantically trying to think of a way to explain things so that Fáinne will understand and I suppose Fáinne is just glad to be home.

Eventually, though, she lifts her gorgeous dark head and says, 'Isn't it true what I said, Mammy, isn't it?'

I brush her hair back from her damp face and kiss her on the forehead. 'What did you say, baby?' A pathetic stalling manoeuvre.

'I *told* you.' She sounds annoyed, which, I guess, is a good thing. 'I said,' – she takes a deep breath – 'that everyone has a daddy, but not all daddies live with their families.'

'That's right,' I agree.

'So who *does* my daddy live with?'

I swallow hard.

'Well?' She pulls away from me and, head cocked to one side, studies me. Not for the first time I feel inadequate in front of my child.

'I don't know,' I mutter.

Her eyes narrow; eerily, she reminds me of my mother. 'You don't know?' Her voice is loaded with disappointment.

'But,' I gulp, 'I can find out for you if you like.' Jesus. What had made me say that?

'Really?'

And then, like a life raft in an ocean, I remember the diary. 'I've a picture here if you'd like to see him.' I scrabble about on the floor, trying to locate the diary. Finding it, I pull out the photo. 'That's him there in the navy shorts.'

She stares at it. Softly, as if she's afraid of it not being true, she breathes, 'That's *my* daddy?'

I ruffle her hair. 'Yeah.'

'But I can't see his face.'

'I know, but you can see the rest of his body, can't you?'

She's considering this when she spots me. At first she's not sure that it is me because she looks hard at the photo and then hard at me. Eventually, her petite finger jabs at the photo and she says delightedly, 'Is that you?'

'Uh-huh.'

'You look *nice*.'

The surprise in her voice makes me laugh out loud. 'Do I not look nice now?'

A silence. 'You look OK now,' she concedes, somewhat reluctantly. 'But you look nicer there. I like your smile.'

'Thanks.' I begin to tickle her. She's really ticklish and has the most infectious laugh. 'What do you mean I look OK?' I try to sound offended. 'What do you mean?'

She's wriggling about, half laughing, begging me to stop. Arms flailing, trying to fend me off, she squeals, 'You just look nicer in the photo – happier.'

I stop tickling her then. I pull her on to my lap and both of us look again at the picture. I guess I do look happy. A big sloppy grin is plastered to my face. I was in love, that's why I looked so good. And even though a shadow covers his face, I can still remember every detail of it. The glossy dark hair that was never really cut in any particular style, just mussed about. It gave him a sort of 'just-out-of-bed' look. The huge girlish brown eyes that my daughter has inherited; the way they shone

11

when he laughed. The sallow skin; the permanent stubble on his chin; his huge, wicked grin that transformed his face from merely handsome to down and dirty sexy. He smiled a lot when he was going to do some daft stunt.

'Did he love you, Mammy?' Fáinne asked. 'Did he kiss you a lot?'

I pull myself back to the present. 'Oh.' I roll my eyes. 'Big slobbery kisses on the lips.'

'Ugh.' She makes a face and giggles. 'Gross.' She takes the photo from me and looks again at it. Her finger touches her father's body. 'So, will you get him so that I can show everyone I have a daddy?'

I feel sick. How on earth will I find him? Almost eight years is a long time. I'm about to suggest that maybe we could have a stand-in daddy. That maybe Gray, her god-father, would do it, but I know she won't go for it. 'Maybe I could look for other photos of him and you'll see his face then,' I offer feebly.

'You said you'd find him.'

'I mightn't be able to.'

'You will,' Fáinne says with the confidence all kids have in their parents. 'I know you will.'

Like I said, I hate disappointing her. 'Yeah,' I mutter, feeling sick, 'course I will.' I can't help but bask in her approving smile.

After I put her to bed, I ring Maddie. Maddie is my best mate; she's been there through it all – she was in the labour ward when I had Fáinne, much to the disgust of my mother. And it was funny, because when Fáinne was eventually born, Maddie screamed so much that every doctor in the vicinity came running in case there was an emergency going on. 'A fat lot of use she was,' my mother often gripes. And she's

12

Fáinne's godmother, also much to the disgust of my mother. 'It should be family,' she always maintains. But there was no way I was asking Tracy. Anyway, at the time Fáinne was born Tracy was tearing around the world, changing her name to Mona Lisa and building up her modelling career, and I wanted a godmother who'd be around for my daughter. The godfather bit was a problem too. Having no brothers made it difficult and there was no way I was having my father as godparent to my baby – that'd be too weird.

So I picked Graham, a guy from college. I'd met him first when he'd taken some photos of a play I'd been in in college (he was a student too only he was studying Fine Arts and Photography) and we'd become really close after a while. Not in the romantic sense, but after what happened with Jason, I'd realised what a good friend Gray was. Anyway, he has been very dutiful, bringing birthday presents to Fáinne and taking her to football matches and buying her new Barbies whenever they come out. If it weren't for Fáinne we might have drifted apart years ago, but he's still a good mate as well as a class-A godfather.

That was fate too.

'Hello?' The phone is picked up at the other end. Maddie has a really joyful way of answering the phone. A sort of 'Hellll-oh!'

'Maddie, it's me.'

'Who?'

'Me. The one who always bloody rings you and whom you never recognise on the phone.'

'Luce!'

'Well done.' I wait while she laughs slightly before plunging in. 'Listen, I have a problem.'

'No!' She makes a big mock-shocked sound. 'Get away! Lucy Gleeson with a problem – I don't believe it!'

13

I snigger a bit. Then remember why I'm ringing. 'It's a biggie.'

'Goody. Your life is what makes my life interesting.'

'I told Fáinne that I was going to trace Jason.'

There is a silence.

'*The* Jason?'

'Yep.'

More silence. I think she thinks I'm joking.

'You're joking.'

'Nope.'

More silence. Then, 'How and what for?'

'I don't know and because he's her dad and she wants to know about him.'

'So tell her about him. Show her a photo. Jesus, Luce, how can you after what he did?'

'I did think about getting someone to pretend . . .' I sound pathetic.

'That's pathetic.'

I don't know what to say to that. 'I know,' I eventually agree, even more pathetically.

'I mean' – Maddie's voice rises – 'say you do find him, what are you going to do? Wow – say if he's married? Say if he has a pile of kids of his own?'

I really haven't thought that far ahead. All I want from Maddie is some back-up. Anyway, Jason didn't seem the marrying sort. Coward that I am, I don't want to go it alone. 'So you think it's a bad idea?'

'I think it's about the stupidest idea ever,' she confirms.

'But don't you think Fáinne deserves to know who her dad is?'

'She might but he doesn't. He was a bit fucked-up, Luce.'

I change tack. 'Aren't you even curious about what happened to him?'

'No.'

'Not even a teensy-eensy bit?' I put on a baby voice: 'A lickle-ickle bit?'

'Not even a fuckin'-wuckin' bit.'

'So you won't help me?'

'I never said that,' she replies. A pause. 'I mean, if you're determined to ruin your life by tracking down that scum, you might as well do it in style. I mean, there is no one like me for helping people fuck up.'

I know what she's really saying is that she'll be around to pick up the pieces.

'Thanks, Madd.'

'I hope you're still saying that when he shits all over you again.'

'Have you seen my garden? I need the fertiliser.' I grin as she starts to laugh.

3

September 29th
College back today and I was thanking God or whoever is responsible
for the universe that at last the holidays were over. I was so sick of
them, mainly because of my poxy part-time job in my mother's local
hairdresser's. All my mates went abroad and what do I do? Wash hair
for blue rinses.

At first it wasn't too bad. It only really got unbearable when all the
auld biddies discovered that I was Dora Gleeson's daughter.

'Are you the model?' was the question on everyone's lips.

'No,' I had to keep saying, over and over, 'that's my sister Tracy.'

And it didn't matter what I did, all they wanted to know about was
Tracy.

'Oh, so what is Tracy doing? Your mother was telling us that she
was doing a lipstick promotion last week.'

And whole days were lost to me as I listened to them talk about
Tracy and her fabulous modelling career. Don't get me wrong – I'm not
jealous of Tracy. Well, maybe only a little because she's earning pots
of money and I'm stuck in college studying a 'go-nowhere-fast' profes-
sion. At least that's what my mother calls it. 'You could be a model too
if you put your mind to it,' she keeps telling me. It's like if I studied
hard enough, I'd get better-looking or something.

I guess I look OK, only compared to Tracy I'm just a faulty photo-
copy. You know, exactly the same but not as perfect. I'm smaller for
starters. I also eat a lot more than she does which makes me heavier.

I've actually got thighs and an arse and she hasn't. My hair has a kink in it and hers is glossy straight. Our eyes are the same shade of blue, we both have fine straight noses and our lips have the same full-ness. I like my lips a lot actually; they've a nice shape. That's the work Tracy gets at the moment: lipsticks. Anyway, if I'm not careful this whole diary will be devoted to Tracy. I do not want to talk about Tracy any more.

She is the bane of my life.

So, heading into college today was a relief. It felt like I had a life again. I was even looking forward to getting my timetable and assign-ments and all that stuff. Most of all I was looking forward to seeing Maddie and Gray. I hadn't seen either of them all summer. Maddie took off to France to be an au pair and spent months out there. She kept in touch via the odd letter but it wasn't the same. Anyway, her au pair job crumbled within a week – she took the kids out for a walk one day and couldn't find her way back. She couldn't even remember the street she was working on. After a big search by the kids' parents, she was located and fired. I couldn't stop laughing when she wrote me that story.

I'm looking forward to seeing Gray too. He went travelling during the summer as well, but his folks are loaded so it was no problem. He's big into photography and he took his camera with him. He sent me back some cool pictures of weird landscapes, but even though I knew they were good and everything, I would have preferred one of him. You know, a normal photo, with people in it. Gray is brilliant though; when he was a kid he was offered a job on a paper after winning some national competition and then they discovered how old he was and they had to withdraw the offer. Gray says he was devastated. I'd be too. It'd be like me getting a job on a film and being told afterwards that I was the wrong height or something. Jesus!

Anyway, I cycled into college. Mam, of course, had given me a list of instructions on how to avoid getting run over by articulated trucks. Then she'd spouted all the statistics to do with cyclists getting run over and how dangerous the whole thing was. I mean, that really gave me confidence. Dad laughed and told her to stop it and she got all huffy with him.

Nothing new there.

I didn't tell them that I cycle because it saves on bus fares which means that I can order extra drinks in the student bar at the weekends – have to get the priorities right. It took me thirty minutes to get in which was good, as I hadn't exercised all summer, unless you count sweeping up hair. I locked my bike and wandered over to the canteen. Maddie, Gray and I always take the same table, unless of course there's someone sitting at it, in which case we'll take the one beside it or the one beside that. The campus was buzzing; everyone was flinging arms about their mates and squealing and swapping fags and photos. I hoisted my bag over my shoulder and sauntered down the steps into the canteen. It was fairly quiet and Maddie and Gray hadn't arrived, so I bought a coffee and a croissant and made my way to our table.

Some guy was sitting at it.

I plonked down at the table beside him. I'm sure he thought it was odd because there were tables everywhere and I had to take the one beside him. 'I'm just waiting for my friends,' I said. 'It's just we usually sit at your table and if I don't sit near it they won't know where to meet me.'

'Oh, right.' He looked at me and it was then I noticed how gorgeous he was. Or maybe not gorgeous, just incredibly sexy. He grinned at me, a really slow grin which seemed to take ages to spread across his face. 'And here was me thinking I was having a lucky day.'

He was so sexy that his feeble joke sent me into spasms of giggles. I was mortified for myself which made me blush. 'Get away,' I said, before realising that that was such an un-cool thing to say.

He merely smiled, looking half embarrassed, half amused.

I turned back to my coffee. I ignored my croissant because I could never eat them with any degree of style. Bits of crumbs tend to go everywhere and my fingers get all greasy.

18

'Jason.' He held out his hand. 'Jason Donovan.'

'Oh.' I couldn't help but smile.

'Yeah.' He shrugged ruefully. 'I've had all the jokes. My dreamcoat is fine; I'm over the split with Kylie.' He paused. 'So, who are you?'

I put down my coffee cup with such haste that it slopped out all over the place. I burnt my hand. 'I'm Lucy,' I said, fighting back a huge gasp of pain. 'Lucy Gleeson.'

'And what is Lucy Gleeson studying?' He angled his body towards mine. Denim jeans, bleached and faded, a navy and grey rugby top and the most glorious face you can imagine.

'Drama,' I squeaked. Already my heart was pounding. 'You know, acting and stuff.'

'Wow – dead impressive. I'm doing Fine Arts. What year are you in?'

'Second.'

'Me too.'

He looked older than nineteen. I mean, he had a boyish look about him but his eyes looked older or something.

'I should be in fourth year,' he said. 'I did first year and got a bit bored so I travelled a bit but that was boring too and so I'm back.'

So he was older than me! Wow. Maybe he was in his twenties, that'd be mad.

'Hiii!' From behind I was enfolded in a huge hug.

'Maddie!' I hugged her back.

'Let's see you.' She stood back to look at me. 'You look great.'

I grinned. If anything, she was the one that looked great. And it wasn't her looks, Maddie was not really beautiful or anything, it was just her. She lit up the place with her huge personality.

'Maddie, this is Jason.' I indicated Jason. 'He's doing Fine Arts.'

'Wow.' Maddie was frank in her admiration. 'For the first time ever, I wish I knew about sculptures and shit.'

Jason laughed.

I sort of wished I'd made him laugh.

19

'Folks!' From behind came another voice I recognised.

'Gray!' both Maddie and I said together.

'How's it going, guys?'

Graham looked good. It had obviously been hot when he was away because he had a great tan. His hair, normally brown, was bleached blond in places and he'd grown taller. I reckon he's about six two now. He dumped his haversack on the floor and grinned broadly at us. 'Great to see yez. Sorry I'm late, the guys on the soccer team had a meeting this morning.'

Graham plays soccer for the university team. He's quite good apparently though I've never seen him play. He takes it really seriously too, always training and stuff.

'This is Jason.' I introduced Jason, determined that from now he was going to be a part of our little gang.

'Hey, Jason Donovan.' Gray grinned. 'Long time no see.'

'You know him?' Gray soared in my estimation. Never ever had Gray been of any use in finding good-looking guys. All his mates were spotty and weedy.

'He's only meant to be the best forward ever.'

Jason shrugged. 'Well, in this college that doesn't say much.' He turned to me. 'I'm on the football team. I met Gray this morning. I used to play when I was here before.'

'Great.' Maddie nudged me. 'We're great supporters of that team – we go to all the matches. Can't wait to see you play.'

Gray looked from her to me but said nothing. All I could think of was that at least it wouldn't be the last time I met Jason.

I have a feeling that this year is gonna be the best yet.

I put the diary down and close my eyes. I can remember that meeting. Everything about it is etched on my brain. Maybe on some subconscious level I knew it was a significant day. Maybe, if I'd done things differently, the memory

20

would have faded, but it was the choice made that day that led to everything else.

I had made the choice to have Jason as my friend.

4

MY MORNINGS ARE a bit mental. I get up around seven and drag Fáinne from the bed. She's the complete opposite of me – I'm terrible in the mornings while she is at her sunniest. I slouch downstairs and she dances. I pour myself some Bran Flakes – my one nod to healthy eating during the day – and pour Fáinne her Rice Krispies. I douse both cereals with milk and we eat them. Fáinne talks all the way through and I pretend to listen.

This morning, Fáinne hurtles down the stairs in her pink Barbie dressing gown wondering loudly what the toy will be in the Rice Krispie box. My eyes barely open, I grab a bowl from the press and watch blearily as she rips open the cereal box and scatters food everywhere.

'Ooops, sorry!'

''S OK.'

'I had a lovely dream last night.' She gleefully finds the toy, tears open the wrapping, studies it and discards it. She pokes me hard in the arm. 'Did you hear me, Mammy? I said I had a lovely dream last night!'

'Did you?' I attempt a smile. 'That's nice.' I pour myself a strong coffee to wake myself up.

'All about you and me and Daddy.'

I freeze. The coffee overflows. 'Shit!'

'We were living in this house.' Fáinne stares about her

happily and shovels some cereal into her mouth. 'All bof us and we visited Nana just like a real bamily.' Her voice is muffled because of the food in her mouth but I can understand her.

'That was a funny dream.' I try to keep my voice light. I begin a mop-up operation on the coffee so I won't have to meet her gaze.

'And he took me horse-riding just like Jenny's daddy does with her.'

'You don't like horses.'

'I know, but my real daddy makes me not be scared of them. Just like the way Jenny's dad does.'

'Right.' I don't know what to say. I know one thing: I want to strangle Jenny. Fáinne is grinning up at me and my heart rolls. 'Look, Fáinne,' I gulp, 'we have to find your daddy first and maybe he mightn't want to live here.' Her smile falters. 'In fact I don't think he will,' I say, determined to get the point across. 'He'll have his own house by now.'

'It was only a *dream*, Mammy. She glares at me as if I'm stupid. 'I only *dreamt* it.'

'Yeah, I know but—'

'The coffee is dripping on the floor.'

Apparently the subject is now closed.

At half seven Fáinne goes up to wash her hands and face. I pour a second coffee for myself and when she's finished splashing about in the bathroom it's my turn to wash and dress.

It's a bitch working in a vet's surgery actually. Talk about having to wear unadventurous clothes. I spend my day on the counter, talking to clients about their pets. The worst is when the animals have to be put down – kids crying and parents bawling: it's a nightmare. That's why I don't have a pet myself;

even though Fáinne is mad for a dog, I don't know if we could cope with the heartbreak if something goes wrong.

Anyway, my job is messy and smelly and bright clothes are out just in case someone arrives really upset and dark clothes are out in case someone arrives really upset. I've a little collection of trousers and jumpers especially for the occasion. My 'older person clothes', Fáinne says. I always look really spinsterish in them but as my mother keeps reminding me, I *am* a spinster.

By eight-thirty we're ready to go. I've sort of woken up a bit and I force myself to chat to her as we drive to my mother's. Mam takes her to school for me, you see. She's dead good like that. I mean, she moans and complains about everything else but for Fáinne she'd do anything. She even brings her to drama for me on a Wednesday though she thinks it's a waste of money. Anyway, after what happened the last time Fáinne went to drama, I'm going to cancel the classes. I do wish though that I could bring Fáinne to school myself. I just want to see her in her school uniform. I want to see her running across the schoolyard to talk to her friends. I want to see her laugh with them. I want to reassure myself that she's happy, that people like her. Mam says that of course people like Fáinne; I mean, who wouldn't want to be her friend? she says.

Most days, I'm home around five thirty after picking Fáinne up from my parents.

'Now listen, baby,' I tell Fáinne just as I pull into my mother's driveway. 'Don't say anything to Nana about looking for your daddy, all right?'

'Why?'

'Because, well, maybe Nana mightn't like to know our business, OK?'

24

'But it's Nana's business too. He'll be related to Nana.'

'Just don't tell her, all right?' I make my voice stern. If my mother found out I was looking for Jason, she'd freak. And to be honest, in the cold light of day, I don't know if it's a good idea. Every time I think of a possible meeting scenario, my heart heaves and I feel sick. How will I get the words out? What do I say? And what will happen if he refuses to see Fáinne? What'll I tell her?

'OK, Mammy.' Fáinne sighs resignedly. 'I won't tell Nana. It'll be a surprise for her, won't it?'

I almost laugh at her choice of words. 'Mmm, yeah.'

Mam is at the front door. 'What's keeping you?' she calls, coming down the drive to meet the car. As usual, she looks great. No matter what time I manage to get Fáinne over, Mam is always up and dressed and made-up. Even when we were kids, she had to look perfect. I used to like it when I was in school, it was important to have a decent-looking mammy waiting for you when you got out. Now, though, it drives me mad. I keep wondering how she managed it. Two kids and she could do her make-up in the morning. I have one and I can barely get dressed.

'Mammy is just telling me something,' Fáinne says mysteriously as she gets out. She pulls her bag after her. Another Barbie present from Gray.

'Oh?' Mam quirks her eyebrows.

'Bye now.' I blip my horn and reverse up. 'See you later.' Fáinne blows me a kiss.

I'm in work for nine. I'm responsible for opening the clinic before all the customers come in. We have a two-hour surgery in the morning, an hour in the afternoon and two hours again in the evening. Wednesdays we open late and we're open on Saturdays for three hours. Saturday is by appointment only while the rest of the time it's open clinic. I don't work in the evenings: I come in at nine and knock off around five. The hours are great really, they suit me for minding Fáinne. Clare, the other receptionist, comes in in the afternoons and does the evening shift and Saturdays. She is a bit weird – she can be in great form one day and jump down your throat the next. When she's in good form, she goes on and on about what a wonderful husband she has, how much money she has, how she's only working to amuse herself, but when she's in shite form she gives Doug grief for not charging people properly and snaps the heads off all the customers.

The clinic is run by two vets, Doug and Jim. Doug is the one I see most of, he works a lot in the mornings and afternoons just like me. He also works in the evenings from seven until eight, then Jim takes over. He mainly does call outs. He says it suits him because he can't sleep at night.

I pull into the car park in front of the surgery and am surprised to see someone waiting. Then I look at who it is and I'm not surprised at all. Mr Devlin and his dog are regulars. I think he comes so often because he's lonely. His wife died last year and ever since he's poured all his energies into his dog, who just happens to be the most vicious animal you're ever likely to meet. Small and curly-haired, her snarl can make your blood run cold. Doug had to get stitches once when he was giving her an injection. She stayed all nice and quiet and then, just as Doug was about to plunge the needle in, she hurled herself at him. Doug had to be carted off to hospital and we had to shut for the day. Mr D. is a gas though; he doesn't seem to realise what a horrible dog he has. Because he comes so often, Doug, hopeless businessman that he is, only charges him about a tenth of what he should be charged, which drives Clare mad, of course.

'Hello there, Mr D.' I slam shut the door on my rickety

car and it shudders. 'How's Paddy today?' That's the name of the dog.

Paddy looks well: she's all dressed up in a tartan coat. In fact, she's better dressed than her owner. Mr D. doesn't even have a coat and his jumper and trousers are tatty. And it can't be for lack of money because he lives on one of the most expensive streets in Dublin.

'Oh, just fine.' Mr D. is a bit deaf. He shouts everything at the top of his voice. He also limps – I think Paddy bit him once when she was a puppy. 'She's here for her monthly defleaing medicine. I wanted to beat the rush so I came early.'

There never is a rush in the mornings unless it's some emergency or other. 'Good thinking,' I say, grinning. I think about patting Paddy and decide against it. 'Hey,' I say instead, in that ridiculous voice that we reserve for kids and animals. 'You've put on a bit of weight, haven't you, girl?'

Paddy bares her teeth in a silent growl.

'A big belly on her all right,' Mr Devlin says in a mock-severe voice. 'It's middle-aged spread, that's what it is.'

I unlock the clinic door and Mr D. follows me in. 'And how are you?' I ask. I go behind my desk and flick on the computers. 'All right?'

He loves being asked about his health, partly because it's not good. 'Not great,' he concedes with a weird mixture of pride and woe. He shakes his head and leans on the counter. 'I had a bit of a cough last night and I think it's going into my chest.' He demonstrates by coughing into my face. 'Hear that?'

'Awful. Cuppa?' I go into the kitchen and plug in the kettle. Mr Devlin continues to shout at me.

'I will, thanks. Anyway, I've a sort of tightness along my breastbone, so I reckon it's going to get bad. I'm going to visit my doctor in the afternoon.'

27

'Well, I'm sure he'll take care of you.'

'Oh, I'm not so sure. A friend of mine had piles and he wasn't much good with him. You don't want to hear about the trouble my friend had with those piles.'

He's right there. I make the tea to a backdrop of him talking to Paddy.

'Now, for Jaysus' sake, be good for the vet,' he tells her sternly. 'Be a very good girl and I will get you a nice treat.'

Paddy snarls.

'Nooo. Not that. Something beginning with a W.'

Paddy snarls louder. I deposit the cuppa on the counter and watch them. Mr D. stands looking sternly down at his dog, like some kind of decrepit schoolteacher.

'A W?' he says, making a 'w' sound.

Snarl. Snarl.

'No, not Bonio. A W, I said.'

Paddy barks and snarls and makes darting motions for her master's legs.

Mr D. jumps nimbly out of the way but he's grinning broadly. 'Waistcoat! Well done.' He turns to me. 'Isn't that clever now? That's how she says "waistcoat": a sort of bark and a snarl.' He picks up his tea and takes a gulp. 'Jaysus, that's hot. Trying to burn me mouth, are you?' The tea gets spat back into the cup as I blurt out an apology.

'Aw, not you again.' Doug's laughing voice cuts through Mr Devlin's gasping. He stands just inside the door and grins at the two of us. 'I thought I'd killed you and the dog off the last time.' He pats his leg. Paddy looks cautiously at him and gives a reluctant wag of her stumpy tail. Doug grins across at me.

Mr D. – we never call him anything else – chortles. 'Hard to kill a bad thing.'

'Well, I'll have a damn good try now.' He winks at me

over his head. 'Come on in. I'll just get set up. Monthly flea, mite and worm is it?'

'Not that she has any now,' Mr D. clarifies as he follows him up the corridor dragging Paddy like a wet rag behind him.

Things are busier in the afternoon. Loads of howling, snarling and meowing. One dog had attempted to chew the counter before being restrained.

I'm thinking that Fáinne will be out playing in the yard now. She'll have eaten her sandwiches and put all the crusts carefully back into her lunchbox. She's a bit weird like that – she likes to bring all her rubbish home and throw it in our bin. 'I don't like it being lost in the school bin,' she explained once. After lunch, which finishes in ten minutes, she'll go back into her classroom and start working again. I miss her during the day.

The phone rings.

'Phone, Lucy,' Clare says. She's in a bad mood today.

'It's that thing there that's ringing,' I say brightly. 'The black thing right beside you.'

'Phone,' she says again.

I stamp and snort and pick it up. 'Hello, Yellow Halls Veterinary Surgery?'

'Yellow, Yellow, Yellow.'

I know the voice. I know the only eejit on the planet that insists on saying 'yellow' for 'hello'. For some reason he thinks it's arty or cool or something. 'Les,' I mutter. 'You can't ring me at work.'

'This is an emergency.'

'What – you've lost your personality?'

My agent laughs. 'Acting is wasted on you. You should be in stand-up.'

29

'The only thing I'd stand up would be you, Les.'

He laughs again, though not as heartily. 'Well, just for that, you'll have to beg me to tell you all about this audition I've got lined up for you.'

My heart lurches. Normally when casting agents ring Les, they're desperate. 'What's it for?'

'Ah, ah, ahhh,' Les teases. 'Say "pretty please".'

'I can't think of you and say pretty,' I deadpan.

He sniggers. 'Pity so.'

I glance around. All the customers are ignoring me, trying instead to get their animals to stop eyeing each other up with a view to decimating each other. Clare is cursing under her breath so she must be doing the accounts. 'Pretty please,' I mutter.

Les grunts in satisfaction. 'It's an ad,' he pronounces.

I feel a bit disappointed. For one fleeting moment, I'd hoped for a film part or a soap part. Still, ads tended to pay well.

'It'll pay well,' Les goes on. 'They're looking for a . . .' He pauses and I hear the sound of paper being shuffled about. '. . . for a twenty-something woman, good-looking but not a total babe.'

'And you thought of me, how nice.'

He misses my sarcasm. 'You've to smile smugly, which should be no problem to you, and you've to say to camera' – he puts on a girly voice – '"I like my man protected."'

I ignore his defective acting ability. 'So when is it – the audition?'

'You haven't heard the best part yet,' Les crows. 'Do you want to hear the best part?'

'If it doesn't take too long.' There was a call coming in on the line.

'Post off these first thing in the morning,' Clare says in

her nasal voice, jabbing me in the arm and dumping a load of letters in front of me. 'I've marked them all as urgent.'

'Emergency.' I point at the phone. 'Well?' I hiss to Les.

Les takes a deep breath. 'There'll be a big billboard campaign and the company plan to run a series of ads featuring the same woman over and over. It'll be big – like the Nescafé one a good few years back.'

Now my heart does quicken. 'And all I have to say is "I want my man protective"?'

'"Protected",' Les corrects me. 'So I'll put your name down, will I? I'll get you a time.'

'Early evening,' I blab. 'Around five-thirty.'

'Will do. Ta ta.'

'Les, what's the ad for?'

There is a small silence. I presume he's looking up his file. 'Protective clothing for men,' he says eventually. 'They'll explain it all when you go in.'

'Great. Thanks.'

'Ta, ta,' he says again.

The line goes dead.

5

WHEN I ARRIVE to pick up Fáinne my mother meets me at the door with a look on her face that would stop a nuclear reaction.

I ignore the impending storm and breeze out a 'hi'.

She disregards my greeting. 'So,' she says, hands on her hips as she follows me into the kitchen, 'I hear you're determined to *ruin* your life.'

My mother is master of the overstatement. She never comes straight out with what's annoying her, instead she implies things. It's a device she's always used to get me to confess to stuff she mightn't even know about. I decide to wait and see what's bothering her. I know it can't be about Jason because Fáinne would never have told her.

'Hiya, baby.' I grin at my daughter and dump my handbag on the table. 'Good day?'

'Jenny says you're a liar, Mammy.' Fáinne looks at me accusingly. 'And Nana says that you're still nineteen. But I told her that you're not.'

'What?'

'That waster!' My mother almost snarls. 'You're—'

'Fáinne, come on.' My father holds out his hand to Fáinne, interrupting Mam mid-flow. 'Let's see if we can find any conkers on the trees out the back.'

Fáinne looks uneasily at me. 'Nana is cross with you, Mammy.'

'Well, there's nothing new in that,' I say lightly, causing my mother's shoulders to hunch up behind her ears. 'You go and look for conkers with Granddad.'

They'll be looking for ages because the only things growing out back are blackberry bushes. My mother must be really furious with me over something if everyone else has to leave the room. Still, I've got an audition; I can floor her with that if she starts on about my wasted life.

Fáinne and my father go out, Fáinne holding on to his hand and skipping along.

Mam sniffs. 'Huh – out at the first sign of trouble.'

I decide that I might as well sit down – this looks as if it could be bad. I sit with my back to my mother. 'Dad's looking after Fáinne,' I say, coming to his defence as always. 'Kids don't like hearing rows.'

She flinches a little at this. Then she comes around the table and sits opposite me.

'Well?' I ask. I make a production of looking at my watch. 'What's the story?'

'I could ask *you* the same question.'

'Mam,' I say, trying to sound patient, 'I've Maddie coming over tonight – I have to get back.'

'Is she going to help you?' Mam leans across the table at me. 'Is she helping you look for him?'

My blood runs cold. Jesus, I think, she *knows*. 'Look for who?' I squeak out guiltily.

Mam says nothing.

'Fáinne wants to meet him,' I blab.

'Oh for God's sake, she's only a child – she doesn't know what she wants. Show her a picture of him or something.'

'I did and she wants to meet him.' My voice rises. I don't

know why I'm defending myself. It's really none of her business. 'She has a right to know him.'

'He has no right!'

The words hang in the air. I don't reply. Maddie said more or less the same thing the previous evening.

Mam glares at me for a second, before continuing, more calmly, 'She told everyone in school that you were going to find her daddy, Lucy. When I went to collect her, she was being called a liar by her so-called "friends".'

I wince.

'Oh, I ran them, I can tell you.' Mam gives me another glare. 'Little bitches,' she hisses. Then, after she realises that her glare has beaten me into submission, she continues in a surprisingly calm voice, 'Why on earth couldn't you have looked for him without letting her know? I mean, I don't think you should do it, but if you're determined, why couldn't you just look for him without getting her hopes up?'

I realise just then that, of course, that would have been the sensible thing to do but unfortunately I've never been one for the sensible thing. I'm convinced that for some people the sensible thing is hidden away at the moment they make their choices. My mother is a rock of sense, but rocks are hard. 'It just came out,' I mutter.

'Well, miss' – she always calls me 'miss' when she's annoyed – 'you think long and hard about what you're going to do. What do you want him back in your life for? What if he wants to see her? Or his family want to see her? They'll have rights too, you know.'

'Yeah.' I glare at her. I fold my arms, like I'm nineteen again, and pout. 'I know all that.' I hadn't thought of that at all. Christ.

'You are not a child any more, Lucy.'

I don't say anything.

'You're a mother now – you've responsibilities.'

I hate this. If anything, she's the one not letting me grow up by constantly reminding me of my responsibilities. 'I'm going to get Fáinne,' I say. I pick up my bag from the table. Grudgingly I mutter, 'Thanks for minding her.'

'You know we love it.' Her voice softens and for an instant we make eye contact. I turn away.

'Fáinne!' I call, rapping on the kitchen window. 'Time to go.'

Mam shakes her head again and mutters something I can't catch. I clamp down my irritation and watch as Fáinne tugs my father's arm, urging him to hurry up. He's smiling at her and trotting alongside her. They come in the door and I'd have to be blind not to see him look anxiously at my mother. She shrugs and tuts and busies herself wiping down the draining board.

'No conkers,' Fáinne gripes. 'Granddad said that the trees aren't listening to him at all. They keep making berries instead.'

'That's not the only thing that doesn't listen,' my mother mutters.

'Well now!' my dad says loudly, in a hopeless attempt to restore some harmony. 'Well now!'

'Thanks, Dad,' I say.

'Not at all.' Dad rubs Fáinne's head. 'She's a great girl, aren't you?

'And so's my mammy.' Fáinne looks at me adoringly and I feel guilt creep right up through me. 'She's going to get me a daddy.' Then her hands clamp over her mouth and a look of horror crosses it. 'Ooooh, I wasn't meant to say that.'

'Like mother like daughter,' my mother says from her position at the sink. She's smiling though, at Fáinne, of course.

She turns to a small bowl on the worktop and hands Fáinne a euro. 'For some sweets after your tea.'

'Thanks.' Fáinne grins delightedly and hugs her. My mother hugs her back. She's never hugged me like that.

'Bye now,' Mam says to me.

'Yeah. Bye.'

Dad walks to the car with us. 'She's just worried,' he says as I strap Fáinne in. 'That's just her way. She got upset down in the school yard.'

'I'm used to it now, Dad,' I say, trying to be flippant. I sit in the car and roll down the window. 'Without me, she wouldn't be like that.'

'Oh, now, that's not true—'

I cut him off by starting up the engine. 'Bye.'

'Bye, Granddad, bye!' Fáinne waves vigorously from her seat. 'Bye!'

Dad blows her a kiss.

6

FÁINNE IS OBSESSED with her daddy. All through dinner she pesters me with questions. Did he like soccer? Did he take pictures? Was he funny? What colour hair had he? Was he tall? Did he like to go out with pretty girls? Did he get hangovers?

I soon realise that Fáinne is basing all her questions on what her granddad and Gray do, as they are the only men in my life at the moment.

As I shovel some half-burnt waffles on to her plate I try to be honest. 'Your daddy was funny. He used to make me laugh. He was a great soccer player and he supported Liverpool.'

Fáinne winces. 'Me and Gray like Bohs.'

Bohs is an Irish soccer team; Gray is fanatical in his support of them. He has Fáinne brainwashed. He loves bringing her to see them play; he buys her all the merchandise and most Friday nights he'll take her to a match if he's not meeting his mates. I go along sometimes but I end up admiring the players' legs and hairstyles and if I really want to annoy Gray, I wolf whistle every time the Bohs striker gets the ball. I can't remember the guy's name but he's a fine thing.

'Do you think Gray would mind, Mammy, if I started to support Liverpool too?'

'I dunno – I shouldn't think so.'

'I'll ask him.' Fáinne cuts into her waffles.

I put my own plate down and sit opposite her. 'What's this about the kids in school calling you a liar?'

She looks guiltily at me. 'Nana said they were bitches. Is bitches a bad word?'

I want to do the mammy thing. I want to tell her that it's not nice to call someone a bitch. Instead, I shake my head. 'If they were being bitchy, then it's the right word, don't you think?'

She considers this. 'I think they were being bastards, Mammy. That's the word I think.'

I don't say anything. I chew a waffle, trying not to laugh. The waffle soon wipes any semblance of a smile from my face. It tastes awful. Everything I cook is awful. The only decent meals Fáinne and I have are at my mother's. I should really get recipes from her but I know I'd only get a lecture thrown in as well.

'Bastards,' Fáinne says again, obviously enjoying the sound of the word that she's normally not allowed say.

'So they were calling you a liar?' I prompt, hoping to get the subject back on track.

'Uh-huh.' Fáinne nods. 'Jenny, see, was going on and on at break time, about her daddy and how wonderful he is.' She rolls her eyes and I try not to grin. It's a love-hate relationship between the two. 'So,' Fáinne continues, 'I just said, "Well, I have a daddy too and my mammy is going to get him for me."'

I cringe. 'And?'

'And Jenny made a face and said that you can't just go *getting* a daddy. And I said that I *knew* that, that you were going to look for him, that he'd disappeared but that you would find him.'

Christ!

'And she said that I was a liar. And after school she started calling, "Liar, liar, pants on fire," and I said' – Fáinne shook

38

her hair back from her face and smiled proudly – 'that at least my pants were *clean* not all dirty like hers and she pulled my hair and said I was a liar and then Nana came and called her a bitch.'

I rub my hands over my face. I want to laugh. I want to cry. 'Right.'

'Then Nana asked me what had happened and I didn't tell her but Jenny did. Jenny said that I was a liar for saying that you were looking for Daddy.'

'Right.' I'm going to kill Jenny.

'And that's it.' Fáinne spoons the last of her beans into her mouth. 'Can I have ice-cream?'

I get up to get her some. My own dinner is uneaten. 'Will you be disappointed if I can't find your daddy?' I ask, my back to her. 'I mean, eight years is a long time. I don't know where he is.'

'Go on the radio,' Fáinne said. 'Declan D'arcy will find him for you.'

When had she ever listened to Declan D'arcy? His radio show was a laugh but it was hardly suitable for seven-year-olds.

'Gray listens to him,' she says. 'And one time they had a woman on who was looking for someone who was Les Bean. And they found someone for her.'

I want to kill *Gray* now.

'Right.'

I watch as she eats her ice-cream. She's dressed in her usual attire of jeans and a soccer jersey. A Bohs jersey. The tomboyish clothes can't hide how lovely she is, how young she is. I want everything for her. I'm scared that somehow I'll let her down.

Maybe I already have.

*

Maddie arrives over at nine. Fáinne has just gone to bed with warnings that if she comes down she won't get any sweets for a week. To be honest, she's actually very good at going to bed and staying there, but I do not want her over-hearing any part of the conversation between Maddie and me.

Maddie hasn't changed since college – well, physically anyway. She's still small and round with a riot of brown tumbling curls and a huge smile. She still wears clothes that border on the hippie: she's dressed tonight in a loose white cotton blouse with an embroidered neckline and wide, embroidered sleeves. She's wearing a long purple skirt with tassels at the end and black Doc boots. Her hair is tied up with a purple and yellow scarf. This shows off her dainty ears complete with long jingly earrings. She looks great, as always.

'Hiiii,' she says loudly, shoving a bottle of plonk into my hands. 'How's the Private Investigator?'

'Shut up.' But I grin, motioning towards the stairs. 'Don't let herself hear you. She's obsessing already.'

Maddie's brown eyes darken. 'That is not good, ma petite chatte.'

She's a French teacher. After college, she suddenly realised that theatre was not for her and she did a H-dip and now teaches French in a rough and tumble community school. She's living with one of the business studies teachers; he's very conventional, very ordinary and I would never have put them together in a million years. But they've been together for almost three years now and that's the longest Maddie has ever been with anyone. His name is Clive and he *looks* like a Clive, if you know what I mean.

Maddie moves on into my tiny sitting room and plonks herself on the sofa. 'Gimme a drink, I'm gasping.'

I pour us both some wine and we sit a second in silence.

'So,' she says, 'Fáinne really thinks you're going to find Jason, does she?'

I nod.

'And if you don't?'

'Jesus, how hard can it be?' I say back. 'We just have to have a plan of action.'

'Look at what happened the last time we had a plan of action,' Maddie says.

We both think for a second and then, despite the painful memories, I begin to giggle. 'OK, so I got pregnant and upset my folks and ruined my life and—'

Maddie laughs. 'Operation Chasing Jason: ey?'

'That plan went a little wrong.'

Maddie laughs harder.

'But I wouldn't be without her now,' I say, nodding in the general direction of Fáinne's room.

'I know.' Maddie pats my hand, still grinning. After a bit, she says, 'Well, I was thinking it all over last night and the first thing we have to do is to ring the college and see if they'll give us an address to work from.'

I like the way she'd said 'we'. 'That's a very good place to start,' I say in my best Mary Poppins voice. Which reminds me. 'Hey, I've an audition!'

'No!' Maddie looks impressed.

'For an ad.'

'Oh.' Maddie doesn't look impressed.

'Well, a series of ads. And billboards.'

'Oh – good one. Who got you it?'

'Les.'

'Feck off!'

Everyone in my year at college landed good agents. Les had been good too. Once. 'So' – I swirl the wine around in

41

my half-empty glass – 'maybe this face will be appearing on a TV near you soon.'

'It will,' Maddie says confidently. She always had more faith in my acting abilities than I had. 'You're great on telly. You stole the scene in *Fair City* the time you were on.'

I laugh. I'd sat in the background in the pub while two of the main characters had a fistfight. 'Ta.'

I pour myself some more wine and attempt to top up Maddie's glass but she's hardly touched hers.

'You driving?'

'Naw – Clive is picking me up.'

I 'oooh' and 'aaah' a bit but she ignores me. 'So, when are you going to ring the college?' she asks. 'The sooner the better.'

My heart gives a jolt, making me feel sick. This is really happening. 'In a couple of weeks, I suppose, when the colleges start back.'

'Sure, if that turns up nothing, we'll go to his flat, the one he used to rent, d'you remember?'

How could I forget it? Like everything else about the guy, it's etched on my mind in Technicolor three-D.

7

October 1st

Sad pathetic person that I am, I actually went to a football training session tonight. I dragged Maddie along, who didn't mind too much, to be honest. All those men's legs would be worth seeing, she reckoned. Only they weren't. Gray's football team are the ugliest, hairiest bunch of lads going. Well, with the exception of Jason — who was the main attraction anyway. Maddie said, kind of crossly, that she hoped all the standing about in the cold would lead to something. She hoped that I wouldn't just stare at Jason and get nowhere. I pretended that I didn't know what she was talking about. I'm not much good with lads. None of them ever seem interested in me. Maybe it comes from having a mega babe as a sister.

Anyway, after training, the lads all came out of the dressing rooms. Jason still had his shorts on but he'd changed his T-shirt. His dark hair was all mussed and wet and he looked GORGEOUS. And I got all tongue-tied and started hopping from foot to foot and it was Maddie who eventually asked Gray and Jason if they were going for a pint. Gray was up for it but Jason shook his head. He was wrecked, apparently. He didn't look wrecked. He looked lovely.

The lads kept hassling him to go and I really thought he would go, but he didn't.

'Naw,' he said in his delicious Kerry accent, 'I'll go back to the flat.' He sounded regretful.

Then Maddie said that I was heading in that direction and that

43

maybe he could walk me to my bus stop. Jason looked confused. Gray looked confused. I was confused – I'd planned on going for a pint.

'She's wrecked too, aren't you, Luce?' Maddie said, really pointedly.

Gray laughed and tried to make it sound like a mad coughing fit.

I went red, like I usually do, and gabbled out some rubbish about only coming to watch the training before heading home.

Jason didn't seem to think there was anything odd and he smiled (oh, his lovely smile) and said that of course he would walk me to the bus stop.

And off we went.

Hardly knew what to say to him. I haven't been on my own with him since that day in the canteen. But we chatted about music (we both like the same stuff) and art (I haven't a clue but he is big into it) and football (as above – only I had to pretend that I knew something about it). He lit up and offered me a smoke. I slagged him off about smoking and playing football. He just grinned and lit up another fag. He has a dead sexy way of smoking: fag cupped in the palm of his hand as he takes big drags from it. Then we arrived at my bus stop. He waited until the bus arrived and we chatted all the time. He's dead funny in a quiet sort of a way. Or maybe because I fancy him so much I just laugh at whatever he says – I dunno.

Looks good, ey?

October 8th
Didn't go into college today. Normally when things are bad at home, I love heading to college, just to take my mind off things, but today I knew I wouldn't be able to. Mam and Dad had a ferocious row last

night. *Apparently Dad left the immersion on and the hot water burnt Mam's hand and she had to get it bandaged and she said that Dad had done it on purpose and he said that that was ridiculous. (Which it was.) Anyway, then she gave him a list of everything he does that is ridiculous and it was a long list and he said that if she found him so ridiculous then he would move out. And she said fine. And he said fine and then there was a lot of door banging and slamming and I just lay in my bed wishing for morning to come so that I could get out of the house.*

For the first time ever, I wished Tracy was home.

I spent the day wandering around the parks and playgrounds and shops. I couldn't face college and Maddie's all-time good humour. Even the attraction of maybe bumping into Jason couldn't entice me.

I sneaked back into the house when I was sure that Mam and Dad were both gone out.

Only Mam wasn't. Out, I mean. She was in the kitchen. She'd obviously decided not to go into work that day. 'Who's there?' she called.

'Just me,' I said back. 'I've a half-day today.'

'Fine.' Her voice sounded sort of sniffy and choked up. I wondered if she was crying only I hadn't the nerve to go into her. So I went up to my room instead.

October 15th
Dad is sleeping in the spare room. They don't tell me this but I know. Neither of them are talking except through me and, as I go out of my way not to be there most of the time, the house is like a grave.

October 17th
There were auditions for our end of year show today. It's a big deal as it attracts agents and if you've a main part, obviously you're going to have a better chance of getting noticed. We're doing A Midsummer Night's Dream *and I tried out for the part of Puck. Yeah, yeah, I know – he's usually played by a guy but I don't see why. Puck is a*

fairy, he has to be small and slim and light on his feet: how many guys can do that? Not many on our course anyway. They're all massive lads and so I reckon I've got a chance. Maddie went for the part of Hermia, though she says she doesn't care if she gets it or not. She's losing interest in acting, she says, it's such a false profession. I laughed when she said that. Of course it's bloody false – it's why I like it. I can be anyone I want to be when I'm on stage. Maddie, though, is too happy being herself.

    Lucky her.

8

THERE'S SOME SORT of a flea epidemic going around. Every animal in the surgery today seems to have it. Their owners are baffled. 'He's off his food and his fur is all clumpy,' they tell me. I've seen enough flea ridden animals to make a diagnosis, but unfortunately I'm not qualified. Instead, I smile brightly and tell them to take a seat. Doug will be minted by the end of the afternoon, which won't be a bad thing as Clare keeps grumping that he only just made his rent payments last month.

All the pet owners are in good form: there's nothing that bonds people quicker than common illness. Every conversation I overhear is in the 'Oh, but my pet's scratching harder than your pet' vein.

Mr Devlin arrives in just after lunch. Paddy hasn't got fleas; instead, she's in for her yearly check-up. And another flea shot. Mr Devlin is wearing a plaid coat and Paddy sports one too.

'Paddy is twelve now,' Mr D. tells me proudly. 'And she's only beginning to slow down. A bit like myself.'

'Yeah, I'd say you were a mad goer in your day.' I pull out Paddy's file.

Mr D. blushes. He's never struck me as the blushing type. 'Oh, well, I had a way with the women all right,' he agrees. 'But Paddy now, she is not into other dogs at all – she'd eat

47

the leg off anything that came near her.' He changes his raspy voice into something scary and high-pitched as he turns to his dog. 'Isn't that right, Pad?'

Paddy barks.

'She knows she's far too good for them. One time a German Shepherd assaulted her, right outside our gate. Right up behind her he came and *assaulted* her.'

I try to keep the grin off my face. The image of a German Shepherd and a skinny tiny rat-like dog is hard to take. 'Well, keep her out of here today,' I say. 'You don't want her getting assaulted by fleas.'

Mr D. shudders. 'Paddy never had fleas in her life. Once a month I get her treated, as you know yourself.'

'I do.' More like once a fortnight. With the amount of flea stuff on Paddy, I reckon the whole flea population currently residing in our clinic could be wiped out.

Paddy yawns and lies down. Mr D. nods at his dog. 'She likes you. It's not in everyone's company Paddy will fall asleep. She's a great judge of character – aren't you, Pad?'

Paddy whines.

Behind me Clare sniggers. She thinks Mr D. is an awful idiot. He thinks the same about her.

I'm chuffed. I like that I'm liked. I reach behind me and pull out a doggie biscuit from the stacks of them on the shelf. 'Here, girl.'

Paddy almost hurls herself up at the counter to snap it out of my hands. I fall backwards on to Clare who glares at me. 'Watch it, will you! And don't be wasting the supplies.'

'She loved my wife.' Mr D. ignores Clare's outburst. 'Would follow her around all day. When she was sick, she lay down beside my wife on the bed and wouldn't budge. She snarled at anyone that came near – even me.'

48

'Really?'

'Yep. See this?' He pulls up his sleeve. His shirt is skanky. 'See that?' He points to a scar running from his elbow to his wrist. 'Opened me up one day when I tried to catch Eileen's hand – that was my wife's name – opened me up and I had to go to Emergency. We had to throw a blanket over her and shove her in a kennel any time one of us wanted to talk to Eileen. She's very loyal, that dog.'

Paddy snorts as she munches on her dog biscuit.

'I always thought I'd go before Eileen,' Mr D. continues. I don't know what to say to that.

'She was the healthy one; I was out working all hours and here I still am. The dog loved her   she sat on her lap and danced around her and, I swear, she bleedin' *cried* the day before Eileen died. Spent all night howling.'

'Oh.' Soft idiot that I am, I can feel tears prick my eyes. 'That's sad.'

'Dogs don't cry,' Clare whispers dismissively.

'Yeah – it *was* sad. Paddy howls when she senses things. I think she sensed Eileen was going.'

Paddy looks at me and starts to howl.

'Well, I'm not going anywhere.' I giggle uncomfortably. I throw her another biscuit and she falls on it.

'Are you telling Lucy all about that wild weekend you had last week, Mr D.?' Doug startles us both as he appears. He grins at me. 'I met him when I was out, and with a very attractive woman too.' He winks at Mr Devlin who doesn't take to the joke at all.

'A friend,' he snaps. 'An old friend of Eileen's.'

Doug laughs. 'She wasn't old. I don't think she'd like you saying that about her.'

I giggle but Mr D. withers him. 'I was telling Lucy about the way Paddy can foretell death, as a matter of fact,' he says sternly. 'It wasn't anything to laugh at. You won't be laughing when it's your time to go.'

'I hope I will.' Doug widens his golden-brown eyes. 'I want to die drunk as a skunk.'

'Huh – you'd probably smell like one too.'

Doug and I laugh and Mr D. grins reluctantly. Doug hands me back a file and asks who's next.

'John Lynch's Dalmatian,' I say, passing him a brown folder. Despite everything being on computer, Doug likes the feel of paper in his hands. He thinks it reassures the clients, especially the older ones.

He tucks it under his arm and flashes us both a smile. 'Give Mr D. a cuppa, Lucy, will you? It'll be a long wait.' He looks at Paddy. 'All ready for your check-up, Paddy?'

'I've told her what it will involve,' Mr D. says seriously. 'So she's prepared.'

'Good.' Doug nods seriously. 'I always like my patients to know what'll happen.' He hits me gently on the head with John Lynch's folder and goes to the waiting room to call out the next patient himself.

He's not a bad guy to work for.

Later, when it's quietened down a bit, I look up the number of my alma mater. I feel a bit sick at the thoughts of phoning the college actually. Maybe it's because it's the first step and once it's taken there'll be no going back. Maybe it's because I wonder what the guy on the other end of the phone will think of me. He's bound to want to know why I want Jason's address. It's kind of funny, Maddie, Gray and I knew Jason for a year and yet we never really learnt anything about him. And the little we did learn, well, by then it was way too late.

I find the number in the Golden Pages and, finger shaking, I begin to dial. The phone has only just started to ring at the other end when a client comes in with his rabbit. Clare is out at the bank so I'm on my own. Clare always gets to go to the bank except when it rains – then it's my turn. Reluctantly I put down the phone and look up at the client. He points to his rabbit. 'She's off her food and her fur is all clumpy.'

'OK.' I take a note of his name and send him to the waiting room. Then, with my heart now about to explode out of my chest, I redial and listen to the 'bleep, bleep' at the other end of the line.

'Hello, enquiries?'

'Oh, hi. Hi,' I stammer out. 'Eh, I'm, eh, looking for an address of a student who attended the college about eight years ago.'

There's a bit of a silence from the woman in enquiries. I know she's thinking I sound like a moron. I vow that when she comes back to me I will speak with authority.

'Eight years ago?' she repeats.

'Yes.'

'Hang on, I'll put you through to admissions.'

More bleep, bleeping. I take deep breaths, trying to get my breathing under control. If Maddie were here now, she'd grab the phone off me and tell me to not be such an idiot. She'd be forceful. Assertive. A bit of role-playing is called for. I have to pretend I'm Maddie.

'Hello, admissions?'

'Hi.' Gulp. Deep breath. 'My name is Madeline Carver and I attended college there about eight years ago.'

'Yes?'

How come men always sound friendlier than women on the phone? I begin to relax.

'Well, I had a friend there at the time. His name was Jason Donovan – not the pop star,' I joke feebly, 'the other guy.'

The man gives a token laugh.

'And, well, we lost contact and I want to locate him now and I was wondering if you'd have an address for him.'

Silence. Then, 'Oh, well, I'm sorry,' the man says, 'I can't really release that type of information, Madeline. It'd be private. Sorry.'

'But I have to find him.' I sound pathetic.

'Well, I'm sorry I can't be more help. It's not college policy to give out names and addresses of students.'

He does *sound* sorry. But his sorriness is no use to me. I ask myself what Maddie would do. She'd probably explain. 'Look,' I say, 'I need to find him. I'm dying.' *Oh God. Oh God. What have I said?* I apologise to God in my head, asking him not to punish me.

'Oh.' The man sounds taken aback.

'He was a very dear friend,' I say, in my best dying voice. 'I know he'd like to know.'

The man is torn. I feel sorry for him. I feel awfully guilty but desperate times and all that.

'We-ell,' the man says eventually, 'the best I can do is to ask you to send in a letter requesting the information and maybe we can write to him for you – how's that?'

It's better than nothing, I guess.

'Will it take long?' I ask, trying to imply that I haven't got long. *Oh God. I'm sorry. Please forgive me.*

'We'll give it priority,' the man says nicely. He really believes me. He's probably not so horrible as to go about pretending that he's dying. 'I'll give you the address and you can send your request to me personally.'

'Thanks,' I say. I scribble down the address.

'And take care,' he says.

I feel like a heel.

I put down the phone to find Doug staring horror-struck at me. 'You're dying?' he whispers. 'Jesus.'

I must have been damn good. I allow myself a little bit of pride in my performance before shrugging and muttering, 'Just dying to make contact with an old friend. I never, eh, finished my sentence to the guy on the phone.'

Doug doesn't know whether to laugh or be disgusted at me. He looks relieved though. He hands me a file, takes up the next one and just as he's leaving the cubicle, he turns back and says, 'D'you know what my first thought was when I heard you say it?'

'Talented as I am, Doug, I'm not psychic.'

He smiles slightly. 'I was pissed that you hadn't told me so I could find a replacement.'

I giggle. 'Cold bastard.'

'Yeah, I must be,' he agrees cheerfully. 'Anyway, glad you'll be around for a while yet.'

Gee, it's nice to know I'm wanted somewhere.

9

GRAY HAS A new girlfriend. She's tall and blonde and he leaves her sitting in his car while he pounds on my front door. I had been trying to write the flipping letter to the college and just as I'd pinned down the exact expression I needed, Gray's hammering distracts my easily distracted thoughts.

I know what he's going to say and I consider ignoring him. I've been sort of avoiding him these last couple of weeks – not returning his calls and being too busy to talk to him when he rang me up at work – but now he has me cornered. I decide that attack is the best form of defence.

'What?' I say in a really narky voice, flinging open the front door.

It doesn't bother him. Instead, he strides into the hall, forcing me to step back. He smells all clean and sort of spicy. His hair has been cut and he's dressed for going out somewhere posh.

'What are you playing at?' he barks. He's narkier than me. He shoves his hands into his trouser pockets, totally ruining the look of them. 'I was talking to Maddie.'

'Good,' I say. I make a huge effort to sound normal and upbeat. 'So you'll know that I'm looking for any old photos of Jason in case I need them. You did piles of head shots of him the time yez were in the cup final, remember?'

Gray rolls his eyes.

'So if you could look up something that would be nice,' I say innocently.

'And don't you remember what an absolute tosser he was? Have you forgotten?'

Gray is annoyed, which doesn't happen often. He looks kind of cute. His shoulders are hunched up, he's biting his lower lip and if he's not careful he'll draw blood. His neatly cut hair even looks ruffled now. 'Chill,' I say.

His shoulders hunch up even more.

'Look, I have to do this. Fáinne needs to know.' I'm getting tired of explaining to everyone. I punch him playfully. 'Now, if you're going to shout and wake your godchild, I'll have to shove you out. If, however, you're going to help me, well, then, I'll give you a big cuddle.'

He glares at me in exasperation. 'I'm saving my cuddles for her.' He thumbs in the direction of his car. The blonde girl seems to be filing her nails.

'Nice,' I comment.

He grins briefly. 'She is.'

Neither of us says anything for a second. I hate fighting with Gray, we've only ever had one major blow-up and I never want it to happen again. So I reach out and touch his hand. 'It'll be fine,' I mutter, half embarrassed.

'What – my date or your life?' He's still annoyed.

'My life. Your dates are always disasters.'

I'm rewarded with a grin. 'This one is different. She's a model; I think she reckons I'll be able to do a portfolio for her.'

'Aw, to be used by one so beautiful. Must be hell.'

'Don't you go getting used,' he says softly, his grin fading. 'And if you're determined I'll have a look for some shots.'

'Gray!' I want to hug him but I don't want to jeopardise his date. Instead I squeeze his hand. 'Ta.'

'Yeah, well . . .' He doesn't finish. He begins to back out of my door, holding my eyes with his. 'See you Sunday, right? There's a match on and I promised Fáinne I'd bring her.'

I make a face. 'Do I have to go?'

'Nope.'

The relief of that. 'I'll have her ready.' He waves at me briefly. 'Don't do anything I wouldn't do!'

'So, everything goes then?'

Cheek.

Everything goes. I bloody wish, I think as I sit back down to my letter. Men are not exactly queuing up to go out with me. Well, eligible single men, that is. And any that are reckon they're on to a good thing. They think that because I have a child, I'll just jump into bed with anyone. Jesus! If anything, I'm more cautious about whom I see. Much as I love Fáinne, I do not need another child, thank you very much. And I don't want Fáinne getting confused if she sees me with other men.

Well, there's no fear of that, actually. I haven't exactly *had* any other men since Jason. Oh, sure, I've had a few dates, but once Fáinne got mentioned, my dates could have rivalled Linford Christie for getaway speed. And what's more annoying, not one of them admitted that Fáinne was the problem. It was always *Oh, I don't think things are working out* or *You don't seem to be emotionally available.* The last one was by a Yank, wouldn't you just know it? And of course I wasn't emotionally available, I do have a daughter, don't I?

Anyway, all this thinking doesn't solve the problem of what I'm going to write in the letter. I reread it again. *Dear Sir, I wish to obtain information on a Jason Donovan who attended your college eight years ago.* I change it to *I wish to contact Jason Donovan who studied Fine Arts at your college eight years ago.*

56

Mmmm. I was never very good at letters. Ask me to write a story and I'm away but anything remotely official and I get stumped. I want to stress in the letter that it's important for me to contact Jason without actually writing down in blue Biro that I'm dying. It's one thing to lie over the phone but writing it down just seems *much* worse.

I stay stumped for another ten minutes before I admit defeat and ring Maddie. She's a French teacher. She probably has her kids writing stiff formal French letters all the time – sounds almost pornographic.

'Hello.'

Damn. It's Clive. He always makes me feel as if I'm a kid with dirty fingernails. 'Clive, hi.' My cheery voice sounds very forced. 'Is Maddie there?'

'No.'

'Oh.'

Clive doesn't say anything for a second. I can almost hear him wondering what he should do. His social intercourse isn't great. Though, according to Maddie, his other type is explosive. 'It's Lucy, isn't it?'

'Eh – yeah.' I quash my dirty thoughts.

'Do you, eh, want me to give her a message?'

'Yep. Can you tell her to ring me – I need some help writing a letter.'

'Well, I can help if you like.'

No, I don't like. But I don't want to offend him. Clive is the sort of guy that *likes* helping. He's the kind of guy that could sort the world out if you let him. Not that that's a bad thing, it just makes us ordinary mortals seem very inadequate.

'Eh – Well, it's, eh – Well, I have to write to the college asking for information on a guy I used to know. Jason.'

'Jason? Is he—?'

'Yep.' I blush.

'So, read out what you have,' Clive instructs me.

Haltingly, I read it to him. I'm back in school again. I gulp and stammer and hiccup.

Clive is silent. Then, 'What's wrong with that?' he asks, much to my surprise. 'Doesn't that say it all?'

'Well, yeah, but I want to make it seem more urgent.'

'So tell them it's a matter of urgency.'

'Oh.' I'm surprised I never thought of that. Well, I did, I just didn't write it down. 'So, I'll just say that this is a matter of extreme urgency?'

'And that you'd appreciate a prompt reply.'

'Great.' I feel all warm and fuzzy towards Clive. Sometimes dry shites can be very useful. I hastily jot down what he's just said. 'Tell Maddie I said "hi",' I say then.

'Will do. Bye now.'

The phone is put down.

I laboriously finish off the letter and shove it in an envelope. I don't think about what I'm doing. I figure that if I get uncomfortable opening this particular door a chink, well, then I can just close it again, can't I?

10

WHEN I ARRIVE at my parents' house on Monday evening to pick up Fáinne my mother meets me at the door. She's holding a shocking pink, very perfumed letter and she starts flapping it in my face.

'It's a letter from Mona Lisa!' Mam always calls Tracy by her model name. It's really irritating.

'Who?'

'Tracy,' Mam snaps.

We always do this – it's like I've now given her permission to call her Tracy again. I'm surprised to hear there is a letter from her though. Tracy's letters are about as rare as good boy band singles. According to her, she's just too busy to write or phone or learn how to use computers so that she can e-mail. Not that it would be much use anyway. Mam and Dad are deeply suspicious of modern technology. Even the remote control for the telly is viewed as exotic. Mam doesn't know how to set the video (which I bought for her one Christmas). 'Sure if I like programmes I'll go out of my way to watch them,' she said when I told her just how handy a video recorder would be. That was the last time I ever surprised her. Now it's the traditional M&S vouchers. Or something from Arnotts. Their video is the luckiest in Ireland. I'll bet it thanks the day it was brought into the Gleeson household. Talk about an easy retirement.

Anyway, Mam waves Tracy's precious letter about and almost sings, 'Tracy is coming home next month and she'll be staying well into the New Year.'

'Oh.'

Mam steps aside for me to go in and then she follows me up the hall, still waving the letter. 'Isn't it great?'

I know Tracy is my sister but I don't feel excited at meeting her again. We've never got on. She specialised in getting me into trouble and stealing my friends. It was just as well I never wore make-up or she'd have stolen that too.

Still, I try to sound happy for Mam's sake. 'Why's she coming home? Is she taking time off modelling or something?' I wonder if maybe she's too old for modelling now. She'll be thirty soon (in December) but she doesn't look it. It's her fab bone structure, you see. Well, so Mam always says.

'Yes.' Mam nods, still looking really excited. I wonder where Fáinne is. She normally runs to meet me: it gives my ego a much-needed boost after a day dealing with sick animals. There's a thump of what can only be a football in the back garden and glancing out of the window, I see that Dad has her playing in goal while he takes penos against her. She's completely fearless, she throws herself on to the ground and I wince in pain for her.

'I wish he wouldn't do that with her,' Mam says, following my gaze. She begins stirring a pot of stew. The smell is yummy. If heaven exists, it would smell of stew and roasting meat. 'Tracy is taking four months off modelling.'

I get the feeling that Mam wants me to ask why. So I don't. I wonder idly if Tracy is pregnant. But Mam wouldn't have a big happy smile plastered across her face if she were. I remember how it was for me – Mam literally went into mourning. But then again, she's mad about Fáinne now . . .

60

'She's doing another project, you see.' Mam reads directly from the letter as she stirs. 'A big project.' She stresses the 'big'.

So she *could* be pregnant.

'Mammy!' Fáinne spots me and abandons her makeshift goal. She pounds up the back-door steps and dances into the kitchen. Her dark hair is tangled and there is mud all over her good school shoes, which she tramples into Mam's kitchen tiles. 'Granddad couldn't score against me. I saved everything!'

Dad winks at me behind her back.

'Good girl!' I grin.

Mam tut-tuts. Letter momentarily forgotten, she mutters her usual, 'That godfather you have for her is a bad influence. He's turning her into a boy.'

She's always hated Graham because of his godfather status.

'I'm a *girl*, Nana,' Fáinne whoops. 'I can't turn into a boy! Don't be silly!'

'And you.' Mam whirls on Dad, who's drying his mucky hands on the tea towel. 'You shouldn't be playing football at your age. You'll have a heart attack.'

'Thanks,' Dad says, smoothing himself down and rubbing leaves and bits of broken branches from his hair. 'It's nice to know I'm on my way out.'

Mam smiles a little. 'You know what I mean.' Then she turns to me. 'Girls shouldn't play football, maybe get that godfather fella to bring her somewhere more suitable.'

'Her dad played ball,' I remember suddenly. 'She probably takes after him.'

'Did he?' Fáinne is wide-eyed. 'Really?'

'Now, let's set the table.' Mam attempts to divert my daughter's attention and I resent her for it. I can tell Fáinne what I like. She's mine.

'He was pretty good too,' I add.

'He was good at running all right,' Mam mutters, glaring at me.

'Was he?' Fáinne asks.

I can't answer for a second because there's a lump lodged in my throat. When Fáinne asks again all I can do is nod. Then I croak out, 'Coat, Fáinne. We're going.'

Fáinne knows something has happened but she doesn't know what. She looks from me to her Nana.

'Sorry,' Mam says, sounding sorry. She fiddles with the bright pink letter in her hand. 'I don't know what made me say that.'

I gulp. 'Coat,' I say again.

'Please, Lucy, I'm sorry.' Mam indicates the pot on the cooker. 'I made enough for the four of us.'

Of course, she knows that by saying this, Fáinne is going to start jumping up and down demanding to be fed something decent. If God has some great universal plan, he certainly fucked up when he made me a mother. I am hopeless. I can't do motherly things: cook, sew, cover schoolbooks or make mobiles. I try but I just can't hack it.

'Come on, Luce,' Dad cajoles. 'And your mother will be able to tell you Tracy's news. Have you told her?' he asks my mother.

'Just about to,' she murmurs, looking anxiously at me.

Fáinne hasn't started jumping up and down, much to my surprise. Instead, she turns to my mother and says, 'You've made my mammy sad. That's not nice.'

I feel tears prick my eyes at her words. She's right. I am sad.

Mam flinches. 'I know, honey.' She rubs Fáinne on the head. 'I didn't mean to. Your daddy was a good footballer and he must have been nice because you are so lovely.'

'She's nice because her mother is a damn fine thing too,' my dad pipes up, tousling my hair.

Jesus, I feel like a three-year-old being cajoled out of a bad mood. I blink back tears, feeling stupid at my emotions. 'OK,' I mutter, unable to look at them, 'I'll stay.'

It's like they deflate in front of me. 'Good,' Mam says abruptly, though she sounds relieved. 'Good,' she says again.

Dad smiles at me. 'She's made a lovely stew for you,' he said. 'I've been smelling it all afternoon.'

I try to return his smile. I still feel a bit raw.

Fáinne clasps my hand in hers. 'Come on, Mammy, and see the picture I did for you in school.' She gently leads me out of the kitchen. It's just what I need.

The dinner is a strained affair. Mam's comment about Jason being a good runner hurts more than it should. It was eight years ago, it's in the past, we've all accepted it and moved on. So why it should hurt so much, I don't know.

Mam seems unsure of what to say to me as I answer her in monosyllables. I'm not sulking, honestly, it's just awkward.

'Oh,' she says as she begins to clear the dinner plates. 'I never told you about Tracy.'

I'm not sure I want to know.

'It's big news,' Dad says. 'Very big.'

There's an expectant silence as they wait for me to ask. 'Sounds dead exciting,' I murmur.

'It is.' Dad leans across the table to me. 'She's only after being offered a part in a film – quite a big part – and it's being shot in Ireland.'

Both of them beam at me.

I feel as if I've been punched in the stomach. 'But . . .' I stare at them. 'But she's a *model*.'

'And now she'll be an actress,' Mam says proudly. 'Imagine!'

An *actress*. My *sister*. I hate myself for the indignant feelings that flood up through me. I should be glad for her but, for God's sake, she's only ever modelled clothes for a living. She hasn't spent four years doing a drama degree; she hasn't waited years to be discovered; she hasn't ever done any acting in her entire life – well, not counting the speech and drama classes that she gave up after four weeks because she had to learn a poem. 'Imagine,' I parrot weakly. 'Imagine.'

'She'll be like you, Mammy,' Fáinne says.

She won't be like me, I want to shout. I'm bloody *qualified*. Suddenly my ad audition doesn't seem so exciting. 'How did she get the part?' I ask, trying to sound enthusiastic. 'Did she audition?'

'Someone liked the way she looked apparently,' Dad says, oblivious to my mounting irritation, 'so they told her to go for an audition and she got it. It's a big budget thing and she's the main female lead. She says it'll be scary because they'll all want to knock her because she's a model but she doesn't care.'

'That's Tracy all right,' Mam says, dishing out some apple tart which I don't want. 'She just goes for what she wants and damn the begrudgers.'

Of which I am one, I realise, to my shame. I shovel some tart into my mouth and try to chew it. It'll stop me moaning.

'So when's *your* audition?' Dad asks kindly.

I feel patronised. 'Wednesday.' Jesus, I hope I get it now. Imagine Tracy in a film and I can't even get a crappy ad. Story of my life.

'Well, good luck with it. Sure, if Trace can get a big film with no training, an ad should be no problem to you. You were in college for ages.'

I can't quite figure out how to take that. 'Yeah.'

'Mammy *will* get it,' Fáinne says loyally. 'I even told my teacher that Mammy was going to be on the telly.'

Great.

'Don't go about telling people your business,' Mam chastises gently. 'Things like that are private.'

For once I agree with my mother. 'You can tell your teacher about your aunt instead,' I say, trying to be generous about my sister's good fortune. 'Tell her that you've a film star aunt.'

'Oh.' Mam turns to Dad. 'A film star for a daughter: how does that sound?'

Dad winks. 'Not as nice as a gorgeous woman for a wife.'

Mam blushes and I find myself smiling. It's nice when they go on like that. Fáinne makes gagging noises and we all laugh. Well, I try to laugh.

Honestly.

11

THE AUDITION IS held in a small studio in the city centre. I arrive at five-thirty, make-up caked to my face, and sit down beside a very anxious-looking girl who's actually sweating. She smacks of desperation, which is a sure sign she won't get the ad. I'd smile at her only I'm afraid my make-up will crack. Les had advised me to do myself up. 'Ya don't look half bad when ya make the effort,' he'd chortled down the phone. 'Slap on a bit of make-up, get yourself a short skirt and a nice blousy thing. Sensible but tarty.'

It just showed Les's complete lack of experience with women, I thought as I zipped myself into a blue denim mini. No one could look tarty *and* sensible. I decided to go more for the sensible angle – after all, who'd want a tart advertising their precious product?

'Linda Ryan,' someone calls and the girl beside me jumps up, squeaking out a 'me'. She's gone for the tarty angle big time: black mini, fishnets, plenty of cleavage. She totters into the audition on heels thinner than the plot of a *Charlie's Angels* movie. Now it's my turn to sweat. I don't normally, only this audition means so much to me. I have to get it to prove to myself that Tracy isn't the only one in our house capable of doing something with her life. It's pathetic, I know, but it's how I feel. It's how I've always felt about Tracy – that I had to compete with her.

Ten minutes later, the nervous tarty girl staggers out. She smiles at me as she passes, obviously feeling well pleased with herself. This gives me great hope. If she stands a chance, then so should I. 'I like my man protected,' I murmur to myself over and over. It'd just be my luck to forget it.

'Lucy Gleeson?'

'Me.' I try to look composed. I stand up from the hard grey chair and sashay towards the woman. If Tracy can bloody act then surely I can catwalk sexily.

'Now?' the woman says snottily.

I flinch and walk more quickly.

There's a camera in the room and the woman with the clipboard sits behind a table. Another man, who looks important, is sitting at the table also. He's probably the director, I think, feeling panic rise in me. I smile at him, hoping to lick arse. He smiles back. The cameraman tells me where to stand and hands me a red box. 'Right,' he instructs, 'just tell me what you look for in a man.'

'What I look for in a man?' I gulp. I hadn't been expecting this. I look blankly at them. 'What I look for in a man,' I repeat.

'Now?' the woman says again.

'Well,' I bite my lip. 'Just someone who, who . . .' I'm bloody stuck. I don't look for anything in a man. Mostly I go out with them just because they're there.

'You're not a lesbian, are you?' the director asks anxiously. 'Not that I've anything against lesbians, but I can't have one in this ad. You must understand that.'

Jesus!

'Pure hetero,' I reassure him brightly. I think of my fantasy man. I think of what I liked about Jason. I think hard about Jason. 'Well,' I start again, 'I like someone who can make me laugh, who can get on with my mates, who makes life exciting for me.' I pause. The cameraman is busy filming and the other two are looking intently at me. Reassured, I go on, 'I guess I'd have to be attracted to his looks and he'd have to be interesting to talk to and have the same interests as me and—'

'Good,' the man behind the table says, smiling. 'Now, say the line. Hold up the condom box and say the line.'

Condom box?

I'm auditioning for condoms?

I can't believe it.

I've trained for years to get to this moment in my life.

'Now?' the woman says nastily.

Oh fuck it. I'll kill Les when I see him. In fact, I'll go see him right after this bloody audition. Con-fucking-doms. Jesus.

I hold up the red box. I do not want this ad but neither do I want to let myself down. I toss my hair back, stare intently into the camera as if giving the world an important message. Licking my lips, I say huskily, 'I like my man protected.' I hold my gaze. I see the cameraman bringing his hand down and I relax. I don't wait to be told to leave. I stomp out of the room as fast as I can in my tight denim mini.

I phone my mother and tell her I'll be late. She's excited. She thinks that my being late means that they've been so impressed with me at the audition that they can't bear to let me go. I let her believe it.

I drive, my hands gripping the steering wheel so tightly that after about twenty minutes, they start to cramp. My face begins to ache a little too and I realise that I'm clenching my teeth really hard. I'm annoyed; I'm gutted. My big chance has been blown away in a puff of smoke. How can I be taken seriously if I do an ad for condoms? I didn't even know that they *had* ads for condoms. What the fuck is Les trying to do for me?

Les lives on the south side of the city. He has a small house that could be nice if he bothered to do it up. I shriek to a stop outside and, slamming my car door, I march up his cobble-locked driveway. He's in because his car is there. Les walks nowhere.

I press his buzzer. And stop. And press. And stop. And press. And press. And press.

'I swear' – Les's rough-edged voice comes from behind the door – 'I'll pay you next week. The fucking milk was sour again.'

'Pity it didn't kill you,' I shout in. 'It might have saved me a job!'

'Lucy!' He actually sounds happy that it's me, and then his tiny mind processes what I've just said. 'What's up?' he shouts out warily.

'Can you open the door first?' I say, not wanting to shout my business out on the street.

'Is this about the audition?'

I don't answer.

Curiosity gets the better of him and the door opens.

Les is ugly. No hair, high forehead, a beaten leathery face with a prominent chin that wouldn't look out of place on a hammer-headed shark. He's small, around five feet two, and is skinnier than Kate Moss. 'Yes, Les,' I say, stepping into his hall, which smells of days-old chips, 'this is about the audition.'

He begins to back-up towards the kitchen. 'Well, you can't blame me if you didn't get it,' he blusters. He attempts a wolf-whistle. 'You look *great*.'

'I don't know if I got it or not,' I half shriek. 'But I know I don't bloody want it. What made you think I'd do an ad for condoms?'

His attempt to look surprised is pathetic. 'Oh,' he says, in a sort of swanky voice, 'aren't *you* the choosy one. I didn't think work was exactly *falling* from the sky for you.'

I can't say much to this.

'And what's wrong with a condom ad? It'll be the first in the country.'

'Well, there must be something wrong with it if you didn't tell me it *was* a condom ad,' I snap. 'Protective clothing, you said.'

'Which it is,' he countered.

'My arse, it is.'

'No, for my arse, actually.'

'Les, I'm not laughing. You conned me. I'll never be taken seriously if I do that ad.'

'So don't do it,' he says. 'Don't do the posters and the follow-up ads. Don't get the huge fee and get noticed. Don't do it. Simple.'

And it was simple, I suppose. But my dreams were shattered. And I had to blame someone and that someone was him because he'd given me hope in the first place. 'From this moment, Les, I'm no longer your client, right?'

He pales but he recovers. 'I'll have to consult your contract.'

'Oh, the one that says I have to know what I'm auditioning for at all times?'

'It doesn't say that.'

We glare at each other.

Then I realise that I haven't actually got anything more to say to him and I turn about.

'So if I get a call from Hollywood for you, I'll just forget it, will I?' Les shouts out after me.

'Just tell them they must have rung the wrong number,' I counter.

He slams the door loudly.

I pat myself on the back for such a clever comment but it's a minor victory. I'm back to square one. I'm still waiting to be discovered.

12

October 22nd

Had a lovely day today in a weird sort of way.

I couldn't face going into college as the parts had been decided for the end-of-term play and I was terrified that I wouldn't get the one I wanted. I knew bunking off was only delaying the inevitable, but I just wasn't in the right frame of mind for rejection. I was afraid that I'd burst out crying in the middle of the mall and make a complete show of myself. Only, I wouldn't be crying over the part, I'd be crying over the silence at home.

I did get the bus to college though – I mean, I meant to go in and then, just at the last minute, I decided not to bother. Instead, I headed into the city centre to have a wander around the clothes and music shops and cheer myself up. There is nothing better than blasting your head with loud music when you don't want to think.

So I ended up in town, wandering from shop to shop and eventually found myself in HMV. I was scanning the bargain bin when someone tapped me on the shoulder. It was Jason. Can you believe it?!

'No lectures today?' he asked and he was grinning at me.

I shrugged. Tried hard for nonchalance. 'Decided to take a break.'

He laughed. 'Me too. Whatcha looking at?'

I told him I was looking for bargains. So we trawled the bin together and found nothing, well, not unless we were into the Furies or opera or boy bands. Which neither of us were. We left the shop and without consulting each other, we started to walk up Grafton Street towards the

Green. Jason must have intended to go to college too because he had his bag with him. He slung it over his shoulder and asked me if I wanted to go for a coffee.

'Mmm.' I made a face and smiled, trying not to look too thrilled. 'I might be able to squeeze it in – I'm soooo busy today.'

Another grin. 'Come on so.' We went into the shopping centre and got coffees in the Kylemore. Jason kept staring at me over the rim of his cup. 'I wouldn't have put you down for the bunking sort,' he said eventually.

I didn't really want to talk about it. 'I'm full of surprises.'

'Yeah.' I reckon he liked that about me 'cause he smiled. Then he said, 'I thought you liked your course.'

'I do. I love it. But, well . . .' I shrugged. My voice trailed off. I stared into my half-empty cup.

'Lucky you,' he said after he realised I wasn't going to say any more. 'I hate my course, that's why I didn't go in.' He looked straight at me as he said it and my heart flipped.

'So why do it?' I croaked out.

'Well, I thought I'd like it,' he said in this really endearing, earnest way, 'I mean I like art and stuff but I just don't like the way they teach it.'

'Is there nothing else you could do?'

He gave a bit of a laugh. 'No. Anyway, I promised my dad that I'd stick it out.'

'Your dad?'

He shrugged. Gave another laugh. 'Yep.' He said nothing more.

'And?' I prompted.

'That's it.'

'I wouldn't have put you down as the dutiful son.' I didn't mean it as an insult, but there was something about Jason that wasn't quite . . . I dunno . . . right, I suppose. It was nothing I could put my finger on, there was just something amiss. It was like there was this huge gap between who he said he was and who he actually seemed to be.

73

My remark hurt him, I think. He dropped his gaze from me. 'Thanks,' he muttered.

Without thinking, I touched him. Just a small flap of my hand across the table. It was gorgeous. Even now, remembering, gives me delicious shivers. 'Naw, I meant that you're not a boring, traditional sort of guy.'

He smiled. 'I'm full of surprises,' he said, copying me.

'Yeah.'

As if on cue, we both drained our cups and stood up. He looked at me; I looked at him. 'The Green?' I said.

And we left the shopping centre and walked into St Stephen's Green, which is a gorgeous park right in the centre of Dublin. We didn't even talk much, just walked together, occasionally bumping off each other. I wondered if he was as conscious as me about it. Eventually, I dunno why, I muttered, 'I actually didn't go in today because they're giving out the parts in the end-of-term show. I was scared in case I don't get the one I want.'

He looked surprised. Then wistful. Then said, 'Do you want to go in now and I'll look for you and I'll tell you what you got?'

'No!' The thought horrified me. 'God!'

'You'll have to know sooner or later.'

I knew he was right. And I knew I wouldn't be able to sleep tonight for thinking of tomorrow and I knew that I could chicken out tomorrow as well. And I knew that Maddie would start ringing me, wondering where I was – if she hadn't already. I took my mobile from my bag and flicked it on. Two missed calls. One from my mother. One from Maddie.

'OK,' I agreed reluctantly. 'Just go and look and I'll wait outside the building.'

'What part do you want?'

I didn't tell him. At least if he didn't know what I wanted, he couldn't worry about letting me know.

So we caught the bus back to college, he went into the Drama building and came out ten minutes later. 'Saw it,' he said.

I couldn't even talk. I stared mutely at him, feeling sick.

'Puck?' he said nervously.

The scream I let out made him jump. I caught his arms and danced about with him.

He wrapped his arms about me and hugged me. Hard. 'Must be nice to want something so much,' he said into my hair. 'Well done.' Then he let me go and stood smiling at me.

'Thanks for today,' I said, unable to stop beaming. 'Thanks a lot for today.'

He reached out and touched my shoulder. 'Anytime you need a bunking-off mate, you know where I am.' He grinned. But it didn't reach his eyes.

On impulse I hugged him. I dunno, I think he needed it or something. 'And you know where I am,' I said back.

He shook his head. 'You'd never pass that course of yours if I took you up on that.' And he laughed.

But I think he meant it.

October 23rd

My mother, as it turns out, had rung to tell me that Tracy is coming home next month. At least the news has given her and Dad something to smile about.

At least they're talking again.

13

MADDIE'S HOUSE IS warm, comfortable and inviting. Well, technically it's Maddie and Clive's house but I always associate the big squashy sofa and the beaded lamps with Maddie. Clive does not fit comfortably into this environment – at least not in my mind.

It's Sunday afternoon and Maddie has invited me and Gray for dinner. She does this a lot. I think she likes us to be together. If it were left up to me, I'd see them down the pub for a few pints and a laugh, but Maddie likes us to talk. She thinks it brings us closer and maybe it does. It's nice to feel close to people even if it's not my family.

The minute I walk into Maddie's hall I can smell dinner. Chicken satay, my favourite. 'Mmm,' I sniff, handing Maddie a bottle of wine. 'Smells gorgeous. Jesus, I'm so hungry I'd eat my own cooking.'

Maddie laughs and then, putting her finger to her lips, she points in the direction of the sitting room.

'What?' I whisper.

'Gray has Audrey with him,' she whispers back.

'Audrey?' I don't know any Audrey.

'Ssh!' Maddie pulls me down the hall. 'Tall? Blonde? Model type?'

'Oh – the girl from the car?' I'm surprised. I hadn't thought Gray would be big into Audrey, but then again, Gray has weird taste in girlfriends. His last one, which was a while ago, had been mad about cats. She even wore cat sweatshirts and had cat earrings. Her house, according to Gray, had been covered in cats. And when she talked, she'd literally purred. Gray had gone out with her because her voice reminded him of an Alfa Romeo starting up – it was only after he'd got to know her that he'd found out about the cats. All his girl-friends were gorgeous – being a photographer, beautiful women went for him; I think they thought he could get their photos into society pages and stuff like that. Some hope. The pages Gray is responsible for are the sports pages – only he never tells the women that. 'What's she like?' I murmur. Then, 'Did you invite her?'

'No,' Maddie says. 'But she seems normal enough. Well, normal for Gray anyway. She's a bit young though.'

I giggle. 'She'll suit Gray so.'

Maddie thumps me and shoves me in the direction of the sitting room. 'I'll go check dinner. Clive is watching it and he'd spoil the Last Supper, so he would.' She waddles off into the kitchen and I think to myself that she's put on weight. Not that that would bother Maddie. 'Being fat is a sign of contentment,' she always says. I ask her why Clive is so skinny then and she belts me.

Grinning, I enter Maddic's lovely sitting room, dying to see Audrey up close. Gray has his feet plonked on the beanbag and he's watching football. His arm is slung around Audrey's shoulders and she's snuggling into him, though she looks as if she's not exactly used to snuggling into Gray yet. They haven't got that familiarity that close couples have. Her body is sort of stiff and she jerks away from him when I enter.

'Hello,' I say.

'Hi,' she chirrups.

She's stunning. Long, loose blond hair, long legs, probably loose too. I shake my head – that's just being nasty, I tell myself. She's dressed in a tiny white skirt and a tinier white top. Her tan, fake or natural, complements it beautifully.

Gray pulls her to him again and I feel like a definite outsider. 'Hiya, Luce.' He grins. 'This is Audrey.'

Audrey smiles brightly. Too brightly. She's nervous and I feel a bit sorry for her. I sit in beside her, feeling like a hippo in my long skirt. And I wouldn't mind but it's the one that makes me look the *thinnest* of all my skirts. 'I saw you in the car the other night,' I say.

'That's right.' Audrey nods eagerly, then runs out of anything to say.

'And you're a model?' I prompt. If there's one thing I know it's that models love to talk about what hard work modelling is.

'That's right.' She gives a tinkle of a laugh and then stares back down at her hands. 'Though I'm not working on anything at the moment but I'm hopeful. You know.'

More silence. Whatever Gray sees in her, it's not her conversational skills.

'Lucy's sister is a model,' Gray offers, hoping to help the conversation along. I could kill him.

'No!' Audrey looks excited. 'Maybe I know her – what's her name?'

I don't want to say it.

'Tracy Gleeson,' Gray says for me.

Audrey's perfect face puckers up and she's about to shake her head when I add, 'She's known as Mona Lisa Gleeson.'

'No!' Audrey's jaw drops so fast, she almost gives herself lockjaw. '*The* Mona Lisa?'

'So you know her then,' I say lamely.

'*Everybody* knows *her*.' Audrey beams. 'And you're her

sister?' She cocks her pretty head to one side and studies me. 'You don't look like her at all.'

'Thanks.'

Audrey blushes. 'I didn't mean . . . I mean . . . I just—' She takes a deep breath. 'Are you a model too?'

She's only asking it to be polite. All she'd have to do is look at me to know I'm not a model.

'She's an actress,' Gray says staunchly. I think he's trying to be nice. I wish he'd keep his mouth shut.

'No way!' Another death-defying jaw drop. Audrey's high voice goes up another octave. 'What have you been in?'

I squirm.

'She did the ad for Super Stain detergent last year,' Gray says proudly. 'She was the woman with the horrible hands.'

'Oh, I remember that!' Audrey yelped. 'I remember that!' She looks at my hands. 'Did they use your own hands?'

'Yep.' I bite my nails; it got me a part.

Audrey squeals and turns to Gray. 'Wow, imagine, I've met an actress who's a sister of a famous model.' She sounds overwhelmed. Her awe is genuine. She's impressed by me. I feel all sort of nice towards her. 'I was in *Fair City* too,' I say. 'In the big row scene. I was the woman drinking pints at the bar.'

'God!' Audrey says. Then she pauses and I can almost see her brain working. 'Hey, wasn't there something in yesterday's paper about your sister – that she's going to be the lead in a major movie?'

Great. 'Yep.'

'Wow!' Audrey is almost hyperventilating.

'Fuck off!' Gray is gawking at me. 'Thought you were the actress, Luce.'

I smile weakly.

'What's this?' Maddie pokes her head around the door,

79

brandishing my opened bottle of wine. 'Something I should know?'

'Tracy has only got herself a part in a film,' Gray says.

'No way!' Maddie's eyes widen in disbelief. 'How did she manage that?'

'She's a very *talented* model,' Audrey says, looking aghast at Maddie. 'I'd like to go into acting too, once my modelling career takes off.'

Maddie and I ignore her. Gray looks embarrassed.

'And how did your audition go?' Maddie asks.

I cringe. Admitting it in front of Audrey is humiliating. 'It was for condoms,' I mutter.

'So?' Gray asks. 'Did it go well?'

Typical man. 'I'm not doing an ad for condoms,' I hiss. 'Jesus, my sister acting on the big screen and there's me advocating condom power – no thanks!'

'It'd be a blast.' Gray laughs. 'Jesus, loosen up, Luce.'

'Fuck off.'

Whatever atmosphere there has been now evaporates. I've told Gray to fuck off countless times before but never in the horrible way I've just done. And in front of his new girlfriend too. I feel guilty but not guilty enough to apologise.

'Dinner's ready!' Clive saves the moment by appearing at the door in a frilly apron. He's brandishing some sort of Chinese cooking instrument and looks like a total wally. 'I've made some incredible soup to start with.'

'I made that soup.' Maddie injects some lightness into her voice. 'Don't be taking all the credit, you.' She pushes him gently and he nibbles her ear, catching her about the waist.

It's a lovely gesture that makes me feel quite lonely. Two couples and a spinster.

'Right, let's eat.' Gray gets up from the sofa. He holds out his hand to Audrey who lets him haul her up. Then he turns to me. 'Come on, Luce, I thought you were starving.'

I can't look at him. I recognise the gesture for the peace sign it is and it only makes me feel worse.

Any subject to do with me is carefully avoided during the dinner. I just can't wait to go home, cuddle up to Fáinne, maybe spend a bit of time messing about with her hair before kissing her asleep. It's amazing how comforting thoughts of my child are whenever I'm upset. She loves me, we don't fight and I would do anything for her. It's what keeps me going really.

Audrey entertains us with stories of her modelling – or lack thereof. She seems to have overcome her initial bout of shyness and to be honest, she's a nice girl, quite sweet and not as hard-edged as I remember Tracy being when she started off. She's done some minor work but her main ambition is to do *Cosmo* or *Vogue*. 'I'm not a catwalk model like your sister,' she tells me. Then she sighs. 'But your sister can do anything really – she's got the face *and* the body.'

I smile and pick at my chicken.

'So tell us,' Maddie asks. 'Is modelling hard work?'

I smirk and am surprised when Audrey laughs. 'Not if you love it,' she says. She shivers a little. 'And I *do*. I love the clothes and make-up and getting my picture taken. I just love it. And Gray says I take a good picture, don't you?'

Gray nods. He's got his smitten, bemused face on. It strikes me then that he really likes Audrey. He keeps peeking at her, smiling at her and finding excuses to touch her. 'I took a whole heap of them last week for your portfolio, didn't I?'

Audrey squeezes his arm and looks around the table. 'He's the most *amazing* photographer. He's wasted in sports journalism, I keep telling him. He should be on a fashion shoot.'

We laugh as Gray looks pained.

Maddie chortles. 'Gray prefers men in shorts to women in shorts, don't you?'

'Once the men in shorts are running after a ball, I could watch them all day,' Gray agrees.

Clive, who has appointed himself host, begins to clear the plates. 'Was yours all right, Lucy?' he asks as he sees my half-eaten chicken.

'Great.' I manage a smile. 'The wine has filled me up, I think.'

Maddie has concocted some weird chocolate and cream thing for dessert. Of course, I've no problem eating that. That's comfort food. Audrey chatters on and on to Maddie. I let the conversation flow over me and wonder what the hell is wrong with me. I was looking forward to tonight; I'd even bought a new top in honour of the occasion and now I'm ruining it for myself and everyone. I have to stop it. It's not fair on Maddie. I force myself to concentrate on Gray's story about some premiership footballer and just as I'm about to contribute a witty remark about balls and shooting, Clive stands up and taps his wine glass with a spoon. 'Attention please,' he says loudly.

Maddie rolls her eyes as we become silent.

'Youse are probably wondering why we had youse over tonight,' Clive continues.

From the look on Gray's face, he hasn't wondered and neither have I. I want to laugh suddenly.

'Well,' Clive goes on in his posh voice, 'we're going to put you out of your misery.'

'Hang on here a second,' Gray says, and I get the impression that he's the tiniest bit drunk, 'no one is putting me out of my misery – that's illegal, so it is.'

I start to giggle.

Clive isn't amused and if it is possible to scald with an

acidic look, Gray would have been hospitalised with third-degree burns.

'People,' Maddie says mock-sternly, 'this is no joke, you know.' I think she's glad I'm laughing.

'No,' Clive agrees seriously. 'It *isn't* a joke.'

Gray grins at me and I find myself smiling back at him. A *real* smile. I want to say sorry now but I can't. It's too late. Clive has launched into a boring speech about how he'd met Maddie when she'd told him, in French, that she'd like to shag him senseless. Now, that doesn't *sound* boring, but coming from Clive it sounds both boring *and* unbelievable.

'And she didn't know that I spoke *fluent* French,' Clive goes on proudly, really getting into his stride. He's building for his punchline, which will not be funny, as we've heard the story about a million times; only from Maddie it's funnier.

'So he said that he'd take me up on it,' Maddie interrupts, 'but that he'd need at least ten years of good shags before he'd be senseless.'

Audrey is the only one that laughs. Clive glares at Maddie in exasperation.

'They already know the story, sweet thing,' she says mildly, patting him on his skinny bum.

'And now,' Clive goes on, daring her to say any more. 'It's not *quite* three years but I must be senseless because I've just asked Madeline to marry me.'

'Awwww,' we all say.

Maddie laughs. 'And I must be even worse because I said "yes".'

'Awwww,' we say again.

Clive produces a ring from his pocket and places it on her finger. 'We chose it last week,' he says, wrapping his arm about her shoulder and kissing her.

'Oooh!' Audrey puts her hands up to her mouth and looks

83

delighted. 'That's *great*. I love weddings and proposals and stuff.'

Maddie looks really happy. And I'm really happy for her. I wish it wasn't Clive though. I wish it was someone whom I didn't feel so awkward with, someone whom I wouldn't mind chatting to on the phone if Maddie wasn't in when I rang. But she's chosen him and she loves him and I make myself be happy for her. I watch as she hugs Gray; I watch as she hugs Audrey. I stand up and wait my turn. When it comes, I want to cry. 'Congratulations,' I say and my voice is all shaky.

'Don't start,' Maddie warns. 'Don't! You fucking eejit!'

I laugh and cry at the same time. 'Let's see the ring then,' I say, blinking rapidly. 'I hope he spent a decent amount on it. I know these economics teachers!'

Clive actually laughs. Maddie holds out her hand and a lone diamond winks and gleams in its bed of white gold.

'Fab,' I say.

Audrey demands it be taken off as she wants to make a wish. I watch her placing it on her finger and making her wish after which she turns it three times.

'I'll have a go of that,' I say. I take the ring, close my eyes and don't know what to wish for. There's so much I want. In the end I settle for boring old happiness. Then I wonder if wishing for happiness means that I'm not happy. So instead I wish for a big acting part.

Gray declines a wish. I don't know how he can do that. I wish on everything: the first star in the evening; the first day of a new month; pulling the wishbone on a chicken; and so far I haven't won the Lotto, found a man or got a major acting part but then again there's no time limit on a wish, is there?

Audrey is still squealing. 'Wow,' she says, 'I'm having a

great time tonight. Meeting famous people and seeing people getting engaged. Gray never told me he has so many connections. You've got great friends, Gray.'

'I know.' Gray gives me and Maddie a squeeze.

I give him one back. We're friends again and I feel happy to be there.

14

I WAKE UP THE next morning with a thumping headache. After the dinner, Clive had surprised us all with four bottles of champagne. Real champagne. Very expensive champagne. And I'd got very, very drunk. Bits of the night remain with me like jagged little fragments lodged inside my head but huge amounts of it are grey. I sang, I remember that.

God, I sang.

I want to crawl and die with humiliation. I'd taken a taxi back to the flat and horrified my mother who was babysitting for me. I remember that. I'd told her that I had every right to get drunk if I wanted to and she'd made me see that I hadn't any rights as it happened because I had Fáinne and she depended on me. And she'd stormed off after first making sure that I wasn't going to make chips or turn on any electrical equipment.

In the harsh sobriety of morning, I can sort of see her point. What if I'd drunkenly set the house on fire? Could I have rescued Fáinne? The questions make my stomach heave so I lie very still.

It must be early enough because the bin truck is trundling along outside and the room is fairly dark. I hate waking up early because it gives me lots of time to think and when I think I start to feel overwhelmed by the responsibilities of my life. Only it isn't really my life any more because it's tied to my child. And if things happen to me, they happen to her. And I couldn't bear anything to happen to her. When I start to think like this, I begin to wonder if my mother feels the same about me. Does she love me so much that she'd curl up and die if anything happened to me?

I laugh to myself at the very idea. The only thing about my mother that curls up is her hair. I mean, I guess in her own way she does love me but just not as much as I do Fáinne. Or maybe it's just that Fáinne's life is still so new. Maybe when she tarnishes it a bit, I'll turn into my mother.

But I don't think so.

In fact, that'll be my next wish. Please don't make me turn into my mother. I grin at the thought.

Out on the landing, there is a patter of feet. A tousled head pokes in the door. 'Mammy,' Fáinne whispers, 'are you awake?'

I wonder should I pretend to be asleep because I still feel sick but I can't resist the thought of her warm body snuggled into mine. I like holding her. 'Just about.' My voice sounds as if someone has hacked at my vocal cords with a power saw.

'Can I come in?'

In answer I push back the duvet and Fáinne bounces into the bed. My head jars.

'Have you a hangover?' Fáinne asks. 'Gray says they're a bitch.'

'No,' I lie. 'I'm just sleepy. Let's just lie here and be quiet.'

'OK, so.'

Fáinne couldn't be quiet if her life depended on it. She talks and talks for the next hour. She talks about Jenny and how she thinks Jenny's dad is thick. She wants me to make her jam sandwiches for school because everyone else has jam sandwiches. She wants them wrapped in tin foil because

Barbie lunchboxes are babyish. She is going to grow her hair as long as Rapunzel, she wants a Bratz castle or Supervan from Santa or maybe a dog. I tell her Santa doesn't do dogs. She says she hopes that Jenny's dad runs away from her mammy, and she can't wait to meet Aunt Mona Lisa again. And of course her daddy. And then she gives me a list of all the things she wants for her birthday.

By the time we get up I feel as if I've done a day's work.

It's almost a relief when Fáinne gets out of the car at my mother's. I'm too much of a chicken to go up the path with her today. My mother will have told my father all about my appalling behaviour last night and I can't bear their disapproval, not when I'm still feeling so fragile.

'Bye, Mammy,' Fáinne shouts loudly. 'Take care of your headache.'

I wince. My mother has just arrived at the door for the last bit of Fáinne's well-meant advice.

'Bye, baby.'

'I'm not a baby.' Fáinne waves vigorously as my car pulls out of the drive. I see my mother staring after me and I pretend that I don't see her.

By midday my headache had abated. It's impossible not to feel well when all I see are sick animals all day. At twelve o'clock, the last of the morning casualties leave and I close the door and breathe a sigh of relief. Doug pokes his head out of his surgery. 'Are they all gone?' he asks cautiously.

'It's safe.'

He too looks relieved as he joins me in the small kitchen. 'Jesus, save me from fleas and worms and ticks and mites and—'

'Stop!' I laugh and put on the kettle.

Doug rummages about in the fridge. 'Did you forget your lunch today or something?'

'Couldn't face it – I got a bit drunk last night.'

'I thought you looked crap this morning all right,' he says, sitting down and opening up his own lunch. 'Sort of yellow.'

'Thanks.' I pour us both a coffee and sit opposite him.

As usual, my mind registers just how good-looking Doug is for a vet. I mean, I always think that vets must have been swots in school and swots generally aren't that good-looking. But Doug is a fine thing. He's tall, I reckon about six feet one with black hair that's in all these messy curls. His face has a chiselled look about it and he always has just the right amount of stubble. His eyes are a sort of yellow-brown, really unusual, with enormous curly lashes. Dark lashes that sweep up at the ends. Spiky, as if he's loaded them with mascara. And he has a lovely smile which shows off a dimple just to the left of his mouth. But – and it's a big but – he has horrendous dress sense. He wears horrible hairy jumpers and desperate trousers. And he seems to favour brown for some reason. And the animal smell that hovers about him takes a bit of getting used to. Well, it hovers around the whole surgery actually, so maybe it's not from him. But still, to look at him working on a sick animal or calming a terri-fied one with his slow murmuring way of talking is a complete turn-on.

Well, I think so.

We get on well too, which is good.

Normally we have a ninety-minute lunch but today, because it was so busy in the morning, we only have an hour.

'So where were you last night that was so good?' Doug asks, peeling the wrapper from his chocolate bar. His eating habits are almost as appalling as his fashion sense.

'In a mate's house. She got engaged and we celebrated a bit too hard.'

'Jesus.' He stretches out his long legs and shakes his head. 'Sounds great. It's ages since I've been plastered.'

'So arrange to get plastered.' I wish I'd brought a lunch now, my stomach is rumbling. 'You can do it at our Christmas party, I'll mind you.'

His eyes light up. 'Mmm.' He takes a bite out of his bar and studies me, his head cocked to one side. 'Sounds nice.'

For some reason I blush. 'You wouldn't think me minding you was nice if you saw the state of my poor daughter,' I stammer out feebly.

Doug laughs. His dimple flashes in and out. 'You've a gorgeous daughter, she looks like you.'

I drain my coffee. I know he's only flirting with me, but I can't handle it. 'She looks like her dad,' I say firmly, standing up. My head gives a thump at the sudden movement and I wince.

'There's Solpadene in the press,' Doug offers. 'You look as if you're going to be sick.'

'I'm fine. I just need some air.' I pull on my coat and head outside. It's just what I need.

At five, we're just about to close up for tea when the phone rings. Clare legs out the door pretending not to have heard while Doug and I stare at it in horror. I will him to tell me not to answer.

'You go,' he says resignedly. 'I'll deal with it.'

Of course, now I feel guilty so I snatch up the receiver. 'Yellow Halls Veterinary Surgery, how can I help you?'

I want to die as a rough-edged voice yells a triumphant, 'Yellow.'

'Yes?' I say back in a clipped tone.

'It's your ex-agent here,' Les says cockily.

'Sorry, don't know anyone by that name, you must have a wrong number.' I put down the phone.

Doug looks relieved. He pulls on his jacket and grins at me. 'I'll lock up – you go on.'

'Ta – you're a star!' The phone rings again just as I'm putting on my scarf. 'Probably the same person,' I say. 'Let's leave it.'

But he won't. He's so completely dedicated. He rolls his eyes and picks up the receiver. 'Hi, Doug Kelly here, what's the problem?'

Of course it's Les and he obviously tells Doug that he wants to speak to me. 'For you this time – some fella.' He hands me the phone.

'Hello, who is this?' I'm getting redder and redder.

'I already told you that, it's the guy you fired last week. The guy that sent you for the audition you just got.'

It takes a moment for it to sink in. I've actually got the bloody audition. Typical. Why the hell is he phoning me to tell me? I lower my voice and hiss, 'I didn't want it then and I don't want it now.'

'Right.' Les puts on this big regretful voice. 'So you don't want the money involved either?' He names this extraordinary amount of money.

'Quit the shit,' I say, though my heart is pumping.

'And you don't want the exposure: billboards, magazines, follow-up ads. Yeah, I can see that compared to being a receptionist in a vet's place you'd hate this. Yeah, sorry for wasting your time.'

Les doesn't put down the phone. Instead he's waiting for me to say something, only I can't. I'm completely dumbstruck. Do I want to do such a tacky ad? Nope. Do I need the money? I could certainly do with it. But I'm an *actress*, for God's sake. They don't do condom ads. 'Les—'

'Please take it,' he says then, his wheedling tone startling me. 'Jesus, maybe you don't need the money but I do. Christ, I can't even pay my milk bill at this stage. Aw, go on, Lucy. You'll thank me for it!'

Thank him? Thank him for getting me a condom ad? Thank him for making me responsible for paying his milk bill? I've fired him, for God's sake. 'Les, I—'

'Pleeeeease!'

Out of the corner of my eye, I see Doug pacing up and down. The poor guy is probably dying to get home. He's got surgery again at seven. 'I'll think about it,' I mutter, hating myself for saying it. Where are my principles? Where is my artistic integrity?

'Good girl.' Les chortles. 'Let me know tomorrow, yeah? Bandini needs to know by then. Sooo, I can take it that I'm still your agent?'

I hang up on him.

Doug looks questioningly at me. 'Problem?'

'No.' I'm a terrible liar. I blush like mad.

Doug stares at me for a second, then nods. 'Right, so.' He shoves his hand into his jacket pocket and pulls out his keys. 'Let's run before we get caught again.'

Shit – I need to tell someone. An impartial someone. A Mr Joe Soap who watches the telly and who doesn't know me, not really. I mean, if I tell Maddie and Gray, they'll tell me to take the ad but neither of them seems to care what other people think. I, on the other hand, am obsessed with what other people think. And, frankly, I worry about being associated with condoms. Am I a prude? A snob? I hope not.

'I've been offered an ad,' I tell Doug as he holds the door open for me.

'No way?' He looks dead impressed. 'Is that what the phone call was about?'

'Uh-huh.'

'So you'll be on telly, like? Wow.'

I gulp hard before admitting, 'It's, eh, for condoms.'

He pauses in the act of locking the surgery. 'Condoms?' He sounds surprised. 'I've never seen an ad for condoms.'

'Well, you will now.' I try to sound light-hearted but fail miserably.

Doug stares at me. 'Am I missing something? Don't you want to be on telly?'

I nod miserably.

'Is it work? There's no big deal getting time off. Clare will do your shifts, you know her – she'd work all the time if she was let.' He gives me a gentle nudge. 'Plus, I reckon a famous receptionist will do the place a world of good.'

His grin makes me sniff. Then, to my horror, a tear plops on to my cheek. 'But it's for *condoms*,' I wail. 'Condoms!'

'Try the pub up the road, luv,' a passer-by yells. 'You'll get them in the jacks.'

It makes me laugh a little and Doug, who obviously is completely shocked, smiles too. 'Thanks, mate,' he yells back. Then he turns to me. I'm still sniffing and wiping my nose on my sleeve and trying to compose myself. 'What's the matter?' He bends down to look into my face. 'Is it not a good thing?'

I shake my head. 'No, no, I'm fine. Forget it.' I want to run as far away from him as I can. 'I'd better go and pick up Fáinne.' Sniff. Sniff.

'You need a coffee.' He reopens the surgery. 'I'll make you one.'

'No, I—'

'You can't let your daughter see you in that state, it'll frighten her.'

93

He has a point. 'But your dinner?'

'My frozen pizza, you mean?' He turns off the alarm and bounds into the kitchen. He throws his jacket across a chair and flicks on the kettle. 'Sit,' he orders.

I sit, feeling stupid. 'I'll be all right in a minute.'

'So, it's not tears of joy, then?' Doug asks, taking out the coffee jar and emptying about five spoonfuls of coffee into two mugs. 'I thought acting is what you always wanted.'

'Doing an ad for condoms isn't acting,' I half snap. 'It's tacky and cheap and . . . oh my God, it pays so well!' I start to sniff again.

Doug places my coffee in front of me and sits down beside me at the battered table.

'You think people won't take you seriously, is that it?'

'Yep. And my mother will kill me. She'll say I'm squandering my talent or something like that.'

Doug is quiet for a bit. I think he's feeling uncomfortable; he keeps shifting about on his chair. Eventually, he mutters, 'Well, being a receptionist is hardly using your talent, is it? I reckon doing a ad, no matter what it's for, is using what you've got.'

'Even if it's condoms?' I'm like a kid looking for reassurance.

'Condoms are good – they stop the spread of Aids. You ever seen someone with Aids?'

I shake my head.

'Well, neither have I,' he admits ruefully. 'But if we did, I reckon we'd think that condoms aren't cheap or tacky. We'd think that they're a lifesaver.' He takes a biscuit and jabs it in my direction. 'You tell your mother *that* if she gives you grief.'

I think about his words. I sip my horribly strong coffee and eat a few more biscuits. And I decide that he's probably right. I touch his sleeve. 'Ta, Doug.'

'Forget about anyone else. You've got to do what you want, what makes you happy. It's the best thing in the end.'

'Is it?'

'My folks went spare when I went into veterinary medicine,' he says cheerily. 'In fact, they're still going spare. But they'll get used to it. Eventually. Do what you want – right?'

I nod. I don't know if I'll feel that positive about it – all I think is that maybe I'll feel better doing it than not doing it and that'll have to be good enough for the moment.

15

Dear Madeline,

I wish to inform you that Mr Jason Donovan is not contactable at the last known address that this college has for him. We are sorry that there is nothing more we can do in this matter and wish you much luck with your search.

Yours sincerely,
Tom Kilbane

16

SATURDAY MORNING. MADDIE and I are standing outside a crumbly, grey, three-storey building with a narrow, over-grown garden. Steps lead from the street up to the front door. Maddie turns to me. 'Are you sure you want to do this?'

I nod. Just looking at where Jason lived is giving me goose bumps. It hasn't changed much in the last eight years. It looks a little more dilapidated, a little more unloved. I wonder what it'll be like inside because eight years ago it was a pit.

'Right, big deep breath and up we go,' Maddie says, propelling us both up the steps and on to a potholed path.

We reach the front door. As before, there is a buzzer for each flat. Jason's one now reads *Byrne/Gaynor*. 'Wasn't Byrne the surname of the guy who used to live with Jason?' I can't help it, I sound excited. 'Wasn't his name John Byrne or something?'

'Byrne is a pretty common name,' Maddie says. She's not even looking at me. She thinks I'm mad. The same way she thinks I'm mad for not telling my mother I got the condom ad. She can't understand the fear I have of that woman. Maddie has fought her mother tooth and nail all her life and it doesn't seem to bother her in the same way fighting with my folks bothers me. I watch as she presses the bell. A long ring. She's hoping this comes to nothing. She's hoping that I'll let it drop.

'Ye-ah?' a sleepy male voice enquires. 'Who the fuck is this?'

'Open up and you'll soon find out,' Maddie says brightly.

There is radio silence from the other end. Then a cautious, 'Do I know ya?'

'Not at the moment, but you soon will.'

'I, eh, don't really encourage women I don't know into my place,' the voice replies.

'Well, you're the only man on the planet that doesn't, so,' Maddie says.

I laugh.

The voice laughs too. 'I'll meet you in the hall. I hope you're not a saleswoman because you're wasting your time. I've no money.'

He buzzes us in and my heart starts to hammer. Maddie pushes open the door and it's as if we've stepped into a time warp. The peeling wallpaper, the cracked lino, the smell: all the same. I half expect Jason to bound downstairs.

'What a kip,' Maddie whispers. Her earrings jangle like Christmas bells as she talks. The sound is weird in the musty house.

A kid, who can't be more than nineteen, arrives down to meet us. He has obviously got dressed in a hurry. His jeans are creased and his shirt looks as though he slept in it, which maybe he has. He stops on the last stair and studies us.

'Hi,' Maddie says in her cheerful voice. 'I'm Maddie and this is Lucy.'

I smile at him; if I speak my voice will shake.

'Hi, Maddie, hi, Lucy.' The kid nods. 'So, what's the occasion? Why me?' He attempts to brush himself down. 'Friday night, party night,' he says with a cute sort of smile.

We both smile back. 'We're looking for a bit of information,' Maddie says, 'about a guy that used to live in your flat.'

'Yeah?' The kid shrugs. 'Well, I've only been in it about two months, since I started college. I dunno who lived there before me.'

'And your flatmate?' Maddie says. 'How long has he lived here?'

He shrugs. 'Dunno. He's a bit weird – doesn't say much.'

'Is his name John Byrne?' I ask.

'Uh-huh.' The kid nods and his eyes brighten. 'Hey, is he who you're looking for?'

'Not exactly,' Maddie says. 'Can we talk to him?'

'I think he's in,' the kid says. He sounds excited now. He begins to walk up the stairs. 'Come on, youse can knock on his bedroom door. I'm not going to; he'd probably kill me. My mother thinks he's, like, an axe murderer or something and she keeps telling me to find someplace else to live but it's cheap here and the money I save I can spend going out.'

'Wise decision,' Maddie says, making a face at me. How anyone could live in the place is beyond us.

The kid opens the flat door for us and points to a brown door at the end of the hall. 'Be my guest,' he says.

For the first time Maddie looks uncertain, but I'm not. We've come this far, we might as well go the whole way. I march down the hall and knock politely on the bedroom door. The kid stands well away, his arms folded. Maddie, bless her, comes and stands beside me. No answer, so I knock more loudly.

Still no answer, so Maddie, gaining courage from me, pounds on the door. It's as if the whole room shakes.

'Wazissit?' a slurred voice says. It's thick, with a flat Navan accent.

'There's two girls here, Johnno, and they want to know about a guy that maybe you shared with.'

'Fuck off!'

99

'Charming guy,' Maddie says.

The kid sniggers.

'How old is he?' I ask.

The kid makes a face. 'Really old – maybe in his thirties, could be more.'

Maddie rolls her eyes. 'Ancient,' she mutters. Again she knocks on the door. 'Hey, Johnno, please answer a few questions – it's dead important.'

'Fuck off!'

'It's about Jason Donovan,' I call out.

'Jason Donovan used to live here?' The kid sounds impressed. 'Jesus, wait till I tell me mother. She'll love it, so she will. Is he not in some musical now or something?'

Neither Maddie nor I bother to explain because from the bedroom there are sounds of activity. It's as if Johnno has jumped from his bed and landed with a huge wallop on the floor. There's a lot of stamping and cursing going on and the kid says nervously from behind us, 'You've annoyed him now.'

I half expect a Fee, Fi, Fo, Fum from behind the door. Maddie and I move back as the sound of stomping footsteps comes towards us. The door is flung open on shaky hinges, revealing a giant of a man, dressed in stripy pyjamas. 'Did someone here say Jason fucking Donovan?' he roars.

It's the same flatmate, I'm sure of it. My heart begins a slow hammering.

Maddie tries to be humorous. 'I believe what was said was Jason Donovan.'

'If you knew that fucker like I know that fucker you'd say Jason FUCKING Donovan,' Johnno bellows into her face.

'So you know him?' Once again, I sound hopeful.

The giant turns to me. 'Knew,' he says viciously. 'I *knew* him. I never want to ever set eyes on him again. If I met him in an eternity it'd be too soon.'

'His music isn't that bad,' the kid says.

'FUCK OFF, YOU!' the giant roars.

The kid fucks off.

'And you two' – he turns his gaze on us – 'What do you want with that waster?'

Maddie nudges me. My mouth opens and closes like a goldfish. I don't know what to say. 'We want to meet him so we can tear him limb from limb,' Maddie says calmly. 'We want to first take his legs off and roast them over an open fire and give them to him to eat.'

Christ!

Johnno looks impressed. 'What did you say your name was?' he asks.

'Maddie.' She holds out her hand. Indicates me. 'And this is Lucy.'

Johnno dismisses me; instead he bestows a brown-toothed smile on Maddie. 'Coffee?'

Maddie gulps. Drinking coffee in this place would be as risky as jumping into a shark-infested ocean. 'Fine,' she squeaks.

Johnno, scratching himself in all the places he shouldn't, strides out into the kitchen. The kid is at the table, drinking a coffee himself. 'Out,' Johnno orders and the kid smiles apologetically at us before exiting. Johnno holds out a chair for Maddie and she sits down. I sit on the old sofa. The same old sofa I first sat on years ago. Johnno busies himself switching on the kettle and rinsing out some mugs. Two mugs, I notice with relief. Kettle boiled, Johnno makes himself and Maddie coffee and then, as if I don't exist, he says, 'So, what did the prick do to you?'

Maddie looks to me for guidance. I shrug. 'He hurt my best friend when she needed him most,' she says tactfully. 'He—'

101

'He was good at hurting people,' Johnno spits. 'Good at letting people down. Will I tell you what he did to me?'

I don't think it's a question because Johnno doesn't wait for an answer. 'He stole from me,' he says. His voice rises. 'He stole my biscuits, my food, my fucking booze. He shit all over my hospitality, he shit all over me, he fucked off and left me owing loads of rent. If you get in touch with that wanker, you put him on to Johnno.'

'I will.' Maddie nods and I'm half afraid that she will. 'Can you tell us anything about him to help us?'

'Yeah, he was a bastard.'

'We know that,' she says and Johnno laughs. A surprisingly nice laugh. Maddie continues, 'Where was he from? Wasn't it Kerry somewhere?'

'Dingle,' Johnno says. 'A prick from Dingle.'

'Anything else?'

Johnny screws up his pretty-screwed-up face. 'Football, he liked that. And he had a girlfriend. I only met her once – mad about him she was.'

I cringe. I was young; we were all young.

'His family?'

'He didn't have a mother,' I say then. I never told Maddie or Gray that before, but I guess it doesn't matter now. Maddie stares at me and I mutter, 'He told me that once.'

For the first time Johnno looks at me. Then he positively stares. 'Hey, you the girlfriend he had? Are you the one he hurt?'

I nod. I haven't thought about the hurt in a long time.

Johnno jumps up. 'You need a coffee.'

Maddie looks at me behind his back and we grin at each other. The man is seriously mental.

Johnno shoves a coffee into my hands. 'Yeah,' he says, 'you've been screwed around like me, haven't you?'

I want to say that I think I've coped with it better than him, but I can't. I'm too afraid.

'I dunno about his mother,' Johnno says, sitting down again and talking to Maddie, whom he seems to have taken a shine to. 'He never said, but I do know he didn't get on too well with his dad. He visited here one day and they had this big argument. Big bruise Jason had after it. Serve him right, I say. What do you say, Maddie?'

'Hear, hear.' Maddie raises her coffee mug and Johnno laughs.

'May he rot in hell!' Johnno toasts.

'And so say all of us,' Maddie toasts back.

We both leave the flat feeling as if we have to be decontaminated. We even smell of must and damp. I can't wait to go home and rinse my hair.

'Phew.' Maddie pretends to collapse against a lamppost. 'That was heavy going.'

I giggle. 'You charmed the jocks off him.'

'Which was a big deal' – Maddie nods – 'seeing as they probably haven't been off him in decades.'

'Ugh!'

We both laugh more than we should. I think we're just relieved that we've escaped. Maddie though has had to promise sincerely to contact Johnno if we ever do catch up with Jason. 'I'll come with ye,' he promised, cracking his knuckles and leering in a very disturbing manner.

'So, what do we have?' Maddie asks.

'Born in Dingle, no mother, didn't like his dad, played for the local football team, was a wanker—'

Maddie laughs.

I've reached my car. I unlock it and open the passenger door for Maddie. My car, I reckon, is older than I am. It has no alarm, no power steering, and no central locking. It has a radio and a heater and it goes – minus the suspension. Maddie sits in the passenger seat and it sinks. 'I hate your car,' she moans. 'I always feel like a big fat cow whenever I sit in it.'

'You know it's not you.' I switch on the ignition and my car coughs and splutters before it gets going. 'So, how about some lunch to celebrate our information-digging?'

'I've just said that I feel like a fat cow and you suggest lunch?'

I grin. 'If you feel like a fat cow, you can always order steak.'

She belts me and I swerve. The guy in the car behind blasts us and we laugh.

17

November 2nd
Tracy came home today. When I got in from college, she was sitting in
the kitchen talking to Mam and, honest to God, I hardly recognised her.
First of all, she's got so thin – she was always thin but now she's like
a chopstick on legs. It's the only way to get work apparently. And Tracy
wants to break into catwalk modelling which means that you have to
be super skinny.

Second of all, she looked really grown up. Not grown up as in old,
she was just well groomed. I mean, she always took care of herself, but
now she's immaculate. Her nails are an art form with little glittery
stickers on them and her skin glows. I look like a right heifer beside her.
Bitten nails, raggy hair and a body that actually has fat on it.

'Hi, Tracy,' I said.

'It's Mona Lisa,' Mam corrected. 'Tracy has to change her name,
and her agent thinks that Mona Lisa suits her.'

Tracy nods in affirmation.

'Mona Lisa?' I stared at them both. 'But she was dead ugly!'

Of course Mam accused me of trying to cause trouble and started
giving me grief so I just walked out and left them to it.

Mona Lisa – Jesus!

November 9th
I know before I was dying for Tracy to come home but things are worse
now. All she cares about is herself. I mean, has she asked why she's

sharing with me and not sleeping in her own room? Nope. So I told her. It's because Dad is sleeping in your room, I said. He and Mam don't talk.

I waited for her to be horrified, to be worried. But she just waved her hand about and told me not to be ridiculous. It's only temporary, she said. It'll blow over.

But it won't, I tried to say. I don't think they can stand each other. She just shrugged and went out.

And, on top of that, though not as important, is the fact that Tracy is obsessive about things being tidy. Even her knicker drawer is colour coded, can you believe it? She's such a cow. If I don't make my bed in the morning, she tells Mam. It's my room – it always was – so why do her rules have to matter?

But that's the thing, see: Tracy matters in this house.

November 10th

Jason arrived at my rehearsals tonight. He sat in the back of the hall and I didn't notice him until the director told us to finish up. I grabbed my bag, pulled my fleece over my head and was on my way out when he tapped me on the arm. 'Hey.' It was great to see him. It turned out that he'd come to walk me to the pub. Maddie and Gray were already down there and he'd said that he'd bring me. And he did – just to the pub door. He wouldn't come in because he was broke.

'I'll get you one in,' I said. 'Come on.'

But he wouldn't. I reckon he has a test tomorrow and was afraid to say it in case he sounded swotty or something. 'So you're not coming?'

'Nope.' He gazed down at his hands. 'Have a good night, yeah?'

How could I have a good night when he wasn't there? I'd been looking forward to sitting beside him and chatting to him. I hardly ever see him socially and I wouldn't ever unless I bunked off. So I told him that I was tired too. That suddenly I realised that if I had a drink I wouldn't have enough for bus fare. And would he please walk me to the bus stop?

I think he was surprised but he just smiled. 'Yeah, sure.'

Just walking beside him, up the road and out of the campus, was heaven. Just staring at him out of the corner of my eye was a thrill. As we reached the outer edges of the campus, Jason stopped at this big green hedge. It stretches for about a hundred metres down the road. Jason gave it a poke. 'D'you know something,' he said, 'I've always wanted to walk on top of that hedge. I reckon it'd hold my weight.'

'Get lost!' What a weird thing to think about.

'No, I'm serious.' And he was. 'Look at it.' He gave it another poke. 'It's like solid concrete.'

'You'd fall right through it.'

'I don't think so.' He looked gravely at it. 'I could crawl on it, I bet – spread my weight.'

'That'd be a sight.' I couldn't stop the giggles.

He grinned. 'Yeah, I guess.'

'Come on.' I walked away from the hedge in case he climbed up on it. He stared at it a bit longer before running to catch me up.

We spent the rest of the time talking about my play and his football. He'd scored every match so far though last week he'd been sent off for a hard tackle and was now banned for two matches. Bill – his trainer – was furious with him, as were half the team apparently. It means that he won't be able to play in the cup final.

'Does it not bother you that they're all mad with you?'

He shrugged. 'Naw – nothing new there.' Then he shrugged some more. 'Anyway, the guy I tackled was saying horrible stuff to me, so he deserved it.'

'What did he say?'

'Doesn't matter.'

I reckon it did though, because he looked hard and un-Jason-like for a second before smiling again. 'Who cares, ey?'

I loved the way he pretended not to care. I couldn't do that.

November 12th

Dad picked me up from rehearsals tonight. We rehearse twice a week: Wednesdays and Fridays. Coming up to the performance, it'll probably be every night. Anyway, tonight it was after midnight when we finished up. Jason waited for me again and he stayed with me until Dad arrived, which was really decent of him. Only he wouldn't say 'hello' to Dad or anything. He walked off as soon as Dad pulled up. Dad was really quiet driving me home. I chatted to fill in the silence but I know now that he wasn't listening because he interrupted me mid-flow and said, 'It must be tough on you, Lucy, the way things are between your mam and me.'

I couldn't look at him. It's weird when your parents start treating you like an equal, isn't it? I just nodded.

'We're going through a bad patch right now,' he said. 'We think a bit of distance might help things.'

A bit of distance?

'What?'

The upshot of it all is that Dad is leaving. Soon.

18

GRAY GIVES TWO sharp 'bips' of his car horn and I curse. 'Mammy!' Fáinne is dancing about from foot to foot in the hallway. 'When are we going? Gray's here and he's been beeping his horn for *ages*.'

'Run out and tell him I'll be ready in a second.' I can't find my good boots. The ones that I splashed out over a hundred euro on. They are of soft tan leather and they dress up any outfit, even faded denim jeans and a brown and cream stripy jumper. Fáinne opens the front door and runs down the path, her black hair flying out behind her. I hear her telling Gray that I'm on my way. Gray does his usual, 'Who's this girl? I don't know any girls this big,' and I smile. Old trainers, old slippers and old boots are piled high in the hallway as I frantically tear the place apart. I even find a pair of shoes that I'd forgotten I had.

More horn blasting.

'Oh fuck off,' I mutter.

Eventually I give up and pull on a pair of black boots: last year's pair with big clumpy heels and square toes. I keep clothes and shoes in the hope that they'll come back into fashion and some of my things have actually: my polo-necks have and so has my denim mini-skirt.

'Are you coming or not?' Gray yells.

'I'm ready.' Slamming the door behind me, I jump into the front seat of his car.

'Those boots don't match, Mammy,' Fáinne says accusingly.

I ignore her.

Gray looks at my boots but wisely says nothing. So I mutter an irritated, '*What?*'

'You could have made more of an effort, Luce.'

'I did make an effort – I'm dressed, aren't I?'

Gray shrugs and starts his car. For some reason, I've been biting the head off him lately. 'Thanks for the lift.'

'No probs – can't have you late for meeting your beloved sister.'

I smirk. Gray smirks back.

'Yeah, we don't want to be late, sure we don't.' Fáinne says. 'I wonder what she'll be wearing. Remember we saw her in the paper in that gold dress – I wonder will she be wearing it?'

Jesus, I hope not.

'So what's wrong with your car?' Gray asks as he takes the turn for the airport motorway. 'Did it just stall this morning?'

'Yeah.' I glance at my hands. I guess I could have filed my chipped nails for the occasion but I never noticed them last night. How come that is? It's the same with my house: I never notice how dirty it is until my mother visits. 'My car didn't want to meet Tracy either.'

'Not nice,' Gray chastises.

'Who else doesn't want to meet her?' Fáinne says. 'Will you be meeting her, Gray? She's famous, you know.'

'Aw, I won't be staying around,' Gray replies, trying to sound as if he's sad about it. 'You'll have to get a lift back with your nana – I've a hot date this afternoon.'

'Wow!' I elbow him. 'Sounds good.'

'Are you going to Spain?' Fáinne asks.

Gray and I laugh. 'He means that he's going out with someone lovely,' I explain to Fáinne, who doesn't look impressed. Gray heading to Spain would have been much more exciting. 'So' – I turn to Gray – 'is it Audrey?'

'Uh-huh.'

'Serious, huh?'

He shrugs.

'Is – it – serious?' I tease, jabbing him in the arm. Gray is shy about his love life. Not that he's ever had much of a one: more a string of dates. Audrey has been around for six weeks at least and it's a record as far as I know.

'It's . . .' He pauses. 'It's early days, but I like her.'

'Wow.'

'But not as much as Fáinne.' Gray turns to grin at Fáinne who lights up. 'She's my number-one girl, aren't you?'

'Yep.' Fáinne smiles at me. 'Gray is going to marry me when I grow up.'

'Really?' I pinch Gray on the arm. 'You never told me you were heading into the priesthood.'

He laughs. 'I thought you were going to say that I wasn't good enough for her.'

'That goes *without* saying.'

As we get nearer the airport, my stomach begins to roll. My mouth goes dry and I'm only half listening to the conversation in the car. As Gray drives towards the set-down area I want to run as far away as I can. I can see the terminal building looming up and it sums up the way I feel. Gray indicates and, driving into a free space, he stops the car. 'Well, ladies, here you are.'

'Great!' Fáinne pulls off her seatbelt and looks expectantly at me.

111

'Where are you meeting your folks?'

'At the bottom of the escalators in the departures area.'

'You know where that is?'

'Uh-huh.'

I can't move.

Gray places his hand on mine. I notice that his nails look clean and well cut. His hands are warm and strong. I feel like crying. I feel like crying a lot these days. 'Nervous?'

I nod.

'Come on, Mammy, let's *go!*'

I wish I'd found my tan boots. I knew I'd feel like this but for some reason back at the house I hadn't cared.

'You'll be fine. OK, so your boots don't match, but you look *great*.' Gray squeezes my hand. 'Tracy couldn't wear horrible boots and get away with it.'

I manage a grin. 'I'll ring you later.'

'I mightn't be there but leave a message, OK?'

I hate that he's not going to be there. Why couldn't Audrey have just lent him to me for the day?

'I'll be looking out for you on the news.'

'Stop!'

'Mammy!'

'Fáinne, I'm coming. Have patience.' I feel horrible the minute I say it, but Fáinne is too excited to notice my snappy tone. She's going to go through the window with excitement if I don't leave soon. 'Ta, Gray, enjoy the hot date.'

'Will do.'

I get out of the car and slam the door. I don't look back as he pulls out because I'm afraid I'll run to him and beg him to take me home.

Mam and Dad are waiting for me. I reckon they've probably been there since last night just so that they won't miss their fabulously famous daughter. Mam is wearing her purple suit, the one she wears to all her important occasions. It's her one bow to designer gear and it does look fantastic on her. A long soft skirt that folds and sways about her ankles. A jacket of the exact same shade though made from heavier material encases her slim frame. Underneath the jacket, she has a cream and purple camisole. Her hair has been coloured a rich honey and her make-up is so perfect and natural. She looks about forty and I cringe as I come towards her. I know she'll be eyeing me up but that she won't say anything.

Dad is quite dapper too. He is wearing his tan overcoat, brand new tan trousers and a check shirt. He has had his hair cut. They look a stylish pair and not at all related to me.

'Hiya, Nana!' Fáinne dashes towards them, barging into busy commuters who look annoyed before smiling at her and telling her that it's OK. She's so cute, even at seven, that I reckon she'll have an easy coast through life.

'Fáinne!' My mother opens her arms and Fáinne runs into them. 'You look so pretty today!'

And she does. She's wearing her Christmas clothes a few weeks early as I couldn't afford two new sets of clothes and I didn't see why I had to either. How many other people dress up to meet their aunt off a plane?

'Hiya, Luce,' my dad says. 'What happened? We were getting worried.'

'Car broke down. Gray had to give me a lift.'

'Oh dear.' Mam looks pained. 'And how will you manage without it?'

'Dad might have to pick Fáinne up in the morning and I'll walk to work, if that's OK?' I hadn't intended broaching the subject so early in the day.

'That's fine.' My dad pats Fáinne on the head. 'Nothing like an early morning drive to blow the cobwebs away. I'll drive you to work too, Luce, if you want.'

'Ta, that'd be great.'

'And pick you up.'

'Aw, no, I'll be fine.'

He looks doubtfully at me.

'Just bring Fáinne home around six and I'll be there to meet her.' I didn't want to give Mam the chance to say anything about Tracy and how would Tracy manage if she had to go somewhere. As far as I knew Tracy didn't drive. She'd never had the time to learn apparently.

Mam, holding on to Fáinne's hand, begins to make her way through the crowd. 'Let's go,' she says, 'the plane is due in in twenty minutes.'

The arrivals floor is bedlam. Cameras are everywhere. Guys with microphones are setting up. Photographers are looking around for someone to snap and then some eagle-eyed reporter spots us. 'There they are!'

There is a stampede as about twenty guys rush headlong towards us. Microphones are shoved in our faces and a torrent of questions assaults us. I am vaguely aware that my picture is being taken and I lower my head. God, I wish I'd bothered with make-up. Fáinne is beaming proudly into the lens of some TV camera or other. 'How does it feel to be meeting your auntie?' they ask her.

'I can't wait.' Fáinne shivers deliciously and bats her huge eyes at them. 'She's so cool and wears cool clothes and I want to be just like her, so I do.'

'God forbid,' I mutter under my breath and Dad shoots a sharp look at me.

'And you' – a microphone is shoved up my nose – 'have you missed your sister?'

114

'Yes.' I want to add that I've missed her like a ruptured appendix but I can't.

'All we want is to be left alone to welcome her back,' my mother says in her posh voice.

'Left alone, my arse,' Dad hisses fondly to me. 'The woman is loving it.'

And she is. She glides like a swan away from the gaggle of reporters and they, sensing that she's the boss, follow her like kids after the Pied Piper. Mercifully, Dad and I are left on our own.

'It'll be fine,' Dad says, surprising me. 'You'll see.'

'I know,' I say casually. 'It's only Tracy.'

Oh fuck – it's only Tracy.

At one-thirty, fifteen minutes late, Tracy's plane lands. At one-fifty, the passengers begin to swarm out into the arrivals lounge. All the waiting reporters greet each person that's not Tracy with a groan. Eventually the shout goes up, 'She's on her way! She's on her way!' Even those who don't know who's 'on her way' stop what they are doing and look expectantly towards the arrival gates. Dad, Mam, Fáinne and I get shoved up front. Fáinne is hyperventilating with excitement beside me. I push my hair behind my ears in the vain hope that it will suddenly look nice.

Everyone waits. And waits. People begin to push from behind. And suddenly she is there.

Bulbs flash, TV cameras click on and Tracy stands with a laser beam of a smile on her face, accepting the adoration as if it's her due. Her teeth are even more perfect than I remember, her smile dazzles and I think that's the reason she got a film role. She *would* set the screen on fire. Except that she can't act.

She's dressed in white: a white frilly blouse, white flared

trousers that hug just the right amount of thigh and white stiletto sandals, the straps inset with fake diamonds – at least I reckon they're fake. Draped across her shoulders is a white fake fur coat.

'She's like a princess,' Fáinne whispers reverently.

Mam can't contain herself any longer. She rushes from the crowd and embraces Tracy. The cameras have a field day. Dad goes in next and he drags Fáinne along with him. I stand on the edge of the crowd, not willing to put on a show for anyone. But Tracy does it for me. She pretends that she doesn't know me at first and then joyfully embraces me.

'Welcome home,' I mutter.

'Thank you.' She holds me by the shoulders and looks hard at me. 'It's great to be back.'

'Can we have a few words, Mona Lisa?' a handsome reporter asks.

'Just because you're so cute,' she replies flirtingly, her Irish accent tinged with an American twang.

The reporter blushes like a schoolboy and his TV friends whoop and cheer. Tracy smiles as if she's used to it. Which she probably is.

She's dragged to one side and I can't hear the questions she's being asked. Mam stands beside her, beaming proudly, holding Fáinne by the hand.

'Coffee?' Dad asks.

'Sure.'

We walk in the direction of the bistro and Dad buys two coffees and two squishy cream cakes. 'They won't be finished with her for ages yet.' There is pride in his voice. 'We'll wait here until they're done.'

It's gonna be a long day.

19

ONE OF THE problems with not having my car is that I'm dependent on Dad to drive me home. OK, I could have got a taxi but money is tight and until I get paid for the ad that's the way it's gonna be for a while. So, instead of heading home after the airport, which is what I would have liked, Fáinne and I end up beside Tracy in the back of this fab limo that the film company have provided for her. Fáinne is bouncing off the seats in excitement and Mam is thrilled. She tries to look as if she's used to limos.

'I can get the driver to drop you off outside your house,' Tracy says helpfully to me.

'No way, Mona Lisa,' Fáinne whimpers. 'Nana is having a special dinner for you and she's invited us.'

'Good.' Tracy beams and Fáinne snuggles into her. I try my best not to glower. Tracy is jetlagged but, give her her due, she tells an enthralled Fáinne all about Hollywood and modelling and going for screen tests. She drops names into the conversation like little golden sweets for Fáinne to pick up on.

'You've met Christina Aguilera?' Fáinne breathes.

Tracy nods. 'Uh-huh. She was at a party I went to and we had a great laugh.'

'Did you get her autograph?'

'No.' Tracy pouts. 'If I had only known that you liked her I would have.'

'Next time, will you?' Fáinne pleads.

'Promise.'

I feel a momentary stab of envy. Why can't I impress my child like that? Why can't I meet famous people and do all sorts of wonderful things? 'Come away from Tracy, Fáinne, you'll dirty her blouse.'

'Not at all.' Tracy wraps her arm around my daughter. 'What's a blouse compared to a hug from the prettiest girl in Ireland?'

'*Isn't* she pretty?' my mother says from the passenger seat. 'I'm always saying to Lucy that she should enrol Fáinne in an agency – the child would get loads of work.'

'I don't want my daughter out earning money,' I mutter. 'That's my job.'

'Oh, for God's sake' – Mam waves her manicured hand about – 'she'd love it – she's a born performer, just like her aunt.'

There is an uncomfortable silence. Then Tracy says, 'If I remember rightly, it's Lucy who's the performer. She was always the star in our school plays.'

Talk about *patronising*. 'Yeah, well, I never got to star in a Hollywood movie.'

'Oh, do tell us about the movie,' Mam thrills. 'It sounds so exciting.'

'And then Mammy can tell you about her ad,' Fáinne pipes up. 'That sounds exciting too.'

My blood runs cold. Jesus. How does she know about that?

'An ad?' Mam says, puzzled. 'You never told us you got an ad. Is that the one you went for a few weeks ago?'

'She told Gray,' Fáinne said. 'I heard them talking about it. I think she was going to tell you at some stage, Nana.'

'Well, thanks.' Mam sniffs, annoyed. 'Telling some stranger before your own mother.'

118

'It's great though,' Dad says quickly, to head Mam off.

'How come you didn't tell me?' Mam knows something is up. She can smell deception like others can smell a garlic overload.

'I, eh, well . . .' I frantically try to come up with something. 'I didn't want to ruin Tracy's thunder.'

Silence.

Everyone is thinking it but they're all too polite to say it. There is no way a crummy ad could ruin the excitement of starring in a Hollywood blockbuster. 'Oh.' Mam smiles vacantly. 'That was thoughtful.'

'That's our Luce,' Dad chimes in.

'Thanks,' Tracy says.

I shrug.

'What's the ad for?' Tracy asks.

Christ.

'Protective clothing,' my mother tells her. 'Isn't that right, Lucy?'

I could tell them now. I could ruin their day if I had a mind to. But the truth is I can't. They look so happy to see Tracy and, to be honest, I'm scared stupid. 'Sort of,' I mutter. 'I haven't exactly been told how it's to be yet.' Which is true.

'And when do you shoot it?' Tracy asks. She's trying to sound professional, as if she knows what she's talking about.

'Next week – it's to air before Christmas.' I don't say anything about the billboards or follow-up ads. If they've to find out, it's better to do it in gentle stages.

'Well, good.' Mam beams at me and I smile back. 'Well done, Lucy.'

'Yeah, well done, Mam.' Fáinne snuggles up to me now and I wrap my arm about her and look challengingly at my sister. She smiles back at me and I wonder what she's thinking.

*

When we arrive at Mam's house, the neighbours come out to welcome Tracy home. Most of them have known her all her life and, as she steps out of the car, they applaud loudly. Shouts of: 'Welcome home, Tracy,' and, 'It's great to see you, Tracy,' compete with the cheers. She dazzles them with her smile. Even though Fáinne has done an admirable job of creasing her blouse, she still looks good. Some younger kids run up to her to ask for her autograph. Fáinne keeps a firm hold on her coat while she's signing and bossily tells all the kids to get in line. I laugh despite myself.

Mam goes on into the house and puts on the kettle to make tea. The neighbours follow her in and produce cakes and buns and sandwiches and before we know it, the house is jammed and there's a party in full swing.

I feel guilty that Dad can't take a drink because he has to drive me home. 'I'll get a taxi, Dad,' I tell him, hoping it won't cost too much. 'Don't worry.'

'Are you sure?'

'Uh-huh.'

'I'll pay for it.'

'No you won't.' I roll my eyes. 'You'll have enough of a job paying for the carpets to be cleaned after this lot go.'

He laughs. 'You could be right but, sure, isn't it great – look at your mother, she's thriving on all the attention.'

I follow his gaze and see my mother at the centre of a group of neighbours. She looks young and vibrant and alive. Her face is animated and I know it's because of Tracy.

'Where's Tracy?' Dad asks, obviously thinking about her too. 'Don't tell me the guest of honour has abandoned ship.'

It sure looks like it. I reckon she's got bored and decided to ring some Hollywood friends or something. Oh Christ, I'm being a bitch. I shake my head to clear it and try and smile and think nice thoughts about my sister. She looks lovely, that's one nice thought. Her coat was nice, that's thought number two. Then I draw a blank.

I slug back some more wine and hope it will help the nice thoughts to come. At least it'll blank out the horrible ones. A neighbour comes up and begins to talk to Dad. They're discussing football results so I wander away.

Around five-thirty, just before the news, I decide to go. More people than ever are jammed into the house and the whole thing is getting louder and louder. I reckon Fáinne is better off at home than listening to her granddad give any more drunken singing performances. He has already murdered 'The Wild Rover' and my mother has sung a very off-key 'Over the Rainbow' and now one of the neighbours is swaying dangerously as he attempts to warble 'Bridge Over Troubled Water'.

'I'd rather jump into the troubled waters and drown than go home with you!' someone calls out and everyone laughs.

I ring for a taxi and then look for Fáinne. I haven't seen her since the beginning of the party when she'd been outside with Tracy. Now I feel a moment of panic as I try to find her. She isn't in the kitchen or in the garden, so I go upstairs. As I approach the top of the stairs I hear voices.

'Fáinne?'

'In here, Mammy.'

She's in my old room. And so, I see with surprise, is Tracy. There are wrapped parcels strewn all over the bedroom floor. Fáinne is wearing a weird costume which she has pulled on over her Christmas dress. When she sees me she does a twirl. 'Do you like it, Mammy? Mona Lisa says it's one of the elf costumes from *Lord of the Rings*.'

'I just bought it for her – I didn't know what to get her,'

121

Tracy explains from her vantage point on the bed. 'I didn't know if she'd be into dolls or what.'

'Isn't it lovely, Mammy?'

'Gorgeous.' I grin. 'You can wear it next Halloween when you go trick or treating.'

'Or I can just wear it every day,' Fáinne says.

'Yeah. Sure. I hope you said thank you.'

'Thank you!' Fáinne throws her arms about Tracy who hugs her back.

'You're very welcome.'

'And Mona Lisa got you this.' Fáinne locates a present from the masses on the floor. 'Isn't she nice buying everyone presents?'

'Great.' I hold the present in my hands, without unwrapping it. 'Ta.'

Tracy looks embarrassed. 'It's only small.'

'It's the thought that counts.' I wonder why I'm saying such stupid things. Normally if anyone gives me a present, it doesn't stand a chance. I rip the paper off with as much excitement as if I'm undressing Brad Pitt. I love them. I love giving them. I love getting them. But I can't open this one. Not in front of her, anyway. 'Thanks again.'

'No bother.' She stands up from the bed. 'Fáinne was just helping me unpack my cases.'

'She has *lovely* clothes, Mammy,' Fáinne says. 'Come here and I'll show you.'

'Oh, I don't think Tracy—'

'Mona Lisa, Mammy.'

'Well, I don't think—'

'It's fine,' Tracy says. 'Go and look.'

I have no choice. Fáinne walks confidently to the wardrobe and opens it to display the most beautiful array of clothes I have ever seen in my entire life. Silks, satins, velvets, shiny materials that seem to glow with all the colours of the rainbow, corduroy, denims, silvers and golds.

'This is the gold dress she wore in the photo shoot for that lipstick,' Fáinne informs me. 'And normally she just wears jeans. But just look at these, Mammy.' She pulls out a pair of denims, knocking some other stuff flying.

'Fáinne!'

'It's OK, I can fix it up. It'll all be a muddle in a couple of days anyhow,' Tracy says. I think of her bossing me about over the mess I used to make in the bedroom and telling Mam tales about how untidy I was and I wonder what has happened. Tracy comes to join me as Fáinne unfolds the jeans.

'Look, Mammy!'

The jeans are washed denim, flared with cool triangular pockets and embroidery all up one leg. They literally must have cost an arm and a leg. I would have killed for a pair of jeans like that.

'They are the business,' I say, too impressed to do anything other than sound impressed. 'Where did you get them?'

'New York. I designed them myself and got someone to make them.'

'Pays to have money, huh?'

'Yep.' Tracy tosses her glossy hair behind her shoulders and beams at me. 'Fáinne wants them when she grows up.'

'And I can have them.' My daughter looks adoringly at her aunt. 'Isn't that great?'

'Great,' I agree, loving her excited face but hating the fact that it's not her mother she's going all ga-ga over. 'But for now put them back and get your coat – we have to go.'

Her face drops. 'Why?'

'Because you've school in the morning and I've work and I've booked a taxi.'

As if on cue, my dad yells, 'Taxi is here, Luce. Where are you? Taxi!'

Downstairs, the opening chords of the news begin. I have to get out before I see myself on the telly looking scruffy. 'Come on, Fáinne.'

'I don't want to!' Fáinne folds her arms and glares at me. 'I want to stay. Granddad will bring me home.'

My dad, at this stage, wouldn't be able to drive a golf ball never mind a car. 'You're coming now!'

'Nooo.'

I feel embarrassed that's she's behaving like this in front of Tracy. It's as if I have no power over her. 'Yes!'

'No.' She dodges behind Tracy.

'TAXI, LUCY!'

'If you go with your mammy,' Tracy says, 'I'll visit you and take you somewhere nice.'

Her head peeps out. 'Really?'

'Uh-huh.'

'Mammy, did you hear that?'

I hate that she's said that. She'll never bring Fáinne out. 'I did and I hope she means it.'

'Course I do.' For the first time Tracy sounds annoyed. 'I'll see you next week for your birthday, OK? But in order for it to happen, you have to get your coat on and go home with your mammy.'

'OK.'

'I don't like bribing her,' I say. Oh God, I'm being a bitch and I can't stop and, to be honest, Tracy hasn't shown her horrible side yet. 'Your coat is downstairs.'

'Hey, hey,' one of the neighbours calls, 'Fáinne is on the news!'

Everyone downstairs goes: 'Awwwww!'

Fáinne legs it out of the room and it's just Tracy and me.

Tracy gets up from the bed and begins picking up the clothes that have fallen from her wardrobe. 'Don't you want to go and see Fáinne on the telly?' she asks, not looking at me.

'Don't you want to go and see yourself?'

She shrugs. 'God, no.' She folds up a gorgeous sky-blue and green top. 'Everywhere I go, I see myself.'

'Hard life, huh?'

She detects the sarcasm in my voice and flinches. 'It's all right.'

'I thought you'd be staying in a hotel,' I say then. I can't help it. When she lived at home, she couldn't wait to get away. And now . . .

'I'm sick of hotels,' Tracy mutters. 'They all look the same after a while.' She stares about the old room. 'This is nice for a change.'

'Well . . .' I indicate the room, the house. 'Enjoy the rest of the party.'

I begin to leave when she calls my name. 'Your present.' She tosses it to me and I catch it.

'Oh, right, thanks.'

We look at each other. She says suddenly, 'It is nice to see you, Lucy. I hope . . .' She swallows. 'Well, I hope we can be friends.'

She hopes we can be friends! I'm not that hard up for friends – I feel like saying this but I don't. 'Sure. Whatever,' I say dismissively. I leave the room and go and catch the tail end of Fáinne as she beams prettily from the TV.

20

THE MECHANIC RINGS me at work to tell me that my timing belt had gone. Luckily though, he adds, as I wasn't going at speed, the damage to my engine is minimal.

'Damage to my engine,' I say faintly.

'About four hundred euros' worth, that's assuming I can lay my hands on the parts – that's an antique yer driving, missus.'

Four hundred euro. I could probably buy a car for cheaper than that. And where was I going to get four hundred euro anyway?

'D'you want me to fix it?'

Visions of my faithful car being towed to the scrapyard and mashed up into hundreds of pieces make me shudder. I love that car.

'The shocks are gone too, but you probably knew that.'

I hadn't. 'Is that serious?'

'Naw. Not good for the suspension though – but your suspension is knackered anyway.'

Mr Devlin and Paddy come in. He gives me a nod and indicates the waiting room. 'Doug said to come in – he's giving Paddy an X-ray or something?'

I wave him in. I turn back to the phone and steel myself and ask the hard question. 'Is it worth getting it fixed?'

'No.'

'Oh.'

'It's a heap of scrap. You could buy a car cheaper. I've a lovely one here for three hundred euro. Ten years old but as smooth as melted chocolate. No power steering, dodgy heater, good radio. Hundred thousand miles on the clock. I'd say she'd go another fifty at least.'

I feel like I'm betraying my best friend. My poor car all abandoned, thinking it's coming home . . . I shake my head. It's a *car*, I remind myself. Lots of metal and rubber. 'I'll come and look at it – maybe tomorrow if I can?'

'Fine.'

The phone is hung up at the other end and for the next ten minutes I sit staring into space feeling truly terrible.

I spend the rest of the morning working out how I'll manage to cope after spending three hundred euro on a new car. Will the insurance go up? What about my motor tax? And Christmas is coming and Fáinne wants her Bratz Supervan and make-up. And there are other presents to buy. Thinking of presents, I still haven't opened Tracy's one. It's shoved down at the bottom of my bag and for lack of anything better to do, I pull it out and unwrap it. It's a bottle of perfume. The kind I always sprayed on myself whenever I went into Arnotts in the city centre. Expensive perfume smelling, I always thought, of the sea and sand and holidays. I feel ridiculously touched that Tracy even remembered that I liked it, but maybe it was just a fluke. Or maybe she got it as a present and passed it on to me. That was much more likely – she had never liked that smell. I open the bottle and inhale its scent, and then I spray it on my wrists and neck. It's gorgeous.

'Lucy, when you're finished?'

Doug sounds weird.

I jump and turn to him. 'What?'

'Ring Mr D. and ask him to come in next week after hours, will you?' He throws Paddy's file in front of me. 'Early next week. All right?'

'Sure – what day?'

'Any day. Monday if possible.'

'Is there something wrong?'

Doug rubs his forehead. 'Uh-huh, I think so. I should have spotted it earlier – maybe months ago. Fuck.' He winces. 'I've just got to run a couple more tests to be sure. Maybe an ECG. Have him bring Paddy in.'

He flashes me a rueful smile and picks up his next file and calls the patient in.

Doug offers me a lift home at five. His humour seems to have improved though he's still a bit morose about Mr D. In the car, he puts on the radio. I'm glad he has it tuned into a pop music station and not some boring news programme. I hate guys that listen to the news and offer their opinion on every issue raised because that means that when the news gets really interesting – like the break-up of some celebrity marriage – I always miss it because News Boy is lamenting the state of Israel or something. Doug starts tapping his steering wheel in time to a Westlife track and I grin.

'It's catchy,' he defends himself.

'Yeah, like flu,' I say back.

He laughs. 'So, I guess you're a music snob.'

'I like folk,' I say. 'Dylan, Chapman, Cohen: all the singer-songwriters.'

'The stick-your-head-in-the-oven brigade?'

'No!'

He grins at my indignant face and changes the subject. 'So what's the state of play with the car now?'

'Gone to the great scrapyard in the sky.' I have a catch in my voice when I say it and I hope he doesn't notice.

Doug winces. 'Tough. So what are you going to do?'

I shrug. 'Apparently I can get a replacement car for three hundred euro. I'm going to look at it tomorrow if I can get my dad to bring me out there.'

'Out where?'

'Malahide.'

'Sure, go now – it's only ten past five and ten minutes will get us over there.'

'Us?'

Doug nods. 'I'll check it over if you want.'

I look at him in his smelly jeans and equally gross jumper. I am right – the smell is from him as well as the surgery. 'You?' It's awful but the amusement in my voice is not amusing.

He doesn't take offence. Instead he gives me a sideways glance and nods. 'My dad owns a pile of garages – it was meant to be my inheritance until I became a vet. He used to make me work every summer on the cars when all I wanted to do was roll about in muddy fields and play with dogs and stuff.' He laughs. 'Caused a pile of trouble at home, but at least now I know my engines.'

'Oh.'

'And my bodywork.'

'Yeah, well, you're a vet. That's like being a doctor.'

He laughs again. 'I mean, I can tell if a car has been crashed, you idiot.'

'Oh.' I *feel* like an idiot – of course that's what he meant.

'So? Will we go over?'

I don't have three hundred euro on me but I guess it'd be handier than going the following night. 'Right.' I pause. 'But don't you have to get something to eat before surgery tonight?'

'I'll survive. I have until seven. Anyway, Clare sometimes brings in buns for me.'

'No way!'

'Yep. She looks after me, so she does.'

Lick-arse, I think. I wonder does he know how much she gives out about him too? I smirk. 'Tell you what: I'll cook for you if you look at a car for me and you'll have no need of Clare's buns.'

'I beg your pardon? Clare's buns? Sounds nice.'

'Well?' I ignore his innuendo.

'Deal.'

You know the way you always think of mechanics as 'heave-ho' sort of lads? Well, my mechanic is more a 'hi-ho' guy. He's small, thin and keeps scratching his head as he talks. If he had hair, I would bet that he had lice, but he doesn't – have hair, that is – so scratching his shiny dome is obviously a habit, and a disconcerting one at that. He defers to Doug in our conversation, which annoys me: after all, I'm the one buying the car. In fact, Doug seems to have forgotten me completely too as Jimbo (that's his name) leads him to my 'new' car. At first glance, it looks nice. It's a gorgeous bright green and has rounded headlights in the front. I feel a sense of betrayal at how excited I get just looking at it. Doug paces around the car, looking up and down and tapping the bumper and doing all sorts of things that look impressive. Then without saying a word, he sits inside and pops up the engine. I take it as my chance to see the interior. It's so clean and bright. Little pockets are everywhere. There is even one at the back of the front seat. The radio looks complicated with loads of little dials and buttons and I love it. Even the heater resembles something from NASA. I can't wait to see what it looks like in the dark: will the dash lights be red or yellow or what? If it was up to me, I'd buy it. I begin to wish that Doug wasn't here because if he finds something wrong with it, I'll go mad.

'Ye-ah.' Doug pulls his head out of the bonnet and makes a face. 'It's all right.'

'It's a beauty,' Jimbo says. And then, deferring to me for the first time since I came, he says, 'You like it, don't you, Lucy?'

Doug shoots me a warning look. 'Eh . . .' I wince. 'It's, eh, all right.' How can I be such a bad actor?

'Three hundred is a bit steep,' Doug goes on. He sinks his hands into the pockets of his jeans and, for some reason, I'm riveted by the sight and feel my heart begin to beat a little faster. But that's the excitement of car buying for you. 'Two hundred and you've got a deal.'

'Forget it.' Jimbo walks off.

'Doug—' I say frantically and he withers me.

'You won't get any more for it,' Doug says loudly. 'How much can you afford, Lucy? That is if you *really* want it.' He makes it sound as if I'd be mad to really want it. Then he holds his hands up. Two fifty, he's telling me.

'Around two thirty,' I say, getting into the spirit of it.

Jimbo turns around. 'Two forty and you've a deal.'

I want to shout with victory, but Doug says, 'Two thirty-five.'

'Yez drive a hard bargain.' Jimbo screws up his face. 'Cash?'

'Sure.'

Jimbo shoves out his hand towards me and I shake it. Doug winks at me over his head and I want to hug him. Two thirty-five is still a lot for me but it's better than it was. 'I hope you can cook,' Doug whispers as we go to sign the papers.

Shit.

*

As we enter my house, Doug tells me that I've got a real bargain. 'Great car, great engine.'

'Great colour,' I say.

'Women.' He sits down at my kitchen table and looks around. 'It's nice in here.'

I thank God that I wasn't home yesterday because it certainly wouldn't have been as tidy as now.

Because it's winter and it's dark out, I switch on the ceiling lights and they give a nice warm glow to the walls. The patches on the walls that are dirty are nicely concealed by shadows. 'So, what would you like?' I feel a bit awkward in front of him. I wish I were the sort of woman who could go confidently about her own space rustling up nice dishes at the drop of a hat. 'I've, eh . . .' I glance into the fridge. 'Eggs, cheese.' Up to the freezer. 'Pizza, chips, burgers, fish?'

He tries not to grin. 'Pizza and chips sounds nice: I haven't had that since yesterday and the day before and the day before.'

'Jesus!' But before he can tell me he's joking, I whip them out of the freezer and turn on the oven. 'I'll put a few on for Fáinne too,' I say. 'She'll be back in a little while.'

'Will I put on the kettle?'

'Sure.'

He gets up and I'm suddenly aware of how he fills the room. I arrange the chips on a tray and shove them in the oven. Then place the pizza on a shelf. Doug bumps into me as I'm throwing the pizza wrapper in the bin.

'Sorry.'

'Sorry.'

It's weird. He is my boss after all but it's never felt that way. He's so relaxed most of the time. Doug grins and moves sideways to get by me and as he does so my hand brushes his chest – well, not his *actual* chest, just his shirt. I jump as if I've been electrocuted and he looks at me.

'Sorry.'

'For?' He looks genuinely puzzled.

'Just for the smallness of the kitchen.'

'I like it.'

I don't quite know how to take that.

'It's cosy,' he explains, looking around. 'And it's probably right for you and Fáinne.'

'It is.' I manage to dispose of the pizza wrapper just as the doorbell rings. It's my dad and Fáinne and I bring my dad in to introduce him to Doug.

'You're not going to let her cook for you?' Dad exclaims as Doug explains his presence. 'You're a brave man.'

'Dad!'

'Has he signed a disclaimer?'

'Get out!' I push him towards the door and leave Doug entertaining Fáinne with stories of his rescuing of wild animals.

'Still, I suppose he's a vet so he'll be used to stopping undercooked meat from rearing up and biting him.'

'Dad!' I say again.

From inside the kitchen I can hear Doug laugh. Then Fáinne tells him that really, Granddad isn't joking and I am a dreadful cook.

'So he's your boss?' Dad says as he pulls his gloves back on. He winks at me. 'Nice-looking fella.'

'I'll pass your admiration on to him.'

'Oh now, that's not what I meant.'

'He got me a bargain car, that's all I know.'

'If you can't afford—'

I put my hand on his shoulder and he stops. 'I can,' I say firmly. 'Don't worry – please.'

133

Dad pats my hand with his gloved one. 'OK. So, will I drive you to pick up this car tomorrow or what?'

'Doug says he will.'

Dad smiles. 'Really? Nice boss you have there.'

I don't want to even *go* there. All a guy has to do is grin at me and Mam and Dad think it's love. And while Mam jumps in with dire warnings of what might happen if I were to choose the wrong guy, Dad thinks it's great that I have a social life. God, if only he knew.

'See you tomorrow morning, Dad – all right?'

'Yes. Bye.' He pauses halfway down the hall. 'By the way, Tracy says would it be OK to take Fáinne out next Friday evening for her birthday?'

I'm so stunned that Tracy actually remembered that all I can do is nod.

Doug eats everything I put on his plate. I reckon if I'd given him shite, he'd have scoffed it. I like him because of it. After he polishes off the last slightly charred oven chip, he pats his stomach and grins at me. 'That was great – the most stuff I've eaten in ages.'

'Not the best then?' I tease.

'Almost the best,' he offers.

Fáinne has exited: *The Simpsons* are on and from the television room, I can hear Homer telling Bart that winning is everything.

Doug and I both laugh at the same time.

'Coffee?'

'Yeah, sure.' He looks at his watch. 'I'm not on for another twenty minutes. Hopefully it'll be less crazy tonight. I'm telling you – it's one of the busiest practices I've ever been in.'

'Where else have you been then?'

134

'I've worked all over.' He takes a biscuit. 'London, Manchester, did a stint in Spain – that was fun: hadn't a clue of the language.'

I grin.

'I like it here though, being my own boss. The people are more easy-going too.'

'And the staff are probably nicer,' I offer.

'Definitely.' He smiles and our eyes meet.

I turn away quickly; I'm not one for eye contact. I stir his coffee vigorously and place it in front of him. Smirking, I say, 'You must have been a right school swot to end up a vet. Betcha you were always stuck in a library when you were a kid.'

'Naw.' He shrugs. 'Always stuck in a calving shed, that was me. Me ma says I grew up with the smell of shite in my skin.'

I laugh.

'Don't rush to disagree now or anything,' Doug says, sounding offended. He chomps on another biscuit, but he's smiling. 'I just loved animals, I guess. The whole vet thing came easy to me. Yeah, I swotted for my Leaving 'cause I needed the points but in college, I found it easy. Bit like you with the acting, huh?'

'Yeah – I needed it to become a receptionist all right.'

'And a fine one you are too. Brilliant diction, great projection. And just think, when the animals get restless, you can entertain them with Shakespeare or something.'

'Feck off!'

He smiles, a big warm smile. It's like the sun has just come out.

I spill my coffee all over myself.

21

November 20th

Dad moved out today. It was a Saturday and I had no lectures or rehearsals, so I couldn't escape the house. I could have called into Maddie's or Gray's, but I would have felt bad about it. I mean, if I really had to go somewhere, well then, it couldn't have been helped, but as I didn't, I just felt that I had to stay and say goodbye to him. He looked pathetic with his black suitcase all packed up. And his plastic bag with his toothbrush in it. Tracy was crying, bawling her head off and getting all the attention as usual. I just kind of watched the whole scene in a detached sort of way as if it wasn't really happening to me.

'I'll call over the weekends,' Dad promised as he hugged me. 'We'll go to films and do things, OK? You haven't lost me. Your mother and I just have to sort ourselves out.'

'But why can't you do it at home?' Tracy wailed.

'We tried that.' Dad hugged her then.

And after a few more screeches from Tracy, Dad climbed into his car and drove away.

It was all so weird. Normally when he drives away, he comes back. But not this time. I left the house then. I just wandered around, not really thinking. Feeling a bit guilty because I was a tiny bit glad that now at least the rows would stop.

November 23rd

Tracy told Mam that she's leaving just before Christmas to do a shoot in Galway. Mam is surprised; she thought that Tracy would stay until after Christmas. Lucky Tracy, I think, she's going to be missing Christmas at home. I'm dreading the thought of it.

November 27th

Maddie, Gray and I had arranged to go to a film tonight. When Mam heard she offered to lend me some cash. Guilt money, I thought. Then she said, 'It's on condition that you bring your sister. She's really upset, Lucy. This whole separation has come as a huge shock to her.'

A huge shock? I'd told her. I'd warned her.

And what about me? I wanted to say. What about me that had to listen to the endless rows and cope with the horrible silences and who couldn't even invite her mates over in case they'd sense the atmosphere? What about me? 'I'm not bringing her,' I said.

Mam's lips thinned out and she folded her arms. 'Well, in that case, you can't go either.'

'That's not fair,' I wanted to cry, but couldn't. Instead, I got angry. 'How is that fair?'

'Bring Mona Lisa.'

'Her name is Tracy and I'm not bringing her.'

'She wants us to call her Mona Lisa. It's the least I can do.'

I said nothing. What was the least she could do for me?

Mam looked as if she might cry. 'Please, Lucy,' she said. And to my horror, she started to sniff. 'Please, Lucy. Your sister has no one to go out with. Go on, please.'

I didn't know what to do. I wanted to put my arm around her, but I couldn't. I've never really put my arm around my mother in my whole life. 'Don't cry,' I said instead. 'Please, Mam, don't cry. I'll do it, OK?'

She gave me a watery smile and wiped her eyes. 'Thanks, Luce, you're great.'

That made me feel good. For a while. Until the film and its after-math. You see, Tracy dressed up in all her nice clothes and washed her hair and painted her face and totally charmed Gray and Maddie who spent the night talking to her. And my sister can be very charming. She didn't mind them calling her Tracy. And I was like a spare, sitting beside the three of them. Maddie did ask me what was wrong and I said, 'I thought I was supposed to be your friend,' and she laughed.

But she doesn't understand. Tracy does this to me all the time. Just when I meet nice people, she comes and takes them away from me. She did it all through primary school – all my mates wanted to play with her in the yard. They came to our door looking for her and only played with me when she wasn't there. I used to die when she eventually turned up and they abandoned me. I'd cry for ages and Mam would keep telling me that we should all play together, but she didn't understand.

One of my boyfriends dumped me for her too. Only she wouldn't go out with him then. Serve him right.

If she takes Maddie and Gray from me, I'll never forgive her. The sooner she goes to Galway the better.

After the film, she told Gray about her lack of a social life. 'I've been away for so long, I've lost contact with all my friends,' she simpered. Gray fancies her, it's so obvious – anyway, he bloody well told her to come out with us whenever she wanted.

'In fact,' he said, 'next week our football team is in the final of a cup match – come to that, there'll be a party afterwards and I know Luce and Maddie are going.'

Maddie giggled. 'He'd do anything to rent a crowd for his football, wouldn't he, Luce?'

'Yeah.'

And they kept talking away.

I feel, right at this minute, as if I've lost everything important.

And then Jason, for some unexpected reason, pops into my head, and that makes me smile.

November 28th

Dad brought me and Tracy out to see a film today. It was weird, going to the cinema with my dad. Like, at nineteen, you think you're past all that. He came to the door, very nicely dressed, almost as if he was taking us out on a date. Mam made sure she was out at the time. He took us to some awful film about a couple separating.

'Bad choice, ey?' he said after it had ended in complete mulch.

Tracy laughed but I couldn't. I couldn't do much of anything really. From crying every night, I hadn't cried since Dad had told me he was moving out.

Dad caught our hands and squeezed them. 'It'll all be fine,' he said. 'I promise.'

Neither Tracy nor I said anything.

'And if you want to talk about it,' he said then, 'I'm always here, OK?'

Talk about what? I wondered. What was there left to talk about?

22

IT'S SO LONG since I've done television work that I feel ridiculously inadequate as I arrive at the building where my part of the ad will be shot. According to Les, three women were chosen. The first woman has to squeeze a gorgeous man and say, 'I like my man with muscles.' The second one squeezes another hunky guy and says, 'I like my man with a nice ass.' And I, star of the ad, squeeze a box of condoms bearing the garish name 'KING CON' and say, 'I like my man protected.'

The other parts of the ad have been shot, so there's only mine left. I arrive early, thanks to my bright green car, and am taken straight to wardrobe. 'Now,' the wardrobe lady says, 'I've your stuff right here.' She goes to a hanger and pulls out a pair of red jeans and a red and white stripy top. Whey-hey, I think, I'm colour-coordinated with a box of condoms. Because I've already given my measurements to her, the jeans fit like a second skin. The red and white top, plunging in the front, leaves very little to the imagination. And I mean that. I've got very little. On go a pair of red crocodile-skin high boots and it's off to make-up and hair.

My make-up is hot red lipstick that I would never wear – but it does enhance my pouty lips. Foundation is ladled on to my face, followed by blusher – red – and my eyes are done up in a myriad of pinks and reds. My eyelashes can barely

140

open with the amount of mascara on them and my eyebrows are picked out in the blackest of pencils.

Then my hair. I have nice hair. Thick and glossy with only the slightest hint of a wave. Most of the time it sits on my shoulders and I love the feeling of it swishing about my face as I turn my head this way and that. People like my hair.

'You've got very thick hair,' the hairdresser says, in what I note is a disapproving voice. 'I was hoping for it to be easier to manage.'

'Sorry,' I say meekly.

'Mmm.' She walks all around me and eventually decides to French plait it across my head and intertwine some red ribbon through it.

'Red is big in this ad, isn't it?' I remark dryly.

'Colour of passion,' she says back, deftly plaiting away. 'We wanted someone with red hair initially but then you came and the director was mad about you.'

'Oh.' I sit up straighter in my chair. 'That's great.'

She sniffs. I don't think she feels the same way. She continues her work in silence.

Eventually I am ready. I stare at myself in the full-length mirror and can hardly believe it's me. I look young and very contemporary, half punk, half rock chick. I actually look as if I've got attitude. Maybe – the faint hope flutters in my heart – maybe my mother won't recognise me when I get plastered over bus shelters. I mean, *I* hardly recognise me.

'Time,' someone calls from outside.

Nervously, feeling like a complete fraud, I walk on to the set. To my horror, Les is there, bouncing about and grinning manically. 'Hey baby!' He walks towards me, his arms out in a big welcome gesture. 'You look great. Doesn't she look great, everyone?'

People on set nod politely. Half of them are wondering

who he is and are afraid to offend him in case he's important.

'Can we get started?' the director calls, coming on set.

Frantic activity.

I'm ushered to a place in the spotlights. Behind me is a backdrop of a red sunset.

'Stay still and when we call action, say your line,' the assistant director says, fussing about with my hair and patting it into place.

'Lights!'

'Check!'

'Sound!'

'Check!'

'Camera!'

'Check!'

'Action!'

'Hi, I like my man protective.' Fuck! Shit!

'Did she say protective or protected?'

'Protective,' I say, blushing. 'Sorry.'

Everything gets set up again. Les gives me the thumbs up. My face is dusted with powder.

'Lights!'

'Check!'

'Sound!'

'Check!'

'Camera!'

'Check!'

'Action!'

'Hi, I like my men protected.' Men? Fuck!

'It's "man",' the director shouts. 'We're not trying to make you out to be a slapper!'

'Sorry.'

'It's six words.' He comes towards me. '"Hi – I – like – my – man – protected." Hug the condom box, lick the lips and for Christ's sake look sexy. Pretend it's a man or something.' He turns and walks off.

I remember my favourite day with Jason. The one when we climbed Howth Head. The one where he told me about himself – or so I'd thought. I remember the way we'd kissed and he'd stared into my eyes and turned my heart to mush. I'd loved that day. It had been perfect. I pretend it's that day in my head. I pretend because I've never felt the same way about anyone else since. Ironic really that the person they pick to advertise condoms has a child. I wonder whether, if they knew, it would bother them.

'Lights!'

'Check!'

'Sound!'

'Check!'

'Camera!'

'Check!'

'Action!'

'Hi, I like my man protected.' And I cuddle those condoms.

'Cut!'

'Fabulous,' the director says. 'Good girl.'

Then I have to pose in front of the backdrop for photographs. Because of Gray, I know that setting up the equipment will take ages, so I sit around and try to look interested in what's happening. Les comes over to me and attempts conversation. 'It'll air before Christmas party season,' he says. 'Probably early December.'

'Yeah.'

'We should be paid for the TV part of the campaign by next week. I'll send you on a cheque.'

'OK.'

He hops around from foot to foot before asking, 'Are you in some sort of a bad mood?'

143

'No.'

Pause. Then he gets down on his hunkers and looks at me. 'Look, Luce, I read about your sister in the paper and I know it's a bummer for you. I'm sorry that this is all I could get – you deserve more, I know that.'

I'm touched by his words. By his faith in me. 'Yeah. Thanks, Les.' I pat his shoulder and tell him it's fine. Everything is fine.

He gets up and walks off.

I don't know how Tracy does it, it's so boring. Smiling on cue, pouting on cue, licking my lips on cue. But they think I'm good at it. The photographer tells me I'm the best actress/model he's had, ever.

At five o'clock I'm finished. I take off my clothes – at this stage I'm wearing a red glittery top and black and red jeans – and slip back into my comfortable jeans, my tan boots (which I found under all the dirty clothes in the bathroom) and my blue V-neck jumper. I scrub off all the make-up, pull my hair out of its party style (lots of knots sitting on top of my head all held together with masses of hairspray and pins) and leave.

I'm back to being me again.

It's a relief.

23

It's Fáinne's eighth birthday and she's on a high. I've just handed her a sparkly skipping rope that she wanted when the front-door bell rings. Before I can get to it, Fáinne has raced down the stairs and answered it. 'Mona Lisa!' she whoops. 'Wow! What are you doing here?'

'Happy birthday, Cutie,' I hear Tracy sing. 'I'm bringing you out for your birthday, didn't your mother tell you?' Tracy stands in our hall and the place, as usual, is a mess. Fáinne's school bag and tracksuit are dumped right at the end of the stairs, my jacket is hanging up on the banisters and the phone book is open on the floor. Pens and pencils and notebooks are beside it, with scrawled messages all over them.

'Bringing me out?' Fáinne says. As I come down, she whirls on me and says accusingly, 'You never said, Mammy!'

'I thought Tracy might forget,' I mutter. And it's true, I had and I couldn't bear to see how upset my daughter might be then. 'She's very busy, you know.'

'Not that busy,' Tracy says, and she sounds hurt. Then she smiles a little too much. 'So, miss, are you ready?' She takes in my daughter's jeans, trainers and Bohemians jersey. 'Won't she need a coat?' she asks me.

'I'll get it.' Jesus, I hope it's clean.

'But, Mammy' – Fáinne grabs my arm – 'Gray rang last night, and, oh, I told him that he could take me to the football match today.' Tears spark in her eyes. 'I didn't know Mona Lisa would be here!'

Great!

'Oh, well . . .' I look apologetically at my sister.

'But I want to go with Mona Lisa now!'

I don't know what to do. 'But you told Gray—'

'But that's only because you didn't tell me that Mona Lisa was coming!' She's going to throw a wobbler and to be honest, I don't blame her. 'If you had told me that she was going to bring me out I could have said "no" to Gray.'

'I can bring you out some other time,' Tracy says. 'There's—'

'No!' Fáinne glares at me. 'It's Mammy's fault.'

'You should have asked me before telling Gray you could go with him,' I snap. I don't want her fighting with me in front of Tracy. 'You don't just go saying you can go places without asking me!'

'I never ask you – you like the break on a Friday!'

The little bitch! 'What?'

'You said that to Gray before – I heard you!'

Before I can answer, the bell rings. Gray's familiar outline is visible. 'That can't be my quiet little godchild shouting,' he jokes as I open the door.

Fáinne glares at him.

'No way!' He makes a horrified grimace. 'And what has happened to her funny little face – did the face fairy come and steal it away because she is EIGHT today?'

'That's stupid,' Fáinne snaps, folding her arms and pouting.

'Ouch!' Gray glances from me to her and then spots Tracy. He stiffens. Flushes. 'Eh, hiya, Tracy.' He nods.

Gray used to fancy Tracy big time. They went out together until she dumped him – at least that's what I think

146

happened, he never told me the full story but I know she hurt him.

Tracy manages a smile. Even when it's not her magazine smile, it's still devastating. 'Graham,' she says warmly, 'how's things?'

'Not bad,' he mutters to his shoes. 'Yourself?'

'Not bad either,' she says back. 'Anyway, I'll go now.'

'No!' Fáinne grabs her. 'I'm going out with you today – sorry, Gray.'

'Fáinne!' I'm mortified. 'Gray has come to bring you out and you've got on your football jersey and everything.'

'Mona Lisa' – she turns to Gray – 'that's her proper name, you know, well, she asked me out too and she got here first.'

'Well, that's lovely.' Gray shakes his head and winks at me. 'My best buddy on a Sunday and now look, she's dumping me. Well, that's all right. I'll just have to find another girl to treat.'

'You've got Audrey now,' Fáinne says brightly, making me smile. 'She loves you. You can bring her.'

Gray pretends to consider. 'Suppose so. Only it's not her birthday and she's not as good at cheering as you are.'

'I'll teach her.' Fáinne's face is bright with hope that maybe she can wriggle out of her football date. 'I'll make her the best shouter for Bohs ever.'

'Right.' Gray nods. 'Come on, so, she's in the car.' He holds out his hand for her. Fáinne's face drops and Tracy laughs. Gray grins at me and turns back to Fáinne. 'Well?'

Fáinne stares sullenly at him. 'I didn't mean *now*.' She bites her lip and shrugs. 'I'll be busy with Mona Lisa, see, and I can't do it right now. Maybe tomorrow.'

'But the match is today and we were going to eat out after for your birthday.'

'Yeah, well . . .' Fáinne attaches herself to Tracy. 'We're

in a hurry now, see? Maybe tomorrow?' A pretty smile. 'OK, Gray?'

She reminds me suddenly of her dad and my heart twists.

Gray winces. 'I'm not used to being stood up, you know.'

'I'm not standing you up,' Fáinne says. 'Just, just making it for another time. For next week. I promise, Gray. Next week I'll go with you.'

He makes a big deal of considering. Then he nods. 'Right – OK, so.'

'Yeah?' Fáinne can hardly believe her luck. 'Really?' As he nods, she throws herself into his arms and hugs him. 'Thank you. Thank you, Gray.'

He hugs her back and I want to hug him myself. He's so bloody decent.

'Oh. My. God.' Audrey startles everyone with her shriek from the window of Gray's car. 'Oh. My. God!'

'Is she all right?' I ask, about to leg it down the path to see how she is.

Gray looks mortified. 'She's spotted you,' he mutters to Tracy. 'Sorry about this but she thinks you're great.'

'Oh. My. God!' Audrey squeals again. She waves furiously from the car window. 'Hi! Hi!'

'Hello!' Tracy calls back, though less enthusiastically than Audrey. 'How's things?' Audrey is stunned into silence.

We laugh and Tracy makes her way down the garden, Fáinne skipping alongside her. She stops at Gray's car and pokes her head in the window.

'Oh. My. God!' Audrey is hyperventilating, her hand clutched to her throat.

Gray and I are left alone.

'She's just not cool, is she?' Gray says, amused. 'Not cool at all.'

I don't know whether to agree or not so I say instead,

'Sorry about the mix-up – I forgot Tracy was coming.'

'No bother.' He shoves his hands into his pockets and grins ruefully. 'Sure, why wouldn't the kid want to go out with her – there was a time I wanted to go out with her myself.'

'Yeah, well, let's hope Fáinne cops on as quick as you did.'

He ignores the comment. Instead, he says, 'She looks tired, doesn't she?'

We both look as Tracy climbs into Gray's car. Fáinne jumps into the back. Audrey is chirping away excitedly.

I make a face. 'I wish I looked like that when I was tired.'

He grins. 'So, what are you going to do now? D'you want to come to the match with me and Audrey? I've got a spare ticket seeing as your daughter stood me up. Stand seats and everything.'

I wonder what I am going to do. Housework does not appeal, worrying about my ad is a waste of time, Maddie's not feeling the best apparently so I'll just probably spend the afternoon wondering how I'm going to track Jason down – which seems another waste of time as he's obviously not living at his old house any more. Maybe a football match is just what I need.

'We can go for a drink after?' Gray waves a ticket in front of my face. 'And I'm driving?'

'Sold to the desperate-for-a-date girl in the blue jeans.' I grin. 'Hang on until I get my jacket.'

24

AUDREY TALKS ABOUT Tracy all the way to the match – only she calls her Mona Lisa. She goes on and on about how Tracy seems so *normal*, how she is just so *ordinary*, how she's just like a *regular* person. Then she talks about Tracy's beauty regime, about how Tracy never goes to bed without cleansing her face, how much toner Tracy uses on a wad of cotton wool, how many calories Tracy consumes in a day. I swear, she knows more about my sister than Tracy knows about herself. All Audrey's information has come via fashion magazines and Audrey can see exactly what the magazines mean when they talk about Tracy's luminous skin.

'Her skin is lovely,' she says dreamily. 'Isn't her skin lovely, Gray?'

Gray shrugs.

'Luminous skin, that's what she has,' Audrey says for the millionth time as she examines her own face in the passenger mirror.

'She's probably just been living beside a nuclear reactor,' Gray remarks.

I laugh and Audrey looks from one to the other of us before she gets the joke. 'Oh you.' She belts Gray who rolls his eyes and makes her promise to shut up. 'But look,' Audrey goes on, 'if you met some big photographer fella – I dunno, the guy that's named after the drink – wouldn't you be excited?'

'Who's named after a drink?' I ask.

'David Bailey.' Gray laughs. 'She means David Bailey. And, yeah, right, I would be excited but come on, who have you just met – a human coat hanger, for Christ's sake.'

'That's awful!' Audrey squeals. 'Awful.'

And she starts all over again.

She keeps talking all through the match. I'm not big into football but neither am I big into wondering what sort of material the goalie's jersey is made from or wondering where the girl sitting behind us got her particular shade of lipstick.

I tune out after a while and focus on the match. Gray is groaning in despair as his team has just conceded a second goal. Things are not looking good.

'CORNER!' we both call out at the same time.

A clap goes up.

Audrey squeals. 'Was that a goal?'

'Corner,' I say absently.

'Is that good?'

'Yeah.'

She stops talking and screws up her eyes to watch the centre forward take the corner. He curls it into the box and the striker hits it full force into the back of the net.

'GOAL!' about twenty of us scream as Audrey jumps.

People stand up and cheer. Gray embraces Audrey and she looks startled as he hugs her tightly, then she grins and just as she's enjoying it he lets her go and hugs me. A huge guy beside Audrey slaps her on the back, making her cough, and someone else catches her and swings her around. Gray begins a chant. Others join in. Soon the whole stand is singing and Audrey, mouth agape, looks on in horror at her previously quiet boyfriend.

'Come on.' Gray grabs her about the waist. 'Sing!'

'I can't,' she says, sounding dismayed. 'I can't.'

'We are red, we are black, we are on the AAA-TACK! Na-na-na-na-na-na-na-naaaaa!' he roars. 'Come on, Aud!'

She shakes her head and sits down. 'No. No, it's fine. Honestly.'

Gray and I laugh.

Unfortunately the attack doesn't last long. The other team score within minutes and that's the way it stays until the match ends. Gray is pissed over it.

'I feel like getting drunk,' he mutters. 'Bloody disastrous result.'

'Well, you can't.' I grin. 'You're driving.'

Audrey laughs at his grumpy face. 'It's only a match. Cheer up.'

I wait for Gray to snap at her. A match is never just a match to Gray. He takes it all very seriously. But, to my surprise, he smiles dotingly at Audrey and wraps his arm about her waist. 'Yeah, you're right.' He sneaks a quick kiss on her ear and she snuggles up to him. They look nice together, even if she doesn't have a clue about football. And, as usual, I'm the big green gooseberry.

The pub is jammed. The three of us eventually find a seat in the corner beside a radiator. It's not as nice as the fire at the other end of the room but the heat is welcome. Gray goes up to the bar to get in the drinks and Audrey and I make ourselves comfortable. I throw my jacket into a corner and pull my trainer-clad feet on to the seat. Audrey folds her jacket and very neatly puts it on top of mine. She then crosses one slim leg over the other and fastens her hands firmly on the radiator. 'I'm never going to another match,' she twitters,

152

creasing her cute face up in an expression of loathing. 'All that standing about in the cold would ruin my skin – I hope you put on plenty of moisturiser today, Lucy.'

'Loads,' I lie gamely.

Audrey smiles in relief. 'That's good. You've nice skin, and standing about in bad weather won't do it any favours.'

I'm flattered that she's admired my skin. No one else ever has. I vow to buy some moisturiser asap.

'Gray has nice skin too,' Audrey continues as she places the backs of her hands on the radiator. 'I keep telling him he should moisturise but he won't.'

I smirk at the image.

A sigh. 'Gray is great, isn't he?'

'Yeah,' I agree. 'A bad skin-carer but great.'

Audrey sighs in a dreamy way again.

Silence. Well, silence between us. The pub is buzzing. The guys beside us are wondering when their drinks are arriving.

Audrey takes her hands from the radiator and examines her nails. She frowns at one tiny little chip in her nail varnish and I immediately screw my hands into little fists so she won't see my disastrous attempts at filing. 'I like Gray a lot,' she says, still looking at her hands. 'He's the nicest guy I've ever gone out with.'

'That's good.' And it is good, I think. I pick up a beer mat and begin to play with it.

'What does he think of me?' Audrey says. Her casual voice wobbles and her face goes all red. I can see that examining her nails was just a decoy to save her having to look at me.

I gawk at her. 'Oh, he, eh—'

'No. No! Sorry, forget it.' She waves her hands about, still not looking at me. 'That was silly. I mean, you're his friend, you don't need to tell me what he says.'

Her face is really red and I can't help but stare at it in

fascination. I feel like I'm in a teenage time-warp. There is no way I'd be that desperate to ask anyone what she's just attempted to ask me.

'I mean what he says to you is *probably* private.'

She gives me this weird hopeful look and I surprise myself by saying, 'He likes you too. I don't think he's ever gone out with anyone for as long as he has with you.'

'No!' Her eyes light up. A big silly grin covers her face. 'Oh. My. God. Really?'

'Uh-huh.' I'm not going to say any more. I feel stupid enough as it is. Though I envy her her excitement. I know what that feels like.

'Ohhhh.' She cuddles herself. Then she puts a hand on my arm. 'Thanks, Lucy. I can see why Gray likes you so much too. You're *great*!' A squeeze.

I 'ohhhh' back at her because that's what she expects, I think. Then she giggles. 'I didn't get the job for the hand cream – was I telling you about that?'

I shake my head. What job? What hand cream?

'And I was really upset over it and Gray bought me a huge bunch of flowers to cheer me up and he brought me to dinner and he told me I had lovely hands. Wasn't that nice?'

'Brill.'

'And when I didn't get the lipstick job, he bought me some perfume.'

'Great.'

'And the leg job was gone when I arrived for the casting.'

What jobs has she done, I wonder?

'But Gray said he likes my legs the best of anyone's. He's so sweet.'

A cheer goes up from the table beside us and I'm glad of the diversion. Audrey and I turn to look.

'At last!'

'Thank Christ.'

'Thought you'd done a runner, ya miser!'

The miser is gorgeous – over six foot with a cute grin. He's also Doug. He's dressed in a Shelbourne jersey and faded denim jeans and he looks clean and unsmelly. For a second I consider doing a runner – I mean, who wants to meet their boss when they're out? – but he notices me. Another cute grin as he dumps his friends' drinks and comes towards me. He stands by our table, hands half in, half out of his pockets 'Well, hello, receptionist, how's things?'

'Great.'

'Ohhhh!' Audrey squeals, poking me. 'Ohhhh!'

Doug either doesn't hear or doesn't notice. He sits down beside me and I have to move closer to Audrey to let him in. She gives me another poke in the arm and I shake her off.

'Were you at the match?' Doug asks.

'Yep.' I gaze at his jersey and make two of my fingers into a cross. 'Be gone, Satan!'

He laughs. 'At least Satan knows what team to support. Yez can't have been up for those other eejits?'

'They were very good,' Audrey pipes up.

Doug glances at her. 'They were,' he agrees seriously. 'Very good to let us win.'

'Yeah,' I smirk, 'they let you win – yez couldn't have done it on yer own.'

Audrey claps her hands. 'Brilliant, Lucy! That was brilliant!'

I'm faintly embarrassed for her. Gray is right – she isn't cool.

Doug sneers and turns to his mates. 'Here lads, pass me over my pint, will yez?' His pint is passed to him and he looks questioningly at us. 'Mind if I join yez – those feckers will fleece me for another if I don't get away.'

His mates call him a jammy bastard getting to chat two gorgeous women up. And so Doug invites them all to join us. By the time Gray arrives back, Audrey and I are being entertained by a horde of guys. Well, Audrey is being entertained by a load of them; I've only Doug chatting to me.

'Hey, everybody,' Audrey says, wrapping her arm about Gray, 'this is my boyfriend Gray.'

Doug splutters on his pint as his mates mutter reluctant hellos to Gray.

'They thought they were on to something there,' Doug whispers to me.

'And you didn't?' I slag.

'No,' he says, sounding surprised.

'Oh, right.' I take a slurp of my pint. 'So you don't set your sights too high then?'

He grins. 'Well, I'm talking to you, so that should answer that.'

'Fecker! I'll only let you away with that 'cause you're my boss.'

'And that's Lucy's boss,' Audrey is explaining loudly to Gray. 'He supported the other team.'

'We all have our problems,' Gray says equally loudly and this is met by good-natured booing from the lads.

Doug holds out his hand. 'Hiya, Doug Kelly.'

Gray shakes his hand. 'Great to meet you. You're the guy that got Luce the car – fair play.'

They chat a bit about cars. As they do, I stare at Doug's face, his dark stubble, his smile; my eyes wander over the expanse of his shoulders, his chest, down to the crotch of his jeans. Nice.

'I didn't know you liked soccer.' Doug startles me and I realise that the car conversation has stopped. I pretend that I'm looking at my trainers. I rub some dirt off with my finger and then see that my finger is now mud caked.

'You never said you went to soccer matches,' Doug continues, blessedly not noticing my flaming red cheeks. What am I thinking of? I force myself to look at him. I wipe my finger on the dull brown seat and hope no one notices. Doug's dimples flash in and out as he smiles. 'Well, not that your team can actually *play* soccer but—'

I belt him and he catches my hand and we both get embarrassed. I mean, he *is* my boss. He lets me go and says some more horrible stuff about our soccer team. And for some reason I don't tell him that I'm not actually a big soccer fan. Maybe it's because I don't want him to go and find someone else to talk to. I like him talking to me. And yeah – he's nice eye candy.

I'm not sure what time Fáinne is due back so I leave after an hour. Gray has offered to drive me home but I decline. Audrey is cosied up to him and he looks happier than I've ever seen him. His arm is around her and he's playing with a strand of her blonde hair. I reckon he's glad Fáinne didn't come.

'See yez love birds,' I joke, pulling on my rain jacket, 'Talk soon.'

'Yeah, bye, Lucy,' Audrey shouts. She's plastered. 'Tell Mona Lisa thanks for talking to me.'

I'll tell Tracy no such thing. 'Sure.'

'I'll walk you to the bus stop if you want,' Doug says, standing up. 'It's dark out there now.'

'Aw, such a nice guy,' one of Doug's friends calls. 'So caring, so com— com—' He drunkenly struggles with the word. 'Nice,' he finishes.

'I'm a vet, we're meant to be nice to animals,' Doug says, which is met by laughter from his mates.

'Stay.' I push him back down on his seat. 'I'm fine.'

He stands back up. 'Please,' he hisses. 'I can't take any more people telling me about their pets. That girl Audrey' – he flicks his eyes to Audrey, who is watching us avidly and nudging Gray – 'she keeps talking about her mother's poodle and how best to groom it. She doesn't seem to know the difference between a vet and a . . .' He frowns. '. . . and a guy that clips pets' hair.'

I start to grin.

'And I told her, I'm a vet, I said. Oh, she says, so you don't work with animals then.'

I laugh out loud.

'I can't take it.' A forlorn smile.

The smile does it. 'Oh, come on, so.' I wait while he pulls on his jacket. It's a horrendous padded thing and immediately spoils the effect of his faded jeans. Obviously he has no girlfriend, which somehow cheers me. Jacket on and zipped up, we step outside. The silence hits us both and I think we become slightly tongue-tied. Well, I do.

Eventually he says, 'Gray's a nice guy.'

'Yeah.' I tell him that Gray is one of my best mates and that he's Fáinne's godfather. And I say an inane, 'Your friends are great too.'

And he tells me that he grew up with most of them. He asks me how I got into soccer and I cringe.

'Fáinne's dad played it,' is about all I can manage.

I see him looking strangely at me. Then he says, 'Played? Is he—'

'I don't see him any more,' I mutter, a bit sharply.

'Oh.' A small smile. 'Right, well, that's stalled that thread of conversation.'

I smile at his jokey tone. 'Sorry for snapping.'

'Sorry for being so tactless.' He gives me a nudge with his elbow.

'You're fine.' I pause. Then, 'He doesn't know about Fáinne. I'm trying to find him at the moment. The whole thing is a bit sensitive.'

'Oh. Right.'

'And don't say it. Don't ask me what I'm going to do when I find him. I don't know.'

'I wasn't going to.'

I'm mortified. 'Yeah well . . .' My voice trails off before I add, 'Everyone else has.'

'I'm not like everyone else.'

'You're right there.'

He laughs. 'Things always work out,' he says, suddenly serious. 'If you think it's the right thing to do, do it.'

I don't know if it is or not, but I'm doing it anyway. I reckon I'll decide when my back is to the wall. 'Thanks, Doug.'

''S OK.'

He then starts to chat about his friends, telling me funny stories about them and it seems to take only a short while until we reach the bus stop. There is a bus just pulling in. 'Well, see ya,' I say.

'Yeah. See ya tomorrow.'

We stare at each other in a really weird way. I mean, he's staring at me so I stare back and it becomes hard to leave. 'Bye, so,' I eventually mutter.

He reaches out and touches my sleeve, then just as quickly pulls his hand away. 'Bye.'

It takes me a second to realise that I'm seriously turned on. By what, I don't know. Maybe it's just that I haven't had a guy in so long or something. I thought sexual frustration only happened to spinsters in their forties but maybe not. 'Bye,' I stammer out and then turn quickly away. I leg it on to the bus.

All the way home I keep wondering what he'd be like to kiss. What those lips would feel like pressed on mine. What his hands would feel like on my skin. And for the first time, I don't mind going into work the next day. A nice fantasy is just what I need to keep life interesting. But that's all it is.

Fantasy.

25

December 5th

Massive hangover this morning as it was the soccer club's Christmas party last night. Details are a bit blurry but I know for sure that it was brilliant. It was held in a pub (surprise) and was just a big informal gathering of the team and their fans. Maddie and I had never been to their Christmas party before – mainly because we'd never been fans before, but it was great because there were loads of guys and us. Well, me and Maddie and Tracy. Up until Tracy arrived in the room, Maddie and I had been the centre of attention. It was great – I've never been the centre of attention in my life and then in came Tracy and, I swear, most of the lads gravitated towards her as if she were some enormous flame and they insects just waiting to be burnt.

And they will be burnt. Especially Gray, who seems to be big into her.

Maddie and I had gone straight to the pub from rehearsals, but Tracy had come via home. She looked good if a bit overdressed. Gray, of course, made it his job to introduce her to everyone and Tracy, putting on a big, shy, awkward act, blushed prettily and told them all how great it was to be there.

'And you're Lucy's sister?' some guy asked.

'Yes.'

'You don't look like her.'

There was general agreement to this and I wanted to die.

Just as I was in the middle of the dying, Jason slid in beside me and I got hot and sweaty and elated and chuffed and panicky. I mean I didn't think he'd come because most of the lads were being horrible to him as he'd been banned from playing in the final and the team had lost. Apparently if Jason had played they might have won. 'Hiya, Luce,' he said in his gorgeous way. I love the way he says my name.

'Hiya. So you came.'

He nodded. 'Fuck them.' He gestured around the table. 'I wasn't going to let them see I cared.' Pause. 'Which I don't.'

People stared 'cause his voice was a bit loud. He was a little drunk, I think – his eyes were glassy though still a brilliant brown. And his grin was cute and he looked fab. 'Course you don't.' I patted his hand – I didn't care as I was a bit drunk too. 'Whatcha having?'

He ignored me. 'Who's the princess?' He looked over at Tracy, who giggled.

Fuck, I thought. It'd be like every other time in my life. I might as well get it over with. 'Tracy. She's—'

'I'm Lucy's sister,' Tracy interrupted me. 'Mona Lisa.'

'Naw.' Jason gave me an incredulous look. 'You're joking!'

'No,' I said.

'No,' she said.

'You don't look like her at all.'

I wanted to die.

'I mean, that's one of my favourite pictures but the name does not suit you.'

Tracy flushed.

'Her real name is Tracy,' I said.

'I'm called Mona Lisa in the business – I'm a model – because of my smile,' Tracy said a little snottily.

'Right.' Jason nodded. 'Suits you better.' He then turned back to me and gave me a lovely smile. 'So, Lucy, d'you enjoy the match?'

Maddie elbowed me. 'Get in there,' she muttered in a big deep voice, so that Jason wouldn't hear, I think. 'Operation Chasing Jason – come on.'

'Well?' Jason was still looking at me, still smiling at me, still ignoring my sister. I wanted to hug him, just out of gratitude. 'Yeah.'

Maddie stood up and gave me a lewd wink. 'I have to go now.' She smiled, poking me in the back. 'People to see, you know how it is. Bye, Lucy. Bye, Jason. Don't be bold, now.' A dirty laugh.

I wanted to die even more then but Jason seemed to have barely heard. He was barely listening to my amateurish retelling of the match either. He dug his hand into his pocket and pulled out a ragged tenner. 'Drink, Luce?'

'Carlsberg, ta.'

'No problem.'

Up he got, swaying slightly, and I watched him move towards the bar. Some of the lads talked to him, others ignored him. Bill, the trainer, came towards him and must have started giving him earache. Jason actually shoved him off and Bill wagged his finger. They glared a bit at each other; Bill threw his hands in the air and stalked off. Jason stared after him for a moment before shrugging and moving again towards the bar. When he returned to me with two pints of Carlsberg, he was smiling as if nothing had happened. 'Did Bill have a go at you?' I asked.

He was sitting really close to me. I could smell aftershave, cigarettes and booze on him. His shoulder brushed mine. His arm brushed mine. 'He thinks he's the boss of me,' Jason said. 'But he's not.'

I laughed.

'No one can tell anyone what to do, isn't that right, Luce?'

'That's right.' God, I wished I believed it.

'Yeah, you're my kinda girl.' Jason lifted his pint up into the air. 'Cheers, gorgeous.'

He called me 'gorgeous'. 'Right back atcha.'

We clinked glasses.

It was the highlight of the night.

December 13th
Opening night of our play. I was really really nervous but hardly anyone

turned up. Not many people come on the first night of a play; there were more people on the stage than in the audience. Dad came though and he told me I was great. He looked sort of lost, sitting all by himself.

Maddie asked why he'd come on his own and so I told her. 'They've split up,' I said. I can say it now, out loud, and not wince.

'Oh.' She didn't know what to say, which was a first.

'He left our house last month.'

She hugged me then. It was unexpected but I think she did it 'cause she couldn't think of anything to say.

But I didn't cry.

December 18th

Packed house for the last night of the play. Apparently there were agents in the audience which caused mad excitement. Still, the chances of being taken on by an agent in second year are minimal, but there is a chance so we all put on a great show. We've sort of eased into our parts now and are relaxed enough to experiment with each other. I don't mean say the wrong lines or anything, just confident enough to be more spontaneous in saying our lines. It makes for a more energetic show.

Afterwards, Mam and Tracy came backstage and Tracy was made up when someone from the cast recognised her face from some magazine or other. And Mam was so proud of Tracy being recognised.

So bloody proud.

December 19th

Great night. Started badly though but got much, much better. It was our cast Christmas party but as it was in the pub anyone could come.

Of course, Gray, idiot that he is, invited Tracy. Oh, says he (last night), why don't you come, Tracy. It's only a fun drink. I could have killed him. It's so obvious he fancies her. And it was my night and I'd been looking forward to it for ages.

When we got to the pub, I sat as far away from her as I could. I couldn't bear to listen to another modelling story or hear what wonderful things she's going to do when she's in Galway for Christmas. Maddie told me to chill out. I snapped at her and she stalked off in a bit of a huff.

Then Jason turned up just as I was downing my third pint. I wanted to get drunk at that stage, get really drunk and forget about everything and everyone. It's funny how I wanted it so much; I've never been like that before. I especially wanted to forget Jason. He hadn't even bothered to go to see me in my show. He'd promised but hadn't turned up. Anyway, he sat beside me and I ignored him.

'Luce,' he says and his voice was sort of hurt.

So I looked at him.

'Sorry about last night,' he said. 'I hurt me eye – banged into a door.'

His eye was black and yellow and looked really painful and I felt guilty for glowering at him. I reached out to touch it.

'It's not sore now,' he said, pulling away.

I nodded. Drank some more. He ordered in a pint for himself and we drank in silence. But a nice silence.

Then at some stage Jason said that he'd miss walking me to my bus stop now that term and rehearsals were over. He said it in a low voice, leaning in really close to me, his forehead almost brushing mine. Oh, I said, you can always ask me out and then you wouldn't miss it. His forehead tapped mine. Electric shock time. I will so, he said. I will so.

And suddenly his hand was in mine, rubbing the back of my palm and sending dizzy signals right through me.

Then he pulled me up from the table. My legs almost buckled though whether it was from desire or booze, I don't know. The two of us left the pub and staggered outside. And his kisses were even better than I imagined.

December 22nd
Tracy left today. It's not for long though – she's coming back in January. She told me to leave her stuff alone while she was gone and not to

touch any of her make-up. (As if.) She even locked it in the spare room so I couldn't get at it. She dumped it on Dad's bed and I wanted to shout at her to get out of Dad's room, but I didn't. I wasn't going to let her see I cared.

Gray drove her to the bus. It was weird, seeing them together. They don't fit right. He asked if I wanted to come with them but I said 'no'. Mam went though – suddenly Gray is a nice guy 'cause he's seeing Tracy.

Dad turned up at the bus too apparently.

I hate her for leaving.

December 26th

Miserable miserable Christmas. Just me and Mam eating our turkey and ham. Even the thoughts of Jason don't cheer me up. In fact, thinking of how happy I feel when I'm with him only makes things worse at home.

Dad rang to wish me a happy Christmas and I couldn't hardly answer him there was such a lump in my throat. I wished he was there. I couldn't bear to think of him in his flat all alone. Then he talked to Mam who just said words like: 'fine', 'yes', thank you', and hung up.

Jason didn't ring.

I think he's gone home.

Tracy rang Christmas night. She talked to Mam for ages. Mam laughed when she was on the phone to her. It was nice to hear her laugh but I wish I'd made her do it. I think I'd only made her miserable.

I can't wait for college to start back.

26

Tracy is all over the papers. Images of her on the film set, dressed up in her sexy costume, are everywhere. I feel a stab of envy – which I know is horrible – when I see the banner headline proclaiming that she's the next Julia Roberts. What wouldn't I give to be told that?

But here I am, sitting in my spotless little cubicle like an animal in a zoo, which is apt, I suppose. Most of the animals this morning are just in for injections which is good. I normally love mornings like this because no one is too upset or worried and I can chat to them and fuss over the cats and dogs and generally have a bit of a laugh. But images of Tracy spoil today for me. Instead of being sociable, I spend my time typing up reports. As I do so, I think of Tracy being fussed and petted ten miles away on her film set.

'Lucy.' Doug startles me as he comes in.

I wish he'd stop doing that. At least once a day I jump in fright at the sound of his voice. 'What?' He looks taken aback at my tone but I'm in no mood to make apologies. 'Well?'

He's back to smelly white-coat vet mode. Hard to fantasise about. 'I was wondering if you'd stay on a little late tonight – maybe until six?'

'*Six?*' Maddie is due over for a coffee so that we can discuss what to do about Jason. Apparently Clive has come up with a good suggestion and she wants to discuss it with me. Of course, she prefaced it by saying, 'Are you still determined to ruin your life?' And I told her that I was. So she told me that she had a sure-fire burn-out idea. And I replied that I was very excited to hear it.

'I wouldn't ask if it wasn't important,' Doug continues apologetically. 'It's Mr Devlin – I reckon six will be the very latest you'll be off.' He is standing in the doorway and a shaft of sunlight is coming from behind him. He looks tired and I'm ashamed of being so selfish.

'What's wrong?'

He crosses to me and throws down a file. 'I did those tests on Paddy – just checked with Jim to be sure and, well' – he bites his lip – 'Paddy has congestive heart failure.'

'No!' Congestive heart failure basically means death. Yeah, it can be controlled for a time with drugs but only for a short time. 'Are you sure? I didn't hear her coughing or anything.'

'She's retaining fluid which is why she's so pot-bellied, her heart is enlarged and her QRS is all over the place.' He pulls open a page which means nothing to me and jabs at some printouts. 'See.'

I'm flattered that he thinks I'm intelligent enough to understand the ups and downs of the graph. 'Oh, yeah, right.' I hope I sound knowledgeable. 'I'll just phone my mother and let her know I'll be late – see if it suits her.'

'Great.' Doug smiles gratefully at me. 'Thanks, Luce. Just let Clare go at the normal time and you stay on, OK?'

'Uh-huh.' I dial my mother. I know even before I ask that keeping Fáinne will suit her. She'll be thrilled. She'll be able to feed my daughter a decent meal. Fáinne will be delighted because it might mean a meeting with the next Julia Roberts. All in all, the only one upset will be me because I'll feel guilty about not being with my own daughter when I say I'll be with her.

Mr Devlin arrives dead on five. When I see him, I feel so sick that I can't even chat to him properly.

'Hello, Lucy.' He smiles, coming up to the counter. 'How's things?'

'Oh.' I roll my eyes, not wanting to look him in the face. 'Still waiting to be discovered.'

'And you will be,' he assures me loudly. 'There aren't half enough decent singers out there. You should go on that programme on the telly – what's it called? *You're a Star.*'

'If I could sing, I would,' I say patiently. 'I'm an *actress*, Mr D.'

'Right.' He's already lost interest. Not for him the artistic life. 'So what does Doug want? D'you know?'

'All set for Christmas?' I change the subject and blurt out the first thing that comes into my head.

He snorts and reminds me of his dog. 'I wouldn't be ready for Christmas if I had ten years to get ready for it. It's all a load of bollix. Buying presents; pretending to be happy. Jaysus, most people would be happier if they had a few bob in their pockets instead of spending it on Christmas.'

'Oh.'

'Mind you, the wife always treated Paddy to half a turkey, so I'll do that, I suppose.' He wanders about the hallway and comes back to me. 'So, does Doug have something to tell me about Paddy's 'BIG the other day?'

'BIG?'

'The X-ray moving thing?'

'ECG.'

'That. Yeah.'

'And you don't cook a pudding or anything at Christmas?' I'm sweating. Where the fuck is Doug?

Mr D. looks at me as if I'm bonkers. 'Pudding? Jaysus, where would I be going with a pudding? Everyone hates pudding anyhow, they all just pretend to like it 'cause it's Christmas.'

'So it's all just a big Christmas conspiracy?'

'Too right it is.'

'Mr D.?' Doug startles us both. Honestly, he'd make a great spy. He's as quiet as a cat. 'Can I have a word?'

'You can.' He taps his nose at me and nods. 'Christmas conspiracy.'

Doug smiles cheerily at him, then, his smile disappearing, he turns to me. 'Stay there, Luce. Shove on the kettle, will you?'

'Sure,' I say, standing up. 'D'you want me to bring it in?'

He looks undecided then shakes his head. 'Naw . . . just, you know, have it ready. Lots of sugar.'

I head into the little kitchen. I want to run as fast as I can away from the place. Why the hell did he put me in this position? I know Doug couldn't have asked Clare as Mr D. can't stand her. And she hates him because Doug refuses to charge him properly. I put on the kettle and get two cups down. I arrange tea and coffee on the counter and pull a packet of biscuits from the press. Then I go back into the waiting room and sit on the sofa and try not to listen to the murmured conversation coming from behind the door.

After about five minutes, I convince myself that I'm over-reacting. Mr Devlin might love his dog but, in the end, he'll accept it.

'No!' The half-shout from the surgery makes me jump. I disappear behind my counter and hope that he can't see me clearing up.

There are slightly raised voices and then Mr D. hurries out of the surgery. 'That's not true. Sure you're only a young fella – I'm going to get a second opinion.'

'Have a cup of tea, you've had a shock.'

'A cup of tea, me arse.' Mr Devlin glares at him. 'I'd rather get a new vet.'

'That's your choice, of course.' Doug glances at me and I pretend not to see him. 'But your dog is very sick and the sooner you put her on the drugs the better.'

'Her name is Paddy and I'll not have her a drug addict. Eileen would have hated that. She's able to walk everywhere – there's nothing wrong with her.'

'Mr Devlin, I can show you the X-rays if you want. She's sick – she's got heart failure.'

'She just needs a rest.'

Doug says nothing and eventually the front door slams. After about a minute's silence, I poke my head above the counter. Doug is staring hopelessly at the door. He gives me a feeble grin. 'Well, that went well.'

'He's had a shock.'

'Yeah.'

'I've the kettle boiled – d'you want a cuppa?'

'Only if you've whiskey to go with it.'

I laugh slightly. 'No can do.'

We wander into the kitchen and I make the tea. He takes a cup from me and shakes his head. 'Sometimes I fucking hate this job,' he says.

'Yeah – well, it's tough having to tell someone their pet is sick. Especially someone like Mr D.'

He shrugs. 'Some people don't give a shit. You remember that guy a few months back who wouldn't even pay for the drops for his kitten's eyes? Said they were too dear? D'you remember him?'

I nodded. He was, we'd agreed at the time, a scabby bastard.

'Forty fucking euro and he couldn't bring himself to pay

171

it. That poor cat is probably in agony now. It makes me sick. And there's Mr D., who'd probably spend his life savings on the dog, and it still won't change things.'

'But the drugs work, don't they?' I sit beside him on the sofa.

He shrugs. 'For a while, yeah. But Paddy will need ACE inhibitors and diuretics from the start. Plus she'll need digoxin. Normally I could start a dog on one drug and build it up, but with her, I can't. I tried to tell Mr D. all this but he wouldn't listen.' He puts down his cup and rubs his eyes. 'So he's going somewhere else.'

'He'll be back.' I attempt a giggle. 'Can you see any vet *touching* that dog and staying intact?'

Doug grins slightly. Then he swirls his tea about and says softly, 'I never thought it would be like this.'

'What – the tea?'

Another grin. 'Naw. My life.'

'Your life?' I nudge him. 'You've a great life: living in your own place, going to football matches, being your own boss, making piles of dosh—'

'That last part isn't true,' he mutters.

'Yeah, I've seen the accounts. I take it back.'

He smiles ruefully. 'I thought I'd be great, you know, looking after animals – it's all I ever wanted to do. But instead it's looking after people and wondering how much they're prepared to spend on their animals and hating them for being mean and wanting to shake them for being so thick. D'you know, a girl came in last week wondering why her cat was losing weight and I checked it over and over and couldn't figure it out.' He shakes his head. 'Then she fucking admits that she had it on a vegetarian diet.'

'No!' It's so ridiculous, I laugh.

'Uh-huh. She didn't agree with meat eating. I told her

that she agreed with animal cruelty though and she stormed out.'

'Without paying?'

He nods morosely.

'Doug, I hate to do a Clare on it, but you need to make some money here. Find me her address and I'll charge her.'

He ignores me and continues, 'Nothing is the way I thought it was going to be. I mean I should have spotted Paddy's pot-belly ages ago.'

'And would it have made a difference?'

'Probably not but it just shows how crap I fucking am.'

'Aw, Jesus, bring on the violins.'

He says nothing.

'You're a good vet.' I lean in closer to him. His shirt is horrendous – brown and orange check – but he still looks good. 'All the customers think you're great. Before you came, Jim did your job and he wasn't half as good as you. He was used to the bigger animals and he fecking roared at small kittens as if he was herding a load of cows into a field.'

'Naw?'

'Uh-huh.' I like that he's half smiling. 'He used to roar at them and they would piddle all over the floor and Clare and I would have to wipe it up. I swear, it put me off the smell of bleach for life.'

Doug laughs.

'You're better than him,' I say.

'Thanks a lot.' He rolls his eyes. 'Praise indeed.'

I grin. 'Plus you're heaps better looking.'

'Important in a vet.' He nods, mock-impressed. 'When I went to college, that's the first thing they said to me: you're good-looking, you'll make it.'

'I'm sure they did. And all the women who come in love you.'

'Jesus, stop!' He chokes on his tea. 'I'm a bloody vet – stop, will ya!'

I've embarrassed him now. For the first time I realise that he doesn't actually know how good-looking he is. It's appealing. '*And* you arranged the Christmas party – major brownie points there.'

'I must be brilliant, so.'

'You are.' I nudge him gently and get up. My tea is gone and I reckon he's slightly happier now. I wash my cup out and look questioningly at him. 'So, is it OK to go? You all right?'

'I'm grand.' He smiles at me and my heart does a weird flip-flop. 'Thanks, Luce. Sorry for holding you back – I'll pay you extra.'

'Forget it.'

'Nope, I won't.'

'And Mr D. will be back.'

He nods and his face clouds over again. 'I made a fucking mess of it.' He stares glumly at his hands.

Silence.

For some weird reason I muss his hair up. It's not exactly a professional thing to do but I can't help it. He reminds me of Gray when he's mucked up one of his relationships. 'See you tomorrow.'

He catches my hand and squeezes it. 'Ta.' His hand is warm and strong and big over mine. Too soon he lets me go.

'Bye now,' I manage to croak out.

'Bye.'

Fáinne is snuggled up in bed and I've just finished reading her a story when the bell rings. 'Who's that?' Fáinne sits up. She looks really cute in her Barbie nightdress.

'Oh, probably no one,' I say. If she reckons it's Maddie, she'll want to come down.

'How can it be no one?' She giggles. 'Unless the doorbell rang by itself.'

'No one important, Smarty.' I ruffle her hair. 'Go to sleep.'

'Maybe it's Tracy?' Fáinne says, her eyes bright. 'I'll go down and see.'

'It's not Tracy,' I answer, pushing her gently but firmly back into bed. 'Now go to sleep and if you're good we'll invite Jenny over to play on Saturday and she can help us hang the decorations on our Christmas tree.'

'OK,' Fáinne says, sounding suspicious. 'But you don't like Jenny.'

'I do.' I sound as if I'm protesting too much. 'She's great.'

Fáinne pulls her covers back up as the doorbell rings again. 'And can we get a takeaway? And a pizza?'

She's milking it now but I have no choice. 'Sure.'

'Good, I'll tell Jenny tomorrow.'

Great.

'Night, Mammy. Love you.'

'Love you too.'

I'm just about to close the door when I hear, 'I know it's Maddie,' and she giggles.

Maddie bounces in the door in her usual way. She's puffing madly on a fag and furiously indicates for me to find her an ashtray, as there's a huge amount of ash dangling from the end of her cigarette. I shove one at her just in time and, holding the ashtray, she sinks into a chair and asks for a cup of coffee.

'Just talk quietly,' I say as I shove on the kettle. 'Big ears is still awake.'

'Can I go up to her?'

'Nope.'

Maddie makes a face. 'Just to say hello?'

'She'll want to get up then and we'll never sort anything.'

'Mmmm – maybe that would be best.'

I ignore her. She's still against me looking for Jason though I think her curiosity has been aroused. 'So.' I put some biscuits on the table and sit opposite her as we wait for the kettle to boil. 'What's this great plan of Clive's?'

Maddie grins. 'It's so obvious I dunno why we didn't think of it. He says to place an ad in the local paper down in Dingle. You know: where is Jason now? And to give a mobile contact number.' She stubs her fag out and looks triumphantly at me. 'Brilliant or what?'

'Yeah,' I agree. 'It is. Let's do it.'

Maddie rummages about in her voluminous skirt and pulls a scraggy piece of paper out. Unfolding it, she smooths it on the table. 'Here, take a look at this. It's fifty euro for this ad – I checked.'

Desperately seeking Jason Donovan. Last known address is somewhere in Dingle. Studied Fine Arts in Dublin Arts University; played on soccer team. Six foot, dark hair, brown eyes. Complete wanker.

'You can't put that,' I splutter.

Maddie sniggers. 'He *was* six foot.'

'"Complete wanker",' I jab the paper. 'You can't put that.'

'That's the only bit we know is true.' Maddie grins, then, seeing my face, she shakes her head. 'It was a joke. Of course we're not going to put that in. We'll shove in a mobile number and your name. Just your first name though, we don't want all sorts of weirdos ringing you. Clive says you can use his mobile if you want and he can field the calls.'

'That's nice of him.'

'He is nice.'

There is a lull in the conversation and Maddie unexpectedly places her hand over mine. 'You'll get to like him,' she promises. 'I know—'

'I do like him,' I lie gamely. 'Honestly. What makes you think I don't?' My face goes red as it always does when I lie.

Maddie shrugs. 'You never really talk to him. You never have. And I do so want you to be friends.' She lights up another fag.

'We will be,' I say. 'And you can thank him for saying he'll take the calls – I'd like that.'

'Good.'

Maddie is staring strangely at me. I think she wants to say something else, but doesn't quite manage to do it. Instead, she begins to rummage about in her skirt pocket again. 'Now, Clive thinks a photo would be a good idea too. So, what do you think of this one?' She lays a four-by-six black-and-white photo in front of me. It shows Jason in his blue-and-white football gear – only in the picture it's grey and white. God, he was beautiful. I feel a lump in my throat just looking at it.

'Where did you get that? I didn't think you had any photos.'

Maddie shifts uncomfortably. 'Gray gave it to me in case I needed it. He said he, well, he felt better giving it to me.'

'Fecker!'

'So we'll use this?'

'Yeah.' I can hardly take my eyes from it. Without thinking, I run my finger down his face. 'Yeah,' I say again.

Maddie coughs slightly and removes it from my grasp. 'I need to e-mail this to the paper,' she says, half apologetically.

I want to ask her to give it to me when she's finished with it, but I know I'll sound pathetic. 'Great. Thanks.'

'That coffee would be nice now,' Maddie says.

As I turn away, she hastily stuffs the ad and photo back into her pockets so that when I arrive at the table with two mugs, there's nothing to be seen. And just as I'm about to broach the subject, she masterfully changes it with, 'Clive and I set the date.'

My heart plummets and I don't know why. I feel, I dunno, as if life is moving on without me on board. 'When?' I do a big cheesy grin.

'Autumn next year. Last Saturday in September. We have the church booked and the band and the hotel and everything.' And without waiting for me to ask any questions, she's off. She's so full of her plans that I feel like I'm caught in a whirlwind. I haven't time even to feel happy for her. 'Of course,' she finishes, eyeing herself, 'I'll need to diet, especially if I've just had a baby a few months before that.'

I don't think I've heard right.

She looks at me and nods encouragingly.

'A baby?' My mouth drops open.

'Yep.' She snorts with laughter. '*Me*, a *mother*, can you *believe* it? Clive is awful chuffed that his little boys managed to evade condomville.'

Despite my shock, I giggle. 'Betcha didn't use King Cons?'

'I did. Bloody useless things.'

'Oh Maddie – what can I say?'

She eyes me. 'You can tell me you're happy for me and that you'll return all those babysitting favours and that your child will play with mine and that you don't really want to find Jason.'

'You'll make a great mother.' I hug her.

'Thanks, Luce.' She hugs me back. 'I reckon I'll make a better mother when it's born that I am doing now – can't give up the fecking fags.'

'I spent most of my pregnancy drunk, so you're in good company.'

178

She looks at me. I hadn't meant to sound bitter. She reaches out her hand and clasps mine. 'And look how good you are now,' she says. 'I want to be exactly like you.'

'Well, in that case, drink, eat, live alone and advertise condoms!'

27

IT'S NO FUN being a single parent at Christmas-time. For one thing hauling the Christmas tree into the house requires a major effort. And yeah, I know I could get a pretend one but it's not the same, is it? Or rather it is the same – every single year. I like the idea of my tree being different each year; I like the smell of pine that permeates right throughout our tiny house; I even like when it starts to shed all over the floor. But I bloody hate buying it, shoving it on the roof and having to try and haul it into the house. Some years my dad helps me and some years Gray comes over but this year there was only Fáinne and her sniggering, pigtailed friend Jenny.

'Move out of the way there,' I try and say nicely to them as I pull the tree into the hallway. They move.

'Smells nice, Mam.' Fáinne is excited. She hops from foot to foot. 'When can we decorate it?'

'When I get it standing up,' I pant. I drop the tree and stretch my back. I look all red and smell of sweat.

'My daddy always cuts the end off it,' Jenny says, walking around the tree. 'Maybe when you find your daddy, Fawn, he'll be able to do that.'

I stiffen. Fáinne hasn't mentioned the search in a while – ever since Tracy came on the scene in fact. But Fáinne doesn't seem to mind Jenny talking about it. Kids are great like that. 'Maybe he will, I dunno. Mammy is looking hard and all her friends are helping too so I guess maybe by next year he'll be around. Can I hang the fairy up on the top, Mammy?'

'Sure.' I ruffle her hair and go outside to find our Christmas bucket. We call it that because that's what we put the tree in. I fill it with soil from the garden, shove the tree into it, cover the bucket with tin foil and hey presto: a Christmas bucket. Of course, I need bricks and stuff to hold the tree upright and I've a hook on the wall to loop some string around the tree to secure it.

A while later, the tree is still not exactly straight, but Fáinne and Jenny are getting bored and I don't want that to happen. So I drape the lights in what I hope is an artistic way across the branches and say, 'Right, I'm going to leave the two of you to decorate while I order some food.'

The two girls squeal and Jenny says, 'I love coming to your house, Fáinne, because your mammy always gives us junk food.'

'That's because she's cool,' Fáinne agrees, beginning to pull red and yellow tinsel from a box on the floor. 'That's all I get to eat every day except when I go to my nana's.'

'You're so lucky,' Jenny gives a shiver of delight. 'My mammy cooks potatoes and vegetables all the time.'

'I'd like that.'

'Yeuch!'

I leave them laughing together and go into the kitchen. It hasn't been too bad a day really – I was dreading Jenny coming over but she's been quite good and the fact that Tracy said she'd bring the two of them to the pantomime later seems to have impressed her big time.

'I've two tickets to the panto for Saturday,' Tracy told us on Friday at my mother's. She'd arrived back from filming early because it was bucketing down with rain and the director had called a halt for the day. Tracy waved the tickets

181

in front of Fáinne and said teasingly, 'Noowww . . . wonder whom I could invite?'

'Me!' Fáinne said delightedly. Then her face dropped. 'Oh, I can't, Mammy invited one of my friends around on Saturday to help decorate the tree.' She looked beseechingly at me and I ignored her. She knew the rules: if you agree to go somewhere you can't back out when you get a better offer.

'That's OK.' Tracy shrugged. 'I'll buy a ticket for your friend too – will she be let go, do you think, Luce?'

'I suppose.'

I know it was childish, but I was irritated. Fáinne had been so happy when I'd invited Jenny and now Tracy was usurping it by producing something better. OK, it wasn't her fault and she wasn't to know, but still . . .

'I'll ask her.' Fáinne ran and hugged Tracy, rumpling her blouse. 'I love you, Mona Lisa.'

Tracy giggled. 'Love you back, nice niece.'

And from then on the panto had been top of the discussion list.

'Do you want to come?' Tracy asked me then. 'I can get a ticket for you as well.'

I shook my head.

'Oh go on, Lucy, it'd do you good to have a laugh,' my mother said, getting her spoke in. 'You'll love it.'

And, of course, I got all bristly with her, which I shouldn't have, and I said, 'Why? Have you seen it?'

'She means you'd love it just for the night out,' my dad placated as usual. 'You don't go out much, that's all she meant.'

'Well, I'm fine, thank you. I don't need a social life arranged courtesy of my sister and my parents – I do have friends, you know.'

And they all looked at me in surprise and Fáinne asked what was wrong and I smiled and said nothing and that she was to tell me all about the panto after she'd seen it.

Tracy is being all that a fairy godmother aunt should be at the moment and I can't help wondering why. She's never been nice to *me* in our entire lives. I try to think of the worst thing she ever did to me and I reckon it has to be the time she told all my friends that I had worms. (I did have but it was a secret and I'd taken the medicine for them.) Anyway, Tracy told them all and none of them would play with me for ages.

I can hear Fáinne and Jenny chattering away in the lounge. They're having great fun. I used to feel guilty that Fáinne was an only child, that there was no possibility of her having a sister or brother for years, but thinking back to my childhood, maybe Fáinne is better off. And she's a happy kid despite being on her own.

I figure I should really ring my mother and apologise.

The food arrives and I go to call in the girls. The tree has been decorated and to be honest it looks awful. Awful in a funny way. All the decorations are on the lower branches. Nothing is up high because obviously they were too small to reach. In her hand, Fáinne carries the fairy. Trying not to chortle, I lift Fáinne up and she reverently places the fairy right at the top. The poor thing looks dreadfully lonely up there, presiding over a half-decorated tree.

'Cool,' Jenny says, tossing her pigtails back over her shoulder. 'That was fun. My mammy only has red and white decorations – your tree looks like a carnival, Fawn.'

Fáinne and I laugh and I tell them to go in and eat their tea because Tracy will be arriving any minute to pick them up.

*

183

Tracy is bang on time. She steps out of a taxi and Jenny is almost hyperventilating with excitement. Once again she tells Fáinne how lucky she is to have a famous aunt as all hers are old and boring and only tell her what a big girl she is. And how much she's grown and who she looks like.

When Tracy rings the bell though, Jenny is reduced to awestruck silence while Fáinne takes complete command and introduces Tracy by saying, 'Jenny, this is my famous aunt, you probably know her already.'

Jenny nods dumbly.

'So are we ready?' Tracy quirks an eyebrow. She looks fantastic as usual – even if she is only dressed in jeans and a cord shirt. She's wearing a fabulous sheepskin jacket and brown boots and her hair is caught back in a ponytail.

I give the two girls some goodie bags and a fiver each and tell them to be good. They barely acknowledge me as they skip together down the path to the taxi.

'It should be over around ten,' Tracy says. 'We'll drop Jenny home and I'll bring Fáinne back. Thanks for letting me take them, Luce.'

'No bother. Thank you for taking them.'

Tracy smiles and leaves. You'd know she was a model by the way she sashays down the driveway.

I hate nights on my own. I'm not one of those people that like headspace. Gimme lots of noise, loads of company and I'm as happy as I can be. Even if I'm on my own downstairs, just knowing that Fáinne is upstairs makes me happy. But nights like this one, when there is no one I can call, scare me a little.

I pick up the remote control and put on the telly, hoping for some noisy colourful movie. *Pretty Woman* has just started and it's one of my favourite films. I make myself a big mug of hot chocolate and shove in a few pink marshmallows, curl up on the sofa and prepare to fantasise about some rich guy taking me on and buying me lots of nice clothes. I'm only twenty-seven – there's still hope.

At ten-thirty, just as the credits roll, Tracy arrives back. Fáinne is half asleep in her arms. She smiles drowsily at me and tells me the panto was great.

'Come in.' I feel I have to invite my sister in as I take charge of Fáinne. 'Go on inside, I'll be with you in a sec – I'll just put this one to bed.'

Tracy indicates the taxi. 'I'll just pay him and tell him to come back in a hour, will I?'

'Sure.' An hour? What the hell am I going to talk to her about for an hour?

I take ages getting Fáinne ready, hoping it'll kill some time. But fifteen minutes later, with my child in bed, I have no option but to go down and face Tracy. She's sitting, her long legs tucked under her, on the sofa. 'Is she asleep?' Tracy whispers.

'Uh-huh – she must have had a great night.'

Tracy smiles, all gleaming white straight teeth. 'The two of them were hilarious. They were shouting up at the stage louder than anyone. It was great.'

I half wish I'd gone. 'Wine?'

'Yeah, thanks.' Tracy rubs her hands together and looks about. 'It's lovely and cosy in here,' she says. She pulls a cushion from the seat and cuddles it to her. 'Must be nice just to sit here at night and unwind.'

Huh. It's a complete mess: Fáinne's toys are everywhere and bits of the tree that I've cut earlier have to be hoovered up. She doesn't mean it. Tracy likes order. 'Not as nice as sitting in your penthouse and counting your money,' I joke.

And it honestly is a joke but Tracy doesn't laugh. Instead she stares into the glass of red wine I've just handed her and shrugs.

'So how's the film going?' I've been dying to know. Film sets are my manna.

'Oh, great, yeah.' She smiles brightly. 'Everyone is dead nice and encouraging.'

'And your character? What's she like?'

'A bimbo,' Tracy says with rare self-deprecation. 'The kind that doesn't know her arse from her elbow except when it comes to jumping into bed with the leading man.'

'Sex scenes?' My jaw drops so far, I think I nearly dislocate it. 'No way? What'll Mam say?'

'Well, no nudity – just kissing and suggestion. I don't want Mam to die just yet.'

We both smile and I realise that we've never actually smiled over the same thing in decades. I'm half tempted to tell her about my own ad but I pull back just in time. Tracy and secrets have never stayed together very long. 'Here.' I pour some more wine into her glass. 'Tell me more – it's the nearest I'll ever get to the big time.'

There is an awkward silence. 'You were a great actress,' Tracy says after a bit. 'You should have made it.'

I shrug. I don't want to be reminded of how I should have made it. I don't want to be patronised by her either. 'Tell me about the film,' I press again.

And she does. She talks with enthusiasm about even the stupidest detail so that I get the feeling that she's making it sound far more interesting than it actually is. Still, I would love to be fussed over and lipsticked to within an inch of my life.

'And are there a lot of egos?'

Tracy nods. 'Incredible.' Her wine is almost gone and I

go to pour another. 'It pisses me off, to be honest. I thought modelling was bad, but actors seem to be worse. And the reporters hanging about hoping to catch you in a clinch with the leading man – Jesus!'

'And have you?'

Tracy rolls her eyes and says brightly, 'Men seem to avoid me – I never have that problem. Anyway, if I was involved with someone, I can avoid the reporters – you learn as you go. But, hey, it's the leading men that are doing the avoiding.'

'Yeah. Right.' She's been linked with every famous guy on the planet. There was once a story about her and Tom Sherlock, a married guy, and Mam had almost died. Tracy had denied it of course, but the story had run and run.

'No, honestly.' She waves her hand about and some wine slops on to her jeans. She ignores it. 'I think the way I look frightens guys off. It's easier to get a guy if you're ugly than if you look like me.'

'Must be why I never have a problem then.'

'Stop!' A semi-drunken giggle. 'You're not ugly. And you've loads of friends.' She pauses, seemingly arrested by her words. 'You always had loads of friends.'

'You hang out with all the celebs.'

'Nooo.' She smiles and, putting on an affected Zsa Zsa Gabor accent, she slurs, 'Zey 'ang out wiz me, dahlink.'

I can well believe it. Even though she's joking, I can believe it.

A blast of a horn from outside stops the conversation. It's the taxi. Tracy slugs her remaining wine, picks up her lovely brown bag and jacket and bids me goodbye. 'See you Christmas Day,' she says. 'I'm working all hours until then. Bye, Luce, it was lovely.' She's about to air kiss me and then thinks better of it. Instead she hiccups and giggles. 'Bye.'

I walk her to the door. Her model swagger has deserted

her as she staggers towards the taxi. The taxi driver jumps out and opens the door for her. Tracy thanks him profusely before dropping like a sack of spuds into the back seat. Without even glancing at me, the taxi driver gets back into his car and drives off.

Just before I go to bed, I drop in to look at Fáinne. I love looking at her when she's asleep. It's like I can stare and she won't turn away and in the silence I can feel all the love for her filling me up. I adore that feeling. At times like that, I don't need anything else.

28

January 4th
I slept with Jason!

Yep. I can hardly believe it but it was great and wonderful and I love him to bits and I reckon he feels the same way.

And it all started because I had this massive row with Tracy. She's only back a day from Galway and causing havoc. Bitch.

Anyway, the row all started because I was giving her a rundown of Christmas. She hadn't asked for one but I figured that she deserved one as she'd managed to avoid all the unpleasantness by going to Galway. Plus, and I'm being honest here, I needed to talk about it. Maddie was useless – she kept telling me how awful it must be, how she'd hate it if her folks split up and how most marriages where the couple split have only a small percentage chance of getting back together. Like I really needed to hear that. Anyway, Tracy was putting on her make-up and brushing her hair and generally looking fab while I was lying across my bed feeling quite depressed. 'Christmas was awful here, you know,' I said.

'Mmmm.' She turned around and pouted. 'Is this a nice shade of lipstick, do you think?'

'Mam hardly ate anything and she forgot to get us a present. And Dad was on his own in his dingy flat. And Mam didn't even get dressed up – you know the way—'

'Got it cheap in BT's. It's a nice shade isn't it?'

'—she normally dresses up on Christmas Day, well, she didn't and

189

I think she might be a bit depressed or something. She cries all the time at night and—'

'Lucy, shut up!'

That stunned me. 'What?'

'I don't want to hear it. God, you'd put a dampener on the second coming, so you would.'

It was as if she'd hit me. I felt the physical sensation of being punched right in the stomach. The selfish cow, I thought. All she cares about is her lipstick and her perfumes and her fancy clothes. So I told her that. In fact, I shouted it at her. And she stood up and gave this patronising sigh and so – I hadn't planned it – I picked up the book I'd been reading and flung it at her. It hit her in the face. Right in the eye and she howled. She crumpled up on the floor, screaming.

'Serve you right,' I shouted. 'You'll listen to me now.'

Only the door flew open and Mam came in and when she saw Tracy on the ground, she flung herself down beside her.

'Oh my eye, my eye,' Tracy howled. 'She flung a book at it and I'm sure it'll be all black and I've a casting this afternoon. Ooooh!'

Mam pulled Tracy up and insisted on having a look at her eye.

I ran out before she could give out to me.

Being in the open, I couldn't cry and I did want to. A big hard lump came into my throat and it hurt a lot when I tried to swallow. Eventually, I got it to go away by blinking really hard and thinking of where I would go. I couldn't go to Maddie or Gray as they both loved Tracy and wouldn't understand. And anyway, it wasn't them I wanted to see. It was Jason. He just seemed to think I was great. We clicked in a way I've never clicked with anyone else before. And he made me laugh. The more I know him, the more I like him and the more I don't know him. And 'like' isn't the right word for it – I can't stop thinking of him. When I met him first, he seemed normal, a bit wild but normal. Now I know that he's a lot wild in a really quiet sort of way. Like he walks into trouble when he doesn't have to. For instance, he doesn't seem to go to his lectures much, he says he can't be bothered and then he just laughs.

LAUGHS! I reckon his folks will go mad. And he's stopped showing up for football training and that drives Gray mad. And on the football pitch, he plays like an angel but he tackles like a devil. He seems to get worse every time he plays. Bill the trainer is going mental with him, Gray says. And that's when he bothers turning up for matches. Sometimes he doesn't even show. I reckon it's because of the way some of the lads treated him at the party that time, but Gray says it's just because he's a waster. Gray is such a moralistic pain, sometimes.

I've never been in Jason's flat before and I was calm enough until I arrived outside it. We usually meet in college. I suddenly felt as if I was taking a big step in the relationship by going on to his home territory. Ridiculous, I know, but my heart speeded up so fast that I honestly thought I was going to black out. I almost did when, from behind me, a big cheery voice asked, 'What do you want?' A tall, broad, red-faced guy with mad, fuzzy brown hair and baggy jeans was standing beside me. Country Bumpkin should have been blazing in lights on his forehead.

'I, eh, well, I was hoping to see Jason Donovan in flat three,' I babbled.

'Oh. Really.' Country Bumpkin stuck out his hand. 'I'm Johnno. I'm Jason's flatmate. How you doing?'

So this was Johnno. He looked nice enough. Jason had said he was a bit odd. 'Hiya.' My hand was pumped vigorously up and down for what seemed like ages. Eventually Johnno loosened his grip and began a search of his baggy jeans.

'Here we are now.' He took his key out and inserted it into the lock. 'Good job I met you – Jason wouldn't have answered. He isn't the best today.'

'Is he sick?'

Johnno looked at me strangely and nodded. 'Yep. I guess so.' A pause as he looked at me harder. 'You're not a relation of his, are you? He'd kill me for bringing you up if you were. He doesn't like his relations much.'

'Well, I'm not. I'm a friend from college. I'm Lucy.'

'Hey, Lucy.' He said it as if he knew me. 'I know all about you. You're the girl who's doing the drama, yeah?'

'That's right.'

'Aw, yeah, that's fine, so. He won't mind you coming up.' He began to stride up the stairs. His feet were enormous.

'Why doesn't he like his relations?' I asked, half running to keep up with him.

Johnno shrugged. 'Dunno. Jace doesn't like too many people anyway.' He fumbled with the lock on the battered door. 'Hey, Jace,' he yelled as he turned the key. 'Visitor.'

I heard a groan from Jason's room.

Johnno grinned at me. 'It's Lucy. Do you want her to go on in?'

'Wha'?' Jason's voice, sounding really croaky, came back. 'Lucy?'

'Hiya, Jace,' I called. 'Just wondering if you're up for going out anywhere?'

'I'll be out in a sec. Get Johnno to make you a coffee or give you a can or something.'

Johnno already had the kettle on. A plate of chocolate biscuits was on the table, looking oddly formal among the mess of the flat. 'I usually keep them for my girlfriend,' Johnno explained, almost shyly, 'but you can have some. Sit down.'

I sat. He poured me a coffee and sat opposite me.

'So, you like drama, ey?'

'Uh-huh.' I took a biscuit. 'I want to be an actress. That's the plan anyway.'

'Great.' Johnno didn't seem to know what to say next.

'And you? Are you in college?'

He laughed. A lovely laugh. 'Naw. I work on the building. Good money. I'm saving for a deposit on a house.'

'Too sensible.' Jason's voice from behind startled us. He sat beside me and took a biscuit. 'You're too sensible, Johnno, I keep telling ya.'

Johnno rolled his eyes. 'Beats being senseless,' he joked. He picked up his coffee cup. 'I'm just heading into the shower. Have to clean meself

192

up for herself, you know.' He stuck out his huge hand. 'Nice meeting you, Lucy.'

'And you too.'

We watched as he walked off.

'Nice guy,' I commented.

Jason said nothing.

I noticed that he looked rough. His hair was greasy; his clothes looked as if they'd been slept in. His hand as he put the biscuit to his mouth was trembling. 'Your hand,' I said.

He looked at it. Put the biscuit down on the table. 'Haven't been great the last couple of days,' he muttered. Then, 'So, what's the big occasion?'

'None, just wanted to see you.'

He smiled. He has a lovely slow sort of a smile that takes ages to spread across his face. 'Aw.'

'So – were you sick?'

'Uh-huh. Some kinda bug.' He stood up. 'Another coffee?'

'Thanks.' I handed him my cup and his fingers brushed mine. He paused, hesitated and then took the cup from me. I watched him from behind as he made us both a drink. God, he was gorgeous. His whole personality was gorgeous.

'There now.' He sat beside me again. 'Cheers.' His cup tapped against mine.

'Cheers.'

We didn't talk for a bit.

'So, will you be in college this week?' I asked. 'Do you feel better?'

'I'm fine.' He put his cup down and stared into it. 'I just probably won't go in.'

'You'll fail your exams,' I said.

'You're not my mother,' he muttered, rubbing his face. 'Don't go there.'

I flinched, hurt. 'Sorry.'

He bit his lip. 'Naw, naw, I'm sorry.' He bowed his head. 'I'm just so fed up, Luce.'

I touched him. On his arm. He turned to face me and his eyes turned all smoky. He caught my hand in his and held it. Then neither of us quite knew what to do. So he held my hand and caressed it.

'I thought you promised your dad you'd study,' I said softly.

'Yeah, well, like you said, I'm not the dutiful-son type.' He raised his eyes from my palm and stared at me. 'I like doing things I enjoy.'

'Yeah?' My voice was high-pitched. 'Like what?'

'This.' He bent his mouth to my palm and kissed it, all the while staring at me with his enormous eyes.

'You really are good at that,' I said.

'I'm good at this too.' He stood and pulled me up. He bent his head and kissed me. I tasted coffee. His hands cupped the sides of my face. It was erogenous heaven. His hands snaked around my back and it was as if every part of me he touched burnt my skin. 'Mad about you, Lucy.'

'Really?'

'Yep.' A grin. 'Can't believe my luck. I thought you'd never look at me. I thought you were way out of my league.'

'Get lost.'

'Never. Not ever.' Another kiss.

The sound of the shower stopped in the bathroom. 'Johnno's coming out,' I whispered.

'Come on in here.' Jason pulled me towards his bedroom and I hesitated. 'You don't have to do anything you don't want,' he said.

The problem was there wasn't anything I wouldn't do with this guy.

So, after pretending coyness, I slept with him. Had sex with him. Loved him to bits.

Jason's bedroom (which I feel I have to describe) is amazing. Light floods the room and just opposite the window he has an artist's easel. Amazing drawings of circuits – yep, circuits – were all over the walls. And I know that sounds weird, but they were great drawings. Really detailed. It turned out that Jace had drawn them. That really turned me on – I don't know why. I think it was because he'd never boasted about his pictures before. 'That's for a radio,' he told me, pointing at a small, intricate picture directly across from his bed, where we lay, wrapped in each other's arms. 'Amazing, isn't it – how all those bits and pieces put together can receive and produce a sound?'

'Mmm.' I snuggled tighter into him, feeling really happy for the first time since Tracy had come back. Happy and safe.

'And that one there, that's for a stereo.'

The smell of smoke and heat from him was intoxicating.

'And, like, if one tiny thing is connected wrong, it won't work. Just one tiny flaw and the whole thing crashes. Everything has to be perfect inside.'

'I never thought of that before.' I tried to sound interested. All I wanted to do was kiss him.

'Most people don't.' He pulled me tighter. He turned to face me and his forehead tipped mine. 'I reckon people are lucky. They can be shot to hell on the inside and still work properly, ey?'

I giggled. 'Well, you work just fine.'

And we did it again.

I cry after I put down the diary. I cry and cry and cry. Softly, so I don't wake Fáinne. I don't know why I'm crying really other than the fact that it all seems so long ago and *I* seem so long ago.

29

MADDIE AND CLIVE arrive bearing a bottle of booze, a bunch of flowers and a newspaper. 'There you are.' Clive jabs the paper, which is called the *Dingle Bugle*, and hands it to me. 'A quarter of a page – that should get some attention.'

For a second I don't know what he's talking about and then I see the headline *Tracing Jason* and part of me curls up with embarrassment. What was private is now public – well, public in Dingle anyway – and, OK, no one sees my face or knows who I am, but it feels like they do. 'Thanks, Clive, that looks great,' I stammer out, gawking at the large black and white of Jason and his shiny teeth.

'Will you leave her alone.' Maddie grabs the paper from me. 'I told him not to bring it, Luce.' She jabs Clive in the arm. 'But he was so proud of it – you'd swear he printed the page himself.'

'I thought Lucy would like to see it,' Clive said haughtily. 'That's all.'

'Yeah, well, she's enough on her plate tonight without worrying about that tosser, haven't you, Luce?' Maddie pours a huge glass of wine and shoves it at me.

'The ad is great, Clive,' I say, feeling a little sorry for him. 'Honestly.'

'Yeah, well, hide the bloody paper when Gray arrives, he

is so dead against it. You know him – he never forgave Jason for what he did. Just keep it away from him – let's not spoil the evening for you.'

'When my ad runs on the telly, it'll be spoilt,' I say gloomily as I shove the paper in a drawer. 'I just hope Mam isn't looking at the movie on RTE tonight.'

Les had rung to tell me that my ad was to air around ten-thirty on RTE. For moral support, I'd invited Maddie and Gray around to tell me how wonderful I looked. I knew they'd lie to me and that's what I needed.

'Clive is going to ring your mother at ten-thirty and pretend he's got a wrong number,' Maddie says. 'Aren't you, Clive?'

Clive reddens. 'If you say so, Madd,' he answers dryly.

'I do say so and, what's more, I have Lucy's mother's number programmed into your mobile, so all you have to do is press "call" when the ad comes up.'

'Thanks for invading the security of my phone,' Clive jokes. 'It's nice to know nothing I have is private. Maybe Lucy doesn't want me to ring her mother?'

He says it hopefully but I think it's a cool idea. 'Thanks, Clive – that's great.' His face drops. 'Now all we need to sort out is who can kill my dad?'

They smile.

'Where's herself?' Maddie takes out a Barbie ballerina doll from her bag. 'I thought she might like this as a sort of pre-Christmas present – you know, get her in the mood for all those toys.'

'Don't give her that now – save it for Christmas. She got masses of stuff for her birthday from you – she's spoilt rotten.'

'As she should be.' Maddie places the doll on the worktop. 'She's my godchild and I never get a chance to bring her anywhere – Gray bloody monopolises her. If I can't make her love me, I'll buy her affection. So, where is she?'

'Jenny's.' I resign myself to giving Fáinne the doll. It's true she's mad about Gray and I think Maddie does feel it a little. 'Her mother asked her over some night for a sleepover so I nominated tonight. Clever me, ey?'

The front-door bell rings and as Maddie goes to answer it, I shove a few crisps and peanuts in a bowl and carry them over to the TV. From the hallway I can hear Gray and Audrey's voices.

First Gray congratulates Maddie on her pregnancy. Then Audrey begins to shriek. 'Isn't this exciting! I can't wait to see the ad. Imagine being on the telly! Where is she?'

'Inside.' Maddie sounds amused.

I hear Audrey scurrying along the hall and a couple of seconds later she bursts into the room. 'Good luck!' she says effusively. 'I hope it makes you *famous*!'

'It won't,' I grin. 'More like infamous.'

She frowns. 'In. Famous. Yeah. Yeah. You'll be really in, won't you?' She clasps her hands together. 'This is the most exciting night of my life – well, except for meeting your sister, that is. But that was the daytime, so it doesn't count.' She's like a whirlwind the way she talks.

'Hiya, Luce.' Gray enters, a glass of wine in his hand. 'Nervous?'

'Sick. Wait until you see it – you'll know why.'

'You'll be great.' He hugs me. 'Now, tell me: what lovely food have you concocted for our party tonight?'

'This.' I grin as I indicate the peanuts. 'But I'm ordering Chinese later.'

'I love Chinese,' Audrey nods. 'Especially pizza.'

I extract myself from Gray's arm before I laugh. How does he stick it? 'Sit down,' I splutter out, 'and I'll bring in the wine.'

The film starts late. By the time the ad break comes on I'm a nervous wreck. Each ad seems to last for ages. There's a coffee ad with a gorgeous woman. A breakfast cereal ad with a gorgeous woman. A perfume ad with a gorgeous woman. I begin to wonder if it's a sick joke. By the time my ad comes on, I'll look dull and plain. Each time an ad comes on that isn't mine, my four guests groan. Clive sits, his finger poised on his mobile ready to press his call button.

And suddenly, there it is. Bright green and red cover the TV screen, shocking the eyes. 'Hi,' some blonde bombshell giggles. 'I like my man with muscles.'

Clive walks out of the room with his mobile to his ear. I'm kinda glad he won't see it – I'd be afraid of what he'd think.

'Hi,' the red-headed girl who'd sat beside me at the audition says chirpily, 'I like my man with a nice ass.'

'Oh God, oh God,' I groan.

Maddie squeals as I appear. 'Look, look, Luce.'

'I can't, I can't.' But I peer out from behind my fingers. I look good. Even I can see that. 'Hi,' I say, and I hardly recognise my own voice, 'I like my man protected.' And up go the condoms. Not literally, of course.

Freeze-frame on my sincere face.

And it's on to the next ad.

Maddie, Gray and Audrey burst into applause.

Clive appears back. 'Not a woman that likes wrong numbers, your mother.' He grins.

'You were fantastic!' Maddie, I think, is being sincere. 'You looked *great!*'

'Brilliant.' Gray beams at me. 'That deserves another drink.' He jumps up and refills our wine glasses. Well, everyone's except Maddie's. She's decided to stick with water.

'I'd *never* have recognised you,' Audrey says. 'Wow, you're famous!' And she jumps up from her seat to hug me, spilling her wine all over the floor. 'Sorry! Sorry! Sorry!'

'Forget it.' The relief has made me hungry and energetic. I did look good. OK, it was a condom ad and OK, it was cheap and cheesy, but at least I looked all right. And at least my mother didn't see it.

We're in the middle of discussing it frame by frame when the phone rings. 'Jesus!' Panic grips me. 'Oh, Jesus!'

'It's not your mother,' Clive says. 'I swear I rang her.'

'Maybe my dad saw it,' I gulp. 'Ohhh, Maddie, answer the phone, will you?'

'This is ridiculous,' Maddie says sternly. 'It was a good ad, for God's sake. Answer the phone.'

'Nooo.'

She shakes her head and leaves. When she comes back, she's grinning. 'It's your admirer.'

'Who?'

She glances at Gray and Audrey and they suddenly look guilty.

'Who?' I ask again.

'Your boss,' Maddie says. 'Gray reckons he fancies you.'

'He does,' Audrey nods. 'You should have seen him the night we met him in the pub. And he's *fine*.'

'He doesn't fancy me.' I roll my eyes. 'What does he want anyhow?'

'Dunno,' Maddie says, 'he just asked for you.'

To a chorus of whey-heys I take the call. 'Doug?'

'Having a party, are you?'

'Mmm, sort of.' I glare at my mates who have gathered in the hall behind me. 'Shut up,' I mouth.

'Just rang to say the ad was great.'

'You saw it.'

200

'Uh-huh, me and my flatmates. They want to know when they can get a date?'

'Stop!'

'Seriously.' Doug laughs.

'Thanks.'

'So, I'll see you Monday – if you still want to work for me.'

'Of *course* I do.'

'Glad to hear it.' He pauses. 'See ya, so.'

And he's gone. I turn to my mates who are looking expectantly at me.

'Well?' Maddie demands.

'He liked the ad.' I turn to Gray. 'And he doesn't fancy me – so stop saying he does.'

'He sits beside her in the pub,' Gray says to Audrey. 'He talks to her all night. He walks her to her bus stop. He bloody—'

'—fancies her!' they both say together and laugh.

They've drunk too much wine. With a pang I remember the last guy who used to walk me to bus stops. 'Chinese anyone?' I change the subject before it begins to hurt.

We end up ordering chips and pizzas as Gray apparently hadn't the heart to tell Audrey that pizzas weren't Chinese food.

Les rings in the middle of the meal. 'How's my girl?' he bellows. 'You were fantastic. You looked great, sounded great. I can see a stampede for condoms taking place in the next couple of weeks.'

'Wonderful,' I say, trying to be droll but with half a dozen glasses of wine inside me, I fail.

'It is. It is. I reckon they'll be calling you Juicy Lucy next.'

'I'd rather Beauty Lucy,' I retort, giggling.

'Not the same ring to it at all,' Les dismisses me and I realise that he's actually serious.

201

I don't want to be known as Juicy Lucy. 'Les, I don't want—'

'Bye now. Congratulations.' And the phone goes dead.

I stare at it, wondering if I should ring him back when Gray shouts for me to come inside. 'Luce, come on, Audrey is doing her drum impression. Come on!'

Drum impression? From inside I can hear what sounds like a full set of drums playing and there is Audrey, swaying dangerously in the middle of the floor, making all sorts of weird noises.

'She can do a mean helicopter too,' Gray announces proudly.

It's a great night and it ends about three in the morning. I tell them that they can stay if they want but Gray has a match to cover the next day and Maddie and Clive are meeting Clive's parents for lunch in the city and Maddie wants to make sure she looks decent as nothing fits her any more. So at three, I stand at the door and wave them all off. I'm sure the neighbours will be in to complain in the morning at the noise the four of them make: well, three of them; Clive sort of stands apart as Maddie yells her goodbyes out to the neighbourhood in general.

After the taxi takes them away, I head back into the kitchen and am taken aback to see Jason's good-looking face beaming at me from the paper when I open the drawer to dump the corkscrew in. I take it out and the memory of those days, when I was so happy, sweeps through me and for the first time in years, the memory makes me smile.

Wine is great like that.

30

February 5th

Mam and Dad had an enormous row at the front door today, in front of all the neighbours. Well, not that the neighbours were looking – they'd be far too polite to do that – but they must have heard it. I walked out just as Mam called Dad an idiot (he was bringing us to the cinema and forgot that Mam wanted him to bring Tracy for a casting) and he called her a stupid bossy cow. Dad doesn't lose his temper too much, but he really did today. Neither of them noticed me as I left the house, they couldn't have, they were that stuck into each other. I left as there was no way I wanted to be around either of them after that. I could hear Mam's voice right up the street. I pretended in my head that they were nothing to do with me, but it was hard.

Rang Jason. He told me he'd meet me off the bus at college and that we could go somewhere. It was lovely to see him waiting for me. He looked, and I know this sounds mad, so friendly and safe after what had happened. And I liked the way he smiled at me when he saw me. It's just nice to know that someone out there wants to see me, wants to be with me.

His smile made my eyes water a bit, but I blinked hard and asked him where were we going.

'Howth,' Jace said. 'Let's go to Howth.'

'OK,' I said. 'Let's.'

We caught the Dart to Howth (Jace made me bunk on without paying – he thought it was a great laugh but I was sick in case we'd be caught). When we arrived, Jace for some mad reason thought it would be a good idea to climb Howth Head. He was in a weird mood, sort of hyper, but it was dead attractive. 'Aw, come on,' he cajoled. 'Get fit. Come on.'

I can't resist him and to be honest, I didn't much care what we did, just being with him and getting along with him was enough for me. And his hyper mood meant that I didn't have to talk too much. He pulled me along behind him, laughing as he dragged me. About halfway up, he stopped and studied me. 'Are you OK? You're very quiet.' It was his voice and the fact that he noticed that made me start sniffing. And to my horror, tears began rolling down my face. I haven't cried in months, haven't been able to, but the row and the tension and Christmas and his kindness just seemed to clash together in my head and I couldn't help it. Anyway, even though I rubbed my eyes hard, the tears just kept coming out and running over my chin and dribbling down my neck.

I don't think Jace said anything. In fact, he moved away.

I sniffed and wiped my face with my sleeve and blurted out some sort of an apology. Still Jace gawked at me.

'Sorry,' I blubbered.

'Naw, I am,' he said, sounding shell-shocked. 'Here.' He patted the grass and sat down. 'Sit here. Come on.' He caught my hand and pulled me down beside him. And he said nothing else and the quiet air was filled with my sniffs and hiccups and gulps.

'Sorry,' I gasped again.

'Must be pretty bad,' he offered, without looking at me.

'No, I'm just being stupid.' I tried to stop the sob in my voice. 'Sorry.'

''S OK.'

Silence. The sun came out then. Hit us both full force, lighting up our patch of ground.

'So, what's the problem?'

I swallowed. Telling him was hard. Telling anyone was hard. 'Mam and Dad separated a while back,' I muttered, trying to keep my voice steady. 'They keep fighting. They had a huge row just before I met you

– right in the street and all.' More stupid tears. Oh God. When I think of it now, writing this, I feel so ridiculous.

Jace looked at me. He didn't say anything for ages. His gaze kept darting away from my face and coming back to look at me again. Eventually, he gulped out, 'Does your dad keep in contact with you? Does your mum?'

'What?'

'Well?' He was looking all serious and sombre and a bit scared too.

'Course!'

'Well, that's good then.' He turned away and stared across out to the sea and I followed his gaze. 'My mum just left,' he muttered. 'I came home from school one day and couldn't get into the house. I was eight. I sat and waited for her to come back and at six my dad came home and he let me in and she was gone.'

'What?'

A shrug. His face was unreadable.

'Oh Jace.' What mother would do that? I tried to touch him and he flinched.

'All her clothes, all her shoes, photos, all gone.' His voice was flat, as if he were talking about someone else. 'I'd drawn a picture for her in school the day before and she'd left that. She never came back.' He turned to me and gave a weird sort of smile. 'I don't know where she is.'

'That's horrible!'

He shrugged. 'They fought too. All the time. It was nice and quiet when she was gone. Dad never talked about her after – he just got on with things. So I just got on with stuff too. It's not the end of the world, you know.'

I wasn't too sure about that. 'Does it not make you angry that she left?'

'She must've had her reasons.' He shrugged and tapped his nose and said uncomfortably, 'That's my business, OK? Don't go telling Maddie or Gray, right?'

205

'I won't.'

Pause. 'Swear?'

'Yeah. Sure.'

He stood up and held out his hand. I took it in mine and he hauled me to my feet. 'Come on. Let's keep going.'

On impulse, I hugged him. 'Thanks. And she was mad to leave you – I never will.'

'She didn't leave me,' he snapped, startling me. 'She left my dad.' He pulled away from me and began walking.

I ran to catch him up and caught his hand in mine and he squeezed it.

We cracked open a couple of cans when we reached the top of Howth Head. Jason had them in his bag. The taste of the beer made me feel sick so I couldn't finish even one can. Jason polished off everything. Then he lay back and closed his eyes. 'I can feel the world spinning,' he told me laughing. 'I love that feeling. It's the best feeling in the world.'

Looking at him was, for me, the best feeling in the world. And I felt all sort of protective towards him because of what his mother had done. And I loved him for telling me. So I kissed him.

And one thing led to another.

It was the best sex ever.

February 7th

Brilliant news. I GOT AN AGENT! Yep – when I finished college today, this little man was waiting for me outside the lecture hall. One of my tutors was with him and he introduced himself as Les Lyons. And he wants me. He saw me in my play and he wants me! Apparently he's quite well respected in the business. He gave me a contract to look over and said he'll be in touch.

In total shock.

Mam thrilled for me.

Dad thrilled for me.

February 11th

Jason played brilliantly tonight in football. He scored two amazing goals. Gray didn't play – he asked Bill if he could take some action shots instead. (Gray wants to do sports photography after college.) Bill wasn't too pleased but Gray did it anyway. Afterwards he took a picture of me, Maddie and Jason, only Maddie ducked out at the last minute. Gray has promised to give it to me when he develops it.

Spent the night in the pub with Jace and the lads. Gray left with Tracy (he's become really boring now) and Jace, Maddie and I walked home.

We were locked. When Jace came to the bush that borders the college, he told me to give him a leg-up. If I hadn't been so drunk, I wouldn't have. But, instead, I thought it was a brilliant idea. Maddie was cracking up laughing as Jace put his foot into my cupped hands and hauled himself up.

Once on top of the hedge, Jason stood up, his arms out wide and shouted: 'I'm the king of the world.' And then he started to sink.

We nearly ate ourselves laughing.

Then Jason started shouting out that it was a thorny bush.

We laughed harder.

When eventually he got out, he was cut to ribbons. And his poor face was bleeding. 'Well,' he said. 'That sure answers my question.'

Maddie giggled. 'What question?'

'That I can't walk on top of the bleeding thing.'

'The only thing bleeding is you,' I said.

We all thought this was hilarious.

I laugh as I read. He was great despite what happened afterwards. No other guy has ever made me as happy as he did.

I think that maybe I'm a little in love with him still.

31

TONIGHT IS THE night of the surgery's Christmas party. Both Fáinne and I have been looking forward to it for ages. Fáinne because she's having a sleepover at my mam's and me because I can stay out as late as I want without having to worry about a babysitter. It's years since I've done that. We're all heading out for a meal, and then, after that, all being well, we'll head to either a pub or a club.

Or both.

When I arrive to drop Fáinne off, Dad is waiting in the hall for me. 'No point in you driving into town and having to leave your car there,' he says, pulling on his jacket. 'I'll drive you in and you can get a taxi back to your place. Your car will be safer outside our house anyway.'

He thinks that because I'm heading north of the Liffey it's going to be madly dangerous. I grin slightly and accept otherwise Mam will have to listen to him going on and on all night about my car.

'Bye now.' I kiss Fáinne on the head. 'Be good for your nana.'

'Of course she will.' My mother comes into the hall. She's about to say that Fáinne is always good when she catches sight of what I'm wearing. 'Where did you get that?' She points to my red outfit. OK, it's a little tight but ever since the ad aired (which is about four times now) I've realised that

208

I do look good in tight things. I might not have Tracy's stick-thin figure but what I do have are nice curves.

'You should make the most of them,' Audrey told me. Admittedly after about five glasses of wine.

I deliberately misunderstand her. 'I got my clothes in town.'

'Isn't it nice, Nana?' Fáinne pipes up. 'I like red, don't you?'

Mam gulps. 'Red is nice,' she concedes. 'I've just never seen you wear anything like *that* before.'

She emphasises 'that' to show she doesn't approve. Which must mean I look good. I'm wearing a tight red bustier with sequins and a matching red skirt, tight at the end. In fact, it's hard to walk in but I hope it'll be a car to bar job tonight.

Dad begins to make noises behind us.

'Have a nice time,' Mam says. 'See you tomorrow.'

I kiss Fáinne again, thank them for minding her and climb into Dad's car.

I can see it on the way to town. It's so big, it'd be impossible to miss. A huge blue billboard with me on it. Me in tight red jeans and a barely there top. Me holding my precious condoms. Me sitting beside my bloody dad speeding towards it. I grow cold. Sweat breaks out on the palm of my hands. 'Would you look at that,' I shout out, pointing to an inoffensive old lady walking her dog on the opposite side of the road. 'Did you see what she did to the dog, Dad?'

'Jesus, don't shout, you'll make me crash,' Dad snaps, turning to me.

Crisis averted.

'What did she do to the dog?'

'Kicked it.'

Close one.

*

209

The restaurant is the business – very upmarket. I get out of Dad's car as elegantly as I can in my tight skirt. Dad 'bips' his horn and drives off. Before I go in, I study myself in the mirrored glass window. I look good, I tell myself, as I touch my hair, which has been sprayed to within an inch of its life by my cheap and cheerful hairdresser. She's done some sort of a French plait thing across my head and while it's tight as hell, it suits me. Taking a deep breath, I shove open the heavy doors and hope that I'm not the first to arrive.

The maître d' bows to me as I enter. *Bows*. 'Hello,' he says warmly, 'and you are with?'

'Doug Kelly?'

'This way, madam. They're waiting on you.'

I don't know if I imagine it or not, but as I walk through the restaurant, people seem to be looking at me. I wonder if my zip is undone. Cautiously I run my hands along the back of my skirt. Nope, fine. Nothing is falling out of my bustier either. Maybe it's my imagination. However, just as I spot Doug's table, a fella at the table I'm passing whistles softly.

I look around, then realise that it's *me* he's ogling.

'Do I know you?' I ask, feeling ridiculously flattered.

'Aren't you the girl that likes her fellas protected?'

A whoop goes up from the table, drawing the attention of the whole room.

I flush and turn away.

'Great ad,' he continues hastily. Everyone at the table murmurs agreement. 'You are great in it. Any chance of an autograph?' He shoves a napkin at me.

My autograph?! I have waited twenty-seven years for this. I go pink with pleasure.

'We do not allow our customers to write on the napkins,' the waiter says scathingly. 'This way, miss.'

210

'I'll pay for it,' the guy counters. 'Here.' He shoves the napkin at me again. The rest of the lads at his table are grinning now.

'Please leave our customers alone,' the waiter snaps.

God, I'm like a Hollywood star! 'It's OK,' I stammer. 'I don't mind.' In fact I LOVE IT! I don't say that, of course.

'So, will you sign it?' the guy asks.

I'm about to say 'yes', when I realise that I've got no pen. Just my luck – my first ever fan and I have to let him down.

'Here.' The waiter hands me his notebook and pen and says wearily, 'Sign it if you wish – just don't deface our napkins.'

'Aw, fair play to ya,' the guy says and everyone at the table claps. The waiter smiles condescendingly. With a shaking hand I start to write. Everyone is looking.

'Write "To Joe",' the guy instructs, standing up and looking over my shoulder. *To Joe, all the best, Lucy.* In brackets, I put *Condom Girl*. 'Here.' I rip the page out of the notebook and hand it to him.

'Wow.' He beams at me, looks at my signature. He's a baby really – my guess is he's about twenty. 'Great. Ta.' He hops from foot to foot, then passes my signature to his mates and they all 'oooh' and 'aaah' over it. I stand like a spare, with all the restaurant watching me, and wonder what Tracy would do. I reckon that she'd just carry on walking. Trying not to look madly thrilled, I make my way over to Doug's table.

Doug is there with Clare and Jim. They're all staring at me.

'What happened?' Jim asks. 'Do you know him or something?'

I can't help my huge grin as I stammer out an explanation.

211

Doug and Jim think it's great while Clare looks stonily at me and says dismissively, 'Sure, who'd bother looking at an ad for condoms?'

I hope my mother thinks the same.

'I would.' Jim laughs. 'Telling you, you're going places now, Lucy, getting recognised is the first step. This calls for more wine.'

Doug agrees and another bottle is ordered. I wonder how much they've drunk already – all three of them seem slightly locked.

I sit beside Doug, being careful to pull my skirt up so that my big thighs don't strain the seams. The waitress arrives with the wine and pours us all a glass and then, pen poised, she asks us what we'd like to order.

'Lucy on toast,' Jim says and I giggle. Jim is about fifty and a terrible flirt.

Clare sniffs. 'I'm glad you're not my husband, Jim, I don't approve of those sort of comments.'

Jim chortles. 'I'm glad you're not my wife.'

'Folks?' the waitress says brightly, trying to restore the atmosphere as Clare glares at Jim.

I haven't even had time to look at the menu. I pick it up and gawp. It's bloody enormous.

'Madam?' the waitress says.

'Oh shit.' I wince. 'I'll never read all this.' I hiss to Doug, 'What have you ordered?'

'Number forty-five.' He grins. 'Dunno what it is but it's my lucky number.'

'Forty-five is your lucky number?'

'Uh-huh.' He doesn't bother explaining, instead he says, 'Pick a number and go with it. You can't go wrong.'

I'm feeling giddy and silly and happy. There is nothing like being recognised to boost the ego. 'Fine. Number eight.'

Fáinne's age. 'I'll have garlic mushrooms and number eight.'

Number eight is a vegetarian dish. I'm devastated as the waiter puts it in front of me. Doug splutters with laughter and indicates the half a cow that he's been served. 'Want some?'

'Bloody sure,' I reply. 'This is your fault.' I jab at the risotto. 'I don't even like rice that much.'

'Here.' Doug hacks his meat in half and forks it on to my plate. 'Have some of my veg too and I'll have some of your rice.' I watch his hands as he cuts and scoops. He has beautiful hands. White nails with half-moons that a woman would kill for. I've often watched those hands calming animals and never realised that they looked so gorgeous. All I want to do is touch them. He smells all spicy and, to my horror, my heart speeds up something rotten. Whatever aftershave he has on actually works! It makes me want to rub my face against his, smelling him in great big gulps of air. I want to feel his fingers—

'That all right?' he says, his sharing of food complete. He looks straight into my face, his eyes capturing mine and I suddenly realise that I want him. Bloody hormones. 'Well?' he asks and his spicy smell covers me.

'Fine,' I stammer. 'Thanks.'

But I'm not going to chase him. That's what I decide as I shove some weird purple vegetable into my mouth. It's not him I *actually* want, I think as I gulp down my red wine, it's just a bit of love. And because I get on with him and like him, I have fixated on being with him. It'll wear off.

Clare seems to have fixated on him too. Not in the romantic sense though. She seems determined to tell him about every swab he's ever taken. Or maybe that *is* her romantic preamble, I think in alarm as I watch her toss her darkened hair back from her face and smile at him in a way that can only be described as carnivorous. I sit back and observe her. She's batting her eyelashes at him and showing him the inside of her wrists. That's definite flirtation; I read that in a self-help-capture-a-man type of book.

Doug doesn't seem to notice what she's doing though. I mean, he's nodding back and making intelligent comments about swab-taking but at the same time he's eating. Clare on the other hand has hardly eaten a thing. Neither, I notice, have I. But that's because it's vegetarian and because the conversation makes me feel queasy – back passages feature in it a lot.

'More meat?' Doug breaks conversation with Clare to talk to me.

I don't know why he asks because I've piles left. 'Great.' I know I'm only saying it so that I can observe his hands heaping food on to my plate. I'm saying it in the knowledge that his shirt – which is deep purple and suits him – will brush my bare skin as he passes me the food. I know that I'm turning myself on for no other reason than that it feels good.

'There,' Doug says. 'And that's it. No more.' His smile turns my insides to water. 'The last time I had a meal this good was last Christmas. It's such a bitch not living at home,' he says.

'Well, you'll have to let me cook for you, so,' Clare purrs. 'Brendan and I, we eat a lot of oysters. That's my speciality.' She smirks. 'Besides my buns, of course.'

'Aw, you've very fine buns,' Jim remarks and Doug splutters on his food. Bits of potato go all over the table.

'That's crude, Jim,' Clare withers him. 'So what do you say?'

'You can cook me a few oysters,' Jim answers in Doug's stead. 'My wife could do with them.'

'A bad workman blames his wife,' I tease.

Jim rolls his eyes.

'I'll bet Doug's girlfriends don't need oysters, ey, Doug?' Clare says.

She is *definitely* flirting. God, she's about ten years older than him and supposedly happy as hell with Brendan.

'They don't,' Doug agrees. ''Cause unfortunately they don't exist.'

'Awww.' Clare makes an exaggerated face. She is plastered. 'We'll have to change that.'

'Fancy changing that, Luce?' Jim shouts.

I know I'm blushing and the knowledge that I am only makes me go redder. 'What?' I pretend that I don't know what he's talking about.

'Lucy is not Doug's kind of girl,' Clare says. 'Doug needs stability.'

'I'm stable,' I say, offended.

All three look at me incredulously. 'Aren't I?' I mutter.

Doug makes a face. 'Stability equals boring. Naw, what I need is a rich chick with a massive car and an open view of relationships.'

I giggle. 'I can do the chick part of that for you.'

'One out of four ain't bad.' Doug nods. 'We can work on the rest.'

Of course he's joking. It doesn't stop Jim whooping though. The guy is seriously drunk.

After the meal, it's pub time. Clare can hardly walk, she's drunk so much wine. She clings on to Doug as we stagger into the pub. Jim thinks it's hilarious while I fume. I mean, who does she think she is – she's *married*, for God's sake. What is she doing clinging on to a single man?

'Poor Doug,' Jim sniggers to me as Doug eases Clare on to a chair.

215

I feel instantly cheered. Yeah, poor Doug.

'She's an awful one for the drink when she gets out,' Jim remarks as I sit down. 'I reckon that Brendan fella doesn't let her out much so she has to make the most of it.'

'Oh no, Brendan is very good to her,' I say, reciting Clare's mantra. 'She's always telling me how good he is, buying her nice things and everything.'

Jim quirks his eyebrows. 'Yeah, when he's home. Sure that guy is always away on business trips.'

'I know, but he buys her all sorts of lovely stuff when he comes back.'

'He buys her,' Jim says patiently, as if I'm thick. 'Jesus, the man has it made – a woman looking after his house, being there for him while he gallivants all over the place. The only reason Clare sticks this job is because it gets her out of the house. And she earns her own few bob.' He ruffles my hair. 'Jesus, Luce, you're a big innocent, aren't you?'

Innocent? Me? My mother would love that.

'Drink?' Jim asks.

'Double vodka,' Clare calls out. 'Neat.'

I try to ignore her snuggling up to Doug, who doesn't seem to know where to put his hands.

'I'll have one of those too,' I tell Jim.

So we all have one.

By midnight, Clare is conked out on the seat. As the barman calls last orders, Jim pulls her to standing.

'Uggghhhh.'

Jim grins. 'She's going to be a sore girl in the morning. I'll get her home.'

'You sure?' Doug asks. 'She lives near me, I can share a taxi with her if you want.'

Jim waves him away. 'You won't get out of that taxi alive,

216

Doug. Naw, this night was your idea — you make the most of it.'

Doug grins. 'Well, only if Lucy wants to. I can hardly party on my own.' He turns to me and shrugs.

'I'm on a day off too.' I smile broadly. 'So lead on, boss, where are we going now?'

And even though I know I shouldn't, part of me is celebrating the fact that it's just the two of us.

Like a couple.

32

THE NIGHTCLUB ISN'T what we expected. It's almost too cool, with the obligatory hard chairs, expensive drinks and crap music. The DJ, who's meant to be someone famous, has a haircut that would rival the Empire State Building for height. He's doing really fancy stuff with the vinyl in his booth – throwing it and spinning it and, unfortunately, playing it.

Some people are dancing; Doug reckons that they must be on drugs. They seem to have their own private rhythm as there is no way they are dancing in time to the song – if that's what you can call the pumping, pounding music.

'The last time I heard music like that, me washing machine broke down,' Doug says in a cute bewildered drunken voice.

I splutter my mouthful of Guinness all over him. All over his nice purple shirt. 'Sorry!' Just as well I'm drunk too or I'd be mortified.

'It's OK – I know I'm a very funny guy.' He pulls his dripping shirt away from his body and shakes it.

'I'll pay to get it cleaned.'

'No worries.' He stares about. 'It is totally awful in here, isn't it? Sorry for bringing you – I just kept hearing loads of good stuff about this place.'

'Yeah, me too. Apparently it's the latest celeb hangout.'

'They probably have their own private bar somewhere.'

Doug scans the room and elbows me gently. 'You're a star now – you should ask.'

'Get lost. What would I say?'

Doug pretends to think. 'You could say' – he does a woeful imitation of my voice, which makes me giggle – '"Hi, I'm currently starring in the new ad for condoms and I'm finding my fans a little too excitable."'

'Yeah – they keep coming on to me.'

'And it's all getting really messy.'

'Ugh! Aw, God – stop!'

Doug laughs. 'You did ask.'

'I did,' I agree and we clink our glasses together and our eyes meet and we both turn away I turn away because I'm afraid he'll see that I'm thinking very impure thoughts. And I shouldn't be – he's my boss. He's got Guinness stains all over his shirt and his hair is rumpled. He even has his puffed jacket with him. I concentrate on the jacket to quell my fantasies.

'If you get really famous,' Doug asks, pulling his leg up on to the seat as he angles his body towards me, 'what's the first thing you'd do?'

'I'm not going to get really famous,' I scoff, only half meaning it. Ever since I signed my very first autograph, six hours ago, I've been thinking about it in between thinking about what Doug would look like completely naked.

'But if you did?' he says, pinning me with his gaze. He's madly drunk and it suits him.

'Mmmm. If I did' – I sigh deeply – 'I'd be an ambassador for world peace.'

'Impressive,' he says mock-seriously. 'So you'd leave work.'

'Well, I guess I'd have to,' I say back, equally seriously. 'World peace is a big issue, you know. Can't be solved sitting in your surgery.'

'I'd miss you.'

'Awww. Tell you what – I'd call in to see you and maybe, if I've loads of money, I'd get caterers to cook you a decent meal every day so that you wouldn't eat the crap you're eating now.'

He puts his hand on his heart. 'I'm touched.'

'In the head.'

'Hey – I'm your boss.'

'So?' I grin.

'Well, you should be licking up to me, not insulting me.'

Licking him, more like. 'Sorry, not in my job description.'

He shakes his head. 'I slipped up badly there, so.' He points at my glass. 'Another?'

The DJ puts on a horrendous track – it sounds like a serial killer busy at work. 'Uh, nope. I think I'll head.' I should head off before I ravish him . . . It suddenly dawns on me that we've been flirting. Well, I have. I've been playing with my hair, lightly touching him and generally doing a subtle version of what Claire was doing earlier. And while I'm drunk, I'm not *that* drunk. 'Can't take the music any more.'

'Great.' Doug pulls on his jacket, fighting with the sleeves. 'I was hoping you'd say that.' And even though it's beige and puffy, my thoughts just go, Cor! 'I'll walk you to a taxi.'

Christmas in Dublin and it's impossible to get a taxi. Doug offers to walk me home. The cold night air seems to have sobered us both a bit.

'But it's miles!'

'We'll be hours waiting for a taxi, Lucy.'

I don't want to tell him that my shoes will cripple me and that my skirt, which is already stretched to breaking point, is not a walking skirt. And that I'm feeling all light-headed and I don't know if I'll be able to walk in a straight line. So I link his arm in mine. 'Right,' I say, 'let's go.'

Ten minutes later, I can endure the pain no longer. I warn Doug in advance that I'm going to take off my shoes. Bending down in a tight skirt to remove shoes when your head is spinning is no joke. It's funny and it makes me laugh but it's no joke. I suddenly look about three foot high. My calves, which had been long and slender, are now all wobbly. And worse than that, now Doug can see me for the dumpy midget I am.

'Why don't you pull up your skirt?' Doug suggests as I restart my waddling. 'It's tight at the end, isn't it? It must be hell to walk in.'

I had thought of it but rejected it. Wobbly calves are one thing but fat thighs are another. 'No, it's fine,' I lie.

Doug looks doubtful. 'If you're sure.'

'You only want to see my legs.'

'I most certainly do,' Doug agrees mock-sombrely.

I giggle. 'It might put you off the chips you're planning on buying me.'

'I'll buy you double chips if you show me those legs.'

'Throw in a sausage and we've a deal.'

'Done.'

So I pull up my skirt and Doug tells me that my legs are on a par with any thoroughbred dog's legs – which apparently is a compliment.

We spy a chipper on the other side of the road. Doug attempts to pull me across.

'There are cars coming.' I don't know why I'm laughing. 'I most certainly do not plan on getting knocked down for a double bag of chips and a sausage.'

'No probs.' Doug lets go of my hand and straightens himself up. Then, to my horror, he boldly walks straight out into the road.

'Doug!'

221

I watch through a drunken fug as Doug puts up his hand and cars shriek to a halt. Horns blast and Doug remains standing there, swaying slightly. Then he yells, 'Come on, Lucc, I've stopped all the traffic just for you!'

Someone laughs. Someone else calls him a 'fucking eejit'. It's kinda surreal as I walk over the road to join him. 'Come on, you idiot.' I half laugh, dragging him out of the way of the irate motorists. 'You could have been killed.' It's the kind of thing Jason would have done and it turns me on and frightens me all at the same time. 'You could have been killed,' I say again.

He smiles down on me. 'Worth it.' I blush before he adds, 'They do nice chips here.' Then he buys me chips and sausages and we eat them sitting on a wall, his leg brushing my leg.

After a while we start walking again and it's not pretty. I'm lucky that at home I rarely wear shoes. My feet are tough – covered in hard bits of unattractive skin – but after a while even they start to hurt. Doug props me up. We lurch along and it's lovely, his arm about my waist, my arm holding on to him. The lovely spicy aftershave smell of him. The boozy stench of his shirt. His closeness. His heat.

I pull myself together. He's my boss. He's a vet and he usually smells of animals. Worst of all, he has a Puffa jacket. Well, I have the jacket now. In another grand drunken gesture, he's draped it over my shoulders to keep me warm.

'Another mile left,' Doug says and his face is so close that I can feel his breath wafting across my face.

'How'll you get home?'

'I'll walk.'

'You can stay in my place if you like,' I offer, not wanting him to go. 'There's a sofa bed I can get out for you. Save you heading home in the dark.'

'I'll be all right.' He hoists himself up and staggers a little. 'I'm a big lad.'

I'm sure he is. 'If you're sure.'

He says nothing more but I fancy his grip is tighter on me or maybe it's because I've pushed myself closer to him. Anyway, it's a God-awful turn-on so I stay exactly where I am and enjoy the feel of his fingers pressed into my waist.

Despite the pain and the cold and the long walk, I'm sorry to get home. Doug walks me to my front door and removes his jacket from my shoulders. I feel his fingers brushing my skin and I shiver.

'Cold?'

'Yep.' I smile up at him. He's totally sexy. Totally irresistible now that he's leaving. I want him to stay – just to look at him. 'You can order a taxi from here,' I suggest, my eyelids fluttering of their own accord. 'We could wait until it arrives and you could have a few more drinks.'

'Are you not wrecked?' He looks at my tattered stockings. 'Don't you just want to get to bed?'

With you, I do.

'Nope.' I quash my thoughts. 'Come on in.' I take hold of his arm and the fantasy starts again. 'It's my Christmas party and I'll stay up if I want to.'

'What about Fáinne?'

'At my mother's – we have the house to ourselves.'

He doesn't say another word as I pull him inside.

He rings a taxi and they tell him that it'll take ninety minutes at least. I persuade him that that's fine as I pour us both some wine. Then we sit, him in a chair and me on the sofa. I raise my glass. 'It was a great night, Doug, ta.'

'No probs. Hopefully Clare will think the same when she wakes up tomorrow.'

We both laugh.

223

'She mightn't remember it,' I suggest, grinning.

'I hope she doesn't,' he says ruefully.

We laugh again, then there is silence. Not an uncomfortable silence, just sort of nice. We both sit back and drink our wine and smile at each other. I feel that I might fall asleep. I pull my feet up on to the sofa and tuck them under me. He runs his hand through his already mussed hair and gives me a lazy smile. 'It's nice in this room,' he says. 'Your house is nice.'

His voice sounds very far away.

'Me and Fáinne picked out the colours.' I look at the warm terracotta and cream walls. 'And Gray painted them and Maddie bought all the cushions.'

'Maddie?'

'A mate of mine – she's Fáinne's godmother. I know her and Gray from college.'

'You and Fáinne should come and do up my place sometime, it's awful.' He sighs glumly. 'Word of advice: red and green are shit together.'

'Red and green?' I look in disbelief at him. 'You never did.'

'My two favourite colours,' he says dolefully. 'But shite together.'

'And was there no woman in your life to help you along?'

'Me ma tried but she likes whites and I don't. Lots of rows – not worth it.'

'And no girlfriend?'

'Nope.' A nonchalant shrug. 'I'm not much good at all that stuff anyway – I can't find a girl into football or into flea-ridden animals or into me, come to that.'

'Awww, how sad.'

'Which is why' – Doug reaches across and grabs the wine bottle – 'I'm having another drink. Cheers.'

'Cheers!' I watch him and can't help smiling. He's so attractive with that lazy drunken grin on his face. With his purple shirt all creased. 'For a vet you're pretty useless at everything, aren't you?'

He looks puzzled. 'Are vets *supposed* to be good at everything?'

'I dunno but you seem to be a disaster – you eat *total* shite, your house is red and green, your love life is crap and you have no fashion sense.' Shit! I clamp my mouth shut and hope what I said hasn't registered.

'Fashion sense?'

'Forget it.' I indicate the wine. 'More?'

'I can't forget that.' He widens his eyes, offended. 'What's wrong with my fashion sense? Look at this cool shirt.' He makes a grab for his 'cool' shirt and shakes it. 'I got that yesterday and the girl in the shop said it was nice.'

'The shirt *is* nice,' I say. 'Very nice. More wine?'

'So what isn't nice?'

'Nothing. You're gorgeous, Doug. Totally a babe.' I mean it too, I realise suddenly.

He slowly looks down at himself. 'Is it my shoes?'

'No!'

'The trousers – is it them?'

'They're fine.'

'Well, it's not my jacket – that was expensive.'

I don't answer.

He looks at me. 'It's not my jacket,' he states again.

I shrug. 'If you say so.'

'You *hate* my jacket?' He's genuinely stunned. 'What's wrong with my jacket?'

'It's a Puffa jacket.'

'Yeah.'

'Doug.' I lean towards him. I know I'm drunk. I'm loving

being drunk. 'Puffa jackets are for scangers. You are not a scanger. Neither are you fifteen.' I jab my finger at the jacket. 'Your jacket is awful. I hate it. It ruins what is a perfectly gorgeous guy.' I gulp. 'It ruins what is' – my semi-sober mind struggles to say what I want to say – 'a gorgeous guy's clothes. Sorry, gorgeous clothes on a guy. That's it.' I blush madly and gulp again.

He looks wounded. 'Well, I'm hurt.'

'The truth hurts,' I admit.

He seems to be thinking. Finally he says, 'So you think it would be good if I get rid of the jacket?'

'You haven't got a girlfriend. You have a Puffa jacket – make the connection.'

'That was an expensive jacket.'

'That was an expensive *mistake*.'

From outside there is the blare of a taxi horn. My heart plummets.

'Awww, gotta go.' Doug gets unsteadily to his feet and rather self-consciously makes an attempt to pull on his jacket. 'Sorry for offending you,' he says.

'Go on.' I stand up too and try to help him. We're almost body to body. I shove him gently. 'Get that awful thing outa here.'

I think I say it in an affectionate way. Anyway, whatever way I say it, he pauses, his arm half in, half out of his jacket. He smiles at me and I swallow hard at the look in his eyes. The taxi horn blares again.

Doug's grin fades slightly from his face. He bites his lip. 'You look good tonight, Lucy, you know that?'

My legs turn to jelly.

He grins wryly. 'All that red on you – very nice.' He sways a bit. 'And your hair – very nice.' His fingers touch my face. 'And the way you smile – very nice.'

The touch does it. I move my face up towards his. My lips brush his. I inhale his scent. I pull away slightly and he looks questioningly at me. Then he lowers his mouth to mine and I tangle my fingers in his hair. In answer, he grabs me about the waist and moulds himself to me, his leg crossing over mine. He's got a huge erection and I gasp. 'Can't help it,' he gulps. 'I've been like that all night. Jesus, Lucy, you turn me on something rotten.'

It turns me on more, hearing him say that. 'Come on.' I pull his jacket back off him. The taxi blares again.

'God.' Doug sinks his head on to my shoulder. 'Just let me pay this guy off.'

I giggle as he stumbles towards the door. I hear him outside talking loudly with the taxi driver and my blood is pounding in my ears. I know I'm going to regret this but at that moment I don't care. It's as if it's all happening from far away or something. He comes back in and pauses in the doorway. 'Fecker wanted twenty euro for calling out.'

For some reason we both find this really funny. 'I love your laugh,' he says, walking towards me.

I don't answer.

He comes up beside me. Rubs his hands up and down my shoulders. His pupils are enormous – mind you, that's not the only thing. Erotically slowly, he bends his head to kiss me. And I taste him gently at first and then with a passion I didn't think I had. I love the strength of his arms about me. The way his fingers slide up my back. The kisses on my neck, his hands on the bare skin of my back. The way he groans. The look on his face.

Everything he does to me – I love.

And I discover that for a vet he's not crap at *everything*.

33

I'M AWOKEN BY sunlight pouring in through the window. Strong December sunlight that hurts my eyes. I go to turn over in the bed when I feel something heavy pressing me down. My head is aching and my stomach is rolling suspiciously. For one bizarre moment I think I'm having a heart attack. And then, like a door being unlocked in my brain, the floodwater of memory pours over me.

Doug and me on the floor.

Doug and me in the kitchen.

Dragging Doug up to the bedroom, his hands on my hips, his lips on my neck.

Holy Sweet Jesus, what have I done?

I lie there, frozen, afraid to wake him. What am I going to say? Thanks for the use of your body last night, I'm now a frustration-free zone. Bye now. See you in work. Oh God. Oh God.

To my horror, Doug's hand moves up to my stomach. His lovely fingers start tracing patterns on my skin. I lie, staring up at the ceiling, not wanting to respond.

'Morning,' Doug says. He hauls himself up and, cupping his chin in his palm, grins down into my face. 'That was the best Christmas party I was ever at.'

He doesn't look hung over. And his smile is working its magic on me but I can't succumb any more. It's not fair on either of us. 'I've to collect Fáinne and my car this morning,' I tell him as I push the bedcovers off me. Before realising that I'm starkers. So I do what they do in the films, I try and wrap the quilt around me, only it's heavy and awkward and I look stupid. So I abandon that and try to walk confidently to where my dressing gown is. My thighs wobble and I'm sure they look awful though not as awful as my greyish-white dressing gown. Still, I wrap it about myself and pull the belt really tight. Opening it will be like trying to get into Fort Knox. My head is pounding and I struggle to ask, 'Do you want breakfast?'

He sits up in the bed and my eyes are riveted by his six-pack chest. By his muscular arms. By his bloody gorgeous face.

'Nah. You'll do though.'

I gulp. 'Look, Doug—' I take a deep breath and try to sound reasonable – 'I don't know what came over me last night—'

'Me?'

'—but it was a mistake. I should never have slept with you.'

His grin fades but he doesn't take his eyes off me. Eventually, biting his lip, he says, 'That's bullshit. It was great and you know it was.'

'That's beside the point.' I shrug. 'The point is—'

'We were great together. You wanted me just as much as I wanted you.' A smile that curls lazily upwards. 'And I bet, right now, you still want me.'

'And that's why you're a vet and not a bookie.' I turn to leave.

He says nothing as I pull open the door.

I've poured myself some cereal but I can't face it. I hear Doug upstairs, presumably getting dressed. I wonder how

229

he'll get home – probably on the bus. I wonder who'll want to sit beside him, as he'll smell like a brewery. I stare into my bowl of flakes and tell myself that what I've done is for the best. I don't need a relationship right now – especially not with my boss – and while it will be awkward for a while, we're both adults: we'll get over it and move on. That's the only thing to do in bad circumstances: move on.

Why did I do it? Now, in the cold light of morning I just can't fathom what I was thinking. Me and Fáinne, we're a team. And I've Maddie and Gray if I need help. I've Mam and Dad. What's the point of complicating things? Jesus, what was I thinking? I don't hear Doug until he's at the kitchen doorway and only then because he coughs slightly.

He's fully dressed – Puffa jacket and everything. He looks so attractive with his dark stubble and huge hazel eyes. My heart skips a beat just looking at him and remembering the way I held him the night before. Something in me weakens slightly. Something tells me to go for it. See where it will lead. I feel sick again.

'I just want to let you know, Lucy,' he says, and there's nothing sexy about his cold tone, 'that I don't make a habit of one-night stands. I thought we had something and that's why I stayed last night. No other reason.'

I'm insulted. 'I'm not into one-night stands either.'

'Right.' He sounds as if he doesn't believe me. He shoves his hands into his pockets and turns to leave. 'See you Monday.'

'I'm not.' I stand up from the table, almost upending my chair. 'I was just a little drunk, that's all.' Shit, that makes me sound worse. 'You took advantage of that!'

The silence is terrible. I see his shoulders hunch before he deliberately relaxes them. Slowly, he turns to face me. He seems about to say something and then for some reason decides not to. 'See you Monday.'

And he's gone, with a slam of the door. And I'm left sitting in my sunny kitchen with my soggy flakes.

34

I^{T'S} ALL VERY awkward on Monday. I mean, there is no guidebook for dealing with guys you've had one-night stands with, is there? I reckon it'd sell loads, though I don't know how many women are as stupid as me. I'd need *The Guide to Having a One-nighter with your Boss and Still Remaining Friends.*

The whole weekend has been a bit of a blur, mainly because I was dreading the thought of Monday. I picked Fáinne up from my mam and dad Saturday afternoon and had to endure Mam looking meaningfully at Dad as if to say, 'She drinks too much, look, she's hung over.' Dad however jollied everyone along, which made Mam angry. Fáinne, oblivious to the tensions, had a great big hug for me, which sent my jarring head into orbit and eventually, after thanking them, we left.

'You drank too much last night, didn't you?' Fáinne said when we were driving away.

'No,' I lied gamely. 'I'm just tired.'

'You look sick,' she said.

'Well, I'm not,' I lied again.

Sunday was not as bad. Maddie rang to complain that she was puking in the morning and that Clive was driving her mad by reading out to her from 'Impending Fatherhood' books. He was telling her to eat dry toast and to stay in bed. 'It's like a bloody military operation having a baby in this house,' she grumbled as I laughed. I know she loves it.

When I'd been expecting Fáinne, all I'd had was my mother's hysterical rants about how I'd ruined my life and my father's opinion that everything happens for a reason. 'Yeah, the reason being that she's going to ruin her life,' Mam kept saying. I have to say, at the time, I tended towards my mother's point of view. Though, looking at Fáinne on Sunday afternoon as she headed out with Gray to a film, I'm glad I had her. I'm glad she's in my life.

So, back to Monday. I'm sitting here in my cubicle and it's lunchtime. I have two choices. I can go into the coffee room and talk normally to Doug or I can head down the road to the local bistro and get a sambo there. Doug and I haven't talked much all morning except about work. He looks a bit rough – I reckon he was on the batter the whole weekend.

He comes out of his surgery and, without looking at me, heads into the coffee room. God, I don't know what to do. Maybe I'll try the coffee room and see how it goes. It's not as if I can afford to be buying sambos every day anyway. I take a deep breath, flick my hair back confidently and with an assertiveness I most certainly do not feel, I walk into the coffee room too.

'Lucy.' He nods curtly at me. He pours some hot water into his mug. I notice that he only has his mug out. Huh – he must have thought I wasn't coming. I take down my mug and place it beside his one. He pours some hot water into it too.

'Ta,' I say. I spoon in some coffee, splash in some milk and sit down.

He sits down opposite me.

We nod at each other.

233

Silence.

He unwraps a chocolate bar while I unwrap my sambos. A vision of him naked flashes across my brain. I go red. I wonder if he sees me naked in his head. Oh God, this is a nightmare.

Then he says, and I think it's very rude, 'Sorry, you're sitting on my newspaper.' And I get up, hand it to him and he starts to read it.

I don't know what I expected him to do really. I suppose I deserve it. I mean, I technically did use him only I hadn't thought of it that way at the time. What way did I think of it, I wonder? I try to put myself back there and I realise that I wanted him. I really did. I fancied him, I suppose. And I suppose he fancied me, which is why he's probably a bit hurt.

I don't want to have hurt him.

'Doug?' I say.

'Yeah?' He doesn't lower the paper. He makes no attempt to look at me.

'About Friday,' I stammer out.

He stands up abruptly and folds his paper. 'Forget it,' he says. And he walks out.

I bloody wish we could.

The afternoon surgery is quite busy. Clare arrives late and makes no apologies. She slides into her seat, turns away from me and begins to use the phone. Then she starts a low urgent whispering into the receiver.

Great.

It's about four when a man enters. He's tall and bald and must be in his late fifties. He's vaguely familiar though I can't place him. 'Is Douglas Kelly in?' he rasps out. He's got a sort of intimidating presence about him that makes me wary.

234

'He's in surgery,' I answer. 'Do you want to wait? There's a bit of a queue though, I'm afraid.'

'So – he's doing well then?' the man says in this sneering type of way.

I shrug.

'Can you get him for me?' Pause. 'Now?'

'He's in surgery.' I keep my voice calm. Polite. Firm. This guy seems a bit of a looper.

'Now?' he says. He quirks an eyebrow.

'I'm afraid—'

'Excuse me, miss.' The man raps on the counter. 'Hello, you on the phone?'

Clare looks up. I realise with a shock that her eyes are red. I wonder if she's been crying. 'Yes?' Her voice is as snappy as ever though, and my fleeting sympathy disappears.

'Get your boss for me, will you?' He looks at his watch. 'I haven't all day.'

Clare is about to tell him the same story as I have but suddenly her eyes widen and she nods. 'Just a second.' Out she scurries.

The man turns to me. 'At least someone knows what side their bread is buttered.'

'I don't eat bread.' I can't help it – the words just pop out.

'Well, you might have to start,' the man says back. 'And you might have to forget about the butter.'

'Yeah. Right.' I roll my eyes. I make it sound as if he's a nutter – which he seems to be.

He's about to say something when Clare arrives back in the cubicle. 'Doug will be with you in five minutes,' she says. 'He says to go into the coffee room.'

'Fine.' The man comes behind our desk and in he goes to our coffee room.

'Rude bastard,' I hiss.

Clare tut-tuts. 'He owns this premises,' she says, 'so I hope you were nice to him.'

Oh fuck!

Doug is ages with the horrible man and by the time they finish up, the surgery is packed. Doug comes into the cubicle.

'What was all that about?' Clare asks.

Doug shakes his head. He looks even worse than he did at lunchtime. 'Nothing. Just send the next patient in, will you?'

I call out a name and a woman with a massive Alsatian goes off down the corridor with Doug. The Alsatian is whining and licking Doug's hand. The woman is whining too – she's complaining about how long she had to wait and I hear Doug telling her that he'll only charge her half.

'Jesus!' Clare hears him say it too. 'That man is hopeless. We can hardly pay the bills we're paying let alone have him letting people off money. I'm going to bill her for the whole lot.'

'You can't do that.'

'Watch me.'

'Did we pay the rent this month?'

Clare looks scornfully at me. 'Course I did. That's the main bill we have to pay.'

'Oh. I was just wondering if that's why that guy was in – that maybe we haven't paid.'

'Well, we did.'

But there is something up, I can feel it.

35

March 2nd
Didn't go into college today as I was feeling really sick this morning.
Felt OK in the afternoon though.

Jason rang to see how I was. I told him to call over but he wouldn't.
Gray was over but – story of my life – it was to see Tracy.

He never even asked how I was. He just said hello and then he and
Tracy went out.

March 7th
Tracy delighted with herself. Apparently she has been booked to do some
catwalk show that'll make her famous. All she can say is, 'God, Christy
Turlington made a fortune when she crossed over from face to catwalk.'

It means that Tracy will be moving to Europe again. For a long
time if all goes well. I wish I could move away.

Gray arrives with a big bunch of flowers to celebrate. She's all over
him. When I'm in the room with them, she snuggles up to him and
kisses him on the cheek.

Gray asked me if I'd heard from Jason. Weird. I said, yeah, he
rang me.

More than he did when he missed our match last night, Gray said
crossly.

March 10th
Went into college for the first time in a week today. Still felt rotten but

if I miss any more lectures I'll fail my second year for sure. Maddie gave me all her notes and then asked if I'd heard from Jason. I told her that Gray had asked me that too. I told her that he'd rung me a few times to ask how I was.

She nodded. Then said that Jason had been out all week too. That Gray and the football team were going mad with him – that they were thinking of getting rid of him. He'd missed two matches.

I don't think Gray would get rid of him.

March 13th
Went out with Dad for lunch today. I couldn't eat a thing; feeling sick. It's probably from listening to Tracy talking about her new modelling contract.

Dad asked us how Mam was. I don't think they've spoken to each other since last month. I said that Mam was fine.

When we got back, Mam asked us how Dad was. I said that he was fine. She sniffed and said something under her breath.

March 14th
Jason back in college. He looks rough – maybe he had my stomach bug too. Gray asked where the hell he had been and Jason said he'd been dead sick. Gray then said, in a really narky voice, that he should have at least rung Bill to say he was sick and to not let the team down.

Jason ignored him and took a sip of his coffee.

'You weren't too sick to ring Lucy,' Gray said, not letting go.

'Fuck off.' Jason pushed his coffee away and stood up. 'Fuck off, Gray.' He walked out of the canteen.

'Now look what you did,' I snapped at Gray.

He was going to say something back, but I told him to forget it and I went out after Jason.

Couldn't find him anywhere. I looked all around and it was at least thirty minutes later when I found him in the bar. 'Come join me, Luce.' He patted the seat beside him. 'Whatcha having?'

238

I didn't want anything really, but I didn't want to leave him there. So I sat beside him and he eventually persuaded me to get drunk with him.

After a bit, I asked why he hadn't rung the team. He shook his head. 'Forgot, that's all.'

'And are you sick now?' I asked, rubbing my finger along his lovely face.

'Not if you kiss it all better?'

So I did and we got thrown out of the bar for indecent behaviour.

March 19th

Brilliant news!!! Les has an audition for me. Some big movie. Says the studio asked for me when they saw my picture. Says it's a sure thing

Audition in the next few weeks.

Madly excited. Mam even rang Dad to tell him.

March 20th

I think I'm pregnant.

I remember that last entry as clear as if I'd done it yesterday. There's a big tear streak down the page.

I'd written down those four words and this tear had just splashed right on to the final 't' of pregnant.

I'd finally realised I was pregnant after I'd seen an ad for sanitary towels on the telly. I'd scoffed, wondering who'd be desperate enough to do an ad like that and then I realised that I hadn't had my period in weeks. Yep, it was irregular but this was at least four weeks late.

Looking back, I feel so sorry for the big innocent that I was. I want to hug my younger self and tell her that it's OK now. That things are fine now.

But some part of me wonders if it's true.

36

CHRISTMAS EVE. THINGS at work have slowed down which is good in one way and horrible in another. Good because I'm totally knackered and need the break and bad because Doug has no excuse to be shut up in his surgery all the time. All week, because it was busy, we've managed successfully to avoid any major contact with each other. At lunchtimes, after that disastrous attempt to have a civilised lunch together, I've closed up the clinic and headed down the road to the coffee shop. OK, it's costing me a few euro every day but it's better than trying to make small talk with a guy that spends his time glowering at me.

Clare hasn't noticed that we don't talk as much any more. She's too busy on the phone. I think something is up with her, but she's not the sort of woman you can ask. Right now, just an hour before we lock up for the Christmas break, there is no one in the waiting room and no one in with Doug. I just bet he's wandering around his smelly surgery, watching the clock and waiting to hear me close up so he can sneak out. In normal circumstances, I'd offer to make us both a cuppa. Or he'd come up behind me with his quiet footstep and make me jump. 'What sort of a receptionist are you,' he'd slag. 'Forcing me to make my own coffee.' And I'd joke that I'd have one as well and he'd bring it out to me with a couple of biscuits and we'd chat a bit before anyone else arrived. But now, that's all gone and I hate myself for ruining it. Because it is my fault. I used him and I shouldn't have.

I wonder if things will ever be the same; I fear that they won't. But the least I can do is act normally in the hope that maybe he will too.

I do miss him.

'Right.' My heart is hammering, but I know what I have to do to try and get things back on track. I make my way to his office and tap on his door.

'Come in.'

Doug looks up; he's playing a game on his Game Boy. 'Yeah?' Semi-scowl.

'Coffee?' Now I sound cross. I don't know why, maybe it's because I expected to find him pining away or something. Which is rotten of me, I know. He obviously hasn't missed my company *that* much.

He nods, not looking surprised or anything. I don't think he realises the sacrifice I've made by coming in. 'Yeah. Thanks.'

'Will I bring it in?' Bastard, bastard, bastard, my mind is hissing.

'Yeah. Thanks.' He turns his attention back to his screen and begins zapping stupid little computer men again.

I give into my pissed-offedness and slam the door. I reckon he should be grateful that I'm making the effort.

I make him a coffee with no sugar, which I know he'll hate, and give myself the last two chocolate biscuits. I can hear my mother's voice droning away in the back of my head: *It's no use making up if you're not sincere about it.* Huh, all the times Tracy said sorry and then she'd do horrible things to me again. Like the time she wore my new top and spilt coffee all over it and even though she said she'd replace it,

241

she didn't. Another time she wanted my favourite doll and I wouldn't let her have it and she pulled it off me and broke her head. I cried for days over that. I didn't even care that Mam made Tracy buy me a new one out of her savings. It just wasn't the same doll.

Well, I think as I place Doug's cup in front of him, we'll see if he thinks rotten sugarless lukewarm coffee is the same as nice sugary hot coffee.

'Oh, by the way,' Doug says, startling me. 'This is for you.' He reaches into a plastic bag and pulls out a bottle of wine. 'Here. Happy Christmas.'

I'm immediately gobsmacked and guilty and embarrassed. 'For me?'

'Yeah.' He still looks hostile. 'I got one for Clare too. Bosses do that, don't they – give something to their staff at Christmas.'

I'm hurt at the way he classes me in with Clare. I mean, I don't know what I want him to do but what he's just done hurts.

I reach out to take the wine from him and for the first time since that awful day in my house, we look at each other. And to my horror, I feel a flush creeping up my neck and covering my face. And my heart starts speeding up and I feel attracted to him all over again. 'Doug,' I say, 'I—'

'The wine?' He holds it out to me.

'Oh, yeah. Thanks.' I take it and pretend to examine it. 'Thanks.'

'No bother. Thanks for the coffee.'

'Right.' For some reason I want him to say more, but he doesn't. He takes a sip of the coffee and winces and I feel horrible again. I stand for a bit, like a spare, before deciding to leave.

242

Outside, the bell goes as someone comes in.

'To work!' Doug half smiles and I gulp.

Jesus, he's so attractive.

It's Maddie. She shakes her head as I emerge from the office. 'Jesus, the service in this place is terrible.' She grins. 'Keeping a patient waiting.'

'Ha. Ha.' I stash the wine under the counter and grin back. 'So, what brings you here – besides the fact that as a teacher you have sinfully long bloody holidays?'

'I only got my holidays yesterday,' she says, leaning across the counter. 'And about time too. The kids were hyper. I'm here with news and I knew you were off early so I said I'd pop in and wait.'

'What sort of news?'

'I bring tidings of great joy.' She spreads her arms wide and with the tassels on the end of her coat she looks like a huge angel.

'You're going to have a baby and he'll be born in a manger?' I deadpan.

She smirks. 'You already know that. And nope, the Coombe was my first choice.'

'Lucy, who—?' Doug comes into my cubicle, obviously wondering what the delay is.

'No one,' I say hurriedly. 'This is Maddie, a mate of mine.' I wish he'd stayed in his room, as Maddie is being very childish and whispering 'cor' and 'wow' under her breath. I could kill her sometimes.

'Oh, right.' Doug smiles briefly at Maddie, then looks at his watch. 'You might as well head now, if you want. I'll lock up – I don't think we'll have anyone else in.'

'Sure?'

'Uh-huh.' He nods to both of us and leaves.

243

'Well.' Maddie licks her lips and wriggles her hips. 'I know I'm getting a new dog now.'

I grin. 'You and half the teenage population of Yellow Halls.' I shove on my coat and pull my scarf around my neck. Picking up my bag and my bottle of wine I yell out a 'goodbye' and a 'Happy Christmas' to Doug.

He doesn't reply.

Maddie drags me into a pub, forces me to sit by the fire asks me what I want to drink.

'Water. Still.'

'You have to have something else,' she exclaims. Then adds ominously, 'You'll need it.'

I don't like the sound of that. For some reason I thought her news referred to her and her wedding, not to me. 'Is your news about me?'

'Drink?'

'I'm driving. I've to go into town this afternoon to pick up a Bratz Supervan for Fáinne, and then I've to pick Fáinne up from my mother's, so nope: I'll just have water.'

Maddie leaves and I gaze around. I love pubs. I love the smell of booze in them, the semi-darkness and warmth, the quiet of the early afternoon with December sunlight filtering through the stained-glass windows. The clink of glasses and the low murmur of conversation. I could sit in that sort of a pub all day.

Maddie brings back the water and an orange for herself. 'Food?' she asks. 'My treat?'

'Naw, I'm fine.'

'Well, I'm not. I'm starving and when I'm not starving, I'm puking.' She gets up again and arrives back down with a plate of chips and three massive sausages.

'Gorgeous.' And the smell tempts me and I start to pick at her chips.

'Well, my news,' Maddie says.

'Yeah?' I take the biggest chip off her plate and hope she doesn't notice.

'Hey, I was saving that one for last, you bitch!' We giggle, then she goes all serious again. 'Clive got a call from the *Dingle Bugle*.'

I can't even get the word 'what' out.

Maddie rushes on. 'Not from Jason,' she says swiftly, 'but from the editor. They want to do a story on you – on why you want to meet him again.'

'A story on me?'

'Uh-huh.'

'Jesus.'

Maddie takes a sip of her orange and studies me. 'Well?'

'I don't think I could do that, Madd,' I say slowly. 'I just don't think I could tell everyone that he's the father of . . . Nah, I couldn't, Maddie.'

'Clive says you can avoid that.' Maddie puts down her drink and leans across to me. 'He says just to say that me, you, Gray and Jace were good friends in college, that we had a disagreement and that we'd like to meet up again. We can say that he let Gray down over a match, which is true.' She pauses and her cool grey eyes study me. 'Clive reckons with a story you've a great chance of tracing him,' she continues slowly. 'It all depends on how much you want it to happen.'

How much did I want it? Did I want everyone to know about me? OK, it was just the *Dingle Bugle* but still . . .

'Well?' Maddie asks. 'Do you want it *that* much?'

I wanted it because Fáinne wanted it. Only last night she'd asked me if her daddy would be around for Christmas and I'd told her that I didn't think so. 'But you've Nana and Granddad and me,' I'd replied.

'And Mona Lisa,' she said.

'You don't have to do this,' Maddie goes on. 'We can find other ways of tracing him. It's just that it's cheap – no, free and—'

'No. No. It's a great idea.' I wish my water was whiskey as I take a good slug of it. 'I'll do it. I just don't want Fáinne involved.'

Maddie looks at me doubtfully. 'Are you sure about this?'

'No.' I giggle weakly.

'Then don't do it.'

'I have to.' And that, some part of me acknowledges, is true. 'I really think I have to, Maddie.'

We spend longer in the pub than we should have. Maddie quizzes me on Doug. And though she's my best friend in the world, I don't tell her that I slept with him. I don't tell her because she wouldn't have seen any reason for me not to go out with him and she would nag me constantly about it. Or else she would have told me that unless I had plans for him, I was stupid to use and abuse my boss and I already know that so I don't need a lecture. Instead I let her call him a babe and listen to her expound her theory of how men are always attracted to their secretaries cum receptionists and of how maybe we just might get it together.

'I don't want to get it together,' I say eventually, stopping her mid-flow. 'But what I do need to get is a Bratz van, so I'll say bye, have a good one and see you Stephen's Day – right?' I pick my jacket up from the chair and pull it on, ignoring her startled expression at my swift departure. It's after two and traffic will be mental. 'Hope you get something nice in your stocking.'

'That's not where I'm planning to get anything,' she shouts out as I leave. 'Higher up now, that would be a pleasure.'

246

'Too much information,' I call back.

Someone laughs.

Town is crazy. I pick up the Supervan, which is even bigger than I remember, and am carting it through the streets when I see a familiar figure heading into Roches Stores. I'm tempted to walk on and pretend that I haven't seen him – after all, I've the present to stash away and Fáinne to pick up – but something makes me pause. Maybe it's the slump of his shoulders or the fact that it's the first time I've ever seen him without Paddy. He looks incomplete somehow.

'Mr Devlin,' I call, following him into the shop. He turns. 'Hi? Long time no see.'

It takes a couple of moments for him to recognise me. It's probably the first time he's seen me without a desk in front of me. 'Oh, Lucy.' He smiles, a little guiltily, I think. 'How's things? I suppose I should wish you a Happy Christmas.'

'The same to you,' I say back, wondering what the hell I'm meant to do now. I shift the box to my other hand. 'How's things yourself?'

'Oh, grand.' He nods. 'Just, eh, having a little wander around.' We both look about – it's the women's lingerie section. 'Well, obviously not in here,' he mutters. 'I'm just on my way somewhere to wander about.'

'Oh.' I smile awkwardly. He smiles awkwardly back. 'And Paddy,' I blurt out, seizing on the one thing we have in common, 'how is she?'

It's the wrong thing to say because his smile slips and his gaze shifts from my face to somewhere over my shoulder. 'Fine,' he mutters, fingering the sleeves of his overlarge coat. I don't know why he doesn't invest in new clothes; rumour has it the man is loaded, though I seriously doubt it. But

247

even the modest money he has would surely stretch to a proper coat.

'I thought Doug told me she was sick?' I feign confusion.

'She's fine,' he snaps. 'I just didn't bring her into town today because, well, you know . . .' A pause. 'She's getting old now and she gets a little cranky in crowds.'

'Excuse me.' Someone pushes past us and grabs a pair of knickers. Mr D. stumbles.

'Hey,' I say, 'watch out!'

'Well, don't block up the place,' the teenager says cockily, waltzing off with her newly acquired G-string.

'Full of the Christmas spirit, ey?' I grin and to my horror, Mr D.'s eyes fill up. Then he blinks and looks about a bit and when he turns back to me, he's fine again.

'I can tell you something,' he says crossly. 'She'd never have done that if Paddy was here. Paddy would have snarled at her and frightened the life outa her. That's the problem with people, they've no respect unless you can threaten them.'

Paddy probably wouldn't have been allowed in the shop in the first place, I think. But I say instead, 'Forget her – little wagon.'

Mr D. tries to smile but it comes out all wobbly and crooked.

I gulp; I don't know what to say. I'm no good at comforting old men. So I do what I always do in a crisis – head for the drink. 'Do you want a cuppa?' I know I should be on my way to collect Fáinne but I can't leave the man. 'I don't know about you but I need one. Jesus, the weight of this thing is killing my arms.'

'Oh now, I'm very busy and—'

'You said you were only wandering around?'

'Well, that too. But I'm busy, see, and—'

'Well, right.' I dump the present down on the floor and take a deep breath. If he's not going to come for coffee with me, I decide to say what I'm going to say and to hell with the consequences. What can he do to me, anyway? 'Look, maybe it's not my business but I'm going to say what I have to say and maybe I shouldn't say it but anyway.'

'What?' He looks confused.

'Have you, you know, brought Paddy anywhere else?'

He jerks slightly. 'Do they sell fags in here? I was looking for—'

'Because if you haven't, you should and if you won't, then come back to us. We can get you the drugs for her.'

He opens and closes his mouth, looking as stunned as I feel. I realise that I've been half shouting with nerves and that people are looking at me. There's also this huge security guy making his way over. 'No selling drugs in here,' he yells and I look around. Drugs?

'You.' The security guy catches me by the arm. 'Out!'

'Ouch! Let me go!'

'You've the wrong idea,' Mr D. protests as I'm yanked from the shop. 'Here, Lucy, your present. You've the wrong idea,' he shouts again, running alongside me and Security Man.

'The number of bleeding times I've heard that,' Security Man says. He glares at me. 'Selling to an old man, you should be ashamed of yourself.'

'I was talking about his dog,' I protest as I'm flung forwards out of the door. More people look.

'Original,' Security Man scoffs.

'True,' I yell.

I find myself facing Mr D. He has slunk out behind the security man. 'Keep away from her,' the security man warns.

'Wanker,' I fume, mortified.

249

Mr D. says nothing and we both watch the guard march back into the shop.

'He was on the ball,' Mr D. says wryly.

I give a reluctant grin, though I'm still embarrassed and people who were in the shop are coming out and gazing at me. I pull my coat about myself for comfort and try to ignore their stares.

'Here.' Mr D. hands me Fáinne's present.

'Ta.' I take it from him.

'For your kid, ey?'

'Yep.'

He nods, shoving his hands into his deep coat pockets. 'Christmas is for kids all right. Must be nice to have them and see them enjoy things.'

'It is.' I nod too. 'What about you, do you have kids?'

'No. Paddy took the place of a kid for us, I guess. The wife adored her.' He bites his lip.

'So look after Paddy for her,' I say.

He winces. 'I try.'

'She's sick.'

He pats me on the arm. 'Enjoy the holiday.'

'I would if you'd consider what I asked.' I can't let it go. I hate the stupid dog but he doesn't and he seems so lonely and everything . . .

'I will.' A small smile. 'Safe home and stay away from them auld drugs.'

I laugh. I've said my piece, there's nothing else I can do. 'Happy Christmas.'

He waves his hand.

37

To MY HORROR, Fáinne wakes up at six o'clock on Christmas morning. She pads into my room and pulls gently on my hair. 'Mammy,' she whispers, 'time to get up. Come on down and we'll see if Santa came?'

Her voice quivers slightly. She's always scared that Santa will forget and though I tell her repeatedly that he never forgets good kids, she never really believes it. I was like that as a kid – I could never quite believe that I was good enough.

I drag my eyes open and look at her through half-slits. 'Gimme a second, Fáinne.' I pull myself up in bed and grope for my dressing gown. Fáinne has it in her hand already. She pulls my slippers out of the messy wardrobe and dances about from foot to foot until I'm ready. I try to inject some enthusiasm into my voice as I say, 'Right, let's go!' I follow blearily behind her, trying gamely to smile at her excitement. Truth is, I'm wrecked. I had horrible dreams all the previous night and a six o'clock start is not what I'd intended.

Fáinne pauses before she opens the dining-room door – that's where I put her presents every year – and takes a deep breath. 'Oooh, I hope he got me the Bratz van or castle or puppy,' she whispers as sort of a prayer.

'Only one way to find out.' I virtually shove her in the door, dying to see her happy face. Dying to know that at least I've done one thing to make her day.

'He did! He did!' she squeals and I laugh at her happiness and I laugh at my happiness.

I love Christmas morning.

Christmas Day is spent at my parents' house. Fáinne and I usually head over after midday and stay until eleven or so. This year, of course, Tracy will be there and my mother will be in her element. 'A family should be together at Christmas,' she maintains.

As I park in front of my parents' house, the smell of roasting spuds and vegetables seems to waft out from virtually every house on the road. Fáinne gets up on her tiptoes and inhales deeply. 'Mmmm.' I reckon the key to getting kids to eat well is to feed them the crap that I feed Fáinne. She absolutely adores any kind of vegetable now. Clutching her Bratz van and her Barbie make-up case tightly in her hand, she runs up to the front door and rings the bell.

'Happy Christmas!' my dad shouts as he opens the door. He enfolds Fáinne in a hug and kisses me on the cheek.

'Look what I got, Granddad,' Fáinne shouts, shoving her van halfway up his nose. 'See, it's a Bratz Supervan!'

'It'll suit you so, – ey?' My dad laughs and dodges a punch from her.

I go on into the kitchen. Mam is there, basting the turkey. She smiles at me. 'Happy Christmas.'

Tracy is languishing on a kitchen chair in a beautiful grey box jacket and tiny grey skirt. One fine leg is crossed over the other and she's looking at Mam with a sense of bewilderment. 'We could have gone out,' she says. 'I could have treated you, Mam.'

'I like to cook for my family,' Mam states with a trace of annoyance. 'It doesn't happen too often.'

Tracy rolls her eyes and grins at me. It's the only thing

we have in common, our inability to cook, and it's not something I'm particularly proud of. 'Happy Christmas, Luce,' she says.

I nod back. 'Same to you.' We don't hug; we never have. Instead, I sit at the table and wonder what to say.

Fáinne saves me by legging into the kitchen with her van and her make-up. 'See, I got make-up, just like you,' she tells Tracy proudly. Opening it up, she says, 'Will you make me up? Mammy never wears make-up and I think she'll make a mess of me.'

Tracy laughs and I smile, though I don't really want to.

Dinner is a huge affair and I eat enough to last me through until next Christmas. I also drink an enormous amount of wine. Tracy, I note with surprise, eats quite a bit too. She always had a small appetite from what I can remember and the fact that she's eating surprises me. Mam is delighted. She ladles food on to both our plates. What is it about mammies and feeding their kids?

'So.' Dad, flushed from the wine, leans back in his chair. He winks at me as he says, 'What will we do now, I wonder? We've eaten our food, had our dessert, drunk wine and Coke, pulled the crackers, what's left?'

We all look at Fáinne.

'Pres—' she says.

'Oh, I know,' Dad interrupts her as he jumps up and Fáinne follows him, squealing. 'Time for everyone to go home!'

'No!' Fáinne looks at me in a panic.

'Here's your coat, Lucy.' Dad pulls my coat from the jumble of stuff on the sofa. 'Thanks for coming.'

'But, Granddad,' Fáinne says, aghast, 'what about the presents?'

Dad stops. 'Presents?' he says. Puzzled.

'Yeah.' Fáinne giggles nervously. 'We got some for you and Nana and Mona Lisa and you have to give us some back. Remember we did it last year?'

Dad frowns. Honestly, I don't know who is the bigger kid, him or Fáinne. 'Dora?' He looks at my mother. 'Did we buy presents?'

Mam bites her lip. 'Presents? Why would we buy presents?'

'Because it's Christmas?' Fáinne says, though her voice is doubtful. She looks at me. 'We bought stuff for everyone, didn't we, Mam?'

'We did,' I assure her.

'So then.' Fáinne shrugs and glances at my dad. 'You have to too.'

'Do we?' Dad frowns and mutters and picks up a box from under the tree. 'Something like this, is that what you mean?'

'Yes!' Fáinne grabs it from him and squeals. 'Is this for me?'

Dad nods and we all laugh as she yanks the paper off. Honestly, she's spoilt rotten by them. They've got her a Bratz picnic table for outside her Supervan. I half wish that they'd bought her clothes but then looking at her grinning face as she goes all ga-ga over it, I remember being a kid myself and the crushing disappointment of a soft present. Mam and Dad give me a voucher for Liffey Valley. 'Wouldn't know what clothes to buy you,' Mam says as I open it. 'You're wearing strange stuff these days.' I've got my bustier and skirt on again.

I hand around our presents and then Tracy, grinning, presents Fáinne with an enormous box. 'For my favourite niece.'

The excitement over the picnic table is forgotten as Fáinne stares, wide-eyed, at the box. 'All for me?' she half whispers.

Tracy giggles. 'Every single bit of it.'

254

The box is huge. Bigger than the Bratz Supervan box. Mam and Dad are standing close together; Dad has his arm around Mam's waist and they're looking expectantly at Fáinne. Big smiles all around. I stare at the box, my heart crashing down to my bargain basement shoes, and watch as Fáinne begins to peel off the ten sheets of paper that must have been used to wrap it. Before it's even half unwrapped, I can feel the anger building inside me. I can't even smile at my daughter's excitement; instead, I dig my nails into my palms and will myself to stay quiet. Nausea claws at my belly. I want to cry; I want to shout. Instead, I say, in this weird calm voice that isn't mine, 'Fáinne, you'll have to give that present back. It's too much.'

Mam and Dad roll their eyes and Fáinne continues to tear paper away, jumping up and down and squeaking, 'It's a castle, oh, a Bratz castle.'

'She doesn't have to give it back.' Tracy laughs, waving me away.

They think I'm being polite. They're ignoring me and the way I feel. As bloody usual. 'I was not talking to you,' I snap at Tracy. 'Fáinne, leave it!'

Fáinne pauses uncertainly. 'But, Mammy—'

'No buts. It's too much. Tracy, I'm sure you'll get a refund on it.'

'Huh?' Tracy's perfectly arched eyebrows arch even higher. 'What?'

'If Santa wasn't able to bring it, then Santa didn't want her to have it!'

'You said Santa couldn't get it into his sleigh,' Fáinne said. 'But that doesn't matter now, Mona—'

'You are not having it,' I say through gritted teeth.

'I am. Mona Lisa gave it to me.'

'Tracy is her name and you are not!' I reach out and pull

her away. She starts to cry. 'And stop crying. You've had loads today.'

'You're upsetting her.' Dad crosses to me and attempts to take Fáinne away but I hold on tight. 'Come on now, Lucy, don't spoil the day for the child.'

'Huh – me? It's always me, isn't it? What did I do? I didn't try and upstage Santa, did I?' Even as I say it, I know I probably shouldn't, but I'm sick of it. I saved bloody hard to get Fáinne her present and now she probably won't even look at it. It hurts that I can't give her all she wants but at least I consoled myself with the notion that it would be character-building. 'Tracy can bring it back and get something else.'

'I wasn't trying to upstage Santa,' Tracy says and I hate her soft, calm voice. 'Fáinne told me the three things she wanted and then she told me that Santa couldn't fit the castle in his sleigh so I got it for her.'

'Yeah, Mammy.' Fáinne sniffs. 'That's all.'

'That is not all!' I'm good and angry now. I turn to Mam and Dad. 'It's bad enough when we were growing up that she took all I had – my mates, my toys, my boyfriends – but she is *not* going to buy my child.'

'That's ridiculous,' Mam says. 'Ridiculous.'

'Come on, missy, and let's see what's in the kitchen to eat.' Dad takes Fáinne from the room. I wasn't holding her any more because I've suddenly clenched my fists and turned on Mam.

'It's not ridiculous – you don't have a clue. You always sided with her anyway. Just because she made you look good, you always sided with her!'

'And that's ridiculous too!'

'It's not!'

'It is,' Tracy said and she sounds angry now. Two perfect patches of pink have appeared on her face. 'I am not trying

256

to buy Fáinne. I just thought that the castle would be a surprise, that's all.'

'Yeah – a better one than I was able to give her,' I hiss, because I don't want Fáinne hearing.

'Oh fuck off, Lucy. No matter what I do, you always see the worst side.'

'Oh – *is* there a good side?'

'You've always been jealous of me!'

'I wouldn't be jealous of you if you even had something I could be jealous about!'

'So, you're not jealous that I'm in a film, are you not?' she fires back.

'Oh yeah – playing a bimbo.'

'Well, it's better than being in a condom ad.'

Oh fuck.

'What?' Mam says.

I can't speak. My mouth opens but no sounds come out. 'A condom ad,' Tracy says and she reminds me of the Tracy of my youth. 'Didn't she tell you?' Big surprised voice. The first condom ad to air in the country and Lucy is doing it. The ads are quite sexy – all the lads on the film set want to meet up with her.' She looks at me and shrugs nonchalantly. 'Didn't you tell her?'

I want to kill her.

'Don't tell me you were ashamed to tell her?' Tracy opens her eyes wide. 'Whatever for?'

'Is this true?' Mam whispers.

'It must be,' I say with a confidence I do not feel. 'Tracy always tells the truth, doesn't she?' Then I do the big cowardly thing. I exit the room with Mam following me.

'She's advertising condoms,' she says to Dad, who is busy pouring Fáinne some Coke.

Dad sighs.

'Can I keep the castle?' Fáinne asks.

'No and we're going home. Get your hat and coat.'

'She's advertising condoms!'

'Fáinne. Home. Now.'

'But—'

'Now.'

'You don't have to go.' Dad looks from me to Mam to Tracy who has appeared in the doorway.

I glare at him. 'I do.'

'Come on, so.' Dad takes Fáinne gently and leads her from the room. 'Let's get all your things together and we'll talk to Mammy about the castle some other time – she's tired now.'

I'm about to reply that I'm not tired when he shoots me a look. My dad is a quiet man but you do not mess with him when he looks at you like that. Instead, I said, 'I'll wait outside.'

'You'll tell me about this ad first,' Mam says, following me to the door. 'What sort of an ad is it?'

'It's for condoms,' I fling back without looking at her. 'Ask Tracy – she'll fill you in.'

'It's Mona Lisa,' Tracy chirrups and I want to strangle her.

Once outside, I'm safe. Mam is not going to yell at me in the front garden. So I walk, shaking, to my car and open the door. Sitting inside, I flick on the radio and try to look as if I don't care. I want to get sick. I'm no good at rows.

Two minutes later Fáinne and Dad arrive. She slinks into the back seat after shooting me a glowering look. Dad puts her van and her make-up case and her other presents beside her on the seat. 'Tracy meant the best, you know,' he said. 'She was so excited about giving it to her.'

258

'I'll bet she was.' I fire the ignition. They can never ever see how Tracy buys people.

'It's not something to ruin the day over.'

Which shows that he did not understand one little bit.

'Bye, Dad.'

I watch him in my rear-view mirror as I drive off. He grows smaller and smaller and as we round the bend in the road, I see his shoulders slump as he goes to walk back inside.

Later that night, after Fáinne has sulked her way through the films, I put her to bed. I've tried to have fun with her, but she's being really stubborn. As she climbs into bed, she pulls up her duvet and scowls at me.

I switch on her night-light. 'Fáinne,' I say, 'look, about today—'

'Why don't you like Mona Lisa?' she fires at me.

I freeze. 'I do like her,' I answer. But I blush and my hand sort of hangs in mid-air.

'You don't. You're not nice to her and you never smile at her. And you call her by the wrong name all the time.'

'I *don't*.'

'Yes, you do. And she's really nice and I hate you because you don't like her!' She turns her back to me and I'm left staring down at a pink nightgown. I blink back sudden tears.

I can't say anything. I want to, but I can't. I know all kids say it but she's never said it to me before. I stand up, ruffle her hair and she pulls away. Then I head downstairs and pour myself an enormous glass of wine.

38

'AND IT'S NOT fair – Dad even rang me this morning and wondered if I was going to apologise.' I'm whispering because I don't want Fáinne to hear. 'It's the story of my life – only I thought that being out on my own I'd have left it all behind, but oh no—' I shake my head and Audrey squeals. She's French polishing my horrendous nails and I've just made her go all crooked.

'I'll get some remover,' she sighs, standing up and shooting a look at Gray.

We're at Gray's this year for St Stephen's Day. Normally Maddie or I have a little mini-Christmas for just the two of us as Gray is usually working, but this year he's wangled a free day and Audrey brought up a pile of food from her mother's home and reheated it and now, after dinner, we are sitting, glasses of wine in hand, and I'm having a moan. Fáinne is in the television room watching a movie. She has spent the whole day glowering at everyone and ignoring me. Maddie eventually asked what the matter was and it had come pouring out. Not that I wouldn't have told them anyway. In fact I was dying to. When I row with someone, I like to share the row. It makes me feel less worried about it.

Gray tops up my wine. Maddie takes another chocolate. Clive excuses himself and goes in to watch the movie with

Fáinne. Audrey arrives back and settles herself at my nails again. She's already done Maddie's and they look fab. 'Now,' she warns, 'don't move.'

I hold my hand out and she takes it in hers, then, her tongue sticking out the side of her mouth, she begins to paint.

'Wasn't it a mean thing to do?' I ask.

Silence.

'I mean, trying to upstage my present,' I clarify, just in case they think I mean the condom ad, which I guess was mean as well. Though not *as* bad and *maybe* I had asked for it. 'Wasn't it typical of her?'

Gray shrugs. 'Maybe she genuinely didn't mean it,' he offers.

'Oh, get lost.' I half laugh. 'Of *course* she did.'

'Why though?' Maddie says. 'Why would she do that?'

I stare at them. I cannot believe they are siding with my sister. 'Because that's the way she is.'

Silence.

'She just does things like that.'

'I thought she was very nice.' Audrey looks up from my nails. 'I mean, she went out of her way to talk to me that day and she gave me tips on how to—'

'With all due respect, Audrey, you don't know my sister. You met her once, that's all. One meeting does not make you an expert.'

I'm sorry the minute the words are out because Audrey's face drops and her eyes fill up. Being cross with her is like kicking a puppy. And to be honest, it's not her I'm cross with, it's Maddie and Gray. It's just like all those years ago when Tracy went out with Gray. He tried to drag her along everywhere we went. And sided with her in all the rows. And now he was doing it again and he hadn't even *been* there.

'Audrey's entitled to her opinion just like you, Luce,' Gray snaps.

And now he's sided with Audrey.

Maddie is making a face at me.

My two mates and I'm losing them. One to marriage, one to a relationship. And where am I? Exactly where I've always been.

'Audrey doesn't know Tracy,' I fire back. I think I might cry so I get angry just to keep the tears away. 'Just because she reads about her in crappy magazines, she thinks she does.'

'My magazines aren't crappy,' Audrey gulps.

'No, they're not.' Gray frowns at me. 'Lucy's just having a bad day, that's all.'

'I'm not having a bad day,' I snap. 'I'm not. Your girlfriend is offering her opinion on something she knows nothing about.'

'I know your sister is a model and it's very stressful being a model and maybe that's why—'

'Audrey, you know *nothing* about modelling. There's a difference between wanting to do something and actually doing it – I mean, when have you ever modelled?'

Audrey blinks and then her face crumples up. She drops the nail varnish and it splatters all over the floor.

There is a horrible silence.

Gray puts his arm about Audrey and looks at me in a way that makes me want to curl up and die of shame.

'I think I'll go home,' I say meekly.

No one tells me to stay.

I stand up, my nails only half finished, and call Fáinne. Of course, she ignores me. I leave the kitchen and Maddie follows me into the hall and catches me just as I'm entering the television room. 'Lucy, calm down. Come back to the kitchen. Apologise to Audrey, for God's sake!'

'It was none of her business.'

'She was only offering her opinion, the same as us.'

262

'I didn't ask for her opinion – she's thick anyway.'

'Lucy!'

I can't help it – I'm gutted. My friends sided with Tracy, then with Audrey, and once again I'm left out in limbo. I notice that the nail varnish has come off all over my new jumper. *Great.* 'Fáinne, we have to go.'

'But it's the middle of the film.'

'Yeah and we have to go.'

'But I want—'

'I don't care what you want – home now.'

She flinches at my tone. *I* flinch at my tone. I don't think in her eight years I've ever spoken to her like that.

'I've that film on video,' Clive offers. 'I'll give it to your mammy the next time I see her and she'll let you watch it then.'

Fáinne pouts and guilt fills me up. I've ruined her Christmas with my grumping and I hadn't meant to. I want to be able to tell her to stay and watch the film but I can't face Gray and Audrey in the kitchen. I know I've been horrible, but for some stupid reason, I feel betrayed by him. No guy I've ever gone out with has been more important to me than him. Not that I'm in love with him or anything, it's just that our friendship means so much to me. And now he's chosen Audrey and though I know that it was out of order to snap at her, the memory of his choosing her hurts too much to apologise. Fáinne shoves on her coat and doesn't meet my eye. I pull my jacket on and wordlessly take her hand. 'Go and say goodbye to Gray,' I instruct.

'You should stay,' Maddie says again.

'Can't.'

'Won't,' Maddie snaps.

'Girls,' Clive says jokingly. He playfully pulls Maddie's hair and she catches his hand and I turn away.

263

Fáinne has returned from her goodbyes with a wrapped package. 'For me from Audrey and Gray,' she says, smiling.

'I hope you said thank you.'

'Uh-huh.'

'Right, let's go.'

And I leave without saying goodbye or thank you.

There is a picture of me on my First Communion day in the diary. I don't know what it's doing there but I take it out and stare at it and pieces of memory like shards of broken glass lodge in my head.

I'm wearing a beautiful dress, covered with beads and lace. In my hand is a small round bag and even though I've lost my two front teeth, I look surprisingly cute as I beam into the camera. That's, of course, if anyone is even going to look at the cute Communion girl, for beside her is a gangly girl, dressed in a purple flowery dress. And this gangly girl has the most amazing face. Dark long hair, silky smooth. Huge eyes and even teeth. It is her smile that the camera captures. Dazzling out of the faded picture twenty years later.

I remember that day as I look at the picture. How everyone admired my dress and Tracy's beauty.

39

MAM DOESN'T TALK to me as I drop Fáinne off the following day. Instead, she focuses all her attention on her granddaughter and ignores me. Dad offers me a tentative smile and walks me back out to my car. 'She was afraid you wouldn't bring her up any more,' he says as I climb inside. 'She's been on tenterhooks all morning.'

'I'm not that childish,' I tell him, though I'd been secretly worried in case she wouldn't take Fáinne any more. 'Anyway, Fáinne loves coming here, I couldn't deprive her of it.'

'She loved that present too,' Dad says carefully, 'and you deprived her of it.'

'For good reason.' I'm not going to listen to a lecture. I fire the engine.

'And when were you going to tell us about the ad?' he shouts over the noise.

I stare fixedly out of the window and when I see that he's not going to go I reluctantly turn the car off. 'Dunno. Maybe never.'

'Why?'

I almost laugh.

'Did you think we wouldn't find out? I saw the posters, you know. I knew for a while but I never said anything – I thought you were going to surprise us with it.'

'Surprise you? Yeah, I'd say it would have been a surprise all right.'

'You look fantastic in the pictures.' He reaches out and pats my hand. 'Fantastic.'

I'm not prepared for that. After the hell of the last two days, the compliment caresses me in a lovely gentle way. 'You think?' My voice breaks.

He nods. 'I think.'

'And Mam?' I sound pathetic.

'She hasn't seen them yet. The ad was on last night though.'

'And?'

He shrugs. 'You know your mother – nothing is ever good enough for you. She thinks you should be doing something better.'

Which was his way of saying that she hated the ad.

I turn away and instead try to focus on what Maddie and Gray had said about the ad, what he'd said, what Doug had said and even what Les had said, though once he was getting paid he wouldn't care if I starred in a porn movie. But it's the negative that catches me. I gulp out, 'Bye Dad.'

'Bye bye now,' he said, smiling at me. 'Take care, OK?'

Clare is busy opening up the surgery when I arrive. She always comes in the mornings between Christmas and New Year because we don't have afternoon or evening surgery so it can get quite busy. She's wearing a new jumper, really expensive mohair or cashmere or something. It's cream though and it doesn't suit her. 'Nice threads,' I lie gamely as I flick on the computer.

'Brendan bought it for me,' she says. 'It's typical him. Spending a fortune on me. I keep telling him to go easy but he says he can't. Says I'm worth it.' She looks at me. 'Did anyone buy you anything?'

'I got a Cartier watch from my millionaire boyfriend,' I deadpan. 'Cheapskate.'

Clare actually laughs. 'Oh,' she says then. 'I saw your ad on the telly on Christmas evening. Right bang in the middle of *Sleepless in Seattle*. I don't know why they have to advertise condoms on Christmas evening – but it was good.'

A compliment! Christ.

'I'd never have recognised you – you looked so well.'

Is that a compliment?

'Probably all those lenses they use. I mean, they can make anyone look good, can't they?'

Ugh. I ignore her. It's like my mother all over and I feel powerless to say anything back. Instead, I head into the kitchen to make some tea. 'Bitch, bitch, bitch,' I hiss as I stomp about the place.

'Coffee for me,' she calls out. 'Milk, no sugar.'

'Fucking arsenic would suit you better,' I mutter. As the kettle clicks off, I hear Doug arriving and asking Clare about her Christmas. She tells him it was fantastic. Only she says 'fannnntassssstic'.

'Lucy in?'

'She's making coffee.'

'Right so, I'll go in and put in my order. Can you come in too, Clare?'

'I'm on the counter.'

'Just keep the "closed" sign on for a while. I'm having a staff meeting.'

A staff meeting! Sounds serious. I wonder if he's going to say that he can't work with me any more or something, though he'd hardly announce it in front of Clare. Maybe we're getting a pay rise? That'd be good.

Doug and Clare come into the room. 'Staff meeting, Lucy,' Doug says abruptly to me. So, he's still annoyed then. He waits while I fill three mugs, handing one to Clare, one to him and I keep the biggest one for myself. I wrap my hands around it for comfort.

Doug sits down. We copy him.

'Declan McGrath is selling the premises,' he says, without any preamble.

'Declan McGrath?' I ask.

'The owner of this building,' Doug says. 'He offered it to me and Jim first but, well' – he shrugs – 'I don't know if we'll get a loan for it.'

I hold my mug tighter.

'And what will that mean for us?' Clare asks. She's gone pale.

Doug hesitates. 'Well . . . it means that whoever buys it will decide if we go or stay.' A pause. 'In all likelihood we'll have to go.'

Coffee slops out of my mug and on to my black trousers.

'I've spent the whole of Christmas trying to raise money to buy the place but no one wants to invest in a vet's practice. Especially not one like mine.'

'I told you to charge properly,' Clare snaps. 'If you charged properly you'd have been able to afford it.'

'It's not because of that,' he mumbles but it is partly true and we all know it. Doug is way too soft to be running a business.

'Are there no other premises we could go to?' I ask faintly. I can't believe that I might lose my job. What will I do for money?

He looks at me and shakes his head. 'None suitable. Anyway, we'd have to get planning permission for change of use and we'd need a loan to set it up and, to be honest, I don't have the money. Even if I remortgage my house, it won't cover it.'

268

'And our jobs?' My voice is shaking.

Doug looks hopelessly at me. 'You can look for another one, I don't mind. I'll give yez time off for interviews or whatever. In the meantime, I'm going to go to every bank in the city to beg for money. Jim is going to do the same.'

'How much is Declan looking for?' Clare asks.

Doug names a figure and we gasp. 'Property has shot up around here,' he says, 'and Declan is only doing what any businessman would do. I mean, even our rent is cheaper than it should be. If we even get to stay, it'll rise substantially. In fact, from next month, our rent is going up by a grand.'

Clare gasps.

'I'm sorry,' Doug says.

'It's not your fault.' I give him a sympathetic smile though I feel as if my world is falling apart. How will I ever get such a suitable job ever again?

'Yes it is,' Clare says. 'If he charged decent rates in the first place, we wouldn't be in this mess.'

Doug glares at her. 'If I only employed one receptionist I wouldn't be in this mess either. I took Lucy on because she needed work and she had a kid to support and I took you on because Lucy had to be out of here by six and you wanted to get out of your own house.'

Clare flinches. 'That's not—'

'Jim and I pay you both good wages, enough for three bloody receptionists. Don't tell me how to run my business, Clare.'

Her face reddens and half crumples and she flounces out of the room. 'Well, we might as well open up and see if we can earn some money.'

We hear her opening the door of the clinic and letting someone in. Doug and I sit in silence for a few moments.

Then, without looking at me, he stands up, dumps the

remainder of his coffee down the sink and heads to his surgery.

'No,' I hear a familiar voice shout, later on that morning, 'I want to talk to Lucy, not to you.'

'I am the senior receptionist,' Clare announces haughtily, 'so anything you have to say can be said to me.'

It's Mr D. At least I think it is. I poke my head out of the coffee room and catch a glimpse of a manky brown coat. 'Mr Devlin,' I say cheerily. 'How's things?'

'Lucy, hello.' He turns away from an enraged Clare and smiles at me. 'I, eh, was thinking this morning about our conversation on Christmas Eve and, well, I decided that maybe you were right.'

'Right about what?' Clare demands.

'Right about the fact that you are a nosey old bag,' Mr D. snaps.

I brace myself for the onslaught but Clare just turns away. That's not like her.

Weird.

I cross to the counter. 'So, Mr D., what can we do you for?'

'I asked to talk to you,' Mr D. mutters in an undertone. 'You're nicer than her.' Then, his voice becoming more inaudible, he says, 'I want to get those drugs for Paddy. She needs them.' He swallows and I know this is hard for him. He thumbs in the direction of his car. 'She's outside in my car if Doug will take a look at her.'

'Of course he will,' I say gently. 'You just sit tight and I'll let Doug know – we're not too busy today.'

'Fine. Fine, so.' He folds his coat under him and sits down, glaring slightly at Clare.

*

270

Doug is standing by his operating table with bank statements spread all around.

'Doug?'

He jumps guiltily.

'Mr D. is outside. He has Paddy in the car – he wants you to treat her.'

'You're joking?' For the first time since the party, he grins at me. 'Are you serious – he actually came back?'

'Uh-huh.'

'I didn't think . . .' He doesn't finish. He bounds out of the room and I follow him. A few minutes later, he comes back, cradling Paddy in his arms. He's talking softly to the dog and she's whimpering slightly. Mr D. trots behind them, trying to get a glimpse of his dog in Doug's arms. He's filling Doug in on her condition.

'I hate that man,' Clare says after them. 'He's dirty and smelly and an old Scrooge to boot.'

'That's no way to talk about your boss.'

Clare giggles a little hysterically. She looks completely different when she smiles.

I smile back. 'He's just worried about his dog. She's dying.'

Clare turns back to her papers. I don't know what she's doing but she seems to be fiddling about with loads of figures and stuff. Almost as if she senses my thoughts, she says, 'I'm trying to figure out a way that Doug can afford to buy the clinic.'

I don't reply. Doug had all Christmas to figure it out and he hadn't.

'I can't lose this job, Lucy.'

I freeze. She sounds as if she's going to cry. 'Clare, are you OK?'

'Fine.' Her back is to me but her shoulders heave a little.

'You'll get another one,' I say, a little desperately. 'Sure, you're free all the time – you can work any hours.' I stand, staring at her back, unable to move any closer. *Please God, don't let her be crying.*

'No,' she says and her voice is all wobbly. 'No. I can only work after six or during holidays.'

She wouldn't be telling me this if she didn't want me to ask. Much as I'm wary of her, I don't want her to cry. 'Why? Does Brendan not let you?'

She shakes her head.

'Why doesn't he let you?'

She's really crying now, big heavy sobs. Her head is in her arms. I cross to the door of the clinic and put up the 'closed' sign.

'Don't do that.' She is looking at me as big tracks of tears roll down her face. 'We need the business.'

I gulp out a laugh. She smiles too.

'What's wrong, Clare?' I don't feel nervous now. It's like my dad says, if someone is grumpy and miserable, make allowances for them; they've obviously got a reason. Unfortunately, I'm not much good at it unless I hear the reason. 'Come on, please stop. Do you want to go home?'

'God, no!' More sniffles. She wipes her nose with the back of her sleeve. 'I only work to get away from the place.'

I remember Jim saying something like that at the Christmas party. 'I thought you loved being at home.'

'Whatever gave you that idea?' More sobs.

'Well, you're always talking about Brendan.'

'He's never at home!'

I don't know what to do. I gawk at her.

'He's too busy so it's all up to me.'

She's not making any sense. 'What is?'

'Looking after his mother.'

'His mother?'

272

'She lives with us. And I have to mind her. She needs lots of care. Alzheimer's.'

'Oh.'

'She goes out and gets lost. She needs to be bathed and cleaned. She has to be fed. It's hard, Lucy.'

Whatever I'd expected it wasn't this. 'Yeah, it must be.' I wonder should I hug her?

'And I'm on my own and Brendan's sister comes in the evenings to help but she only comes 'cause I've the job, see. If I didn't have it, I'd never get out. Hasn't Doug told you this?'

'Nope.'

'I thought he told you everything.' She begins to fumble in her bag for a tissue before vigorously blowing her nose. 'You both seem really close.'

'He's my boss, same as he is yours. We're not close.'

'Oh.' She folds her tissue and drops it in the bin. 'Sorry for this. It's just – I can't take it any more. I'm so tired and everything and what with Brendan being so busy, away and all, he can never help.'

'It's *his* mother.'

'He's busy.' She sounds like herself again as she sticks up for her husband. 'He minds her holiday times – like today. He's minding her today.'

Tentatively, I pat her on the back. 'Look.' I attempt a smile. 'You can come around to me in the evenings if we lose our jobs. I'm sure your wages here won't be missed at home – they'll never know.'

She smiles.

'I mean it.'

'Thanks.' She gulps hard. 'Thanks, Lucy. Sorry for . . .' She shrugs and sniffs. 'All this.'

'No probs.' I give her back another pat. 'No probs.'

'Anyway.' She sniffs again and picks up her pen. 'Back to work, now, ey?'

After Mr D. leaves, Doug makes a point of thanking me for whatever it was I said to him. 'He told me he met you on Christmas Eve.'

'Yep.'

'Well, good work.' For the second time since Christmas, he smiles at me. 'You're good with people, you know that, Luce?'

It hits both of us at the same time. I wasn't so good with him, was I? We both flush and stumble out of each other's way.

The 'For Sale' sign goes up just as the clinic is closing. I find I can't look at it. Each hammer blow, as the sign is pounded into the ground, seems to make my heart heave. Doug, however, stands looking, his hands sunk deep into the pockets of his Puffa jacket. Clare is like me; she hurries past it and jumps into her car.

I decide not to tell anyone at home just yet. And just as I make that decision, the phone rings. It's Les. Apparently *Woman's Life* want to do a photo shoot.

Wow!

40

BECAUSE I'M ON a half-day, I head straight to Gray's place. I'm feeling good because of the photo shoot. Maybe I won't need to be worrying about a job. All I have to do now is apologise to Gray and Audrey and ring Maddie and my world will right itself again.

I hope Gray will be in and then again, I half hope I can get by with dropping a note through the door. I ring the bell and my heart jumps as I see his familiar outline in the hallway. But, then, when he answers the door, he's just Gray and I don't feel too bad at all. Apologising will be easy.

'Hiya, Gray.' I smile slightly. 'Is Audrey there?'

'Nope.' He's not smiling back. 'Come in.' He opens the door wider to let me through and I follow him into his kitchen. It's still a bit messy, with bottles and cans all over the place. Gray picks up a bag and begins shovelling rubbish into it. Normally, I'd offer to help, but something holds me back. 'She's gone to a casting though I don't think she'll get it. She was upset this morning.'

'Oh? Why?' I feel I'm being led blind into some horrible cul-de-sac.

'Why do you *think*?' Gray faces me and his eyes, normally full of laughter, are serious.

'It's hardly because of yesterday?' Jesus, she's even more sensitive than I thought.

'Yes, it is because of yesterday,' Gray snaps. He dumps his bag on the ground and glares incredulously at me. 'You were *horrible* to her, Lucy.'

'I only asked her what she knew about Tracy – that's not being horrible.'

'Yes it was. And the way you told her that she wasn't a model – that really hurt her. What if I said that you're not an actress because you get no parts – how would that make you feel, huh?'

I glare at him. 'That's different.'

'I don't think so.'

'Yeah, well, she's obviously got you brainwashed then.'

'Maybe she has but she's my girlfriend and I won't let you treat her like that, Lucy.'

'Oh *sorry*.' It comes out sounding really sarcastic. This is not the way to go but I can't help it. Again.

'Don't be such a bitch.' Gray takes a step towards me and I flinch at his angry look. 'It's about time you realised, Luce, that Audrey is my girlfriend and I like her a lot. No, actually, I *love* her. I'm crazy about her.' He gulps. 'And you seem to think that you can snap at me or snigger at her whenever you like. Just because we have been mates a long time, Luce, does not give you that right.'

'What? I don't—'

'You do.' He takes another step towards me and the anger is gone from his face, but it's been replaced by something else. I can't say what it is, passion or something. He jabs his finger towards me. 'You do it to Maddie too. You don't like Clive for some reason.'

'That's not true!' I go bright red. 'And this has nothing to do with Maddie and Clive!'

'Yes it has. And Maddie might put up with it but I won't. Audrey is funny and sweet and yeah, right, she's not clever like you but so what? I love her and there is no way I will let you talk to her the way you did yesterday.'

I can't say anything.

'And maybe you were pissed with Tracy, but don't take it out on us because we didn't agree with you. Audrey thinks you and Maddie are so cool and you treated her like shit.'

'I did not!'

'You ruined one relationship on me before and I will not let you ruin another.'

'I never did! You always went out with idiots, for God's sake.'

'Tracy wasn't an idiot.'

For a second I don't know whom he's talking about. Then I realise that he means my sister. 'Tracy?' I gasp. 'Sure she dumped you – I ruined nothing.'

'Yeah, she did. And do you know why? Because the way you treated us used to put me in bad form and eventually Tracy just got pissed off with me. I mean, every time we went out you sulked or shot horrible looks at us. And it upset me, Luce. It did. And I wouldn't mind, but you even had Jason at the time. But you wanted it all, didn't you, Luce? You wanted us all dancing attendance on you.'

I gawk at him.

'Well, newsflash: the world does not revolve around you.'

For a second I can't talk. I open and close my mouth like a twit. Then I spew out, 'I know it bloody well doesn't.'

'Really? So why do Maddie and I have to get dragged into your life's dramas? Why do we need to help you find Jason? He was a waster. He'll always be a waster. But you don't have enough guts to do it on your own, do you?'

'For God's sake!'

'And, Luce . . .' Gray's voice dips; he says quietly, 'I'm not giving up Audrey. Not for you or anyone else. But do you

277

know what, she's threatening to give me up because she doesn't want to come between me and my friends.'

'That's ridiculous. Jesus, it was only a stupid argument yesterday.'

'No, it wasn't. You were jealous, Luce. Jealous because I stuck up for Audrey instead of you.'

'I was not!' Angry maybe, I admit.

He ignores me and ploughs on, heaping insult upon insult. 'I'm not your property, Luce. You have to go out and find someone and stop clinging on to me and Maddie. Get a life, for—'

The patronising bastard. The absolute wanker. 'I don't cling on to anyone,' I spit, horrified that he would think so. 'And I definitely wouldn't cling on to a two-bit photographer.'

'And stop looking back and move on,' he continues as if I haven't spoken. 'We're not in college any more.'

I can't believe he's saying this stuff to me. He's my *friend*. Or rather I'd thought he was my friend. We've only ever had a big blow-up once before and that was when I stupidly chose Jason over him. But I learnt. And I never forgot it.

Ever.

'If you want Audrey, fine. I'm not forcing you to choose – she is. And you've made your choice. Bye.' I turn on my heel and walk, head high, back to the car. I hope he doesn't come after me.

I hope he does.

But he doesn't. As I drive off, I see him standing in his doorway looking after me. I rev up my car something rotten and tear up the street. When I get around the corner, I pull in and start to shake.

I shake so badly that I start to cry.

But I'm not crying over him. I'm not.

*

278

By the time Fáinne is tucked up safe in bed, I'm too scared to ring Maddie. I'm still shaking over the row with Gray. I don't know what I'll do if she eats me out of it too. I can't bear to hear how horrible someone else thinks I am. I drink a glass of wine, pick up the receiver, dial a couple of the numbers and then slam the phone back down. In the end however, at around eleven, she rings me. Or rather Clive does.

'Lucy, it's Clive.'

'Clive, hi?' I wonder if he's going to have a go at me for upsetting Maddie when she's pregnant.

'Hi,' Clive says again. 'Hope it's not too late.'

He doesn't *sound* cross. 'Nope.'

'It's about the paper, the *Bugle*. They want to interview you sometime this week – have your story out for New Year, as a sort of New Year Resolution search or something. Are you up for it?'

I could do it if Maddie came too, I know that. But I can't ask. Gray said I was being selfish by involving them. Maybe I am.

'Well?'

I hesitate slightly. 'Will I be on my own?'

'What?'

'Will Maddie be there?' Damn!

'Oh now.' Clive takes a sharp breath. 'She's pretty annoyed with you.'

'Is she?' My voice is small.

'Yeah. When you left Gray's party, she had to eat your share of cake and she's put on five pounds.'

I hear Maddie chortling in the background.

'He-lloo.' Maddie giggles into the phone. 'Don't mind him – I've only put on two pounds all Christmas. So, girlfriend, are you on?'

Her cheery voice makes me wish I was her. Stupid, I know.

'Yeah. Yeah, I am.' I pause. 'Sorry about yesterday, Madd.'

'Aw, forget it – you never should have left though, poor Audrey thinks it's her fault.'

'Well, Gray assured me when I went around there today that it *was* all my fault.'

'He didn't!'

'He's right though.'

'You were upset. Tracy always had that effect on you. Even when we were in college, you'd be perfectly reasonable until she showed up.'

'That's what Gray said too. In a more aggressive way.'

'Aw, he's just annoyed, he'll get over it.'

'I don't think so.'

'You worry too much. Give him time to calm down. I mean, Luce, you just left. He was so bloody proud of having a party in his place, so proud of Audrey, and you went and ruined it – could you not see that?'

'I didn't think I ruined it – I only left.'

'You ruined it,' she says firmly.

'Am I horrible?'

'What you did was a bit horrible, but you are funny and sweet and my best friend.'

I sniff. 'Thanks, Maddie.'

'Now don't be an eejit and start crying,' she admonishes cheerfully.

So I blurt out about my job and about how my mother was annoyed with me.

'Aw, it'll pass. My mother is always annoyed with me. She thinks the fact that I'm pregnant is horrific. She won't talk to Clive now. We think it's a laugh.'

If that was me, I'd never be able to laugh. Maddie is so chirpy and upbeat that I can only smile. 'So, will you come to the interview with me?'

280

'Yep. It's tomorrow afternoon, I think. You're on a half-day, aren't you?'

'Yep.'

'Clive says he'll ring you tomorrow about it.'

'OK, thanks. Bye.' I put down the phone, feeling a little better.

But later that night, after I've peeked in at Fáinne and I'm lying in my bed, I think about what Gray has said. His words bounce across the walls of my brain until they sort of taunt me.

It takes me ages to get to sleep.

281

41

April 1st

Good Friday. I wish it had been. Maddie met me for lunch in town as there was no college. Out of the blue, just as we'd sat down at a table, she asked me if I was OK. I don't know why she asked me – maybe it was because the smell of the coffee in the café had made me wince. She was telling me some story about a fight with her mother and I was doing a good job of nodding and saying 'yeah' every so often. Or I thought I was. Then she leaned in close and cupped her chin in the palm of her hand. 'Are you OK?'

At first I wasn't going to say it. It'd make it real then, see? But she looked so calm and comforting that I just blurted it out. 'I think I'm pregnant.'

Maddie spilled her Coke everywhere. All over her chips. But she ignored the fact that she was dripping wet, she just pushed me out the door of the café.

We didn't speak until we were sitting on the grass in St Stephen's Green. Maddie looked at me and said, 'What did you say?'

And I just said again, 'I think I'm pregnant.'

April 4th

I am pregnant. Maddie spent the last of her student grant on a testing kit. A little blue line told me what I already knew.

Both of us looked at it, then at each other. Then she said, 'Oh fuck,'

282

and I said, "That's what happened, OK." And we both started to giggle. Sort of hysterically, really.

Then we stopped and I looked down at my shoes and Maddie hugged me. I couldn't cry. I couldn't make myself cry. I was crying inside though.

April 6th
Have to tell Jason, Maddie says. She's being very sensible and assertive. You have to tell your folks.

Do I want an abortion, she wants to know.

I don't know what I want.

Had a drink or two.

April 7th
Tracy left today. I think she broke it off with Gray before she went because he wasn't at the airport. I'm glad she's gone. At least my friends are back to being mine. Audition for the film in a week. Les sent me part of the script today. It's about a girl who runs away from home and makes a fortune and comes back and rights wrongs. I reckon I can do it.

April 19th
Haven't gone into college in a few days. Maddie is doing my head in. Gray is doing my head in. He's missing Tracy. He's in a real bad mood with everyone because of it. And he gives out about Jason only to get at me.

And I tell him that I haven't seen Jason.

No one has seen Jason.

April 20th
My first film audition. It was so exciting. All I had to do was read a script to camera. The director told me I was a natural. Fingers crossed.

283

April 22nd

I got the audition! I didn't even have to go for a second one. I can't believe it. On a complete high.

   Mam and Dad thrilled. Dad even invited Mam out for a celebration dinner. She said 'no' but it's still promising.

42

'HEY.' THE REPORTER from the *Bugle* sits opposite me
and Maddie. 'You're the chick from the condom ad,
yeah?' He has a sort of mid-Atlantic drawl to his voice and
his lazy eyes light up approvingly.

'Chick?' Maddie cuts him dead.

He nods. 'Gal, woman, lady, whatever.' He turns to me.
'I love that ad. You especially.'

I know I shouldn't feel flattered, but I do. Or maybe I
should. I dunno. 'Thanks,' I mutter as if I'm used to male
adoration. 'So, can we get on with this interview?'

'Sure thing, yeah, yeah.' He takes out a dictaphone. 'D'ye
mind if I tape yez?'

'Yes,' I say.

'No,' Maddie says, eyeballing me firmly.

'No,' I say meekly.

As he interviews us, my nervousness increases as I'm forced
to lie. We stick to our story. Jason was a friend, we had a
row and we just want to meet him again.

'But why?' *Bugle* Man is not buying it. I feel a grudging
respect for him. 'Why bother? Sure, everyone loses friends
along the way; it's part of life, isn't it?'

'Well, eh—' I stare desperately at Maddie.

Maddie sits up straighter in her chair. Her pregnant size
makes her look imposing and authoritative. 'Maybe it's part

of *your* life,' she says, 'but Lucy and I, we don't like to part on rows with anyone.'

'No we don't,' I agree vigorously.

Bugle Man frowns. 'Nearly nine years ago and you want to meet him *now*?'

'Yes,' Maddie says as if there's nothing wrong with that.

Bugle Man looks at me. 'And you?' he asks me. 'Weren't you the one most anxious to meet him? It was your name in the original ad, wasn't it?'

Maddie kicks me under the table. 'Well . . .' I lick my dry lips. 'I put the ad in myself and when Maddie found out, she wanted to be involved as well.'

'And our friend Gray,' Maddie adds.

'OK.' *Bugle* Man nods resignedly. 'What was the row about?'

His question wrong-foots us. 'That is private,' Maddie says. 'I mean we don't want to drag it all up again.'

'You ever been in a tribunal?' *Bugle* Man snaps. 'You'd be good.'

Maddie laughs loudly and people turn to look. 'All we want to do is find him,' she says in a nicer tone. 'We parted on bad terms and we feel that it's important to bury the hatchet.'

'In his head?'

Maddie laughs again. *Bugle* Man is warming to her. Men generally do. 'OK,' he says doubtfully. 'It's not as good a piece as I was hoping for, but with your ad on the telly' – he nods at me – 'it'll make the front page.'

'I'm also doing a photo shoot for *Woman's Life*,' I tell him. 'That'll boost my profile a bit more too.'

Bugle Man nods. 'OK.' He scribbles something in his notes and flicks a few pages, frowning. 'But there still isn't much news there.'

'Sorry,' I mutter meekly.

'No worries.' He takes out a little camera. 'So, stand together and I'll take a photo. This Jason fella would be mad not to make contact with nice-looking chicks—' He glances at Maddie, who snorts. 'Nice-looking *women* like you two.'

Click.

Maddie cannot believe that Gray and I have fallen out big time. I have to tell her again what happened at his house. We're sitting in her front room – the room I love – and Clive is very nicely making us our dinner. Maddie has warned me not to expect too much but it's got to be better than my own cooking. We are relaxing on her big soft sofa, I've a massive glass of wine in my hand while Maddie, because of the baby, is drinking water. Fáinne is watching the video she missed on St Stephen's Day.

'He said *what*?' Maddie gawps.

I tell her again. She can't believe the Tracy bit. 'Isn't it typical of Tracy? Trying to blame me because he was in a bad mood all the time.'

Maddie frowns. 'Well, you did throw a huge wobbler when he started seeing her,' she muses. 'Maybe Tracy just felt it wasn't worth it.'

'Come on!'

Maddie looks away. Swirls the water in her glass. 'And what did he mean about you clinging to us?'

'I don't know. I don't cling on to anyone.'

She takes a sip of water and frowns. 'Now don't freak out,' she eventually mutters, 'but you haven't really had a relationship with anyone. You do kinda depend on us for everything.'

'Depend on you for everything?' I *am* freaking out. Jesus, what did my mates think I was: a complete loser? 'How do you make that out?'

Maddie shifts uncomfortably. 'Forget it. It came out all wrong.'

'I don't depend on anyone – sure, I've my own house and car and—'

'You do.' Maddie pours me some more wine and it mollifies me. I push her remarks to the back of my mind. Of course she didn't mean it, she was just trying to see Gray's side and failing.

'I just meant *emotionally*,' Maddie continues. 'You know, you don't seem to want to build up a relationship with anyone else. Not even friendships. I mean, the amount of nice guys you've been with and it's come to nothing.'

I shrug. Smile wryly. 'Look what happened with the last serious relationship I had.'

Maddie smiles back. 'Don't let it put you off.'

'It hasn't. I just haven't found the right guy.'

'Maybe because you're afraid.'

Jesus, this was like *Oprah*. I giggle. 'Do you charge by the hour?'

'Free to friends.'

'I'm not afraid, Maddie.' I pause at her sceptical look. 'Honestly – the feeling I had when I was with Jason was brilliant and, yeah, I know it ended in lots of tears but I would give *anything* to have that feeling with someone else and so far' – I shrug – 'I haven't.'

God, I sounded pathetic. A sad single woman looking for a man. But relationships did make you happy. Maddie and Clive were happy. Audrey and Gray were happy. And me? Well, I was happy too. I had Fáinne, didn't I?

Clive shouts from the kitchen that dinner is ready. Maddie holds out her hand for me to pull her up from the sofa. I swear, she has put on weight big time.

'That baby will be a monster,' I joke as she waddles in front of me.

'It'll be beautiful and gorgeous and look like Clive.' Maddie beams up at her husband-to-be and, yep, I become aware of an almost physical pain as they smile at each other.

I'm not included in that smile.

A small flutter of panic then begins as they take one another's hand and Maddie slags him gently about the dried-up look of the carrots. And like some kind of a surgeon, I try to detach from the feelings. I try to quash them. I tell myself that I am not jealous or afraid or clingy.

'Is dinner ready?' Fáinne asks brightly from the hallway.

'Yes, come in.' I indicate a chair for her to sit on and she takes another one.

Maddie raises her eyebrows questioningly. I look away. Yep, my daughter is still not talking. Fáinne is like her mother; she knows how to hold a grudge.

Clive puts some soup in front of Maddie. 'Eat up now, you need all the nourishment you can get.'

'Feck off!' She pretends to punch him and he catches her hand and they kiss.

'Gross,' Fáinne shouts.

Despite the panic and the flutters, I think it's lovely.

43

L ES RINGS ME at home the day after New Year. I'd spent
New Year's Eve working until noon and then sitting at
home, playing with Fáinne. There was a thaw in her attitude to me and I was milking it for all it was worth. But it
had been lonely: no family, no mates. I missed ringing Gray
to wish him Happy New Year though he'd eventually rung
New Year's Day and, after being really abrupt with me, he'd
hesitantly asked for Fáinne.

Anyway, like I was saying, Les rings me and I can tell by
his voice that he's a little annoyed.

'You don't go giving interviews without my say-so,' he
snaps.

'Interviews?'

'Ye-ah, the *Bugle* interview. The "Condom Girl Seeks
Mate" interview. Talk about a double-meaning headline.'

I hadn't even seen the paper. Me. In the paper. I go all
funny and warm inside. 'I didn't know you read the *Bugle*,
Les,' I tease. He's strictly a page-three man plus, of course,
the Arts reviews in the up-your-arse papers.

'I fucking don't,' he says back. 'But lucky for you the
researchers on Declan D'arcy do. They want you to do a
radio interview with the man himself next Tuesday.'

'A radio interview?' I'm dead impressed. 'Really?'

'Really,' he snaps. 'But I swear Lucy, another stunt like

this – Jesus, I felt a right plonker when I didn't even know the interview the researchers were talking about – another stunt like this and I'll have to rethink our working relationship.'

'Just get rid of me,' I offer. 'I won't mind.'

'You're to be in studio next Tuesday by ten. They can do it over the phone if you want, though.'

I'd never been in a radio studio before. 'But what will the interview be about?'

'I dunno, do I – I haven't fucking seen the paper, have I?'

'It's just about me and my mates looking for an old college friend.'

'Right, well then you know what to expect.' He takes in a big whoosh of air before saying hastily, 'Give me a plug, won't you – tell everyone how I got you this ad.'

'How you *conned* me into it, you mean?'

'Condomed you into it,' he sniggers. Then, 'Bye Lucy.' I think he's gone and am about to put down the phone when he barks, 'By the way, who the *fuck* is Clive?'

'Clive?' He must mean Maddie's Clive. 'My friend's boyfriend.'

'Well, tell him to keep his nose out of your business. Jesus, the Declan D'arcy Show were on to him too looking for you. Apparently his number is in the bloody paper alongside your name. You are not his client, right?'

I giggle. Clive as a PR man is so incongruous that I giggle again.

'Yeah, it's OK for you to laugh – you haven't just been made to feel like a gigantic banana.' And he hangs up the phone.

I stand for a second in the hall, savouring the fact that I'm just about to be interviewed on one of the country's biggest shows. Not exactly one of the country's most respected shows

291

but still . . . And then I think that I'll have to lie through my teeth on air, though it wasn't exactly a lie, just not the whole truth. But it makes me uneasy and just as I'm about to pick up the phone to ring Maddie, she rings me.

'Declan D'arcy!' she gasps before I can even say 'hello'. 'Oooh, Luce, this is it. I'm going to tell everyone I know to listen to you. Clive nearly collapsed when his researchers rang. Isn't it great?'

'Yeah!' I feel the excitement build again. 'Great!'

'What's great?' Fáinne asks, half slouching against the doorframe the way her dad used to and my insides turn to jelly just looking at her.

'Your mammy,' I say cheerfully, 'is going to be on the radio. You know the programme that Gray listens to?' She nods. 'Well, that one.'

'Wow!' Fáinne is impressed. 'Does that mean you'll be famous?'

Maddie laughs at the other end of the line. 'Go, girl,' she shouts and I hear Clive telling her not to get too excited and she telling him back that it's too late for that, that she's pregnant. Then she hangs up and I turn to face my daughter.

We eye each other warily. 'Let's be friends, Fáinne,' I say. 'I'm sorry about Christmas. Let's be friends again.'

A small smile as she crosses towards me. 'Are you happy now that you'll be famous?' she asks, wrapping her arms about me. 'Isn't that what you want?'

'I just want a cuddle from you,' I say, squeezing her until she squeals. It feels so good. We end up with her arm about my shoulder and her cheek pressed against mine. I steal a soft kiss and she hugs me harder.

'Imagine, Mammy,' she sighs contentedly, 'you're *almost* as famous as Mona Lisa now.'

Lovely.

44

DOUG LOOKS SURPRISED when I ask for Tuesday morning off. 'A job interview already?'

He sounds concerned and it pleases me. 'Sort of,' I say as nonchalantly as I can. 'I'm going on the Declan D'arcy Show.'

Clare gawks at me. 'No way!'

'The Declan D'arcy Show?' Doug says. He leans on the counter. 'Declan D'arcy?' He doesn't sound excited or thrilled. '*The* Declan D'arcy?'

'Naw, the other one – the one you haven't heard of.'

Clare laughs. Honestly, she seems a lot nicer now that I know what a horrible life she has. I mean, she still snaps and growls, but I don't take it so personally any more.

'What for?'

I blush. Steel myself for the lie. 'Just talking about me and Maddie, that's my friend, trying to find . . . well . . . an old college friend of ours.'

'Oh.' Doug looks uncomfortable. I reckon he knows whom I mean. 'Is that a good idea?'

'My agent seems to think so.'

'What college friend is this?' Clare asks. 'I don't think I'd like to meet anyone I knew in college again. Pretentious shower, the lot of them.'

'This was a nice guy only we, eh, sort of lost touch with him.'

'Oh, right.' Clare turns back to the accounts. 'Doug, do you realise you still haven't given me an invoice for smelly coat?'

'Mr Devlin, you mean?' Doug says sharply. 'And I will bill him. Soon.'

Clare rolls her eyes. 'And there's a fortune missing here for food.'

'Aw shit, yeah.' He digs his hand into his jeans and pulls out a wad of twenties. 'Take this – there's about a hundred there. I took some stuff the other day for the dogs.'

'Dogs?'

'The ones I keep in the back garden at home. Strays.'

That was the first I'd heard of it. 'Strays?'

'I've about six – one is leaving tomorrow. Jaysus, they cost me a fortune. Anyway, shove that money in there and here, take this.' Another forty is pulled from his pocket. 'Put that against Mr D.'s treatment for Paddy, OK?'

Six dogs living in his back garden. No wonder he had no girlfriend. The noise. The smell.

'Happy now?' he says to Clare.

Clare grimaces. 'Forty euro doesn't come near Paddy's treatment.'

'Yeah, well, we'll get the money in the end, right?' He saunters off, whistling.

'I think he wants to go bankrupt,' Clare snarls after him.

But I love the way he's whistling.

45

April 28th

Had a row with Maddie today. Honestly, she's just trying to put a dampener on everything. Everyone in our year has heard about me getting the film part and they're all congratulating me. It's brilliant.

Then, just as Sarah Walker had finished telling me how wonderful it'll all be, Maddie grabbed my arm and told me that she had something to say and I – idiot – thought that it was important.

'You are pregnant,' she hissed at me. 'At least three months. By the time you get to shoot this film you'll be huge. You won't be able to do it, Luce. You won't be able to do it and you know it.'

'It'll be fine,' I said.

'Oh really, how?' And she sounded so smart, saying that.

I shook her off. 'Leave me alone.'

'Have you told anyone? Have you told Jason? Your folks?'

I walked away from her. I do not need this right now.

April 30th

Maddie has threatened to tell Jason unless I do it soon. She says that I have to face up to it. That I can't deny it.

I'm not denying it.

I'm not.

I hate Maddie.

I told her I'd tell Jason soon, there just hasn't been a right time.

Going for a fitting for clothes for the film on Monday.

May 2nd

I felt like a star getting measured and taped and everything. Everyone was so nice. It took ages and it was hard standing up for that long time, but I managed it.

May 3rd

Today was horrible. Horrible. Gray is such a plank. He's been really narky since Tracy left. I swear, it was nearly better when they were seeing each other. Anyway, what happened was that Jason arrived into the canteen today and made a bee-line for our table. I jumped up because, well, I didn't really want to see him just at that moment but Maddie (another friend I could do without) grabbed my arm and held me down. I dunno what's happened since the start of the year but things between the three of us have changed.

So Jason comes over, banging into chairs and tables on the way and annoying people. He doesn't look at me, instead he yells at Gray, 'It's all your fault. You told Bill to dump me off the team, didn't you?'

'No I didn't,' Gray shouted back. 'But if he did then I'm glad.'

Jason, I think, was actually going to hit him but Gray stood up and pushed him and Jason fell over. He walloped his head off a table and knocked over a couple of chairs.

Everyone gasped.

'Sorry,' Gray muttered, going to help him up.

'I'm fine.' Jason tried to get up. He was holding his head. 'Leave me alone.'

He wasn't fine. He struggled to stand and he kept swaying all over the place and there was a massive bump coming up on the side of his head. I never felt so sorry for anyone.

'Jason,' I said.

He looked at me but was grabbed from behind by two security guards who began to haul him out.

'Leave him alone,' I shouted, going after them with Maddie behind me. 'Don't hurt him.'

One of the security guys actually had the nerve to laugh and make a comment about Jason being so wasted that if they pushed him off the Empire State Building, he wouldn't hurt himself. And they threw him on the ground and Jason just sat there, sort of dazed.

I went over to him and he glared at me. 'What do you want?'

'To see if you're OK?'

'Huh.' He stumbled to his feet. 'You haven't called me in weeks, you don't return my calls, what do you care, huh?'

'I do care.'

Maddie tried to pull me away, but I couldn't let him think I didn't care. 'I'm sorry, Jace.'

''S OK, I know you're going to be a big movie star.' He made a big sweeping arc gesture and almost fell over. Maddie caught him and held him up.

'No. It's just, well . . .' I couldn't tell him. Not then. He was too upset over the team. 'Can we meet tomorrow?'

'I don't need your pity.' He began to stumble off.

'Please, Jace. Please.' I grabbed his arm. I should have met him. I should have told him. It was as if at that very minute I accepted the inevitable. I was going to be a mother. I was. 'Can we meet, please? There's something I need to tell you.'

''S OK, you're finishing with me. Fine.'

'No. Not that. Please – when you're not so upset.'

He shrugged. But his face changed. Became softer. Sadder, or something.

'Maybe tomorrow – somewhere on campus? At your flat?'

'No.' He shook his head. 'Here. OK?'

I swallowed. 'Good.' I made to hug him but he turned away. Crying all night.

May 4th

Jason wasn't in college today. I'd been worried sick about telling him and he didn't turn up. Maybe he'd been so drunk he forgot.

It was a bit of a relief actually.

Rowed with Gray. Told him he was horrible for kicking Jason off the team.

'It was Bill's decision and he hated to do it,' Gray said, all calm and contrite.

'Sure.'

Gray looked at me. Made to say something, stopped and then started up again. 'Lucy, are you blind or what? The guy has a serious drink problem.'

'Yeah. Right.'

'He comes and plays and he's half-cut. He's done some terrible tackling. We can't have that on the team.'

'Any excuse. You're pathetic. Just 'cause it's off with Tracy you're trying to ruin me and Jason.'

He jerked a bit at that. 'Where do you think Jason was when he took those years out of college?'

The way he asked me was loaded. My voice shook as I answered, 'He was travelling.'

'He wasn't travelling. He was drying out. Bill told us. OK?' Then he walked off.

I had to sit down. I felt sick.

46

I'M BECKONED INTO the radio studio by one of Declan D'arcy's researchers. Even though it's stupid, I've dressed up for the occasion. I plan to go shopping afterwards and treat myself to lunch in a nice restaurant, then pick up Fáinne from school as Doug has given me the whole day off.

Declan is playing a track by Westlife and he waves at me as I take my seat across from him. I smile back. My heart has begun to pump really fast and sweat coats my palms. The researcher places a glass of water in front of me and I gulp it down. Then I tell myself to calm down, it's only a bloody interview. It's no big deal. I think of all the people rooting for me: Maddie and Clive; Doug, who said he'd listen; Mam and Dad – though I don't know if Mam will listen as she hates Declan D'arcy and hates the fact that I'm searching for Jason even more – and perhaps Gray. Maddie said she told him, but maybe he won't listen.

As the music begins to fade out, I feel a sort of suicidal calm come over me. There is nothing I can do now except to go through with it. I take big deep breaths and compose myself.

'Well now,' Declan says in his husky voice, 'we've a special guest in the studio today. All the lads will know her from the billboards around the country. She's the girl with the condom box: Lucy Gleeson. Lucy, you're very welcome to the studio.'

'Thanks,' I say and my voice comes out normally.

'And, fellas,' Declan says, 'she looks every bit as delicious in person as she does on the ad. She's even doing a photo shoot for *Woman's Life* so yez'll have to go out and buy it.' He turns to me. 'There'll be a stampede now!'

I manage a laugh.

'So, Lucy Gleeson, tell us a little about yourself.'

So I tell him. A very very little. I mention Fáinne, as I can hardly leave her out, can I?

'Pity King Con weren't around then,' Declan says dryly.

I'm insulted. 'I'm glad they weren't,' I say. 'I love her to bits.'

'Like we all do our kids,' he agrees. Then, 'So, Lucy, tell me why you're really here? There was a story in the *Dingle Bugle* about you, wasn't there?'

And I tell him.

'So why now,' he asks. 'Why do you suddenly want to trace this Jason person now?'

'Well.' I take a huge gulp of water and steel myself for the lie. 'Well . . . no one likes to part on a row, do they? And, well, me and my friends were such good mates with him in college that it seemed a pity not to meet up with him again.'

He ignores me. 'But initially it was just your name on the ad. Why?'

'It was just my idea.'

'So it's not a publicity stunt to get your name in the papers?'

'God, no!' A clever marketing ploy like that would never occur to me. 'I decided to search for him before I ever got the part in the ad.'

Declan nods. 'Fair enough. So, go on, tell us a little about Jason. Maybe someone out there will recognise him.'

I launch into where Jason was from, where he lived in

300

Dublin, what he studied, all about the team. It's not so bad.

'And how many years ago was all this?'

'About nine. I know it's a long time but maybe—'

'And how old is your daughter?'

I freeze. Whatever I had been about to say goes straight out of my head. I gawp at him. 'Sorry?'

'Your daughter. How old is she?'

I blink and chew hard on my lower lip. 'Eh, eight. Why?'

'I dunno. Just wondered.' He let it hang.

I have to ask. I have to pretend I don't know what he's getting at. 'Wondered what?'

'If he was, you know, the father of your child. I'm sure that's what everyone is wondering. Is this mysterious Jason the father of your child? Is that why you want to trace him? I mean, how many of us bother looking up people we've rowed with? Most of us are glad to see the back of them. I know whenever I row with my wife, I feel great every time she leaves me.' He chortles, but this time I can't smile back. He leans across the desk at me and lowers his voice, 'So, go on, tell us: is he your daughter's dad?'

An eternity seems to pass as my brain races frantically wondering what I should say. I can't tell the truth: how can I? If Jason is listening, how can I break it to him, live on air, that he's a dad? Before I can answer, however, Declan puts up his hand. 'It seems we have a call on line four. OK, caller, go ahead.'

'That Jason was a complete bastard,' the caller spits. It's Johnno. 'I lived with him – he fucking fleeced me. I was so good to him when he lived here but he repaid me by not paying the rent when he should have. I was saving for a house with me girlfriend at the time and we broke up after that.'

'Eh, Johnno, tone down the language, ey?' Declan

301

chuckles. 'Might offend some of our more prissy listeners!'

'I'm fucking sorry,' Johnno mutters.

Declan rolls his eyes. 'So, he wrecked your relationship, did he?'

'Indirectly, yeah!'

'Ouch!' Declan says. 'So tell us some more about what he was like back then.'

And Johnno launches into a horrible description. It was hard to believe that the guy I'd read about in my diary was the same guy shouting down the phone line. Jason, it seems, has really wrecked his head.

'Well, thanks, Johnno, for that,' Declan says cheerfully. 'Not a big fan, ey? So, Lucy, you still want to go on with the search?'

I nod.

'Pardon?'

'Oh, yeah, yeah, I do.'

Declan holds up his hand again. 'Hey, it seems we have more calls. What?' A laugh. 'Lucy, it seems we have *three* guys here all claiming paternity of your child. A Clive, a Doug and a Graham. Do any of those names ring a bell?'

'Sorry?' I feel suddenly very sick and sweaty. This cannot be happening.

'We'll go to Clive first. Hiya, Clive.'

I wait, paralysed, for the world to start caving in on me.

Clive mumbles something.

'And you're saying that you are the father of Lucy's child, aren't you?'

A massive pause. Then Clive stutters, 'Eh, well, if there are two other guys there, maybe I'm not.'

'Maybe you're not,' Declan repeats dryly. 'I see.' He pauses. 'Hello, Doug!'

'Hi, Declan.' Doug sounds pissed off.

'So you're the father, ey?'

'Eh, well, yeah. Yeah, I am. Lucy's a great girl and, to be honest, you're making her look stupid.'

Thanks, Doug.

'Me?' Declan chortles again.

'Yeah,' Doug agrees calmly. 'You.'

'Do you know this guy?' Declan asks me.

'Eh, yeah.' I wince. 'Yeah.'

'And he's your child's dad, is he?'

What the fuck am I meant to say?

'Tell them, Luce,' Doug says confidently.

'He is,' I mutter.

'So, *who* is the mysterious Graham?' Declan asks cheerfully. 'Graham, what have you to say about all this? Surely you must be mistaken? Doug has clearly laid down his paternity.'

I want to cry. I want to shout. But I can't do anything. This is national radio. Oh God, this is national radio! I cringe as I imagine my dad listening in. Gray tries to backtrack. 'Lucy Gleeson,' he says. 'Oh right, I thought it was Lucy Deeson you were talking to.'

'Lucy Deeson,' Declan says, doing a big mock-confused voice. 'Unusual name. Does she do condom ads too?'

'Yeah,' Gray says lamely. 'In, eh, Iraq though.'

'A Muslim country? They have condom ads there?'

'You'd be surprised,' Gray says, sounding mortified. 'Anyway, sorry for bothering you, eh, Lucy Gleeson.'

'It's fine,' I say back.

But it's not.

'Well, well.' Declan turns to me. 'That was funny, ey? Three guys, all—'

'Can we stop it right there?' I gulp out. 'I didn't come here to make a fool of myself. I came to talk about a search

I hoped to do. I wasn't expecting to be ambushed like this and . . . and . . . I'm, well, I'm disappointed and I think I'll leave now.' I stand up and wrestle with my headphones.

Declan is unperturbed. He starts giving a running commentary on everything that I am doing. 'She's taking her bag from the floor and standing up. She's wearing a lovely two-piece suit that shows off her gorgeous body and she's exiting.' He then launches into a description of Jason, which I mostly miss because I am running blindly down the corridor trying to find my way out. One of the researchers runs after me, but I tell her to 'get lost'.

In my panic, I forget where I've parked and I spend what seems like ages staring blindly about for my car's bright green roof. When I do see it, I run towards it as if it's my oldest and dearest friend. My keys are slippery and I fumble about with the lock. The door pops open and I sit inside, slam shut the door and close my eyes. I can't trust myself to drive. I stay there for ages. People come and go, getting into their own cars, and I keep my eyes shut, like a kid, convinced that if I can't see people, they can't see me.

Driving home is a nightmare. I'm sure that the people in the cars in front are all looking in their rear-view mirrors and recognising me and laughing at me. I don't go into town to shop because I'm afraid someone will know who I am. Instead I go home, crawl into bed and pull the covers up over my head. I want desperately to sleep, to escape the humiliation, to forget about it for a while. I wish I could fast forward time to about ten years from now, when it will all be forgotten about. I do not want to live through the next few weeks.

Of course, I can't sleep. The phone keeps ringing, so I take it off the hook. I switch off my mobile and I go downstairs and pour myself a huge glass of wine. I slug it back, hoping for the lovely floaty feeling wine always gives me – only it doesn't happen. I get even more depressed and ashamed and unsleepy.

At two o'clock the front-door bell rings. I peek out, hoping it's Maddie, but knowing that on Tuesdays she doesn't finish school until after five. To my horror, my parents are standing on the doorstep. I drop the blind and stay very still.

'Well, she's definitely here,' I can hear my mother saying loudly. 'Her car is in the drive.' She rings the bell again.

'Maybe she's gone out for a walk,' Dad suggests.

'Oh, don't be ridiculous, John,' Mam snaps. 'She was totally humiliated on the radio this morning. I'd be surprised if she ever goes out again.'

Well, thank you, Mother!

'No, she's here.'

Another ring.

I'm afraid to move. If there are two people in the world I do not want to see right at this moment, it's my parents.

Suddenly, Mam shrieks. 'Oh my God – say she's done something stupid!'

'Now Dora—'

'No. No. Think about it, John. She's always a bit over-dramatic, she's bound to overreact. Have you got her key? I'm going in!'

I hear the clink of Dad's keys as he goes through them. My mind races – what should I do? Doing something to myself suddenly sounds very appealing but I don't have a stash of tablets or the time right now. Instead, I stomp down-stairs and fling open the door. 'I'm fine. Still safe.'

Mam's worried face is replaced by her annoyed one. 'Why didn't you answer the door?'

'I just wanted to be on my own.'

'Well, you could have answered the phone when I rang, so,' Mam snaps, striding into the hall. 'Do you know how worried I've been?'

'She's been very worried,' Dad says apologetically to me.

Mam walks on into the kitchen and I cringe. It hasn't been tidied since yesterday. In my haste to get out this morning I left the breakfast dishes on the table.

'Are you depressed?' Mam asks, surveying the mess. She begins to tidy up and I want to tell her to stop. 'It's a sign of depression leaving a mess everywhere.'

'I am not,' I say. 'I'm entitled to live any way I want to. I was in a rush this morning.'

'God knows why,' she sniffs. 'You weren't treated very well, were you? Oh, I rang up that Declan D'arcy and got on to his show and gave him an earful, I can tell you.'

'You did not!' Oh shit. Oh God.

'I did. Who does he think he is, humiliating you like that!'

'Mam, I'm a big girl, I can fight my own battles.' I sit down on a kitchen chair and watch as she whirlwinds about my kitchen.

'Your mother was only sticking up for you,' Dad says.

'I don't need anyone to do that for me.'

'Oh yes you do.' Mam nods vigorously as she shoves all the dishes in the dishwasher. 'You haven't exactly made a screaming success of things, have you? You're not exactly ecstatically happy, are you?'

That is it! That is bloody well it! 'Go home,' I say. 'Go home.' I stand up and place my hands on the table and shout at her. 'Go home. I don't need you tidying my house or giving me lectures. I'm tired of being the daughter who makes a mess of things, right? I'm tired of you making me feel second best all the time. Just, just go home to your precious Tracy!'

They both stare at me as if they've never seen me before.

'I'm tired of it,' I say and my voice is strong and loud. 'I'm who I am, I did what I did and that's the way it is – right?'

'Oh, now, Lucy,' Dad says placatingly, 'your mother was only trying to help you. She didn't mean—'

'I know exactly what she meant,' I say, looking at my mother, who has a wet dishcloth in her hands and is squeezing it all over the floor. 'Go on. Go home!'

'I think we should go now, John,' Mam says in a clipped voice. 'Lucy obviously isn't in the humour for company. We should leave her alone.'

'Yes.' Dad seems to deflate. 'Yes. Right.'

Mam puts down the dishcloth. Dad glares at me before putting his arm about my mother and together they walk into the hall.

I let them go. Then I bury my head in the covers and pray like hell that no one recognises me when I go to pick Fáinne up.

47

To go out and face the world the next morning is nerve-racking. And it's even worse facing my parents.

They're both waiting for me in the driveway when I pull up. Mam peers anxiously in as the car draws level with them. She's not looking at me, instead she waves at Fáinne. I hop out, unlock the door and Fáinne bounces out, her pigtails flying, a big grin plastered to her face. 'Hiya, Nana!'

Mam smiles. 'Hello, angel. You look pretty today!' She fusses over Fáinne, leading her into the house and ignoring me. Dad flashes me a smile. 'You look pretty yourself,' he tells me.

'Ta.'

'Well, take care.' He pats me awkwardly on the shoulder. Then, nodding after Fáinne, he says, 'She is an angel, you know.' Then he turns abruptly away and follows my mother up the driveway.

The surgery is deserted when I get there.

Thank God.

I flick on the computer and fill the kettle, dying for a coffee. I flirt with the idea of ringing Gray to thank him for yesterday. But maybe a phone call is a bit cowardly. Maybe I should brave it and call in person at the house.

But what if Audrey is there?

Well, I shall apologise to her too. They can only throw me out. Again. I'd be no worse off than I am now.

Even thinking about it makes me feel sick.

But if I call in at Gray's, I'll have to ask my mother to look after Fáinne for longer and I do not feel like asking her for a favour, so I decide to leave it until the weekend. When I have loads of free time.

Oooh.

My thoughts are interrupted as a tall woman, wearing jeans and a bright blue coat, comes in. She looks annoyed about something. I can tell this by the way she marches over to me and without even a 'good morning' demands to see Doug.

'He's not in yet, can I ask you to sit in the waiting room?' I see that she has no pet with her. 'If you want him for a house call, I can take your name and number—'

'House call?' The woman gives a snort. 'That fella wouldn't have the nerve to make a house call after what happened yesterday!'

I wonder what happened yesterday. 'Well, he's an excellent vet, I'm sure what happened was no fault—'

'Oh, you.' She waves at me dismissively. 'You haven't a clue about—' Then all of a sudden she stops. And stares. And I know she's recognised me and I flush bright red. 'You.' Her eyebrows come together. 'Is this how he takes care of you, is it? When did it happen? When he was flitting about saving all the animals of the world?'

So maybe she hasn't recognised me. 'Sorry?'

'So you should be.' She drags out the sentence. Says it again. 'So you should be.'

I wonder if she's mad.

'Douglas is a good lad. But he's not a businessman. He's wasted in private practice. But, oh no, he was determined. And now I know the reason. Now I know the reason.'

309

We neither of us hear Doug enter. Well, I never hear him anyway. 'Hi, Mam,' he says cheerily. 'How's things?'

His *mother*. Oh Jesus.

She turns to him. 'Tattered-looking as always,' she remarks, staring at his clothes, which are tattered. 'Well, at least I know the reason for it now – supporting a child can't help finance your wardrobe.'

Doug laughs. How he can laugh after she insults him like that, I don't know. 'And you're gorgeous as always,' he says, smiling. At her lack of response, he adds, 'Mam, I like my clothes. And anyway, dogs and cats tend not to go on appearances. They like my smell.'

'I suppose she' – a nod at me – 'liked your smell too.'

'I dunno.' Doug shrugs charmingly. 'Do you like my smell, Lucy?'

I flush again. Christ, no wonder he has no girlfriend. His mother would frighten anyone away.

'Douglas,' his mother says scathingly, 'let's do away with the jokes. What is this about a child?'

Another laugh.

The penny drops and I gawk at her. How can Doug laugh? 'He's not the father of my child. I swear, I never even knew him when I had Fáinne.'

'Fáinne?'

'My daughter. That's her name.'

She doesn't think much of the name, I can tell. 'It means "ring" in Irish,' I say on auto-pilot.

'Wonderful.' She nods, icily polite. 'So, Douglas, you are *not* the father of Fáinne?'

'I think I might have mentioned it to you if I was.' Doug grins and turns to me. 'Jesus, Luce, that was hilarious yesterday, wasn't it?'

'No,' I snap back.

310

'Well, at least you've some sense,' his mother says. 'It wasn't funny at all, Douglas. Do you know how shocked I was – hearing my son admit that he was a father?'

'Not as shocked as I was finding out,' Doug says casually.

I find myself smirking but his mother wilts the smile away with the look she gives me. 'He was only helping me out,' I explain meekly.

'Helping you out?' She gawks at me. 'How is he helping you out by claiming to be the father of your child? How exactly does that help anyone? Why didn't the real father ring up?'

'Well, I *thought* it would help her out,' Doug says. 'It was a bit unfortunate that two other guys wanted to help her out as well but that's the way it goes. Anyway, all's well that ends well. Any files for me, Luce?'

'"Ends well"?' his mother shrieks, producing a paper. 'You think this is ending well, do you?'

It's like a bad dream. My face is plastered over the *Daily Gossip* with the headline: 'Condom Girl in Father Mix-up'.

'Oh God.' I shove my finger in my mouth, ready to nail-bite. I do not need Fáinne to see this.

Doug grabs the paper from his mother and scans it. 'Crap,' he pronounces. 'It's just a rag anyway.'

'Your name is mentioned in it,' his mother snaps. 'I suppose you're delighted with that?'

'Does it say I'm a vet?'

'Yes. Oh, there isn't a thing they don't know.'

'Good. Great publicity for the clinic, so. And, Jaysus, do we need it.'

His laid-back air is genuine. He honestly doesn't care. I admire that. I care too much. I'm beginning to shake. I've bitten a chunk out of my favourite nail.

'The clinic, the clinic,' his mother shrieks, totally losing

311

it. 'That's all you care about. Forget about making something of yourself. You could have had so much more. Oh, forget about all the things you could have done!'

'I have forgotten them,' Doug says and there is an edge to his voice now. 'It's just you that hasn't.'

'How can I? How can I when my only son is determined to ruin his life! And what's that "For Sale" sign doing outside the door here?'

'The owner is selling,' Doug mutters. 'It doesn't concern you.'

'Selling? And have you another premises?'

'Not yet,' Doug says sullenly. His sulky look makes me smile – he's like a grumpy kid all of a sudden.

'Typical.' His mother rolls her eyes. 'Another fine mess. I suppose you couldn't pay the rent or something.'

'That's not what you called in about,' Doug snaps. 'And now that you know I'm not the father of Lucy's child, you can go.'

'Well, at least you haven't gone that far into ruining your life.'

'I'm not ruining my life,' Doug shouts. 'I like my life. I'm happy. You are the one that's ruining it – why can't you just accept that I did not want to do what you wanted me to do, hey?'

'I certainly do not want you phoning up radio stations pretending to be a father of some girl's kid!'

'Yeah, well, add it to the list, so.'

She rolls her eyes and slams the paper down on the counter. A glare at me. 'I suppose you put him up to it?'

'Leave Lucy out of this!'

'I did not!' Her disbelieving look infuriates me. 'I don't ask anyone to do things for me!'

'Go and make us a cuppa, Luce,' Doug says.

'I won't have her accusing me of—'

'Tea?' He pushes me gently into the kitchen.

'I'm only saying—'

'Yeah. I know. Tea.'

I go into the kitchen and, once there, I find that I can't put on the kettle, that my hands and knees and legs are shaking so much that I just can't do anything. So I sit down on the sofa and wrap my arms around my body and try not to cry. Outside, Doug's mother is still shouting. His voice is lower so I don't know what he's saying.

Eventually, after what seems like ages, the door slams shut and Doug comes to me. He stands in the doorway and says nothing.

I look up at him. 'Is she gone?'

He nods and crosses to the sofa. 'I'm sorry, Luce.'

'You? Why?'

'For her. She should never have gone on like that.'

I gulp. 'She's defending her son's honour.'

'Naw, she's defending her own honour. My honour was lost long ago.' A grin. 'Too long ago.'

I manage a shaky smile.

'Coffee?'

'Please.'

He makes me a coffee, pulls out some biscuits and offers me one. Only I can't eat. That paper looms in front of my eyes. How many other papers will have the story in it? I know it's the kind of thing I love to read. I have to protect Fáinne by ringing her teacher and explaining. Only right now, I'm numb.

'You were great yesterday,' Doug says. 'Even the way you left the studio was great.'

'I made an eejit out of myself.'

'Naw. He tried to make an eejit out of you but he didn't succeed.'

'He did.' I sniff. A tear plops into my coffee. 'And this morning I thought it didn't matter and I even braved my mother but now, now it'll be all over the place.'

'Hey.' He moves in beside me. 'Don't.' His arm comes hesitantly around my shoulder. 'Come on. I'm no good at all this emotional stuff, you have to stop.'

But I can't. His kindness is too much and I sniff and sob and rub my nose and all the while he's patting my back. He does have a nice smell. A familiar smell: half clinic, half himself. He pulls me closer to him and keeps telling me not to cry. I rest my head on his chest. On his tatty woolly jumper that suddenly seems so lovely and so him. I want him to kiss me. I need to be kissed. I need to feel that in the whole world there is someone who wants to kiss me. I lift my head up towards him and he gently brushes a tear from my face with his thumb. He stares at me for what seems like an age, his eyes all smoky and dark and lovely. Then he pulls away. His face clears. He asks, 'All right?'

I'm not prepared for the crushing disappointment I feel. I pull away from him too, angry at myself for contemplating kissing him. Will I never learn? I scrub my eyes. It seems that lately no matter what I do, I seem to end up crying. 'I will be,' I sniff.

'You can take today off if you like,' he offers. 'I'll manage.'

It's tempting but I know that eventually I'll have to face people. 'Nope,' I answer. 'Sure, you'll have to face them alone then.'

To my surprise he laughs. 'Luce,' he says, 'I can't wait – business will be booming! We might even make our enormous rent payment this month.'

I smile. Then ask tentatively, 'And have you managed to get any loans yet?'

His grin fades slightly. 'Naw. Me and Jim have been to every bank everywhere. No one is interested. I think you might have to get a new job.'

'And you?'

'I dunno. I suppose I can pick something up. All else failing, I can go work with the auld fella.'

'Aw, Doug . . .'

'I dunno – every bank in the country seems to think Jim and I are chancers. I mean, I even dress up when I go there and it makes no difference. The books are a mess, you see. They think we make no money.'

'Can't you tell them that you just don't charge properly?'

'Would you take a chance on a guy that doesn't charge properly?'

'Good point.'

He nudges me with his elbow. 'Hey, you don't have a stash of cash from your ad hidden anywhere, do you?'

'I wish.'

'We've a few more doors to bang on, so I'm not giving up hope. The auction is a bit away yet. Don't worry.'

But I will. I need this job. 'I'll do my best.'

There is a silence and Doug stands up to leave.

'Thanks, Doug.'

''S all right. Just don't go crying on me again. Guys like me, we're not able for all that.'

'No – I mean for yesterday. I know it turned out a mess but thanks anyway. I was so horrible to you at, well, you know, after—' I stop. Go bright red. We've never talked about Christmas since.

He reddens too. Then shrugs and says offhandedly, 'Yesterday was 'cause I hate that D'arcy bloke, I hated what he was doing to you, OK?'

Why do I not feel happier?

315

'Right. Great. OK. Well, thanks,' I blabber out as he leaves the room.

The day isn't as bad as I expected. Irish people are the sort to recognise you and then pretend that they don't. Just to see you is enough, just to be able to tell the mates in the pub that they saw you keeps them happy. And yep, business does boom. Lots of people suddenly want flea injections for their cats or wormers for their dogs. But as Doug says, it's all money for us so why complain?

And Mr D. comes in with a slightly chirpier Paddy and grumpily wants to know why the place is so packed.

'They all want a look at Lucy,' Clare says.

I could kill her. I think she's a bit jealous of me actually.

'Well, I don't blame them wanting to look at Lucy.' Mr D. chuckles. 'A fine-looking girl she is.'

Obviously he's the one person in the country who doesn't listen to trash radio or read trashy papers.

'And why is the clinic up for auction?' he demands then.

'Owner is selling it,' I say.

'With you lot in it?'

'No, we'll either have to move or go out of business.'

'And where will I go with Paddy?'

Both Clare and I shrug.

'Well, that's very inconsiderate. Very.' He rubs his dog. She must be feeling better because she growls. 'No one cares about the individual man any more, do they, Paddy?' Then, glaring at me and Clare, he says, 'Well, if I had known youse were closing down, I might have gone somewhere else with Paddy. Somewhere permanent.'

'Be our guest,' Clare snaps. She's in a brutal humour.

Mr D. looks taken aback.

'I suppose you don't care that we'll lose our jobs, never mind about your dog.' And off she stomps.

'She's a bit upset,' I say unnecessarily.

'Well, you might lose your job and you're not biting the head off anyone that comes in, are you?'

'Oooh, she can bite my head off anytime.' A young lad has entered, sniggering. He has a Scottish Terrier on a lead. Probably borrowed it from his granny. 'How's it going, Condom Girl?'

'I like my men with some manners,' I say tartly. 'So, let's do the entrance again.'

Mr D. looks in bewilderment from me to the young lad. 'I dunno, you're getting narky too. I dunno. There'll be no business left if yez treat all yer customers like that.'

Then, of course, there are the phone calls. Some papers ring and I decline to answer any questions and some smart alecs ring asking if maybe they could lay claim to Fáinne's paternity. Doug advises me to laugh it off but I can't. It's my daughter they are talking about and however much they want to slate me they should keep her out of it. And this is what I tell them. And one guy apologises, which makes me feel better.

Les rings. He's happy and upbeat about the whole episode. 'No publicity is bad publicity,' he states. 'Publicity like you had yesterday, that's pure gold. Everyone knows you now! Just you wait: you'll be in demand now.'

'Well, I'm not doing the *Woman's Life* shoot,' I tell him. 'I decided last night that I wasn't doing it.'

'But you have to do it!' He is shocked, I can tell from his desperate tone of voice. 'After all the mega-publicity today, you have to maximise your visibility.'

'Yeah, that's what *Woman's Life* are probably thinking too. They'll have me in tarty stuff. I'm sorry, Les, but I've a daughter to think of.'

'Well, try *not* to think of her. Look, other actresses have been right wans and done steamy stuff and they're respected now.'

'Yes, well, I don't want to be a right wan, thanks.'

'So be a wrong one,' Les chortles. 'A very very wrong one!'

'Les, there are calls coming in. Bye.'

Work finishes for me at five. Doug is exhausted – he has another two hours to go and he admits that he has never looked up the arses of so many animals in one day before. 'Business is great, though.' He grins at me. 'Being a father isn't so bad after all.'

Clare makes some kind of disapproving noise to herself which we both ignore. It seems as if the whole country has heard now – and I reckon that if Jason has any sense, he'll never make contact. Maddie phoned and invited me to dinner at her place if I wanted.

'We might as well both share lover boy.' She chortled as Clive told her to shut up in the background. Maddie didn't though. Instead, she shouted, 'Didn't I pick the virile one!'

I'd love to be Maddie. Nothing bothers her. Her good humour wins over everyone. She's like Doug in that way.

Anyway, I told Maddie that I couldn't go to dinner, that I just wanted to go home.

At home, with Fáinne happily informing me that all the girls in her class think it's really cool that I'm plastered across the middle pages of every paper in the country, I allow myself to relax.

Today wasn't as bad as I thought.

There's a lot to be said for good mates.

48

BY THE TIME Saturday comes around, I'm not sure if I have the energy for making up with Gray and Audrey. I mean, I want to, but it's just been such an exhausting week that if it goes wrong, I reckon I'll never set foot outside the door again.

The story about me on the Declan D'arcy show has legs, as they say in the newspaper business. There was a pull-out section detailing my life and wondering what exactly happened during those college years. I reckon if I run short of cash in the future, I can auction my diary. One of the papers even tried to interview my lecturers, who declined. But they dug up a couple of 'good friends' who remained nameless. These people said that I did have a tendency to hang around with weirdos in college. I'm sure Maddie and Gray were chuffed at that.

Tracy was photographed on the film set with a headline about scandal following the Gleeson sisters everywhere. Her denied romance with the married film star was dragged up again.

It was an awful week.

So, here I am, standing outside Gray's house, having been responsible for him being labelled a 'weirdo' in a national newspaper, hoping he's going to accept my second attempt at an apology. It hadn't worked the last time. Last time, I'd figured that he would have me back with open arms, but now I'm not sure. I don't like not being sure of things, I realise suddenly. I like to know what people are like, put them in boxes and decide for myself how they will behave. Only people aren't like that. People can't be boxed off and my judgement is all over the place and it scares me.

I steel myself to ring the bell but before I get to it, the door is opened and Gray stands there. His camera is slung about his neck and he looks as if he's going somewhere. He stops and stares at me.

'Hi,' I mutter. Pause. 'I'm, eh, Lucy Deeson.' I half smile. 'I caught a flight from Iraq this morning to say "hi".'

He grins. *Thank God.* 'Well,' he says in a slightly teasing voice, 'I hope you haven't brought our child with you because I'm going out now.'

I've missed him making me laugh. 'I'm sorry.' It comes out so easily. 'You were right, I was a bitch and I'm sorry.'

He shakes his head. 'Forget it. I was awful to you that day, I said some awful stuff – Audrey was in bits and, well . . .' He opens the door wide. 'Come in.'

'Naw, you're going out.'

'Audrey is here, she'll make you a cuppa. Is Fáinne with you?'

'Naw, she's not.' I don't want to meet Audrey; she probably hates me. I don't blame her. 'I'd better go and—'

'Audrey,' Gray calls. 'Visitor!'

Audrey comes out of the kitchen. She's got something in her hair – some colour or something – and it sticks out all over the place. She stops dead when she sees me.

'Audrey, hi,' I mutter, trying desperately to meet her gaze. 'I've come to say "sorry".' Audrey says nothing so I blunder on. 'I was horrible to you that day and, well, as Gray probably told you, there's something about my sister that sets me off.' I attempt a feeble laugh. 'But, anyway, I was in a bad mood and took it out on you. Sorry.'

Audrey attempts a smile. 'Well, I guess you're *supposed* to take bad moods out on people you like? So *obviously* you must like me and Gray.'

'I guess I do.'

'Well, that's good then 'cause I really want to get on with Gray's friends.' A massive smile. 'Do you want a coffee?'

'Eh—'

'Course she does.' Gray shoves me towards the kitchen. 'Now you two girls have a chat, I've to head out to a match.'

I watch like a drowning woman as he slams the front door. What am I supposed to say to Audrey? It's weird trying to talk to people you've hurt. Hard. I keep thinking that they keep thinking about what I said to them. Maybe I'll tell her that I've to be back early for Fáinne. But before I can lie, Audrey beckons me into the kitchen. 'I'm just going up to finish off my hair colour,' she says. 'Make yourself a sambo or tea or something. We can chat then.'

She makes it sound like a big treat and I can't say 'no' because she was the injured party. And I don't want to offend her again. 'Right, OK.'

Audrey comes down after around twenty minutes and she looks fantastic. She's put some colour and highlights in her hair and it looks great. 'Did you not make anything to eat?' she asks accusingly.

'Eh, no, I'm not hungry. Your hair looks great.'

She smiles like a big kid. Which she is, I think. 'Really?' She flicks it over her shoulder. 'I'm just trying it out. I started work in a hair and beauty salon last week and I like to see what works and what doesn't. Is it *really* nice?'

'Yep.'

She squeals with delight and fluffs her hair up.

'So, how are you fitting the modelling in around your new job?'

'Oh.' Major pause. She shrugs and looks at me through impossibly blue eyes. 'I don't do modelling any more.'

Oh shit. Bugger. Christ. Fuck. 'Not because of what I said?' I whisper. Horrified.

'Uh-huh.' She stares at her nails, which gleam and catch the light. She has some kind of stickers on them and they look cool. 'Well – sort of. I knew I was hopeless before you said it but I just couldn't face it, you know?'

'Aw, Audrey—'

She holds up her hand, which is smooth and gorgeous. 'Don't, Lucy.' She smiles that sort of innocent smile she has. 'Honest, it's fine. Like, it was hard to admit it to myself – I wanted to be a model for so long, but I wasn't right . . . I just couldn't take a hint. No work in two years and I couldn't see it. Wouldn't see it. You did me a favour.'

'No. No, I was horrible.'

She ignores me. 'But then Maddie brought this newspaper over and told me I should apply for this job, the one I have now – and I *love* it.' She smiles brightly. 'It's *great*. Like, I found that modelling wasn't the only great job in the world, there were others. Imagine!'

'And you don't miss the modelling?'

'What modelling? I hadn't done it in two years!'

My admiration for Audrey, which admittedly hadn't ever really registered, shoots up.

'I was, like, so focused on modelling that I couldn't see that there are better things out there. That's what Gray said and he's right.' She takes two cups from the press. 'Tea? Coffee?'

'Coffee, thanks.' She's such a nice person, I realise. OK,

she's irritating too, but really nice. I know what Gray sees in her now.

'Imagine if Gray ever gets tired of me.' She giggles. 'I'll never take that hint. It'll be at least two years before I let him go.'

But I reckon it'll be a lifetime before Gray lets her go.

49

May 6th

I haven't seen Jason in three days. I've called him on his mobile only it seems to be dead. In a way, it's a relief, as I don't know how I'm going to tell him.

Didn't bother going to support the school team tonight.

Haven't talked to Gray since the day in the canteen.

Am avoiding Maddie.

May 7th

Mam remarked that I'd put on weight today. And I have. My boobs seem to have grown. They actually look nice. I pretended not to hear Mam though.

May 9th

Mam said it again. She had a strange look on her face and I suddenly thought to myself, she knows. SHE KNOWS. My heart jumped a bit and I swear, I was going to tell her, but I couldn't. What way could I say it? How do you do it?

Rang Maddie. Cried for the first time over it.

Maddie said that we have to tell Jason.

Going tomorrow.

50

DECLAN MCGRATH ARRIVES in the clinic on Thursday morning with what I reckon is some kind of a 'high flyer' businessman in tow. The businessman is wearing a well-cut suit, he's around thirty (which makes me sick!) and he's carrying an expensive briefcase. 'We're having a look around,' Declan says to a place over my shoulder. 'Ted here is interested in acquiring the property.'

'The site,' Ted corrects haughtily. 'I wouldn't be interested in keeping it like this.'

'Oh, yes, that's what I meant,' Declan says, oily smooth, rubbing his hands together. 'Can you make us a cuppa there,' he asks me, 'while we discuss business?'

I gawk at him. I'm not employed by him. He's putting me out of a job and he wants me to make him tea. The *nerve*. 'You know where the kitchen is,' I say, trying to sound innocent. 'You presumably know what a kettle is.'

Both men look at me. Then look at me again. Ted, I think, has recognised me. I squirm but keep going. 'And I do hope, Declan, that the electricity you use will be deducted from our exorbitant rent this month.'

Declan's jaw drops so far that I'm tempted to reach out and close it for him. 'I'll be having a word with Doug about this,' he splutters.

'About deducting the electricity?'

325

Ted, to give him credit, smirks a little.

'About your attitude,' Declan says. 'Just because you're on TV, don't think you can treat me like this.' He turns to Ted. 'Come on, I'll show you around.'

Both men leave and I allow myself a huge smile.

Doug is accosted by Declan when he wanders out of his surgery a while later. I see Declan whispering furiously to him and gesturing in my direction. I wave in a flirty manner over at the two men.

'Good one, Luce,' Doug calls out cheerfully. 'Keep it up.'

Declan splutters something along the lines of 'even if youse had the money I wouldn't sell it to yez now' and stomps off, slamming the front door behind him.

Doug laughs and ushers the next patient in.

It would be good, however, if Doug did worry a little about the business. Like, I'm sure he *is* worried, just not enough to charge people properly. That very afternoon, just as Clare is struggling in through the door with two enormous suitcases, I overhear Doug telling an old woman not to worry about the tablets for her dog. 'Just pay me when you can,' he tells her.

She's ever so grateful and promises him five euro a week.

Doug glances a little guiltily at me but I don't say anything. I do like that he's kind, and I'd hate him to change, but at the same time, I need my bloody job.

'Hold the door for me, will you?' Clare barks. She's wedged her foot into the entrance. There is one suitcase inside the surgery and one outside. Doug opens the door for her and the old woman squeezes by with her poodle. Clare grunts out a 'thanks' and grabs her other suitcase. When both of them are side by side, she lifts them up and carries them inside the counter.

Doug and I glance at each other and then look at her.

'Holiday?' Doug asks innocently.

'Yes,' Clare says with satisfaction. 'A permanent one from Brendan and his mother and his sister.' She takes off her coat and hangs it up. Then, sitting down, she turns to the books and begins to flick through them while Doug raises his eyes questioningly at me.

'You've *left* Brendan?' I say.

'Where is the invoice for the old woman that just left?' Clare ignores me and turns on Doug.

He flinches.

'Well?'

'She's paying by the week,' he stammers out, like a guilty kid.

'By the week?' Clare raises her eyebrows. 'Are you stupid?'

'Her money will hardly save us,' Doug says sulkily.

'It would *help*!' Clare's eyes unexpectedly brim with tears. She turns away from us and I see a tear plop on to the accounts.

Doug shoots me a desperate look. 'Clare—' he says.

'I'm fine. I'm fine.'

Doug glances at me again. 'Maybe Clare would like a coffee, Luce.'

Great. Thanks.

'I'm fine.' Clare scrubs her eyes.

But she's not. Doug is making big talk-to-her gestures. Talk to her yourself, I want to gesture back. Tentatively, I touch her arm. 'Come on, Clare. It's only a coffee. Let Doug manage on his own for a bit. Do him good.'

'Nothing would do him good except a brain transplant.' Clare sniffs. 'We're all going to lose our jobs and he's still undercharging people.'

'I'm offended,' Doug says mildly. 'Now go inside and let

Luce make you a cuppa from some coffee that I paid for. If you feel that bad, you can leave a contribution.'

Clare gulps out what I think is a laugh.

I make us both a coffee. Clare doesn't seem to know how to react to me. She perches awkwardly on the chair, rubbing her perfectly groomed hands together. 'I'm fine,' she keeps saying. 'I don't know what all the fuss is about.'

'Well.' I hand her a mug. 'It's not every day you leave your husband.'

She giggles, a bit hysterically.

'You don't have to talk about it,' I say, sitting opposite her, my own mug in my hand. 'But if you want to, well, you can.'

She wraps her hands about her cup and takes a gulp of coffee. She doesn't say anything though and I think she's not going to. I reckon Clare doesn't confide in people that easily.

'He's a bastard, you know.'

She says it so low that at first I don't know if she has actually spoken. 'Sorry?'

'Brendan. He's a bastard.'

Am I meant to agree? 'Is he?'

'Yes. Completely.' She drinks some more coffee and, pinning me with her gaze, she says, 'And best of all, he doesn't know I've left him yet. His sister is minding his mother. I had my cases packed before she came.' She pauses and seems to relish what she's about to say. 'Ha, serve them right when I don't come home. I've left him a note in the jacks. Right where he puts his newspapers. He comes home in the evening and sits on the jacks for ages. It's so he won't have to see his mother.'

'Oh.'

'He hardly looks at her. He hardly talks to me. He's in

and out of that house like a lodger. He thinks he can buy me with fancy watches and jumpers, but, well, he can't!'

'Right.'

'Do you know what he said when I told him I might lose my job? Do you know?'

I shake my head.

'Well, you must be able to guess?'

'No.' I laugh nervously. 'I can't.'

'He said . . .' Clare puts down her mug and stares up at the ceiling. 'He said – and this is no joke – he said that that might be for the best as Bronagh – that's his sister – was finding it hard minding her mother. Upsetting, is the word he used. His sister is upset minding her own mother.' Clare looks at me. '"And what about me?" I asked him. "What about me, do I count?" And he said, "It's not your mother, is it?"' She takes in a great whoosh of air. 'And I said no, but that it was my *life*. Or rather my *lack* of a life. Don't get me wrong, I'd do anything for that man but he doesn't seem to care about me at all.'

'Oh he does.' It's an automatic response.

She's suddenly all teary-eyed again. 'No, he doesn't.'

Without thinking, I move in beside her on the sofa and put my arm about her shoulder. 'I'm sure he does.'

Her voice catches. 'D'you know, I've been minding his mother for the last nine years and she's getting worse. She needs constant care. If she goes out of the house, she gets lost. She talks to the television and ignores me. She mashes her dinner up and then won't eat it. And I'm on my own.' She starts to cry, huge sobs that shake her body. 'And, like, we've no children so all his family think that's what we *should* do. And I'd love a little girl or boy, but it's not happening and I can't take it any more. I just can't.'

'Aw, Clare, stop. Come on.' I pull her to me. 'Come on.'

'You're so lucky to have Fáinne. I'd love a little girl.'

'I'm sure things will sort themselves out. I'm sure Brendan loves you.'

'Oh, he does, just not enough.'

I don't know what to say to that, so I just keep my arm about her and hold her until she stops crying. And when she does, she's mortified. She fishes a tissue out of her bag and, wiping her eyes, apologises. 'I don't know what came over me.'

'It's fine.' I smile slightly and wait while she gets herself together. 'Have you anywhere to go now?'

'My sister.'

'Good. OK.'

She blows her nose noisily. 'Sorry for dumping all this on you.'

'No, it's OK. You finish up that coffee and take your time. I'll go and relieve Doug.'

As I stand up, Clare grabs my hand. 'Thanks, Luce. Thanks a lot.'

'No problem.' We smile at each other.

'And tell Doug I'm sorry for snapping at him about that old woman.'

'He needs someone to snap at him,' I say back. 'He's hopeless.'

'Isn't he?' We smile again. 'But he's a good guy all the same,' Clare adds softly. 'He's kind.'

'And broke.'

'I'd take it over inconsiderate and loaded any day though.'

She's got a point.

330

51

A T LUNCH THE next day, I decide to take some positive
action. Clare's worries have transferred themselves on
to me. For the first time in years, I buy a newspaper. I'm not
a newspaper person. Buying a newspaper, I've always felt, is
a mature, responsible thing to do. I'm neither. I mean, even
though I'm twenty-seven, heading for twenty-eight, and I've
got a mortgage, it's as if time stopped in my head when I
was nineteen. I'll probably be wearing flares and tight tops
when I'm ninety. Mutton dressed as lamb, as my mother likes
to say. Anyway, I buy the paper because it's got a jobs section
and I study it for suitable positions.

Nothing appeals. In fact, there is very little that I think
I'll be able to do.

Doug arrives back from his lunch just as I'm circling
'receptionist wanted for busy city centre office' and I hastily
turn over a load of pages until I'm on to the sports section.

He turns them back. 'You might as well,' he mutters
glumly, stabbing the page. 'I got turned down again this
lunchtime.' He's wearing a good suit and looks really well.
How could anyone turn him down? OK, so his suit is brown
and his shirt is brown but he still looks lovely.

'The guy today hated me,' he explains as he digs his hand
into the open packet of biscuits on the table. 'Told me I was
a liability. That my accounts were a mess. That a veterinary

practice should be lucrative. Holy fuck, that's what I said to him. I said if I can make the rent payments, I'd be able to make the mortgage repayments. I told him he could have my house as back-up but he still said no.'

'So that's it then?'

He nods. 'Looks like it. Jim has tried, I've tried; it's not gonna work. Once the auction is over, we'll be out.' He pauses briefly before indicating my paper. 'So you look for something now, Lucy.'

'And you?'

'Yeah, I'll look for something too – maybe abroad again or, if the worst comes to the worst, I'll work for the auld fella.'

'But you'll hate that.'

'It's better than nothing.' He refills my empty coffee cup and pours himself one, then he clinks my mug against his. 'Cheers,' he says unhappily. He's about to add something else when there comes a massive knocking at the door followed by the continuous ringing of the bell.

Doug jumps up, not seeming to notice that his coffee has slopped all over his good trousers. 'Must be serious,' he says, as he legs it out of the room.

From outside, I hear someone shouting and it soon becomes clear that whatever is going on, it has nothing to do with a sick animal. Then an agitated, red-faced man shoves the door of the coffee room open, making me jump.

'Where is she?' this guy demands, glancing about wildly. 'She has to be here.'

'Lucy,' Doug says calmly, 'this is Brendan. Can you tell him that Clare isn't here?'

'Clare isn't here,' I parrot. Brendan isn't what I imagined at all. I thought he'd be tall and handsome and charming, but he's small, quite round actually, with a shiny bald head and tiny anxious eyes. He's wearing an expensive suit, much classier than Doug's, but it doesn't look half as good on him.

'Well, she always works from twelve to five,' Brendan says, 'so why isn't she here?'

Doug and I glance at each other. Twelve is our lunchtime.

'What time is my wife due in?' Brendan barks.

'I dunno,' Doug lies – badly. 'Is she even in today, Luce?'

The front door slams outside and the three of us freeze. Brendan is the first to react. He bounds out of the room with Doug close on his heels. I feel I have no choice but to follow them. I hope there won't be a massive argument. Ever since Mam and Dad fought that time at the front door, rows have always made me uncomfortable.

Clare is standing just inside the door, her arms folded across her chest. She's glaring at Brendan. 'I saw your car outside,' she snaps. 'What are you doing here?'

'Looking for you,' he snaps back. 'What do you think *you're* doing?'

'Going to work.' Clare takes him by surprise as she pushes past him. He staggers back and Doug just manages to keep him from falling.

Brendan shakes Doug off. 'I meant what are you doing by *leaving* me?'

I sit down at Clare's desk and fiddle about with the computer. I want to pretend that I can't hear them, but it's impossible. My hands are sweaty. How must Clare feel?

'I meant to leave you,' Clare states as if it's all so simple. 'Now, Brendan, please get out of here as I have work to do.'

'I'm going nowhere,' Brendan states. 'You're needed at home.'

'I'm needed here,' Clare says with admirable composure. 'And what's more, I'm appreciated here. So please leave.'

'I'm going nowhere!'

333

'Eh, sorry,' Doug says. 'If Clare wants you to leave, you'll have to go.'

'No I don't!'

'I'll be opening up for surgery in a while and, as this is my premises, I'm afraid you do have to go.'

Cor, Doug sounds really macho.

'Won't be your premises for much longer though, will it?' Brendan sneers.

'Maybe not,' Doug says, flinching. 'But for now it is – so go.'

Brendan seems to consider his options. Eventually, he wags a finger at Clare. 'I'll be back.'

'If Arnold Schwarzenegger said that, it might excite me,' Clare replies. 'But from you it just sounds pathetic.'

Brendan's screwed-up little eyes widen. He gulps hard and says, sounding hurt, 'You don't mean that.'

'Bye.'

Brendan glances at the three of us and says defensively, 'I gave her everything. Everything.'

'Including your mother, ey?' Clare snaps.

'She's sick!'

'I know! I've been trying to tell you that for years.' Clare leans her hands on the counter as she shouts this at him.

'I'll be back!' He exits, slamming the door behind him.

None of us quite knows what to do next. The silence sort of builds until Doug mutters, 'You OK?'

'Yeah,' Clare nods. 'Sorry about that.'

'No probs.' Doug shuffles from foot to foot. 'But he's right – this place won't be mine next month so you'd both better start job-hunting.' His voice breaks. 'OK?' He doesn't wait for our sympathy. He heads into his surgery.

I hate Declan McGrath for doing this to him.

52

AUDREY HAS INVITED Maddie and me to Gray's house for a free day of pampering. Apparently, she needs some people to practise her new-found skills on and thinks we'd love it. Neither Maddie nor I are makeover chicks but I feel I have to go to make it up to Audrey and Maddie tags along just because I'm going. Gray was meant to be there too but he turned it down. Maddie grins at me as Audrey makes his excuses.

'He was really sorry,' Audrey explains, filing Maddie's nails into neat ovals, 'but he had some important job on. I asked him what could be more important than taking care of his skin, but he just laughed. Honestly!' She makes an affectionate face. 'Hey, your nails are *great*, Maddie.'

'Pregnancy,' Maddie says.

Maddie is blooming. OK, so she's enormous but her skin is glowing and her hair is shining and her nails are growing. All the important things. I hadn't looked like that during *my* pregnancy. I'd been sick and had suffered from the most terrible nightmares, usually ones involving huge hairy spiders. My hair had grown thick and bushy and I hadn't bothered taking care of it. I'd been a complete mess. Just like now, actually. Two of my job applications have been turned down before reaching interview stage. The jobs *were* slightly out of my league but it still dented my confidence. Hence, major nail-biting. I'm dreading Audrey seeing my hands. I've bitten a couple of my nails right down so they've bled. I didn't even realise I'd done it, I'd be thinking of something, usually my job or money and suddenly I'd find that my nails had been destroyed.

'And now you, Lucy,' Audrey says chirpily. I hold out my ragged hands and she winces. Then she makes a face and, to my surprise, she hits herself. 'Oooh, I shouldn't do *that*,' she moans. Then she says, robot-like, 'No matter how bad a state one of our clients is in, you should never react.' Another wince. 'I'm sorry, Lucy.'

'It's OK. I know my nails are a mess.'

Audrey doesn't answer. She looks at them from all angles. 'I could put falsies on you,' she offers. 'I mean, there is just nothing I can do with what you have. Nothing at all.'

'Sure, falsies would be great.'

'Right. Well, I'll get them, so.' She jumps up and leaves.

Maddie peers at my hands. 'God, you have been busy on them, haven't you?'

'Yeah.' I clench them into fists so we don't have to look at them.

'You'll get another job.'

I can't answer her. If I do, I'll cry and I don't want to spoil the day. Audrey was so thrilled when we said we'd come that I can't go dumping my problems and upsetting everyone. 'So how's Baby?' I ask instead.

'Aw, good, I think.' Maddie pats her bump and grins hugely. 'I've got this thing from the hospital that I have to fill out – did you get one of those?'

'What thing?'

'The baby has to kick ten times in a day apparently.'

I vaguely remember something. 'Oh yeah.'

'Did you fill it out?'

'I can't remember.'

'Like if it kicks all in a row and then doesn't kick for ages, is that one kick or loads of kicks?'

'I dunno.'

Maddie giggles. 'Some help you are. I thought, when I got preggers, oh great, Lucy can fill me in on all the details, she'll understand – but you're hopeless!'

'It's been over eight years, Maddie!'

'Yeah, but how could you forget?'

'Because my dear, there is so much *else* to remember.' I pull gently on her hair. 'You'll see,' I say ominously.

Maddie laughs loudly. 'We are going to have the most perfect baby, Lucy Gleeson.'

'Of course you are. No late nights, no puking. It'll be a doddle.'

'And such a perfect child deserves the perfect godmother – you!'

For a second I wonder if I've heard right, but she's beaming at me, so I must have. My jaw drops. 'Really?'

'Of course, sure you're my best buddy.'

'Aw, Maddie. Thanks. I'll be a great godmother, I promise.'

She cackles at my emotion. 'Well, you'd better get a job, so, 'cause you'll have to buy it loads of presents.'

'No problem.'

A nail makeover, face pack and toe treatment later, Maddie and I are just about to leave when my mobile rings.

'Hi, is this Lucy Gleeson?' a stranger asks.

'Yes.'

'This is Tony Harrison from the *Sunday News*. I was wondering if you'd care to comment on the allegations being made about you.'

'Sorry?'

337

'Is that a "sorry" about what you've done?'

'I don't know what I've done!'

Maddie raises her eyebrows questioningly at me and I shrug back. I share my telephone with her. I get the feeling something awful is coming.

'You don't know what you've done?' Tony Harrison has adopted a faintly sneering tone. 'I believe you were meant to do a shoot for *Woman's Life* and that you let them down?'

'That's hardly breaking news,' I say back, in an equally sneering tone.

'When they'd *booked* you?' He's out-sneering me. 'When they'd measured you up for clothes? Is it a case that condom power has gone to your head, Miss Gleeson?'

'Pardon?'

'"Pardon",' Tony Harrison mimics. 'What do you mean by "pardon"?'

'What do you mean by what you've just said?'

'I mean that you let a perfectly good magazine down at the last minute, that you snubbed their readership, that you hadn't the courtesy to tell them yourself.'

'My agent rang them.'

'But you snubbed them?'

'I was under pressure at the time.'

'Have you found your ex-boyfriend yet?'

'That's none of your business.'

'You made it my business when you went on Declan D'arcy.'

'Fuck off!' Maddie shouts into the phone, deafening me.

Tony Harrison hangs up.

'Maddie!' I stare aghast at her. 'You just told a news reporter to "fuck off".'

'Nosey little shit,' she spits.

'It's his job.' I close my eyes. 'Oh my God, they're going to make me out to be superbitch in the papers now.'

'You're getting frown lines,' Audrey admonishes. 'You have to calm down.'

'I'd rather have frown lines than be in the papers!' I'm hyperventilating. 'Oh God!'

'No you wouldn't,' Audrey says chirpily. 'Come back in and I'll rub a moisturiser on your face.'

'No.' I gape at her. '*Audrey*, I'm going to be crucified in the papers.' Frantically, I flick through the in calls on my phone trying to locate Tony Harrison's number. Finding it, I dial him. He's unavailable.

I try again.

Same story.

'Sorry,' Maddie says meekly. 'I was just so annoyed.'

'I'm ringing Les.' I dial him.

'Yellow!'

I explain what has happened.

'Any publicity is good publicity, Lucy,' he says cheerily. 'They rang me too. I just told them that you couldn't do it for personal reasons, but telling the guy to fuck off was a stroke of genius. Tell your friend "well done"!'

'I will not! You've got to get on to them, Les!'

'Look, telling the guy to fuck off means you're not stuck for work. You don't care about the public's perception of you – which, quite frankly, could be a bit shit when the story breaks – but if you're not stuck for work it means you must be good. So, they'll come banging on the doors for you now.'

'Ring the paper up, Les,' I say grimly. I do not want to be hated. Being hated is my worst nightmare.

'They've got their story, they won't answer.'

'Les, you are my agent, I'm ordering you!'

'OK, but I'm telling—'

I cut him off.

53

I T'S EVEN WORSE than the first time I was in the papers. At that time, it was just gossip and speculation. No one actually *hated* me. But everyone will now. At first I decide not to buy the paper, but that's like deciding not to look at a car crash. I just have to see it. I have to see every gory detail. Torture myself with the horrendous images that will be out there. So I get up on Sunday morning and head down to the local newsagent's, Fáinne tripping along lightly beside me.

'Hello, ladies,' Jean, the ancient owner of the shop, says cheerily, turning as usual to get Fáinne a free lollipop from the jar on the counter. 'How's school, Fáinne?'

'Good,' Fáinne says breathlessly. 'Can I have a red lollipop?'

'Please,' I mutter automatically even though every part of me is recoiling in horror at the headline on the front of the *Sunday News*. 'F*** OFF' it says in big bold letters. Then underneath, also in bold, it says: 'That was Condom Girl Lucy Gleeson's response when asked why she snubbed the readers of *Woman's Life*.'

'Please,' Fáinne says wearily.

Jean laughs as she hands Fáinne a lolly.

I wonder if I should buy the paper. I want to but, at the same time, I don't want to hand over money for something that is slagging me off.

Jean sees me looking at the headline. 'I wouldn't worry about that auld tripe. Load of rubbish. Here, have it free.'

I smile gratefully at her and take it. 'I didn't say that,' I explain unnecessarily to Jean. 'My friend did – they thought it was me.'

'Sure, I know. A girl like you would never say anything like that.' Jean shakes her head. 'I don't know. It's a disgraceful headline. Using the "F" word to get attention. Times have changed. I don't know. And I wouldn't mind, but that same paper has shocking things in it – all the perversions that go on between its pages and they pretend to be outraged by you saying the "F" word.'

'I didn't say it,' I explain once more. It's important that she knows that.

'Of course you didn't,' she says again. 'But can't you see what I'm getting at? Even if you did say it, they're not shocked by it. Not at all.'

'And I didn't snub the readers,' I go on. 'I didn't.'

'You'd never snub anyone,' Jean says. 'Sure, don't I know that? You're a shining example to that child of yours. Well, I suppose it might be nicer if you were married but maybe that's being old-fashioned. Still, Fáinne is a lovely girl. Aren't you, Fáinne?'

'Hmmm?' Fáinne looks up from a Barbie magazine. 'What, Jean?'

'I said you're lovely.'

'I know.'

Jean and I laugh. I buy my two usual Sunday papers from Jean and call 'goodbye' to her over my shoulder.

The article is basically a rehash of the Declan D'arcy show. A picture of me holding my condom box dominates the second page. Then Tony Harrison goes on to explain how

341

the editors of *Woman's Life* felt snubbed by me. How rude it was of me to let them down at short notice. Was my brief flirtation with fame going to my head, Tony wondered?

Little shit.

I wonder what to do. Should I write a letter? Should I just forget it?

The phone rings in the middle of my fantasy of locating Tony Harrison and piercing him with a very painful sword, tipped with poison. It's Les.

'Joe Duffy wants you to appear on his afternoon show,' he says delightedly. 'Would you like that? You can talk to him over the telephone.'

'I would hate that, Les,' I say back. 'I don't want a whole show devoted to me.'

'Joe's a nice man. He'll give you a fair hearing.'

'I don't care. I'm not going on radio again. He'll ask me about the Jason search.'

'Yeah, course he will,' Les says in a big patronising voice. 'That's his job.'

'I'm not doing it.'

'But you can plead your innocence. You can tell the nation your half of the story. Tell them you didn't say "fuck off", though personally if it was me, I'd take credit for that.'

'I'm not doing anything. I'm just going to go to work and try to forget about it. And today I'm going to enjoy my day with my daughter. Bye, Les.'

'I thought you wanted to be famous,' he grumbles.

'Not like this.'

'This, honey,' Les says, 'is the best it gets.'

My arse.

I hang up on him.

*

342

Mam rings of course. Almost hysterical. How could I make a show of myself like that? How could I tell someone to 'F' off? Why didn't I do the shoot? She hoped Fáinne hadn't seen the paper. *She* hadn't seen it. She'd *never* buy a paper like that. A RAG! One of the neighbours had told her about it. Now all the neighbours knew. Why couldn't I be more like Mona Lisa and keep things to myself? Or just smile and be nice, for goodness' sake. Why did I have to tell someone to 'F' off?

'I didn't,' I try to explain. 'Maddie did.'

'A likely story,' she mutters. And then, 'Well, what does it matter who said it: mud sticks. No one will believe that your friend said it. Sure, didn't all your friends ring up claiming to be Fáinne's dad a few weeks ago? I dunno. Where do you get your friends, Lucy?'

And Maddie rings. Of course I forgive her. I couldn't be angry with her for long. And Clive comes on and awkwardly says how awful it is. Gray rings and thinks it's a laugh. Audrey hasn't a clue what's going on.

I break open a bottle of wine and then decide not to drink it. Worse things have happened, I think. Far worse.

Fuck it.

May 10th

Jason wasn't there when Maddie and I called over today. I don't know where he is. He hasn't rung or anything. I'm getting bigger by the day; if I leave it much longer, everyone will know. We rang and rang his bell and no one answered.

Will call again tomorrow.

May 12th

Called again to Jason yesterday. I suppose, deep inside, I knew something was up. He hadn't been in touch — nothing. Maddie came with me again. This time Johnno answered.

'We're looking for Jason,' I said into the intercom.

'Gone,' Johnno spat. 'He's gone.'

And I thought that he just meant gone out, so I asked when would he be back and Johnno said never. That he'd never be back, that he was GONE. And that he didn't know where Jason was, that he'd just packed his bags and fucked off with the rent. That he had no address for him.

That he was just gone.

'He can't be,' I said. I think I turned to Maddie. 'He wouldn't do that to me, Maddie. He loved me.'

She just looked at me. Said nothing. I remember putting my hand on my belly. She hugged me.

I can't believe it.

If I coped all those years ago when my whole life had been bombed out of existence, then I could cope now.

I had Fáinne now.

I knew I would cope.

54

T HE NEXT DAY is my Declan D'arcy nightmare revisited.
I fancy that everyone in the clinic recognises me. But
even though it's all more horrible this time, I'm stronger. I
can do a good pretence of not caring.

'Was that you in the paper yesterday, Lucy?' Mr D. asks,
staring hard at me.

'Yes.' I try to sound cheerful. 'Only I didn't tell the reporter
to fuck off.'

'Well, I would have,' Mr D. says. 'Little shit. It's home
wiping his arse he should be. He's only a young fella trying
to make his name by smearing other people. If you ask me
fuck off is too good for him.' He nods emphatically.

'Aw, thanks.'

'Can you tell Brendan to fuck off if he comes in here again?'
Clare interrupts. 'My husband,' she explains to Mr D.

'I'd say he'd be only too glad to fuck off,' Mr D. mutters,
causing Clare to glower at him. 'You keep smiling, girl,' Mr D.
says to me. 'I look forward to that smile when I come in here.'

'Well, in a little while you won't see it any more,' Clare
snaps, still miffed by his comment. 'We're up for auction.'

Mr D. shakes his head. 'Desperate. The cheapest vet for
miles about and you're closing.'

'He's only cheap because he insists on making a loss,' Clare
says.

'Pardon?'

'He undercharges all the old people. All the young kids. All the single mothers. He basically should run a charity and that's why we're losing our jobs.'

'No!' Mr D. looks to me for confirmation.

I shrug.

'Has he undercharged me?'

I'm about to say that he hasn't when Clare nods vigorously. 'You most of all.'

'Well, you just tell me what I owe you when I come out and I'll pay up.' He sounds indignant. 'I've no problem paying for Paddy. If all my money would keep her alive, I'd pay it.'

'Good,' Clare says and watches him shuffle off with Paddy in his arms. 'One down,' she says. 'About two hundred to go. We'll get the money out of them yet.'

I feel a sneaking admiration for her. Her life has just collapsed too and she's getting on with it. 'Doug will go mad,' I point out, half laughing.

'He's already mad,' Clare says back.

She's got a point.

There is no one in my parents' house that evening when I arrive to collect Fáinne. They've probably gone shopping or something. I hate that I have to go in and wait as it means I'll have to talk to them when they come back. Making myself tea, I locate an inoffensive newspaper in the recycling bin and sit down to read it.

Ten minutes later, the front door opens. I jump up, ready to grab Fáinne and leg it, only it's not Fáinne, it's Tracy.

'Anyone here?' she calls out as she pushes in the kitchen door.

Both of us stare at each other. We haven't spoken since

346

Christmas. 'I think they've gone shopping.' I indicate the kettle. 'You can make some tea if you like – I've boiled the water.' My duty done, I turn back to the paper.

'Ta.' Tracy gets a mug and pours herself a cuppa. Then she sits in the chair furthest away from me.

The only sound is the ticking of the kitchen clock, but it's not relaxing. I know my shoulders are tense and I haven't managed to drink any tea since Tracy arrived. I pick up my cup.

'Brazen it out, that's best,' Tracy says, breaking the silence and making me jump. My tea slops out on to the table.

'Sorry?'

'All that stuff in the papers,' Tracy says. 'Just ignore it. It's horrible but it'll go away if you brazen it out.'

She *would* bring that up. 'Don't gloat or anything,' I snap, looking for some kitchen paper to mop up the tea.

'I'm not gloating,' she hisses. 'Jesus, I know what it's like to have to deal with that crap and it's awful. I'm only trying to help.'

'Thanks,' I say, but I don't mean it. More silence as I wipe down the table.

Then, almost as if she can't leave it alone, she says, 'Why don't you like me?'

'Pardon?' Ultra-sarcastic from me.

'Isn't it funny how you want to trace a guy that let you down big time but to actually talk to me, your own sister, well, that's too hard, isn't it?'

I hate that she's talking about Jason. 'Tracy, just leave it, OK?'

'No, it's not OK.' Her voice rises a little. 'I want to know why it is that you don't like me.'

I glare at her. 'Oh for God's sake . . .' I roll my eyes and fire the wet paper in the bin. 'Just leave it.'

'I made it and you didn't – it's always been about that, hasn't it?'

'No.' I sit back down and grab the newspaper, holding it in front of my face so that I don't have to look at her.

'Yeah. Yeah it is. You've always been jealous of me.'

'Gimme a break!'

'You have!' And her voice is hard and edgy. 'And it's not my fault you got pregnant and chose to abandon everything.'

'I *chose*?' I place the paper very carefully on the table and my voice is low and furious. I hadn't realised up to that point how angry I was. 'I got pregnant. It wasn't exactly a lifestyle choice.'

'You *had* a choice,' Tracy says. 'You could have done that film but you didn't. You obviously wanted Fáinne more than you wanted to do the film. You had that choice and you made it.'

I open my mouth to say something but nothing comes out. I've never thought of things in that way before. But it's true – I never once thought of not having Fáinne. I just assumed that I'd still make it after she was born, which hadn't happened.

'And I'm sick of you being horrible to me every time we meet because I have what you want.'

'That's stupid!'

'No it's not,' Tracy shouts. She's angrier than me, I realise. Standing up, she comes towards me, making jabbing motions with her finger. I sit up straighter in my seat. 'It's true. I have what you want – and do you know why I have it?'

'Because you were the golden child.' I stand up too and shout into her face. 'The one that everyone loved and that everyone gave attention to.'

'Yeah!' To my surprise she's agreeing with me. 'Yeah, I was. And do you know how horrible that is? How horrible it is to be singled out? I became famous because I didn't have a bloody choice – I looked good, I was snapped up and, yeah, it was great for a bit. But now, now you see what it can be like – now you see what happens when the media twist stuff – do you like it now?'

'I'd like the money and the houses and the fame,' I fire back. God, I feel like slapping her. I realise this row has been brewing inside us for years. 'I'd sure like the attention.'

'The houses of which none is home? The money that you can't spend because your horrible jealous sister refuses to let you? The—'

'You tried to buy my daughter!'

'Yeah. Yeah, I did.' Tracy nods. 'And do you know why?'

'Because you haven't charm enough to make her like you as you are!'

My answer shocks her. She flinches, as if I've shot her or something. Then, to my horror, her eyes water. 'Exactly.' She bites her lip and her whole face sort of wobbles. 'Exactly.'

Christ. It's just like her to make me feel awful. I gulp. I think she's going to cry. But she isn't. She turns away from me and grabs her bag from the chair. She's leaving.

'I, eh, didn't mean—'

'You did.' Now she's not shouting. Her long dark hair falls in a veil across her face. 'Tell Mam I called, will you?'

'Tracy – look, sorry.' Jesus, the last thing I want is her on the phone crying to Mam. Mam will skin me.

'No, no, you're *not*.' She is crying. Big fat tears that send great tracks of black all down her face. 'That's all I can do, see. I'm famous for my face, not for my personality. Who cares about my personality? I don't know what my personality is like any more. I don't think I even have one.'

Oh shit! I cross towards her feeling like the horrible person

349

I know I am. 'You do have a personality,' I joke weakly. 'A horrible one.'

She doesn't laugh. She keeps walking. She's in the hall. She's fumbling with the door. And, oh crap, Mam and Dad are pulling into the driveway.

'Don't cry,' I beg. 'Please, Mam will kill me. I've annoyed her enough as it is.' I can't touch her, that'd be too weird.

To my surprise, she laughs. Only it's not a happy laugh. She turns to face me and her mouth is all twisted up. 'Since when have you ever cared what Mam thought? You always did exactly what you wanted. You had as many friends as you wanted, while I was dragged from place to place to get work. Both of them depending on me. Since when have you cared what she wanted?'

I'm so stunned by what she's said that I almost let her open the door but just at the last minute, I shove it closed. Mam starts to knock on it. Dad is taking Fáinne out of the car. 'Since I wrecked my future by getting pregnant,' I answer. 'Since I scrimped and struggled and scraped together a crap life for me and Fáinne.'

'You've a great life,' Tracy bellows, crying into my face. 'A nice house that you can come home to every day; mates that ring up radio stations pretending to be dads to your kid. No one would do that for me. I don't know who my friends are – are they going to go to the press about me? Do they want my money? What? At least you've nothing to offer anyone.'

'Thank you!'

'I didn't mean—'

'What is going on in there?' Mam starts hammering on the door. 'Girls, let me in!'

'Hiya, Mona Lisa!' Fáinne calls cheerfully from outside.

'And you have her and she loves you. I'd love a little girl

350

only what sort of a life could I have with a kid? I hate modelling, it's shallow and horrible and if I could swap places with you, I would – you whimpering cow!'

'Don't call *me* a whimpering cow! What are you doing now except whimpering!'

'At least I have a reason to!'

'Tracy! Lucy!' Dad is hammering on the door now. He sounds alarmed 'Let us in – come on now!'

'I envy you. I've always envied you,' Tracy says in a low vicious voice. 'You had so much freedom. You still have.'

It's as if she's hit me. I blink. 'I envied you,' I say, only I don't sound vicious, just amazed. 'You were all sunshine and nice teeth and I was the big clumsy oaf that messed up everything.'

'No.' Now her voice is softer. 'I would give anything to have what you have.'

I can't believe I'm hearing this.

'Everyone likes you. Everyone always liked you more than me.'

I stare at her. 'You outshone me all the time.'

'No, no, I didn't.'

Mam and Dad are rapping on the door. I'm still wedged up against it. 'Gray liked you better,' I find myself admitting. 'He told me so. He said I ruined your relationship with him.' Our voices, I note, are getting softer and softer.

'I thought he'd hate you if I blamed you,' she says. 'But he didn't.'

'You bitch!' Only I'm smiling. I don't know why.

'You were too.'

And I was. Even at the time, I'd known I was a bitch, but I couldn't help it. I might as well have tried to give up breathing as give up being envious of her. All my life had been spent in her shadow and just when the sun had finally shone on me, a big black cloud had swallowed it all up. And I think, in some way, I'd blamed her. Blamed her because I'd felt I had to match up to her and my chance to do it had gone. Blamed her because she was out of the house when Mam and Dad's marriage was crumbling and I had to deal with it on my own. 'I know I was,' I admitted. 'I wanted to be you. I needed to be you especially when Mam and Dad split up.'

Tracy flushes. 'I stayed away because I couldn't face it,' she says. 'I wished I was you and could be there, but I couldn't. I made sure I had loads of work on.'

The confession stuns both of us.

'Jesus,' I whisper. 'I thought you didn't care. I thought you didn't care about Mam and Dad and I hated that they doted on you.' I look at her. She looks at me.

'Sorry,' she says. Only she doesn't mean sorry for that or for Gray, she means sorry for so much more.

'Me too,' I say, feeling a weird lump in my throat.

And then, just as we're about to do something completely alien, like embrace, Dad shoves in the door and knocks us both flying.

'What is going on here?' he demands. 'Tracy, why are you crying?'

'I'm giving up modelling,' she announces.

'No!' Fáinne gawps. 'Are you?'

'I think we should discuss this.' Mam glares at me as if it's my fault but I'm just as stunned as her.

'I already have,' Tracy says. 'With my sister Lucy.'

And now I know I'm really in for it.

How can Tracy take advice from a girl that has made a show of herself in the newspapers? Mam wants to know.

I try to protest my innocence. 'I didn't tell her to give it up.'

'Like you didn't tell that reporter to "F" off?' Mam says sarcastically.

'Did you tell someone to fuck off?' Fáinne asks, her eyes wide and, I think, impressed.

'No, I didn't,' I snap.

'I'm giving up modelling because I am tired of it,' Tracy says calmly. 'Anyway, in a couple of years I'll be too old and it's better to go now, at the height of it.'

I've always admired Tracy's calm. If it was me, I'd be stomping about the kitchen making a huge drama out of it.

'And what will you do?' Mam speaks in the voice that she usually reserves for me and I feel sort of cheered by it. I like that it's not just me she can give a tongue-lashing to. However, unlike me, Tracy doesn't roll her eyes or make inflammatory remarks. Instead, she answers Mam's question calmly and reasonably. It suddenly dawns on me that she and Dad are alike, which must mean, horror of horrors, that Mam and I are the same.

The shame of it.

'I don't know yet.'

'You don't know!' Mam turns to Dad. 'John, make her see sense, for God's sake. Make her see sense.'

Dad sighs deeply and puts his hands in his pockets. He walks in a little circle. 'Are you happy, Tracy? Now?'

'No. That's why I want to leave modelling.' There is a catch in my sister's voice.

Fáinne goes and takes her hand. 'Don't cry, Mona Lisa,' she says softly.

Tracy hugs her.

Dad shrugs lightly. 'Well, if leaving modelling makes you happy, then I can't see anything wrong with that.'

'John!' Mam's voice is like whiplash. 'How can you say—?'

Dad interrupts her. It's something he never normally does. 'I want my daughters to be happy, Dora.'

'So do I.'

'Well then.'

Mam opens and closes her mouth like a goldfish. 'I do want them to be happy,' she splutters. 'It's all I've ever wanted.' She shoots a weird look at me and I make a face. Then I wish I hadn't. Tracy would never make a face.

'I'll be happy giving it up,' Tracy says quietly. She crosses to Mam. 'I'll be fine, honest, Mam. I have piles of money, I can buy a house here and see you every day if I want.'

'Oh.' A small smile crosses Mam's face.

'You can be a designer,' Fáinne pipes up. 'You make lovely jeans, Mona Lisa.'

'I just might do that.' Tracy grins, hugging her again. Turning to Mam, she says, 'Come on, Mam, I promise I'm not making a mistake.'

We all look at Mam. Isn't it funny how we all crave our mother's approval?

She puts her hand on Tracy's face. 'Once you're sure,' she says in a gentle voice.

'I'm sure.'

And they embrace. And Dad beams.

I'm happy for them, I really am. But no one hugs me.

Then, it's like Fáinne senses it. She leaves Tracy and wraps her little arms around my waist. 'I love you, Mammy,' she says.

And my world is OK again.

55

THE FOLLOWING SATURDAY, I take Fáinne shopping. She's grown so much since Christmas that hardly any of her clothes fit her now. The final money from the ad has come through and I'm treating her to anything she wants. We go into all the shops, examine the pretty jeans and tops and dresses. I point out glittery shoes and fancy hairbands: things that I would love basically. But she's not interested. After a while she turns to me and says, 'Mammy, can I have a Liverpool jersey?'

'A Liverpool jersey?' I know why she wants one but I don't want to get her one. I don't want my gorgeous daughter walking about in jeans and a football jersey. 'Why? Do you want it to hang on your wall?'

Fáinne shakes her head. 'No, silly. You *wear* jerseys.'

'Boys do.'

'And girls too.' She pokes me and looks at me with her father's eyes. 'Come on, Mammy. Didn't you say my daddy supported Liverpool and so, when I meet him, I want to wear it.'

She says it with such certainty that my heart lurches. Oh Jesus. I want to tell her that so far things haven't been looking too good. It's been ages now and nothing has happened. Well, bar the headlines in the papers which Les was ecstatic about. Great publicity for me, apparently. It takes me all my

355

courage to get out of bed in the mornings now. Still, Tracy has replaced me as the newspaper fodder. Her resignation from the modelling world was greeted with total shock, and then with the speculation that she was going to try and make it as an actress. She went on Declan D'arcy and fielded all his questions with such professionalism that the man was fawning over her by the end of the show.

I felt jealous again. But not in a horrible way.

'Mam.' Fáinne tugs my jacket. 'Jersey?'

I jerk out of my reverie and take a deep breath, ready to try to explain to Fáinne that the search was not going too well. She stares at me. I will myself to begin, but we're in the middle of Grafton Street with people milling about everywhere and it's not the time. 'Come on, so, you little tomboy!'

She grabs my arm and looks up into my face. 'You are the best mammy in the world.'

I'd have bought her Grafton Street right then if she had asked for it.

We're at lunch in McDonald's when the phone rings. Well, Fáinne is at lunch, I'm sipping on a cup of tea determined to resist her chips and her burger. I'll grab a healthy sambo later.

'Phone!' Fáinne calls through a mouthful of chips.

She always hears it – I never do even though it's got a really loud ring tone. I begin to scrabble about in my bag, frantically determined to locate it before it stops.

'Yes!' I say loudly into the receiver.

'Are you having great sex there or something?' A loud chortle.

'Les. Hi.'

'I'd hate to disturb you now – are you with Doug or Graham or Clive?'

'That's why you are such a bad agent,' I say calmly. 'You believe everything you hear on the radio and in the papers.'

'Well, I'm not that bad. I only managed to secure you an audition for *Rapid*.'

For a second, I can't say anything. My mouth opens and shuts and nothing comes out.

'Did you hear me?' Les shouts. '*RAPID!*'

'*Rapid?* No way!' *Rapid* was due to shoot next year and was mega-budget. Rumour had it that Brad Pitt was to be the main lead.

'Oh ye of little faith,' Les says good-humouredly. 'Yes way. One week from today in the Film Centre. I'll fax the details to your work, right?'

'God.'

'God had nothing to do with it,' he says. 'I'd rather you thanked me.'

'Why should I? I pay you enough.' But I laugh. 'Thanks, Les.'

'Bye now.' He hangs up.

'Who was that?' Fáinne asks.

I take a celebratory chip from her box. 'Your mammy has a film audition,' I sing out.

She screeches. Hugs me. Yells out, 'Ohhh, you're going to be famous!'

Some guy at the next table looks at her in amusement. Then he looks at me. 'Hey,' he chuckles, 'your mammy is already famous.'

We're on the bus when my phone rings again. Fáinne is busy examining her jersey, which was an awful price.

'Mammy, phone,' she says.

Again the mad scrabble. 'Yes!'

'Hiya, girlfriend, it's Maddie.'

357

'Maddie, hi.' I wonder why she's ringing me. She and Clive have gone away on a coupley weekend to Kerry. Maybe something is wrong. Maybe the baby or . . .

'Are you sitting down?'

'On the bus as I speak.'

'Good.' There is a long pause. 'Clive had a phone call this morning.'

Everything slows down. My heart begins a heavy drum-drumming in my chest. Fáinne's chatter seems far away. 'He did?'

'And it's legit.'

I turn my head away from Fáinne who, thank God, is still looking at her Liverpool jersey. 'Jason rang?' I whisper.

'His dad,' she says. 'Jason's dad rang. Clive asked him the questions we had prepared – the ones about Jason's college course – and he knew them. And he knew the exact years. And he knew Jason's position on the football team – everything. It was legit.'

'Oh. My. God.' I suddenly feel sick. The door has opened and I'm peering inside into pitch black. 'And Jason?' I ask.

'He wouldn't say. Apparently he'll tell you when he meets you. He says he has something for you.'

'What?' This all sounds bizarre. 'Are you sure it's not someone taking the piss?'

'As sure as we can be.' She pauses. 'Are you OK?'

'As OK as I can be.'

'Who is it, Mammy?' Fáinne asks.

'Just Maddie.'

'I want to say "hi" to her.'

'No, sweetie, just have a look at your other clothes.' I turn back to the phone. 'So what now?'

'He's going to contact Clive again to arrange a meeting with you. I think he wants to make sure that you're legit too.

Don't worry, Clive and I will be there in the background, just in case he is a weirdo.' She lets out a long breath. 'It's hotting up now, Luce. Are you sure you are OK?'

No, no I'm not. I'm not even sure if I want to revisit that time again. Then I look at Fáinne and I know I have to.

For her.

For us.

56

'LUCY GLEESON,' I tell the woman behind the desk. 'I'm here to audition for the part of Carmel.'

She flips the pages, glancing at me with total uninterest. I have to admit I like that. It's better than being stared at or wolf-whistled in the street. It's been almost two weeks now and I still keep getting recognised.

'Lucy Gleeson,' the woman says in a bored voice. 'Take the stairs on the right, go up one flight and wait there. We're running late so you'll be a while, all right?'

It's Saturday; I can wait all day if I have to.

When I reach the top of the stairs, there are piles of people waiting to audition. Most of the women are in their twenties and are obviously going for the same part as me. Some of them are gorgeous and I wonder how on earth I'll ever be able to match them. But the casting agency had rung Les and asked for me, so I must have a chance. I find a seat beside a girl who just has to be a model, she's so bloody perfect-looking.

'Why the hold-up?'

She shrugs.

Everyone seems to be studying scripts so I take mine from my bag and study it too. Every so often, I glance about. There are a couple of faces that I recognise: people from soaps and people from ads. One or two have even starred in low-budget Irish movies. I wonder if anyone recognises me. I hope not.

More and more people arrive and the place becomes really crowded. Eventually a rumour goes around that the director has come. You can feel the relief.

'Now things should start moving,' my model companion says.

And they do. Very, very slowly. I reckon that I'll be sitting for another hour or so at least.

'Your mobile,' the girl beside me says, ten minutes later. 'At least I think it's yours.'

It is. I drop my script and stuff falls out of my bag as I try to locate it. 'Hello?'

'Lucy, hiya. It's Doug.'

'Doug – yeah?' Oh shit. My complimentary packet of condoms has fallen out. As part of doing the condom ad, I'd been given two packets of condoms for free. And such was the state of my love life that I hadn't needed to take them from my bag at all. I wonder if anyone has noticed. Should I leave them where they are or nonchalantly pick them up? I decide to leave them.

'I didn't ring you earlier because of your audition but it must be over now, yeah?'

'Eh . . .' I look around. 'Almost.' Someone hands me my condoms. I smile, mortified, before shoving them into a zip pocket in my bag. 'So, what's the problem?'

Doug hesitates before he answers. 'Well, maybe I'll wait until you're done there.'

'Naw, go on.'

'Well, it's Mr D. He rang me yesterday evening. Paddy wasn't too good so this morning I went out to see her and, well, I've to put her down.'

361

'Aw, no!' Quick tears spring to my eyes and the girl beside me shoots me a curious glance. 'When?'

'This afternoon. At four. Now, don't get upset and ruin the audition for yourself.'

'I won't.' My voice wobbles and I have to swallow hard.

'I'm ringing 'cause he asked me to ask you if you'd be there.' There is an awkward silence. I know we're both remembering the only two times I'd assisted Doug in that particular area of veterinary medicine. I'd cried more than the families and only succeeded in making things worse. In fact, one family had ended up comforting me. Now Doug always asked Clare to assist.

'Now,' Doug continued, obviously thinking he was going to put me off, 'I know it's your day off and all so you don't have to but anyway . . .'

'Of course I'll come.' Jesus, what have I said! 'God, Mr D. must be in bits.'

'Yeah, he's pretty broke up all right.'

'I'll see you at four.'

'You sure?'

'Uh-huh.'

'Thanks, Luce. He'll appreciate it.'

I click off my phone and look at my watch. It's three now, I should get seen by three-thirty and would easily make it over to the surgery in ten minutes.

Three-thirty comes and goes and I'm still waiting. Three-forty-five and there're ten people in front of me. At the rate things are going, it'll be after four by the time I get in. I begin to jiggle my feet and fiddle with my hands – all the stuff I do when I'm uneasy – and the girl beside me looks at me in annoyance. 'Sorry.' I sit on my hands.

Three-fifty. Still no movement.

Three fifty-five.

Shit! Shit! Shit! I can't let Mr D. down. I glance at the queue. I'm about nine from the top. Aw, fuck it, I think, I'll take a chance. I'll head to the surgery and race back. I jump up and grab my coat. 'Back in a sec,' I tell the model. 'Can you just say an emergency came up and I'll be back around four-thirty or so.'

'Uh-huh.'

It's a relief to get out into the street. Fresh air and a semblance of sunshine. I pull my jacket on and race towards my car. Starting it, I drive like a banshee towards the surgery. The door is open. Clare is behind the desk but she hardly notices me. She's arguing with Brendan on the phone. His calls have become a regular thing. I run past her to the room at the back of the surgery where all the operations are carried out. 'Sorry, I'm late.' I'm completely breathless. Totally unfit.

''S OK,' Doug mutters. He's not even looking in my direction. He's rubbing Paddy's ears and she's licking his hand and whimpering. She's got really bloated and I can't help staring.

'She looks bad, ey?' Mr D. startles me as he speaks. He's lounging against the wall, his hands in his pockets. His eyes are red and swollen and he won't meet my eye.

'I'm really sorry, Mr Devlin.' I cross towards him. 'The poor auld dog.'

'Yeah,' he agrees, swallowing. 'She won't let me touch her. Keeps growling.'

I smile. 'She can't be too bad, so.'

'She wasn't always so vicious, you know,' he says. 'She'd only bite the odd time. But when Eileen died – that was my wife – Paddy got fierce grumpy. I think she blamed me or something. And I had to take care of her and it was hard,

363

what with being bitten all the time, but you do these things for someone you love – don't you?'

'Yeah.' I pat his arm. 'You do.'

'And she's all I have left of Eileen.' His voice breaks and Paddy looks over at him and growls again.

'It's for Paddy's own good.'

Mr D. nods and I pretend not to see as he wipes his eyes.

Doug holds up the syringe. 'Ready?' he asks quietly. He looks pointedly at me. I give a small nod and gulp really hard and think that maybe if I bite my tongue it'll stop the tears which are already forming.

Mr D. nods gravely. 'Yes,' he says. He catches my hand hard and I wince.

'Right so.' Doug turns to Paddy and begins gently to insert the syringe. 'Good girl,' he says gently. 'There's a good girl.'

Paddy relaxes at his voice. All animals do. I love Doug for his kindness. Paddy lays her head on the table and looks trustingly up at him. The fluid in the syringe empties into Paddy's vein and Doug just as gently pulls it out.

'She'll just fall asleep in a few seconds,' he says softly. 'You can pet her now, if you like.'

Mr D. steps forward and caresses the dog's head.

Doug looks at me and, of course, I'm crying. I feel so stupid; I didn't even like the dog. He pulls out some tissues and hands then to me. 'Here. It's always hard,' he whispers. He pulls me from the room so that Mr D. can say his good-byes.

After a bit, when Paddy has fallen asleep, Doug tells Mr D. that he can take Paddy home and bury her. She's not a big dog and he won't have to dig a very large hole.

'How much do I owe you?' Mr D. asks.

Doug waves him away. 'All part of the service.'

'No, no it's not,' Mr D. says firmly. 'It's part of your job. I'd never have had a lad like you working for me when I was running my business. How much?'

Doug tells him and Mr D. nods. 'I'll pay Grumpy Boots outside, will I?' Then, before Doug answers, he says, 'You and Lucy are great. Two of the finest.'

Doug smiles. 'D'you want a lift back with Paddy? I'll drive you home, it's on my way.'

'No. No.' Mr D. gently lifts Paddy up and puts her over his shoulder. 'I'll carry her home, the same way I carried her here. She'd like to see the places she used to walk one last time.' He holds her gently and rubs his face in her still warm fur. 'Just one last time,' he repeats.

Doug holds the door open for him. 'If you're sure.'

'Yes. Yes I am.'

We watch him walk away.

'Thanks Luce,' Doug says as he begins clearing up. 'You did well. I'll pay you overtime.'

'Naw. I was glad to come.' I lean against the counter and watch as he puts things away. At least I've stopped crying. My nose is all red and swollen though. 'Poor Mr D. He'll be lonely now.'

'He will.' Doug's hair is so shiny – I've never noticed that before. As he bends down light bounces from one curl to the next. 'Still, I've a pile of dogs out me back garden all looking for a home – he might take one of those, in time. I had a litter born last week. He could have one of those.'

A litter out in his back garden? Jesus! I smile. 'Do your neighbours love you or what?'

'House is detached,' he says, taking off his vet's coat and giving me the full benefit of his brownness: brown cords, brown baggy jumper with a hole in the elbow where I get a

365

glimpse of a brown shirt. 'My gran left it to me in her will. I'm the only grandchild.'

'Lucky tosser.'

He smiles. 'So, how'd the audition go?'

And suddenly, I remember. 'Oh Christ,' I virtually shout. 'My audition . . . Oh shit, I've to get back there!'

'You never did it?'

'Nooo.' I grab my coat. 'There was a delay. Have to go.'

'I'll drive you,' Doug calls. 'It's only ten minutes away and finding somewhere to park will only hold you up. When it's finished, gimme a bell and I'll pick you up.'

'Yeah. Yeah. That sounds good.'

It's only seconds, but it seems like ages before he locates his car keys. 'Ready?'

We leg it out of the door.

Doug pulls up outside the studio. It's just gone four-forty-five. 'Good luck, so,' he says.

'Ta.'

'You'll get it, I know you will.' There's a smile in his voice. 'And when you're famous, think back on me working away in some surgery while you're jetting here there and everywhere.'

'I'll come and see you,' I say and I mean it.

'And you'll send around all those cooks to cook my dinner for me?'

He's talking about Christmas, only he's not looking embarrassed. I smile, delighted that he remembers. 'I will.'

'Go on.' He gives me a nudge. 'Hop it.'

And I find that I can't. His gorgeous smile, his mussy hair, his stubble, his general air of carelessness all seem overwhelmingly attractive. And it hits me that if I do get the part I could be taken away from my life here and now. My days

366

at the surgery making him tea and having a laugh will end, my child will probably move to a new house, go to a new school, miss all her friends. I'll barely see Mam and Dad. Maddie and Gray will write but lazy dinners at their houses will be a memory. And I wonder if it's all worth it?

'Go,' Doug says, more urgently. 'I'm double-parked.'

I pop the lock and I still can't move. If I get this, things will change. Do I love *acting* that much? Do I love it more than my life now? Do I love my life now?

'Lucy. Come on.' He's looking at me weirdly. 'Go on. You need this job. Don't be late.'

He's right. I hop out of the car. 'I'll walk back to the surgery and pick up my car,' I say. 'You go on.'

'You sure?'

Sure? Sure about what? I nod.

He pulls off.

It's after five. I'm sure they'll have finished. Still, I run into the Film Centre and up the stairs. There is one person ahead of me. I sit beside her. Just then, someone pokes her head out of a doorway. 'Is Lucy Gleeson here yet?' the person asks irritably.

I'm so surprised to hear my name being called that I jump up and almost fall over myself. 'Here. Here I am.'

'About time,' the woman snaps. 'We've been waiting all afternoon for you.'

All afternoon? For me?

Wow.

I follow the woman into the room where I'm introduced to the director and the cameraman. I hastily explain why I'm late and the director beams approvingly. 'Just like your character,' he says, shooting a smug look at the casting director. 'OK, let's go.' He hands me fresh script.

I act like I've never acted before. This is my future, this is my future, my heart pounds out with every word I say. When the director calls 'cut', I know I've done well. Now, all I have to do is wait.

57

'HE'S ARRANGED TO meet you in the Blue Diamond at eleven o'clock on Saturday,' Clive explains over the phone. 'Will that suit?'

It's all so bloody real now. I can't take it in. I'm meeting Jason's dad in two days' time. 'And Jason?' I croak out.

'He said he'll explain,' Clive says. 'I get the feeling things are a bit difficult or something.'

I feel sick. If Jason refuses to meet Fáinne, I swear I'll kill him. 'OK,' I tell Clive and my voice is normal. 'Grand. And thanks, thanks, Clive.'

'No problem.'

I don't know what else to say to him – I still don't know how to talk to Clive – so I say goodbye and hang up.

I can't sleep at all. At three o'clock, I'm still pondering my minuscule wardrobe and wondering what on earth I can get to go with my brown boots. Everything I purchase these days revolves around the boots. They look good and are comfortable and they make my legs look slimmer than they are. I'm going for a mini-skirt of some sort when the phone rings.

It's probably some drunken saddo. He'll hang up in a second. But he doesn't. Jesus, if it keeps ringing, it'll wake Fáinne.

'Thank God I'm awake,' I mutter, heading downstairs. I hate being woken up at night.

'Hello?' I try to convey to the caller that I am not amused.

'Hey, hey, Lucy?'

It's a voice I can't place, though it sounds familiar. 'Yeah?'

'It's me. Clive.'

'Yeah?' Clive doesn't sound like himself.

'Maddie asked me to ring you.' There is a pause. A sort of silence from him but in the background I can hear all sorts of noise. Then, in a weirdly constricted voice, Clive stammers out, 'The baby. Maddie has gone in.'

'What?' It's late; I can't grasp his meaning. I wonder if I'm dreaming, but no, the tiled floor of the hall is hard and cool under my feet. It steadies me. 'Gone in? What do you mean?'

'She's having the baby.'

'No, she can't be,' I say, confused. 'It's too early.'

'She told me to let you know.'

'But – but – she's only seven months gone – isn't that . . . ?' I can't say it.

'Early, yeah. But, well . . .' Clive gulps out a sob. 'They said they might be able to save it. Anyway, can you come in? Maddie says she wants you.'

My dad agrees to come and mind Fáinne and I head off in my car to the hospital. There's no traffic and I arrive at the hospital in under fifteen minutes. OK, so I've broken the speed limit on just about every road, but like I said, there was no traffic. The suddenness of the whole thing is a huge shock. Jesus, Jesus, Jesus, I keep muttering to myself as I stumble half dressed up the steps to the hospital. It's the most I've prayed in ages.

370

The woman on reception looks up at me. 'Madeline Carver's baby?' I croak out.

The woman looks at her chart. 'She's had a girl.'

'Good. Good. Yeah. Are they both OK?'

The woman shrugs. 'That's all I know. You can wait here. I'll ring the room for you though we don't really allow visitors at this time of night.'

I don't want to visit. All I want to know is that everything is all right. The woman talks a bit on the phone and then, looking disapprovingly at me, tells me to go up. She gives me directions, which I can't follow, and turns away.

It takes me about fifteen minutes to negotiate the corridors. Sounds of babies can be heard all over the place. The walls are decorated with big bright pictures. The worst place in the world to lose a child. Maddie is in a room on her own. I knock at the door, afraid to go barging in. Clive answers. 'Here's Lucy now, love,' he says and Maddie gazes at me. Without saying anything, she opens her arms and I fall into them, hugging her hard.

'How's the baby?'

'In intensive care,' Clive chokes out. 'I'm just going to see her now. It's touch and go, really.'

'Oh Maddie, I'm so sorry. I'm so sorry.' I hug my best mate harder.

Clive stands up. 'I'll go, love. OK?'

Maddie nods. She's wrecked.

'Mind her, ey, Luce?' Clive kisses Maddie on the forehead and she clasps his hand, then watches him as he leaves.

There is a small silence. I don't know what to say. 'Will she be all right, Maddie? What have they told you?'

'I did everything right, Lucy,' Maddie says numbly, in this strange sort of monotone that I've never heard her use before. 'I didn't drink or stretch or even have coffee. I love that baby,

371

I talked to her. I told her – it's a her, you know – that she'd be so happy with me and Clive. I don't understand.'

I don't know what to say. All I can do is rub her hand and push her hair back from her face. She doesn't look like Maddie. Maddie always smiles and laughs. This Maddie needs my help and I realise suddenly that I've never had to do that before. She's been there for me but I've never once had to be a real friend to her. Well, I will now. I'll do whatever it takes. 'I don't know what to say,' I stammer out. 'But she's in the right place.'

'Just tell me I did nothing wrong.' There is an urgency in her voice as she gazes at me. I suddenly realise what I'm doing here.

'You did nothing wrong.' I press her hand. 'I swear, you did nothing wrong.'

She's going to cry. 'I had a pain and she hadn't kicked in ages and I wasn't sure if that was important. And the pain got worse and worse and they told me to come in. The most precious thing to me, Lucy, and I didn't know I might lose her.'

'Come here.' I wrap my arms about her and she cries and cries and cries. 'You haven't lost her. Don't give up on her.'

'I don't know what to do,' Clive says later. He's brought me to the IC unit. Maddie can't face seeing her baby just yet.

The baby is in an incubator, a tiny little thing, about the size of a bag of sugar. Tubes and drips and all sorts of things that I don't know the name of are poking out everywhere. 'All she wanted was you, Lucy. She didn't want me.'

I know it hurts him to say that. Any other time I would have been thrilled to hear those words, but not now. I had resented him but I shouldn't have. Maddie loves this straight-laced, by-the-book guy. She loves him probably because he is good and decent and I've no experience of those type of fellas. 'She will need you.' I take the risk of lightly touching his arm. 'She'll need you to help her bring this little bundle up.'

He shrugs. I don't blame him. It's a crap answer.

'I think . . .' I struggle with the words I'm about to say. 'I think Maddie wants me here because she feels I might understand, what with Fáinne and everything.'

He looks at me. Confused. 'But Fáinne wasn't premature.'

I flush. 'No, but Maddie needs me to tell her that she did nothing wrong, that sometimes these things happen.' I can't look him in the face as I say it. Instead, I focus on a light fitting above his head. My voice comes out in a half-mumble as I confess my most shameful secret. 'When I was expecting Fáinne, see, I was a complete mess. I drank and partied and just generally wasn't in touch with reality. Yet when Fáinne was born, she was perfect. I guess, well, Maddie just needs to know that Amy being early is not her fault and' – I smile a little ruefully – 'and I am the very best one to tell her.'

'Oh.' He nods and rocks a bit on his heels. 'I see.'

I reckon he's horrified. I shrug a bit and keep staring at the light.

Unexpectedly, he pats my back. It's an awkward gesture, but I need it. 'Thanks, Lucy. Thanks for that.'

I've never been thanked for being a fuck-up before. It affects me a lot. I attempt a smile, so he won't see that I'm going to start sniffling. 'It's OK.'

'You're great. I'm always telling Maddie how lucky she is in her friends.'

And here was me thinking he sneered at me. 'And I'm always telling Maddie how lucky she is to have you.'

I know it's a lie, but from now on, it'll be the truth.

58

I TAKE A DAY off work the next day – I reckon Maddie needs me more than Doug. Clive meets me in the corridor and urges me to try to persuade Maddie to see her baby. 'If anything happens,' he says, 'she'll never forgive herself.'

I don't know what I can do. I can hardly say that to her, can I? So, instead, I focus on the fact that I've seen the baby. 'She's lovely, Maddie. There's nothing to be scared of.'

'Lucy, I can't.' Her voice hardens and she turns away from me. 'It's not your baby. It's easy for you to look at her.'

'It's Clive's baby, though, and he has seen her.'

'Yeah, and he doesn't have to live with the guilt of having her too early.'

'It's not your fault.'

'So, whose fault is it, then? Yours? Clive's? It was my body that let that baby down.'

'It's not "that baby".' Clive startles us both with the shout in his voice. He puts his hands on Maddie's face and says urgently, 'Her name is Amy. Amy – do you hear me?'

'Go away!' Maddie puts her hands to her ears, like a kid. 'Shut up, the two of you. Get out! Go on, get out!'

'Maddie, you have to—'

'OUT!'

*

Clive and I head to the canteen. I buy him a coffee. 'How is she doing?' I ask, placing it in front of him.

He stares glumly into the cup. 'Maddie or Amy?'

'Amy.'

'She's fighting.' He smiles a little to himself. 'D'you know, I put my finger into the incubator today and touched her hand. She curled it around my finger and sort of squirmed a little.'

'Aw.'

'And I talked to her. They say that's good for babies, don't they?'

'Yeah. So they say.' My coffee tastes awful.

'I explained that Maddie would be down to see her soon. I know she probably didn't understand but I said it anyway. I don't want her thinking that Maddie doesn't care.'

'Maddie does care.'

'I know.'

There is a silence between us. Not the edgy silences I normally have with Clive. It's a companionable silence: both of us thinking the same thoughts. Clive looks all dishevelled and I feel terribly sorry for him. Normally he's so buttoned up that he's scary. 'She'll come around,' I say. 'You'll see.'

He shrugs and stares into his coffee again. More silence.

'I'm really sorry about tomorrow,' he says then. 'But you know I have to be here, don't you?'

'Tomorrow?'

'Your meeting with Philip Donovan?'

It hits me like a blast of cold air. *My meeting.* Weird as it may sound, I had completely forgotten. Christ. I try to cover it up. 'Oh yeah.' Shit. I'll be on my own. No Maddie as back-up. No Clive. I suddenly realise how much I'd depended on the two of them being there. My big moment and I was going to have to go it alone. 'If you want, I can cancel it and arrange for another time?' Clive is looking at me oddly. 'If you're worried or anything?'

I'm tempted but that'd be selfish. The poor guy has enough to worry about without arranging my life for me. 'It's fine,' I say in a high bright voice that Maddie might have recognised as panicked, but that Clive had yet to. 'I'll get Gray or someone – don't worry about it.'

'You sure?'

'Positive.'

He smiles at me. 'OK, so.' Pushing his cup away, he stands up. 'I'll just head back-up to Maddie.'

I watch him walk away, knowing there is no way I can call on Gray, he'd insist on chaperoning me. Nope, I had opened this door, I bloody well had to see behind it. For the first time in my life, I was going to have to rely on me.

Oh fuck!

59

I WASH, SCRUB, PLUCK my eyebrows and shave my legs. It's all to compensate for the fact that I never bought any new clothes for the occasion. I'm stuck wearing a pair of jeans and my red bustier top. Then I decide that the top is too dressy and so I shove on a jumper, which looks really casual. But, hey, I'm only going to the pub.

I pack Fáinne off to my mother's with some story about a follow-up audition and then, taking a deep breath, I drive to the Blue Diamond.

I'm fifteen minutes early, but I do want to be there first. Before getting out, I take a quick look at myself in my car mirror – which always makes me look awful – and my stomach heaves.

Oh shit. Oh God.

I hadn't tried to find Jason after he'd left. The hurt was too gigantic. He'd made me fall in love with him, he'd made me pregnant, he'd made me trust him and then suddenly, he'd just left. No 'goodbye', no note.

I'd felt as if I'd been bombed inside – complete, utter devastation.

The pub is deserted. I walk in, feeling totally exposed. Going to the bar, I order an orange. The barman attempts to make conversation but I'm in no mood for it. It's as if my head is racing but my thoughts don't make sense. I take my orange down to a table.

Telling Mam had been the hard part. Maddie had been there for that too. We'd stood in the hall, Maddie holding on to my arm, and I'd announced that I was pregnant.

Mam had been putting an extra dinner plate on the table for Maddie and the plate had fallen and shattered on to the tiles. I can still see, in my mind's eye, the shards of the plate as they skimmed and skittered all across the kitchen floor.

That's my life, I remember thinking.

Five minutes later the door of the pub opens and I'm afraid to turn and see who has come in. It's a couple. They're snuggling up to each other as they get their drinks, then they plonk themselves down in my eyeline and begin to snog.

Mam had been unable to cope with the news and she'd rung Dad. He'd arrived over and calmed Mam down. Then he'd sat with me, asked me questions and promised me that if I wanted to keep the baby I could. That he and Mam would do whatever it took. It was their grandchild.

I couldn't look at him. The hurt in his eyes would be too much, so I sat and nodded and agreed.

And after that, I'd spent the next six months blind drunk in a feeble attempt to feel happy and alive. Only when I was confronted with the reality of Fáinne did I come to realise what I'd done.

Again the door opens and this time, glancing out of the corner of my eye, I realise that this is the man I've come to meet. He's tall and grey-haired and the resemblance to Jason is striking. They've the same dark, dark eyes and the same guarded look. The man comes towards me and I swallow, my heart lurching. If he's who he says he is, then this is Fáinne's grandfather.

And after Fáinne had been born, I'd slowly built my world up again. Created a new reality from what was a shell of the former one. But newly built places can never be the same as the original and I sure as hell wasn't. Gone was the kid who chased laughter. I became a doer, determined not to fail my daughter the way I'd failed my parents. And I did a good job but in the process I'd lost my trust. I'd lost my trust in people. The only ones I could trust were Maddie and Gray. I'd lost faith in my own judgement and therefore steered clear of new things. New people especially freaked me out because I couldn't control them — how did I know what they were going to do?

All this hits me in one huge blast as this man, so like Jason, walks towards me. And I realise that I've put myself in that position again. I've put myself in a position where I don't know what will happen and, what's worse, I've put myself in this position with the exact same person that I'd done it with nine years ago.

I feel heat rushing right up through me. I'm sure my forehead is glistening. I place my hands in my lap because they are trembling.

Why have I done this?

For Fáinne. So I won't fail her.

'Lucy Gleeson?' the man says. And his voice is soft and the Kerry lilt makes my heart ache.

I can only nod.

The man places an envelope on the table between us and slides into a chair opposite me. He holds out his hand. 'I'm Philip Donovan, Jason's dad.'

I don't want to shake his hand because mine is sweaty, but I have to. His hand is sweaty too.

There is a small silence. Philip coughs. 'I saw the ad in the *Dingle Bugle* when it first came out,' he says then. 'Only I wasn't sure what you wanted.'

'To make contact with your son,' I say. My voice trembles a little. 'That's all.'

Philip nods. 'May I ask why?'

No, you may not, I want to say. Instead, I answer, 'Well, that's between me and Jason, isn't it? Where is he?'

More silence. Philip gulps. Really hard. He bows his head and I see that his own hands are trembling. 'He died,' he whispers. 'Five months ago.'

Again, as on the bus, I have the eerie sensation of time stopping. Jason is dead. Dead. How can he be *dead*? He was so full of life, energy. He filled up my thoughts. Even when I hadn't tried to think about him, I was thinking about not thinking about him. It was as if he was with me every day. 'Dead?' And even though I haven't seen him in years, I want to cry. And somehow, I realise that I'd always known he would die young.

Philip nods. Tears glisten in his eyes. He blinks hard. A semi-smile. 'He was an awful man for the drink.'

I nod. 'Yeah.'

'He used to joke that he'd been dried out more times than a reused teabag.'

I still can't take it in. *Dead*. It's an anti-climax somehow. I'd wanted to see him again. For me. I'd wanted to see if what I remembered was true. This search wasn't just about Fáinne, I realise. It was about closure. And now that can't happen.

'He died from alcohol poisoning.'

A tear slips from my eye. I wipe it away. However bad it is for me, it must be tragic for his dad. 'That must have been awful.'

Philip nods and looks up at the ceiling; then, his gaze on me again, he says softly, 'He wanted to die, I think. He just hadn't the courage to do it all at once. No matter what he did, he always managed to push a self-destruct button. You met him in college, didn't you?'

'Uh-huh.'

'And I bet in the beginning he was fine – his course was fine, he was getting on well.'

'He was great.'

'Then he went off the rails. I remember that year. I visited him at one stage – his football coach rang me to tell me that he was drinking again – and I shouted at him and fought with him and begged him to give it up and eventually I hit him. Really hard, here.' He touches his eye, swallows hard. 'I'd never hit him before. Never.' He shakes his head and continues. I have to lean across the table to hear him because he's talking so softly. 'Then later in the year the college rang me. Said he was turning up drunk at lectures, that he'd attacked the football captain, that he'd been thrown out of the canteen and that I had to do something. So I made him come home.'

Chunks fall into place. 'You *made* him come home?'

'I told him that unless he came home, I'd disown him. I told him to be packed when I got back, then I went into a church and prayed like I'd never prayed before.'

'Oh.'

'I honestly thought he wanted to dry out that time. But it never lasted. He couldn't live with himself.'

'He left me that time,' I say. 'No note. He was just gone when I called in for him.'

'Then he did you a favour,' Philip says.

I stare into my orange juice. 'He hurt me.'

'He would have hurt you more if he'd been around – I can tell you that.'

Maybe that's true. I never got the chance to find out.

'He hurt everyone he came into contact with,' Philip went on. 'He would have ruined your life. It was good of him to go like he did.'

I still would have liked to have had a chance with him though . . .

'His mother left us when he was a kid. We didn't talk about it. Maybe I should have. I dunno – I mean, if she had just written or something . . .' He stops. 'What hurt him most was that he'd drawn her a picture – Jason was a great artist, even as a kid – and she left it behind. He kept that picture for years after.'

It's as if my heart is sore.

'So he never knew I was trying to contact him?'

Philip shakes his head. 'No. And I was too upset to contact you at first and then I began to worry what it was you were after.' He looks at me. Expectantly.

I feel I have no choice but to tell him. 'He's the father of my little girl.'

Philip gulps. 'Really?'

'Yeah – and she wanted to meet him. I dunno what I'm going to tell her.'

'Tell her that her daddy is dead but that he loved her very much.'

'She won't believe that.'

'Well, I think he loved her mother so I'm sure he would have loved his daughter.' He pushes the envelope across to me. 'This is yours, I think.'

I stare at it. 'What is it?'

'Open it.'

From the envelope, I pull out an unframed oil painting. Only it's not like the circuit ones that I'd once seen on Jason's wall. It's a picture of a beautiful girl. I think it's me.

'Did Jason ever show you his pictures?'

'Yeah – once.'

The picture is beautiful. Colourful. Alive.

'Most of Jason's pictures are all about circuits,' his dad explains. A sort of pride creeps into the way he talks and I look at him. 'What's weird about the pictures he drew are that the circuits don't work – he put in tiny flaws that stop them from functioning properly. Art buyers love them – they're worth a fortune.' Philip nods at my picture. 'This is the only portrait he's ever done. Well, besides the one of his mother when he was a kid. Look, there, right in the corner.'

I peer at tiny handwriting. I can barely make it out. A 'To Luce', is the most I can see.

'It says' – Philip points at the tiny words – '"To Luce, you were too good to hurt. Just remember. Love Jace."'

I stare and stare at the minuscule words. 'It really says that?'

'Yeah. His leaving was his gift to you, I reckon.'

Don't cry, I tell myself. Don't cry. It seems that in the last while I've done nothing but blubber.

'I found it in his stuff after he died.'

He did this picture for me. It was for me. Mine. He loved me a little. My judgement wasn't so bad.

'It's worth a fortune, this picture,' Philip says. 'And it's yours.'

Tears slip from my eyes. In the background, I can see the snogging couple looking over, concerned. Then the girl seems to recognise me and she whispers to her fella. But I don't care. At this moment, it's as if a huge horrible guilt has been lifted off me. He *was* great. He *had* loved me. Fáinne's dad was a good man.

'I've given that Johnno fella a picture too,' Philip says then. 'At least, after all this time, Jason has paid him back with interest.' His voice falters. I catch his hand. He squeezes mine. Even if I haven't met Jason, I've traced him.

I've traced myself. I realise that, all along, it's my own lost self that I've been seeking.

60

TELLING FÁINNE IS the hard part. I haven't even told
her that I was meeting Philip. That night, after her bath,
when she's all curly-haired and squeaky clean, I put her into
bed and sit down beside her.

'Story.' Fáinne hands me a book.

'I have a story I'd like to tell you,' I say instead.

She makes a face. 'But your makey-up stories are always
boring, Mammy. They're babyish. Gray tells great ones. Is
it one of his?'

'Nope. But you'll like it, I promise.'

She studies me. I know she's working out in her head
whether it's worth taking a risk on an unknown story. But
Fáinne, unlike her mother, is a risk-taker. I hope life never
takes that from her. 'Go on, so,' she sighs eventually, as if
she's doing me a big favour. 'Tell me.'

I move in beside her and wrap my arm about her and
she snuggles into me.

'This is nice.'

The love I feel for her rushes up through me. She was
meant to be here, I'm sure of that. 'Isn't it?' I kiss the top
of her head. 'OK, here we go.' I hesitate and she looks at
me. 'Well, there was once a girl, let's call her Lucy, and she
met this great boy. He was funny and handsome and he made

her laugh a lot. And she liked him very much because he made her laugh.'

'Was the girl sad?'

'She was worried, I think, because her own mammy and daddy fought a lot and she needed someone to make her laugh and he did and that's why she liked him so much.'

'Did she fall in love with him?'

I grin. Fáinne likes people to fall in love. 'She did. But the boy had a problem. He kept drinking and drinking and drinking.'

'Maybe he was thirsty?'

'He was very thirsty, but the stuff he drank only made him more thirsty.'

'Like magic stuff?'

'Uh-huh. And then, one day, he realised that he was drinking the wrong stuff but he couldn't stop it and he realised that he loved his drinking more than he loved Lucy.'

'Oh no.'

'And that made him sad so he packed his bags and went to a special place that would help him to stop drinking so he could be with Lucy.'

Fáinne squirms. 'Mammy, can I have *Rapunzel* instead?'

'Just listen, OK?' And maybe there is something in the way I say it, because she nods. 'Anyway,' I continue, 'the boy went away and Lucy didn't know where he had gone and she was angry with him and she had his little baby and she didn't know how to tell him because she didn't know where he had gone.'

Fáinne stiffens. 'Is the baby called Fáinne?'

I pull her closer. 'Yes.'

'And did my daddy drink lots and lots?'

'Yes.'

'And what happened?'

'The boy wasn't able to stop drinking because he had got so used to it. And he didn't know how to tell Lucy so instead he drew her a picture and he told his daddy that if he died, the daddy was to give the picture to Lucy.' I lift up Fáinne's duvet and pull out the picture from where I'd placed it earlier. Gently I hand it to her. 'And here it is.'

She stares at it, not touching it. Then she stares at me. 'Is my daddy dead?'

I nod. 'Yeah, sweetheart, he is.'

'And he drew this lovely picture for you?'

'For us,' I say. 'He didn't know about you but he loved me so that means he would have loved you.'

I watch her lift up the picture and study it, her head cocked to one side. 'Is that you?' she whispers.

'Yes.'

She touches the picture reverently. 'You look like you do in the photo from before.'

'What photo?'

'The one you showed me – where you were happy.'

And that's it – that's what he painted it from, I reckon. 'I was happy then, I guess.'

'And I can't ever meet him now?' Her bottom lip quivers. 'And I can't ever wear my Liverpool jersey?'

'Your granddad supports Liverpool.'

'No he doesn't – he doesn't support anyone.'

'No, your other granddad,' I say. 'Your daddy's daddy. He'd like to meet you. Would you like that?'

'My daddy's daddy?' Her eyes are bright.

'Yep. He doesn't have a wife or a son any more – all he has is you and he'd like to meet you.'

'He must be lonely.'

I don't say anything.

'I think I'd like that,' she says. 'So now I have two grand-dads – Jenny has only one. Ha!'

I try not to smile. 'Would you like me to hang the picture on your wall?'

'No.' She places her hands on either side of my face. 'You hang it on your wall.' Then she smiles. 'Hey, you look like your picture – all sort of happy.'

And I am. For the first time in nine years, I can honestly say that right at that moment, I am the happiest I have ever been.

61

THE CALL COMES just as I'm finishing up work for the
day. Clare is busy making a list of all the things she'd
like to take from her house when she finally divorces Brendan
and I'm left doing the donkey work. Which is apt, seeing as
I'm employed by a vet. Anyway, just as I'm putting away the
last of the evening's files, the phone rings. I ignore it because
if I answer I'll be delayed going over to see Maddie. She's
been home around two days now and she still hasn't seen
her baby. It's worrying, to be honest. Clive spends his mornings and nights in the hospital.

'Phone, Lucy?' Clare says.

'I'm in a rush.'

Just then the phone clicks off and my mobile starts up.

'Phone, Lucy,' Clare says again.

I pull it out of my bag.

'Yellow!'

Les's voice stops me in my tracks. 'Les?'

'The one and fucking only!'

His euphoric tone can only mean one thing. 'Is it about
the audition?'

Vaguely, I register that Doug has come out of his surgery,
bundled up in his Puffa jacket, ready for the off. Clare is
staring curiously at me.

'Is it?' I ask again. My heart is thumping madly.

'It sure is!' I wait for Les to elaborate. He doesn't.

'Well?'

'YOU GOT IT!'

My ear hurts and I have to pull the phone away. A tinny voice screams again, '*You got it!*'

'The part I read for?'

'The main fucking part!' He's singing now. I reckon he's doing a little victory dance as well as his voice is fading in and out.

'No way!'

'Yes way!'

'But don't I have to do a second audition?'

'Nope – he loved you!'

I let out a little scream that makes Doug look at me. He arches his eyebrows. 'Good news?'

'Main part in *Rapid*.' I hyperventilate. 'Oh God!'

'Brilliant,' Clare says, sounding genuinely pleased for me. 'Brilliant, Lucy!'

'So thank me,' Les says.

'Thanks, Les.'

'And another of my actors got a part too,' Les says. 'I'm going to be fucking minted!' With this he hangs up.

I stare at the phone, then stare at my two workmates. 'I can't believe it.' And I can't. My dreams have come true and all I can feel is a weird sort of numbness.

Doug gives a wide grin. 'Well, start believing it. This time next year you'll be huge!'

'No.' I giggle, slightly hysterically. 'That happened the first time I got a film part.'

Both Doug and Clare laugh.

I don't.

*

390

Before I leave the car park, I ring my mother to tell her the news. She's delighted for me. I hear her shouting out the news to Dad. He comes on the phone to tell me how proud he is of me. Then Fáinne gets on and her main mission once she hears the news is to ring Jenny and let her know. 'My daddy is a dead famous artist and my mammy is an alive film star,' she says joyfully. I hear my mother telling her to have a bit of respect.

Then I ring Gray, who's also thrilled. And Audrey who is more excited than I am. 'I'm almost fainting here,' she squeals.

After that, I drive over to Maddie. It hurts that I can't share my news with her.

She's sitting in the kitchen, half-heartedly picking at a piece of chicken that Clive left for her. She's undressed, so she obviously didn't go to work, and her mad head of hair looks lank and greasy.

'Hiya.' I dump a Chinese meal in front of her. 'Eat this. That chicken looks rank.'

'I'm not hungry.'

I pull out two plates from her press and dump some sweet and sour on to it. 'Try it.'

'No.'

'Well, all the more for me, so.' I keep my voice light. 'How's things?'

She shrugs.

'Is Clive at the hospital?'

A nod.

'Did you go in?'

'Lucy, if you've just come here to ask the same questions over and over, I'm going to bed.' She stands up.

'I'm only trying to help you.'

'Yeah, well, don't.' She pulls the cord of her dressing gown tighter around her. 'I don't need help. I'm fine.'

'You do need help and you've always been there for me, so I'm bloody well going to be there for you.'

Maddie startles me by giving a big bellow. 'Huh! And when have you ever let me help you? Huh?'

'What—?'

'Every time I offered my advice you ignored it. You never listen to me, Luce, I always go along with what you want, so *please* don't inflict your views on me!'

'I'm not – I'm only trying to—'

'I told you not to look for Jason and you did. And you found him and obviously it didn't go well because you haven't said a word about it. But you wouldn't listen to me and leave well enough alone, would you? Now, if you really want to help me, get the fuck out of here!'

She's never talked to me like this before. I can only gawp at her as she pushes by me out of the kitchen. And then, from somewhere, words tumble out of my mouth. 'Jason is *dead*,' I say loudly. 'He's dead.' I pause. My voice shakes and I battle to get it under control. 'That's why I didn't say anything. You have enough on your plate.'

She stops, her back to me, then turns slowly around. 'Dead?'

'Yeah, and do you know what?' I'm advancing on her. 'He never saw his little girl. He never saw her and now he never will. And I hate that. I hate that he'll never see her.' I stop and swallow, then, taking a deep breath to keep my voice steady, I continue, 'But you, right, you can see your little girl if you want. You can talk to her and hold her. You have a chance Maddie. Do it now, just in case it's too late one day.'

Her eyes widen. Her face goes red and then white. Maybe I shouldn't have said anything.

'Sorry,' I mutter. 'Maybe I shouldn't—'

'He's dead?'

'Yep,' I nod. 'He died only a little while ago.'

'Oh.' She reaches out to touch me.

Our hands meet. I squeeze her fingers. 'But, Maddie,' I say urgently, not caring what she thinks now, 'you are not dead and your little girl is not. And Jason didn't abandon us, he never knew Fáinne existed. But right now, you're abandoning Amy. And maybe you did nothing wrong during the pregnancy, but I think it's wrong what you're doing now.'

She closes her eyes and sways a little. 'I don't mean to abandon her,' she says, a bit tearfully. 'But I don't know how to cope with it, Lucy. Nothing like this has ever happened to me before. I don't know what to do.'

'The right thing,' I say firmly. 'That's what you do.'

She looks at me as if she's never seen me before. 'I'm scared.'

'I know. But I'm here. And Clive is here.'

'Will you come in with me to see her?'

'Of course I will.'

Maddie squeezes my hand and I pull her into an embrace. 'I think,' I gasp, half laughing, half crying with relief, 'I think it might be a good idea to get dressed first though.'

I drive her to the hospital. She's shaking. 'Maybe the baby will resent me,' she whispers, sounding vulnerable for the first time since I've known her.

'Not a hope. Fáinne wouldn't have resented Jason if he'd come to see her, and she's eight.'

Maddie nods. 'Yeah.'

After parking, the two of us walk towards the hospital. At the door, Maddie clasps my hand. 'Thanks, Lucy. I'm really glad you're here.'

'So am I,' I say back. It's an automatic response, but the words set off an odd chain of thoughts in my head. I *am* glad to be here, I realise. Glad to be helping my friend, glad to be seeing her baby, glad to be godmother to her baby, glad to be able to meet my mates whenever I want to. Glad to go to work every day, glad to have a nice boss. Glad. Glad. Glad. Happy even. It's like the day in the car when Doug dropped me at the audition. Things had suddenly become clear to me, but I'd ignored them. Now I know, with startling clarity, that, like Audrey, I've been chasing a dream. A dream I suddenly understand that I've outgrown. What I want, I've had all along. I don't crave attention from strangers any more. Being whistled at in the street is now my worst nightmare. Maybe I'd only ever wanted to be noticed because I felt overlooked at home. But now, all the attention I craved I could have from people I cared about. And I could give them my attention and be happy to do it. Maddie needs me; I want to be here. How could I help my mates if I went overseas?

'Are you OK?' Maddie asks.

'Fine. I'm great.' I smile at her, dizzy with realisation. 'Come on, let's go and find Clive and your baby.'

I leave at the moment Clive embraces Maddie and they both turn to look at tiny baby Amy in her incubator.

I wish, eight years ago, that I'd had some guy to claim Fáinne as 'our baby'. Some guy to stare in adoration at her. Some guy to care about us. But I hadn't and even if Jason had stuck around, I know now he wouldn't have been good for us. It's as if, with the kiss Clive gives Maddie, all my youthful memories of Jason evaporate and he stands before me as a guy that I once knew, that I once cared about, but a guy that I was suddenly free of.

I know now what I have to do.

62

Doug's house is just like him. Careless and unkempt but seriously charming. To me it is anyway. It's a detached house with an enormous garden. If Doug is surprised to see me, he doesn't show it. He leads me through his red and green hallway and into his grey kitchen.

The man hasn't a clue about colours.

Outside in the back garden, numerous dogs seem to be barking like mad. 'They like visitors,' he explains.

I'm all sweaty palms and deep breathing as I try to keep myself under control. I smile at him and say, 'Don't we all.' I sound ridiculous.

'I just need to finish feeding them.' Doug doesn't seem to notice my discomfort. 'And then I'll make you a cuppa and you can tell me what you want.'

'D'you want me to help?'

'Sure.' He hands me four tins of puppy food. 'You can feed the pups. They're in the kennel on the right. Well, if they haven't torn down the fence and wandered into next door's garden.' He makes it sounds a perfectly wonderful prospect though I'm sure his next-door neighbour hates him.

I follow him into a small, untidy utility room and from there, into his garden. The minute he steps outside the door, dogs race up to him, all wriggling bodies and wagging tails. He pets them, talks to them all and, as I watch him, I suddenly understand that what I've always liked about him is the fact that he's happy. He's content just being him. What I like about my mates is that they're happy.

Doug strides across the garden, the dogs following him, and he beckons to me. I run to catch up with him but stay a step behind, loving his confident walk, enjoying the way the dogs seem to adore him. He leads me towards the puppy kennel. 'In there. You'll find the bowls in there.'

I crouch down and am immediately surrounded by six cute balls of fur. I barely get the food into the bowls before they savage it. Standing up, I see Doug being knocked over by an enormous dog. He's laughing and cursing as he tries to push the dog off but it jumps on top of him and begins licking his face with a huge dripping tongue. I giggle as Doug struggles to get up. Eventually the dog lets him go and Doug dusts himself down. He's filthy, like a great big kid. He loves these animals and his laughter only serves to confirm that I've made the right decision.

'Gorgeous, ey?' Doug says enthusiastically.

'Yeah.'

'Come on, so, I'll get that coffee. What's the occasion anyway – come to hand in your resignation officially or what?'

I don't answer, just tag alongside him into the house.

He scrubs his hands and face vigorously and dries them on a surprisingly clean hand towel before putting on the kettle. Then he pulls up a chair and, turning it backwards, sits astride it. 'Well, what's the occasion? I don't normally have film stars knocking on my door.'

I squirm in my seat. 'Well, that's the occasion actually. I, eh, I've decided that maybe being a film star is not quite me.'

'Huh?'

I lick my dry lips and squeeze my hands together, palm to palm. 'I've a proposition for you.'

'Sounds dead kinky.' He's smiling slightly. 'A proposition from a film star. Nice one.'

'I want to buy the clinic. Or maybe we could buy it together – what do you think?' Of course, I hadn't meant to blab it out quite like that, I'd meant to outline how sensible the plan was, how I'd finance it, all the boring stuff, but no matter, the message is the same.

Doug gazes at me in disbelief. 'You – buy the clinic?'

'I have the money. Well, I think I have.'

'You have?' No smile.

'I have a picture – it's worth a good bit of money. Fáinne's dad did it for me. If I sell it, I can buy the clinic.' My hands are sweaty. I shove them under my buttocks.

Doug stands up. 'Lucy, I really think you should keep your picture. It probably means a lot to you.'

'Not as much as a secure future.'

'Your film will buy you a future.'

'Yeah – but not the one I want.'

Doug slides his hands into the pockets of his jeans and stares down at me. 'You don't know the first thing about running a clinic.'

'Neither do you, but we can learn.' I'm sounding desperate. I thought he'd be delighted. 'Clare can teach us.'

'No.' He shakes his head and turns to look out of the window. 'No, I'm not interested in going into partnership with you, Lucy.'

'Why?'

He doesn't even do me the courtesy of turning to face me; instead he shrugs.

'Well?'

'Luce, look, just go and do your film and—'

'Why don't you want to go into partnership with me?'

My sharp tone shocks him. He turns and gazes straight at me. 'Isn't that obvious?'

'No.'

'How can I go into partnership with someone that I slept with? Hey?'

'That was nothing,' I bluster, mortified. I hadn't seen that one coming. 'It was just a mistake. It meant nothing.'

'It did to me.'

His words cut through my next tirade. I open and close my mouth like a goldfish. Eventually, I stammer out, 'What?'

'I told you at the time – I fancied you like mad. I still do. Working with you does my head in, Lucy. I want to leave.' He gazes at his mucky trainers. 'I'm glad you're going.'

'What?' I can't take it in.

'I'm not saying it again. One humiliation a day is enough for any guy.' He cracks a wry smile. 'I can't be your partner, Lucy. It wouldn't work.' He pauses. 'Anyway, I really think you should keep that picture.'

The kettle clicks off. We ignore it.

'I don't want to be in a film.' My voice sounds sort of lost. 'All I want is for things to be like always.'

'Yeah, well, things change. I can't go into partnership with you just so that you can have what you want. It's not what I want.'

'Well' – embarrassment makes me sarcastic – 'I didn't think working in a garage was what you wanted either.'

'It's better than being around you, Lucy.'

Oh. My. God. Waves and waves of hurt flood through me. I mean, I don't think he was trying to hurt me, but he has. 'Thanks,' I blurt out. 'That's nice.'

'I meant that it's too hard for me to be around you, Lucy. I thought I could cope but it's driving me nuts. Every time you get a personal call, I think it's some guy you're seeing. I know if I get away, it won't be so bad. I need out. OK?'

God, he must really have liked me. I'm ashamed when I think of how I treated him. For years I'd been reeling from Jason's perceived betrayal and I'd done the same thing myself. 'I'm sorry about Christmas,' I mutter. I can't even look him in the face, I feel so guilty. 'Sorry,' I say again.

'Don't apologise.' He nudges me gently, smiling a little. 'Great night.'

And it was. It was a brilliant night. The sex had been fantastic, we'd made love as if we'd been always together. As I meet his gaze, desire for him rushes up through me. I wish he'd grab me and kiss me like he did that night. Just once more, before we both move on. But he won't. Doug isn't stupid.

'Anyway, if your car ever needs fixing, you know where to come.'

I manage a weak smile. It dawns on me that I'm going to lose him. He's going to work in a garage and I'll never see him again – not unless my car breaks down and I travel halfway across the city to get it repaired. I don't want never to see him again.

'Though with the sort of cars you'll be driving, you'll probably have your own private mechanic.'

I don't answer. I've already told him that I'm not doing the film. He obviously doesn't believe me. 'I wouldn't want to torture you with the sight of me.' I pick up my coat. 'I'm sure there're plenty of other mechanics in Dublin.'

His grin fades.

'So, looks like we've a week left together and then you'll be free. Don't say I didn't offer.'

'Aw, Luce—'

'Bye, Doug.' Head high, I march out of his house.

Now what am I meant to do?

63

'**Y**OU'RE LATE,' MAM comments when I eventually get around to picking up Fáinne. 'Telling everyone the good news, I suppose?'

I dread telling her almost as much as I dreaded telling Les. I'd rung Les from outside Doug's. Well, not from right outside as I'd wanted to get away from Doug as fast as I could, but from just up the road. Even though Doug hadn't wanted to take up my offer, I knew there was no way I could do that film. It was enough to know that I'd been offered it. Les had been disbelieving, then furious, then he'd begun begging me to reconsider. But I never would. And it wasn't something I'd spend years regretting either.

No way.

I felt bad for letting Les down though. It seems no matter what I do, I'm going to have guilt following me like a big black shadow.

Mam is staring peculiarly at me.

I try to compose myself. I know I'm going to shatter her hopes. Again.

'You don't look too happy for someone who just landed a film part,' Mam observes, looking at me with her head cocked to one side. 'Tea?'

'I'm not doing the film,' I say and brace myself.

'What?'

'I realised it wasn't what I wanted.'

'Oh.' Her brow furrows, 'Why not? Was it not a good part? I thought it was the main part.'

'I just didn't want to be in a film.'

'But I thought—'

'I know.' I turn away from her. 'I always thought so too, but well, you know me – I never know what I want.'

She's silent. I know she's wondering what to say to that. I reckon she's getting ready to go on the attack. I spot Fáinne's bag underneath the table and start cramming all her little bits and pieces into it, determined to make a quick getaway.

'I suppose,' Mam ventures, 'knowing what you don't want is a start of sorts.'

'Yeah.' I think I'm going to cry. I thought she'd lecture me but she hasn't. As least if she'd acted disappointed, I could have fought back. I'm good at that.

'And it lets you focus on what you do want.' Pause. Then in this really weird gentle sort of voice, she asks, 'What *do* you want, Lucy?'

I shrug. I'm still not looking at her. Why isn't she giving out? 'I dunno – I suddenly realised that I like my life the way it is and that I want to be around my mates and, well, I didn't want things to change.'

'You like your life,' she repeats. 'Oh Lucy.'

Now she sounds as if she *really* might cry. I turn to face her and there are tears in her eyes. 'Mam?'

'Well . . .' She blinks rapidly and says almost defensively, 'You've been so miserable for so long. You were miserable when you were pregnant, miserable when you had Fáinne, miserable when you had the job, miserable when you did that ad – it worried me. You never seemed happy. I didn't know what was wrong. It was awful to watch.'

I wasn't that bad. That unhappy. 'I wasn't that unhappy.'

'Well, you made a great job of pretending to be so.' Now she sounds cross. I'm used to that. My own temper rises.

'Huh – surprised you noticed.'

'And what is that supposed to mean?'

'You know very well what that means.'

'Oh.' Mam rolls her eyes. 'Bring on the inferiority complex.'

'Yes! Yes! Bring it on,' I say. 'Bring it on. Bring on the massive family failure.' I'm shouting and I don't know why. I think it's delayed Doug shock.

'Failure?' She gives me a look. Asks in this really patronising voice, 'How did you fail?'

I almost laugh. 'I had Fáinne, didn't I? Oh, I really let you both down when I had Fáinne—'

'No!'

'But it was my choice and I—'

'We *love* Fáinne,' Mam says. 'We wouldn't be without her.'

'It's easy to say that now.'

'She's the light in our lives, so she is,' Mam says and she really is angry. Bright red spots appear on her cheeks. 'Don't you ever' – and she points a finger at me and her voice is shaking – '*ever* say she was a mistake. She saved our marriage, that child. She gave us something to focus on. She is the best thing that ever happened to us.'

'The best thing?'

'The most *wonderful, precious* thing,' she confirms and she's glaring at me. 'Jesus, Lucy, you must realise how much we love her.'

'Yeah, but—'

'But what?' She is furious.

'But I let you down—'

'You let *yourself* down.'

'Yeah, I failed.'

402

'Never.' The passion in her voice startles me. 'How *can* you say that? OK, you got pregnant at nineteen, but look what you managed to do: you got a job and brought up a wonderful little girl. That's success.'

Her words are enormous. Probably the most significant words she's ever spoken to me in my entire life. They penetrate my head; they tip my world up something strange. Maybe I've just been successful in a different way to what I thought. A better way. Maybe. 'You never told me that before.'

'I didn't think I needed to.'

'You always gave out to me.'

'No!'

'You give me these looks.'

Mam throws her eyes to heaven. 'Because you *annoy* me. It doesn't mean I think you failed or anything else. OK, your house is a mess, your clothes could be nicer, your friends are strange, but what do you want me to do? Pretend?'

I can't find the words to say what I want to say. I don't know what I want to say.

'Just be happy, that's all I want.'

And that's when I cry. I don't know if I'm happy or sad or what. But my mother crosses to me and wraps her arms around me and it's lovely. Really lovely. And I tell her stuff I never thought I would. Of how I always felt a failure compared to Tracy and she tells me again that I was never a failure. She tells me that I'm the best mother she's ever seen. That Fáinne is the happiest kid she's ever seen. And I tell her about Jason and of how he's dead now and of how he left me a picture and of how Doug turned me down for a partnership. How I didn't know what I was going to do now. I don't tell her that I slept with Doug because that'd be too much but I say that I kissed him at Christmas and

403

that he wanted to go out with me and I cry because I've taken a risk and he's turned me down and I cry because I'm happy too. I'm happy that I'm a good mother and I've a good job and I like my house and my life.

My dad pokes his head in the door and quickly hurries Fáinne to the shops.

And she tells me that Doug's pride was probably hurt at Christmas and that that's why he won't go into partnership with me. 'If you want to open that clinic, you do it,' she tells me. 'You do it. Men and their pride,' she mutters as if she's an expert. 'He'll see what he's missing,' she says confidently. 'But don't waste years on him the way you did on Jason. Don't give your life over to him – just focus on the happy things and trust.' She hugs me to her the way I hug Fáinne. 'Just trust.'

And I tell her that I'll try.

64

TWO DAYS LATER, on a Saturday afternoon, Philip
Donovan calls. I had sounded Fáinne out some more
about it and she was adamant that she wanted to meet him.
Dressed in her new Liverpool jersey and blue jeans, embroidered for her by Tracy (well, Tracy designed the stitching,
someone else did it!), she is like someone possessed as she
dances from room to room asking me if it is time yet.

'Soon,' I keep telling her. 'And he's not going to come on
time, no one ever does.'

But I'm wrong. Bang on two o'clock, he arrives at our
door. And Fáinne stops jumping about and hides behind me.
She clings on to my trousers as I slowly make my way to the
door. 'Jesus, Fáinne, cop on to yourself!'

'Hi.' Philip is dressed casually, in a jumper and jeans, and
he smiles nervously at me as I open the door.

'Hiya, Philip, come in and meet Fáinne.'

'Hello, Fáinne.'

Nothing.

I give my daughter a poke. 'Say "hi", Fáinne.'

Fáinne looks up at him and buries her head back into my
side.

'She was so excited all day,' I explain, mortified by my
daughter's sudden muteness. 'Just give her a chance.'

Philip smiles again. Then he surprises me by getting down

on his hunkers and saying, 'Hiya, Fáinne, I'm your daddy's daddy and if you like, I've some pictures to show you of him – just so you know what he looked like.'

Silence.

'Or I can leave them here and you can look at them another time.' He places a brown album on the ground beside her feet.

'Don't mind her,' I snap in a very unmotherlike way, 'have a cuppa. I'll talk to you instead.'

'I want to see the pictures,' Fáinne pipes up. 'I want to see the pictures of my dead daddy.'

'Fáinne!' Jesus, talk about upsetting the poor man.

'It's fine.' Philip is grinning. 'At least she's talking to me.'

'You can go in there with her and I'll make us a cuppa if you like.'

'Will you come?' Philip holds out his hand.

Fáinne takes it. 'Have you baby pictures of him? I think babies are cute.'

When I go back in a few minutes later with a tray of tea, orange and biscuits, the two of them have their heads bent over the photo album. They look surprisingly right together, both good-looking, both sallow-skinned. She has more a look of Jason than she ever had of me.

'Mammy,' Fáinne says excitedly. 'Look, it's the same.'

Philip holds out a picture. 'You haven't changed much.'

It's the one of me and Jason that I have upstairs. Gray must have done a copy for him. Jason must have *asked* him for a copy, so he could paint me. I get all choked up as I look at it.

Fáinne goes back to the album. Philip has a story for every picture. Some of them I'm convinced he makes up so that Fáinne will laugh but there is no doubt that here is a man who loved his son dearly.

I'm suddenly ashamed of myself. Despite losing his wife and his son, Philip doesn't seem at all bitter – not like I would have been. He's a nice person to have in our lives.

Towards the end of the album, he points to a picture of Jason taken a couple of months before he died. 'This was the best day I had with him,' Philip says, smiling.

Jason doesn't look like he used to. I would have passed him by on the street. For one thing, his looks had gone, ravaged by the drink. He's smiling at the camera, his hand shading his face. His teeth are rotten, not the beautiful white grin I remember so well. And he's thin. So bloody thin. His hair is the same though and he still stands with a nonchalant slouch.

God, he could have had such a great life.

'We climbed Howth Head that day,' Philip says. 'Me and him. He liked climbing a lot. Settled his head, he said. That day, as we walked, we talked. We talked about his mother for the first time ever. When we reached the top, we sat on the grass and just looked out at the sea.'

Fáinne makes a face. 'That sounds a bit boring.'

Philip laughs. 'Yeah, maybe it does. But it was the first time we really talked to each other. Your daddy wasn't good at talking.'

'Maybe he needed speech therapy.'

Philip explodes in a laugh. 'Maybe he did. Jesus.' He shakes his head and looks at me. 'Jace would have loved her.'

'Yeah,' I say back.

'It was a good day,' he tells Fáinne, 'because sometimes you don't get to say what you want to someone, but that day, we said everything to each other and I felt he was happy and so was I. There's no point in letting someone go if there's unfinished business.' He looks at me. 'Isn't that right, Lucy?'

'Uh-huh.' Our unfinished business had tortured me for over eight years. Finally though, like Jason, I was going to have some peace.

65

THE HOTEL ROOM is packed. Apparently there has been a lot of interest in the auction, which is bad news for me. I've had my picture valued and it's worth well over four hundred thousand. Can you imagine – just for a picture? The art expert advised me to hold on to it, he said it'd appreciate even more in the years to come, but I can't. I've decided to use it to buy the clinic. The bank should lend me the rest.

I wander towards the front of the room, trying to see if I know anyone here. I've never been to an auction before and am terrified that the guy won't see me nodding or whatever it is you do to place a bid. 'Hiya.' Clare startles me as she arrives with Jim. 'Front row seats, ey?' She plonks herself down and pats the seat for Jim to sit beside her.

'Is Doug not here?' I haven't really talked to him all week. I wasn't sure what I could say.

'He's not coming,' Clare says.

'Doug's not able for all this,' Jim announces. 'He's broke up over it.'

Not that broke up, I think. He wouldn't go into partnership with me. I had hoped that if he came to the auction, he'd see me bidding and realise exactly what he was missing out on. It didn't seem that was going to happen.

'Juicy jelly?' Clare shoves a bag into my face.

Before I can take one, a voice from the seat behind says, 'Awww, haven't you lovely juicy jellies.'

Clare flinches, the bag jerks and juicy jellies fall on to her lap. She turns on the remark-maker. 'What are *you* doing here?'

It's Brendan and he's smiling like a big fat cat. Jim makes a face at me and both of us brace ourselves for the fireworks.

A man takes the podium. The place suddenly quietens.

'What the fuck are you doing here?' Clare's voice rises above the mutterings. Disgusted faces are turned in her direction.

'Quiet please!' The man, I presume he's the auctioneer, bangs his gavel.

'Well?' Clare demands, ignoring him. 'Well?'

'Can everyone be quiet?' the auctioneer says crossly.

Brendan taps the side of his nose and Clare belts him. A murmur goes up around the room. The auctioneer bangs on the counter.

Brendan continues to smile like a guy that's just scored big time. 'I'm here to bid,' he purrs.

'You're not going to buy it,' Clare stammers as the auction gets under way. 'You can't. I own half your money.'

'Not yet you don't,' Brendan says. 'And if I buy it' – he raises his hand into the air and the auctioneer acknowledges it – 'I'll need a damn good secretary to run it. Would you like the job?'

'Fuck off!'

It's hard to ignore the two of them. I do try. I hold my hand up to make a bid.

'I'm buying the bloody thing for you,' Brendan hisses. 'To show you that I love you. And miss you. The least you can do is be happy about it, you stupid cow.'

Oh. My. God.

'Yeah, just like you bought everything else for me,' Clare snaps back. 'I'm not that stupid any more, Brendan.'

'And neither am I.'

I can't help it, I turn around and gaze at the pair of them. Clare looks furious and poor Brendan looks totally hopeless.

'I behaved awfully.' Brendan now has the attention of the crowd. The auctioneer is calling out numbers and no one seems that interested. 'I'm sorry, Clare.'

'Good.' Clare folds her arms and turns away from him. 'Carry on,' she calls to the auctioneer.

'I'll do whatever you want. I just need you back,' Brendan says loudly. 'If you want my mother in a home, I'll put her there.' His voice breaks.

'I don't want her in a home,' Clare snaps. 'I never said that. Ever.'

'I know.'

'All I wanted was help from you. I didn't want jumpers and jewellery and I especially don't want you going buying me a surgery. All I want is some help.'

'You can buy the surgery though,' Jim pipes up. 'Save our jobs.'

I snort back a laugh.

'Fuck off, Jim,' Clare hisses. Her face softens as she turns to her husband. 'Will you help me? Will you get your family to help?'

'Anything.' His pudgy face looks like one of those sad dogs with all the wrinkles in their skin. 'Cross my heart.'

'Aw!' Clare's hard face dissolves and she looks younger suddenly. She reaches over and hugs Brendan hard. He hugs her back.

'Is that a bid?' the auctioneer asks sharply.

'You bet it is,' Brendan shouts up. 'I've just got my lovely wife back.'

411

People laugh but the auctioneer is not amused. 'Three hundred thousand, now who'll give me four?'

I can't help staring at Clare and Brendan. He mouths to her that he loves her, that he misses her. She says that she missed him too. The turf war going on about me suddenly doesn't seem to matter.

'Couldn't let you divorce me without a fight to get you back,' Brendan says. 'I couldn't have lived with myself.'

'Ohhh.'

Brendan raises his hand in the air again and the auctioneer calls out, 'Half a million over there.'

Brendan couldn't have lived with himself if he'd let her go. The words are like hammer blows to my psyche. I realise suddenly that where Jason was once my unfinished business, now Doug is. Or he will be if I don't do something. Why do I want to buy the clinic – really? To keep things the same. But not just that – it's to keep Doug with me. I don't want to lose him. I should have known how I felt. Why didn't I know? Because it had meant taking too many risks. But, Jesus, I'd told him stuff I'd only ever tell my closest mates. I'd slept with him, which was something I hadn't done with anyone in years. I'd cried in front of him. I'd gone rushing out of an audition to see him put down a dog that I hated. All for him. To make him like me. I'd worked overtime for free for him when I'd desperately needed the money. But most telling of all, I'd been prepared to sell a beautiful picture that a guy I'd loved had painted of me in order to keep him with me. The knowledge sweeps over me. I'm paralysed. Scared. Then I think of what Philip said about unfinished business. I can't have it happen to me again. Not again. I jump up to leave. I don't want the clinic. I just want Doug.

'Seven hundred thousand,' the auctioneer calls.

412

I realise he's looking at me. 'No, I didn't—'

'Eight hundred thousand to the man at the back.'

The man at the back is Mr D. He grins up at me. *What is he doing here?*

'Nine hundred thousand to the gentleman in the blue suit.' Blue suit is someone I haven't seen before though there is something familiar about him.

'One million to the man in the second row.'

That's Brendan. I'm glad I'm pulling out.

The bids creep higher. Mr D. surrenders when it gets to a million and a half, after muttering a 'fucking bastards' quite loudly.

It's Brendan and the blue-suited man now.

It goes to one and three-quarters.

One million eight hundred thousand.

Clare pulls Brendan's arm down. 'We could never afford that,' she hisses. 'It's OK anyway, you've got me back.'

Another hug.

'Sold to the gentleman in the blue suit.' The gavel comes down and the man in the blue suit smiles in satisfaction.

As one, Clare, Jim and I realise that our jobs are gone. It's weird. We hug each other and it's more emotional than I thought it would be. Mr D. arrives over just as we let each other go. He looks quite respectable in navy trousers and a black blazer. 'Sorry I couldn't afford it, lads,' he says glumly. 'I thought I could do yez a favour after yez have been so good to me. Of course, Grumpy Knickers would have had to be in charge.' He fires a malevolent look at Clare. 'I mean, no disrespect, Luce, but you and Doug would've wasted every penny I'd invested on freebies.'

I smile wryly. 'Thanks for your faith.'

'Pint?' Jim asks him.

'Yeah, why not?'

They walk into the bar together. Clare and Brendan say their goodbyes – they're all over each other.

I'm suddenly left alone.

On my right, someone is congratulating the blue-suited man. For some reason, I think I've seen him before. He glances over at me and I give him the two fingers.

Dignified, I know.

Pulling on my coat, I head outside and jump into my car. If this is the end of this part of my life, I'm bloody well going to make sure I've no regrets.

66

DOUG IS IN. His car is parked in the driveway and the light is on in his front room. For some reason, a calm has descended on me. I don't care any more about telling him how I feel. Losing him without fighting is a far worse prospect.

I ring the bell. The sound echoes inside the house. From the back garden, the dogs start barking.

No one answers.

I ring the bell again.

And again.

Then I start banging on the windows. 'Anyone home?'

Nothing.

For some reason, it's like I've stepped back years. I'm ringing Jason's flat and he's not there. He's gone. There's nothing I can do. The emotions of the last few hours sweep over me and I find myself pounding on Doug's window calling, 'Doug, open up, please. Open up!'

I'm about to hammer on the door when it opens. Doug, looking bleary-eyed and slightly drunk, stands there, swaying a little. 'What?' He takes a bit of time to focus on me. 'Luce?' Immediately he starts to try to appear not drunk. 'Sorry. I, eh, just had a drink.'

'Or five,' I joke.

He shrugs, not smiling.

'Can I come in?'

'I dunno – the place is a mess.'

'It was a mess the last day too.'

'Was not.' He shakes his head slowly. 'It was tidy then.' He opens the door wider. 'So, what is it this time? Saying goodbye? Heading to Hollywood after all? Who bought the surgery?'

'A guy in a blue suit. Looked a bit of a prick.'

'Oh.' He turns and walks into his front room. I follow.

It is a mess. Books on animals are scattered everywhere. The sofa is an old one, brown and battered. The carpet is beige and the walls are painted beige too. The curtains are beige. The whole effect is like stepping into a digestive biscuit.

'Word of advice.' Doug taps his nose. 'Never go all beige.'

I smile. 'So, how drunk are you?'

He shrugs. 'Not as drunk as I'd like to be.'

'When do you start in the garage?'

'Dunno. I haven't been told yet.'

I stare at the horrendous carpet. 'I didn't bid on the surgery after all.'

He says nothing.

'I only wanted it to keep you.'

'You would have got another vet, just as good.'

'It wasn't the vet I wanted.' I force myself to say the words while looking into his hazel eyes. God, they're beautiful. 'It wasn't the vet I wanted,' I say again, my voice cracking, 'it was the man.'

The words hang in the air. Doug's eyes widen with incredulity. Then slip away from my gaze. 'Naw. Look, Luce, I know—'

I cross to him. I'm inches from his body. I don't care now. After this I might never see him again so it doesn't matter. I touch his arm. The shock of contact jolts me. Desire like

I've never felt before races through me. I rub my hand up and down his arm, moving closer to him.

He stays stock still.

My hand finds its way to his face. The erotic pull of half-stubble. My thumb traces the length of his eyelashes. I move closer still. So close that the thigh of my jeans brushes the thigh of his tatty brown cords.

He looks at me. 'Don't.'

But I can't help myself. I'm like a moth drawn to a flame. 'I want to.'

He gulps. But he doesn't pull away. 'Do you always get what you want?' he asks softly.

'Nope. Hardly ever.'

I knot my fingers in his hair and pull his face down to mine. His lips brush mine; his thumb caresses my cheek. I mould myself to him.

'Well,' he says, and his voice is a bit ragged, 'this must be your lucky day, so.' He crushes me to him. His hand pulls my lower body to his and I feel his erection. Jesus, I want him. We kiss and kiss and kiss.

'You're not going to leave me in the morning, are you?' Doug asks, pulling away. His eyes are almost black.

The longing in his voice is so honest. He really wants me, and he wants me to know it. So, for the first time in eight years, I'm honest with someone other than Maddie and Gray. 'I only ever make mistakes once. This time, I'm never going to leave you.'

That's all I need to say.

He loves me like I love him and that's saying everything.

It's a while later; I'm lying naked on Doug's floor. His finger is tracing little lines from my neck to navel and his eyes are looking into mine with naked – no pun intended – intensity.

'I fancied you from the day I saw you,' he admits. 'To be honest, I was scared shitless you'd become famous and leave me.'

'Thanks. It must've been all your negative vibes that held me back.'

'Naw, I'd never have held you back.' He bends down to kiss me. The front-door bell rings. 'Aw shit!'

'Don't answer it.' I pull him back to me.

'OK, so.' More kisses. 'Are you going to make it worth my while?'

The bell rings again. Then, like me, the caller starts to hammer on the door. 'Douglas,' a woman's voice shouts, 'we know you're in there. Come out now!'

Doug groans, his head on my breast. 'Fuck!'

'Now, Douglas!' the woman orders. Then, on a disgusted note, she adds, 'Really, James, you'd think he'd cut his grass once in a while.'

A man mutters something we can't catch.

'It's me mother.' Doug makes a face. 'And me dad.'

'What!' I glance down at myself, horrified. 'Oh God, get me out of here.'

'Stay there. Get dressed and stay there. I'll handle her. I'll tell her I'm sick.'

He pulls on a pair of jeans and, barefoot and bare-chested, he pads outside to the hall, shutting the door behind him. He opens his front door, and oh shit, his mother pushes her way in. 'Your father and I would like to talk to you, Douglas,' she says in her snotty voice.

'Aw, Mam, I'm feeling a bit rough, OK?'

'Yes, well, drinking never solved any problems, Douglas.'

'Now, now, Glynis, let's just say what we've come to say,' a man's soothing tone – which reminds me of my dad – speaks up. 'Now, Douglas, it's about your future.'

'Aw, God . . . ,' I smile as Doug groans loudly. 'I don't need this today.'

'Well, we think you do,' his mother says briskly. 'Is there somewhere we can talk?'

'I'm sick, Ma.'

'So that's the reason for the state of the place, is it?' she snaps. 'Honestly, do you ever clean up? This hall is like a pigsty. And how many dogs have you now? How do you live with the racket?'

God, she's worse than my mother.

I hastily pull on my clothes and then I try to search the chaos of Doug's front room for my brown boots. Outside the voices get louder. I pay no attention, determined to find my boots, until Doug, sounding panicked, says, 'No, not in the front room. Maybe the kitchen would be better.'

I can't move. It's like my worst nightmare, where I'm running and running and getting nowhere. I can't even propel myself behind the sofa. I just stand in the middle of the room in my stockinged feet and pray that they won't come in.

'Your kitchen is a mess, Douglas. Anyway, those dogs will keep barking all over what we have to say.'

'I'll tell them to shut up.'

'Douglas, this is ridiculous, let us into the room.'

'What's the problem, son?' his dad asks.

'Nothing. I'm just sick, that's all.'

'Oh for God's sake!' The door is pushed open and I come face to face with Glynis. She stands surveying me for a second before turning up her pert nose. 'Is this your nurse, then, Douglas?'

'Yep – she was giving me a massage.' Doug makes a face at me but I can't smile back. His clothes are scattered all over the room. The place suddenly reeks of sex. From behind

419

Doug, a familiar face emerges. Oh fuck. This is worse than my worst nightmare. Blue suit from the auction.

He's handsome. Like his son. No wonder I thought I'd seen him before. I want to curl up and die.

'Oh.' Blue Suit looks at me. 'Hello again.'

'You know her?' Doug looks from one to the other of us in confusion.

'I, eh, waved at him earlier today,' I mutter. Every part of me is dying now.

'A wave, ey?' Blue Suit has the good grace to smile.

'Uh-huh.'

It's then I realise what this visit could mean for Doug. I look at his dad, at his mam and I can't help it. A huge smile breaks out. 'You bought the clinic,' I half whisper. Doug's folks look taken aback.

'We had hoped to surprise Douglas with it ourselves,' Glynis snaps. 'But thank you for stealing our thunder.'

'Oh. Shit. Sorry.' My brown boots are across the room. I think I should put them on and go.

'What?' Doug says, gob-smacked. 'You bought the clinic? But, but Lucy said some . . .' he pauses. Stops. Don't say it, I silently beg. 'She said some really fancy fella bought it.'

'Yes. Me.' Doug's dad smiles at his son. 'I bought it for you. I remortgaged a couple of the garages and decided to invest in a vet's practice. D'you fancy it?'

Doug can't say anything. He opens his mouth to speak but no words come.

'So you'll be happy,' his mother pipes up.

Doug continues to stare at them. 'Really?'

'Really.' His dad crosses to him. 'I shouldn't have expected you to run the garages. It was unfair.'

'I won't let you down,' Doug gulps out. 'Promise.'

It's at that point that I leave. I take my boots and walk to the door. I know hc'll come after me when he's done.

For the first time in my life, I'm actually sure of something.

Of someone.

Epilogue

Two years later

F áinne is on a high. She looks so pretty in her summer dress. She dances into the ward. 'Hiya, Mammy, how are you?'

I reach over and kiss her and she wraps her arms about my neck and hugs me hard. 'Granddad Philip took me to Clara Lara today and I got all wet and I had to go home and change.'

I laugh. Granddad Philip was proving to be a big hit in Fáinne's world. Ever since he'd been to visit – almost two years ago – she'd been in love with him and he with her. It was the best thing I'd ever done, tracing Jason.

Doug and my parents arrive beside me now. Doug kisses me lingeringly on the lips and embarrasses my mother. She gives a small cough and asks if she can see the baby.

'She's in the nursery, Mam,' I say. 'I needed a sleep and they took her off.' Mam sniffs, obviously not approving of me abandoning my newborn child. I'm about to retort something when Doug grins over her head at me.

'Come on, let's go and get her,' I say instead. I get out of bed and my mother and I make our way to the nursery. Doug and my dad follow.

She's gorgeous, my second child. A cap of dark hair, big blue eyes and a small little face. She reminds me of Fáinne and Doug all rolled into one. The two people I love most in the world, so that can't be bad. Happiness rushes through me as I hand her over to my mother. She

422

takes the baby gently in her arms and I marvel as I did ten years ago at the way her face softens.

'She's beautiful, Lucy. Beautiful. And where did you get that babygro?'

'Maddie, Clive and Amy brought it in yesterday.'

'Isn't it cute.' Mam kisses the top of my baby's head. 'Have you decided on godparents?'

'Yeah. Tracy and Clive. Tracy has promised to come over next month for a while once her new shop is up and running so we can have the christening sometime then.'

'She'll be delighted. I know she was hurt over Fáinne.'

I bite my lip and say nothing. Yep, my mother still has the power to annoy – that'll never change.

'And the name?' my dad asks.

I look at Doug. He looks at me. He's grinning and trying not to laugh. I take a deep breath. 'Áthas.'

Deafening silence.

'Áthas?' my mother whispers. 'You can't call a child that.'

'Why not? It means happiness in Irish and that's what she is: a little bundle of happiness.'

'Another makey-up name,' my mother snaps. She turns to Doug. 'Surely you don't agree with that?'

He crosses to me and puts his arm about me. 'Well, she has to have some outlet for her artiness.'

My mother rolls her eyes. 'Jesus, you're some man to put up with her.' She turns to my child and shakes her head. 'Well, God love you, child, being saddled with a name like that.'

423

Other bestselling titles available by mail:

☐	Something Borrowed	Martina Reilly	£6.99
☐	Wedded Blitz	Martina Reilly	£6.99
☐	All I Want is You	Martina Reilly	£6.99
☐	The Summer of Secrets	Martina Reilly	£6.99
☐	Second Chances	Martina Reilly	£11.99
☐	The Rebel Fairy	Deborah Wright	£5.99
☐	Under My Spell	Deborah Wright	£5.99
☐	Lazy Ways to Make a Living	Abigail Bosanko	£6.99
☐	A Nice Girl Like Me	Abigail Bosanko	£6.99
☐	Playing James	Sarah Mason	£6.99
☐	The Party Season	Sarah Mason	£6.99
☐	High Society	Sarah Mason	£5.99

The prices shown above are correct at time of going to press. However, the publishers reserve the right to increase prices on covers from those previously advertised, without further notice.

———————————— sphere ————————————

Please allow for postage and packing: **Free UK delivery.**
Europe; add 25% of retail price; Rest of World; 45% of retail price.

To order any of the above or any other Sphere titles, please call our credit card orderline or fill in this coupon and send/fax it to:

Sphere, P.O. Box 121, Kettering, Northants NN14 4ZQ
Fax: 01832 733076   Tel: 01832 737526
Email: aspenhouse@FSBDial.co.uk

☐ I enclose a UK bank cheque made payable to Sphere for £ . . . .
☐ Please charge £ . . . . . . to my Visa, Delta, Maestro.

[ ][ ][ ][ ][ ][ ][ ][ ][ ][ ][ ][ ][ ][ ][ ][ ][ ][ ]

Expiry Date [ ][ ][ ][ ]   Maestro Issue No. [ ][ ]

NAME (BLOCK LETTERS please) . . . .

ADDRESS . . . .

. . . .

. . . .

Postcode . . . . Telephone . . . .

Signature . . . .

Please allow 28 days for delivery within the UK. Offer subject to price and availability.